Broken and Profane

To Bonnie —
Nice to meet you at
the OP Senior Center.

Jeff Schilt
7/25/12

Also by Jeff Schober

*Bike Path Rapist: A Cop's Firsthand Account of Catching
the Killer Who Terrorized a Community*
    with Dennis Delano

Undercurrent

What a Country, This America
Hans Kullerkupp: A Memoir

Sabres: 26 Seasons in Buffalo's Memorial Auditorium
    with Ross Brewitt

Curriers Express
    a play written with Ryan Collins

Visit www.jeffschober.com

Broken and Profane

Jeff Schober

No Frills

<<<>>>

Buffalo

Nofrillsbuffalo.com

Buffalo, NY

Printed in the United States of America

Schober, Jeff

Broken and Profane/ Schober- 1ˢᵗ Edition

ISBN 978-0615513157
1. Crime – Murder – Fiction.   2. Thriller – New Author – No Frills –
Fiction.
1. Title

No Frills Buffalo Press
119 Dorchester Buffalo, New York 14213
Nofrillsbuffalo.com

In Memoriam
Mary Jo Schober
1937-2009

<u>Chapter 1</u>

From the observation deck of city hall, a man leaned against the concrete railing, watching and listening to the rally in Buffalo's Niagara Square twenty-eight stories below. At this height, sounds of the city evaporated. Yet he heard the minister spewing venom as clearly as if he stood among them on the marble steps.

"White cops and white lawyers in a white justice system will never give the black man his due," the preacher shouted through a megaphone, waving arms and gesturing to those around him. "It is time to insist on justice and see the dream come to life."

Two dozen blacks rallied around the speaker, clapping and shouting words of encouragement.

"This tall polished obelisk behind me," the preacher continued, "points toward God, intending to show the path to righteousness via heaven. But it is made of white marble, symbolic because justice only favors that color. The black man knows this imposing structure is an extended middle finger, sticking straight before the hub of city government, taunting the black man. There will be no justice for our kind. Martin Luther King had a dream and was murdered for it. What we are living now is the nightmare."

"Amen, brother," came replies from the crowd.

From the top of city hall, the man's blood boiled. Humiliation of the assault burned in his throat, tightening his tendons. There had been no justice five nights ago, and now these people claimed they were victims. He was the victim, not them. He had been beaten and robbed. Did anyone care about that?

He was above their lies now. Leaning against the concrete railing, his lips turned downward. Here he felt like God. He pattered about the narrow walkway alone, over the square metal drain grates, and gazed forth in every direction, as if the land and people below were his minions, dropped on earth to serve his purpose.

It wasn't just his attack. His father had been a victim too, along with countless other innocents. His dad, who first taught him about the differences in race, must have known, must have had some eerie glimpse into the future that foretold his doom. On a chilly night twenty years earlier, some fucking nigger in a juke bar on the east side followed his old man to the parking lot and stabbed him with a flattened shank. Despite a roomful of witnesses, the pigs never caught anyone.

This was one of his few spots where he remembered his dad clearly. On a cool autumn day, two decades earlier, his father brought him here. He was so small then that the old man had lifted him into the crook of his arm and held him with both hands. Within those safe confines, he rested his feet on the railing, clutching his father's neck tightly when he gazed down. The older man's skin was a warm blend of olives and musk. Swaddled in his father's arms, he understood contentment. It was a feeling of love he had never been able to replicate.

After the death nothing was ever the same. Mom had been long gone, and dad's girlfriend hightailed it out, unwilling to take on a six-year old who wasn't any relation. He bounced from uncaring aunts and uncles to foster homes. By fifteen, he stopped going to school. He spent time hiding out on the streets, taking meals at shelters and hoping for a warm cubby when the nights turned cold. But all that was in the past.

In the circular panorama were hills to the south, Lake Erie on the west, bridges to Canada stretching north, even the rising spray of Niagara Falls far downriver. To the east, treetops spread until their focus melted and vanished in the distance.

Oh, to raise a high-powered rifle against my shoulder, he thought. *Those fuckers below would be pockmarked with holes.*

A noise stirred behind him. He turned and squinted as a woman with a broom and dustpan on a stick emerged from the fire door. She glanced around, nodded at him, and moved slowly to the corner, sweeping away windblown grit that had accumulated where wall met floor.

She was in her fifties, shaped like a bowling ball with hunched shoulders and a red-polka dot bandana looped over her brillo hair. She wore orthopedic shoes and a denim jumper that stretched to her calves. Her skin was the color of coffee.

Spying between windowpanes, he watched her step onto the observation deck. She kept her head down and swept the outer rim with all the energy of a sloth.

His heart drummed like a jackhammer. This was his chance. Sounds of wind and the rally below faded to an opaque drone.

It took forever before the cleaning lady circled her way around the deck. As she edged from behind the bricks her head was down, focused on sweeping. He stretched over the railing, leaning far enough that he lifted one foot off the ground.

"What you doing, sir?" the woman asked. "Don't you go falling now."

He stood upright, turning to her. Her brown eyes were deep set, the nose flattened putty beneath their sunken pupils.

"This is unbelievable," he said. "You gotta see this."

"What is it?" She leaned her broom against the railing and waddled to where he stood, resting pudgy hands on the concrete rail and looking downward.

"Do you see it? Right below us? You gotta lean over real far."

This close to her, the odor of hair cream mixed with caked sweat was overpowering. He swallowed to keep bile down.

Her curiosity was piqued, so she bent at the waist and stuck her fat ass out. "I don't see nothing," she started to say, words dripping slowly.

If she screamed on the way down, he didn't hear it.

*   *   *

He hurried down seven flights before summoning an elevator to carry him to the lobby. After swirling through the revolving door onto the steps of city hall, he surveyed the area without breaking stride. There was no mangled corpse lying in the road. In fact, there was no evidence of the body at all. He tucked his head and turned right, crossing the street and entering a parking garage adjacent to Niagara Square. Inside the tiered ramp, sounds of commotion filtered to him, but he resisted the urge to turn and look. Taking the stairs two at a time, he climbed three flights to the open-air roof. Against the concrete half-wall, he paused.

Everyone from the rally had stopped blathering and moved like magnets toward the columns of city hall, staring upward, mouths agape. People screamed, raised hands to cover faces, but peeked through fingers at the grisly sight. Businessmen showed revulsion, yet refused to look away.

He followed their line of sight to the parapet above the building's lobby. His jaw clenched, then his lip curled imperceptibly.

This was one of those times when he wished he had continued his education. He didn't know who was history's greatest mathematician. The names from grade school were a jumble. Aristotle? Pascal? Homer? Not one of them could begin to calculate the odds of this.

He watched the proceedings stoically, but inside his soul sang. It was amazing. If he had aimed, he couldn't have done that.

I'll avenge you, pop, he thought. When you left me I was a boy, but I'm a man now. I'll take down as many as I can. The number of their dead will far outweigh the one man I lost, but you were worth more to the world than all the corpses I'll pile up in your honor.

The holy war had begun.

Chapter 2

Mark Bennett sat beneath a spanning oak tree on the concrete patio, sleeves rolled up as he bit into a sandwich. Next to him, Alison sipped iced tea, absently brushing a strand of dark hair from her forehead as she concentrated on her own lunch.

"I can't stand him," she said softly. "It throws my whole judgment into question. How did I ever love the man? What's caused him to change so much that we can't even talk without screaming at each other?"

"I don't know," Mark answered. "Maybe he's not the only one who's changed. You were married, what, thirteen years? A lot can happen in that time."

Alison raised the glass bottle to her lips, silence stretching as she drank. She turned to Mark and forced a smile.

"I'm sorry to keep rattling on about him. You don't want to hear all this."

"Divorce sucks," he said. "No way around it."

"You're very patient." Alison inhaled, as if shaking away a memory. Her voice dipped, and her eyebrows lowered. "Today, after work, I'm coming straight to your house. If I'm there before you, I'm going to take off all my clothes and lie in your bed until you come and make love to me."

Mark stirred; he could picture the scene: clothes scattered on the floor, her naked body twisted into warm sheets, his mouth against her flesh. They had been together nearly every day for the past several weeks, yet he still fantasized, relishing the things they did. This, he realized, was the throes of new love.

"Want to go into your office, lock the door, and pull a nooner right now?" he asked.

Alison stifled a laugh. "You can't have sex in a library. You just can't."

"Maybe you can't. But with you, I sure could." He leaned close and kissed her.

"You're getting mustard on me," she grinned, wiping her lip.

"Oohh... maybe I'll bring some condiments later."

Alison did not notice the sirens, but Mark did. He cocked his head, turning toward their sound on the far side of Lafayette Square. He watched lightbars flash on a patrol car that appeared then vanished behind buildings on Main Street. Another set of sirens chased the first.

"Let me make a call," he said.

As Mark stood, long legs carried him to a pay phone near the library's door. At thirty-three, he was trim and fit. When his face was shielded by sunglasses, people mistakenly thought him to be a decade younger. But pouches beneath his lids belied that, lending him a hangdog aura. While his frame was lean, his eyes were tired, churning into middle age, projecting tangible sadness.

He fished a dime from his pocket and fed it into the slot. Flicking the rotary fast, he spoke into the receiver.

"It's Bennett. I'm on lunch. Is something going on?"

The thin voice on the other end was anxious. "Get over to city hall," he was told. "It's a mess. Chief's wondering where the hell everybody is. He was asking for Connell, but no one can find him."

Bennett's jaw tightened, clutching the phone closer his ear. Thirty yards away, Alison flipped open his newspaper, feathering hair over her shoulders, corralling it into a pony tail.

"I'm on it," Bennett said, laying down the phone. Without a mirror, he adjusted his tie, tightening the knot but yanking it low so it rested an inch below the collar. As he hurried back to Alison, he rolled down his sleeves and buttoned the cuffs.

13

"Sorry, honey," he said, putting lips against her mouth. "I gotta fly."

Without waiting, he trotted down the inclined patio. Strangers moved aside, aware of his haste, some turning with suspicious glances. As his footfalls pounded against concrete, he passed workers who trolled Lafayette Square, munching from brown bag lunches or eating hot dogs bought from vendors.

He had a choice to make: hail a cab or keep running. By the time he flagged a taxi, flashed his badge and explained the urgency... and then, if the driver encountered stoplights...

City hall was five blocks away, less than half a mile.

Mark lengthened his stride.

*   *   *

More flashing lights, a gathering crowd and slowed traffic. The circle in front of city hall held clusters of uniformed police and firefighters. Nervous energy and restrained chaos filled the sidewalk, but Bennett had no idea why.

People in the crowd looked up, pointing. With so much activity around, the sight wasn't clear right away. Only when he followed a stranger's raised finger did he notice what had captured everyone's attention: on the roof above the entrance to city hall, something was impaled on a flagpole.

Bennett squinted, unsure what it was. He jogged through Niagara Square, bisecting the circle. At the edge of the road he stopped, and his stomach tightened at the realization that it was a person, heavyset, clad in denim, shaking in the gentle breeze. The body had been skewered by the pole's pointed end, and had slid down ten feet. Arms and legs dangled like hanging sausages.

"Bennett," the chief rasped, breaking through a wall of police brass. Reluctant to look away, Bennett turned toward the sandpaper voice. A deputy commissioner and several lieutenants milled about, gesturing and aiming fingers upward. "About time somebody got here. Where the hell is Connell? Fuck him, he's too slow. You'll have to be the primary."

His bulk shifted as he stood straighter and angled his gaze toward the parapet several floors above.

"You believe this? That's a black woman up there, stabbed through the stomach. How in hell did this happen? We've already lost control of the scene. Too many goddamn people here."

Bennett's senses shifted to full alert. His neck tingled. If he was the primary, he needed to secure the area and interview witnesses. Was this a suicide? Obviously, the woman had fallen far because gravity and force had propelled her down the metal pole. But where was the site of her jump? He squinted toward blue sky, trying to map the open windows above.

"Oh, hell, look at this," the chief muttered.

A news van, with a logo shaped like a pupil, pulled to the curb. Out spilled a man hoisting a heavy camera over one shoulder, cords snaking behind him. He spread his feet for balance and aimed its lens toward the roof.

"Hyenas just got their lead for the six o'clock news," the chief grumbled. "This is like a field day for them. Three to one odds pictures of this end up tonight on Walter Cronkite."

A fire captain barked across the gathering. "Hey Chief, I need your boys to block off the street," he yelled, pointing to a long red truck. "This ladder can't get the right angle without jutting into traffic."

The chief aimed a thick finger at Bennett. "I want to know who this broad is and why she went for a fly. Close this before supper so there's no shitstorm. There's already a team inside and a group of patrolmen going room-to-room to get witness statements. It's your show now."

As he walked away, he gestured to a lieutenant. "Anybody find Connell yet?"

*   *   *

The dead woman's name was Rosa Greene. She was forty-eight, single, mother of two boys and grandmother to two more. She lived on Auburn Avenue in an upstairs apartment and had worked as a cleaner at city hall for nine months. City hall's maintenance office was a tiny gray windowless room in the basement with enough space for a desk and chair on either side. Its air was stale, dripping with desperation. The supervisor behind the desk was Harris Weronski, a pouchy, red-faced man in his sixties with a bulbous nose and defeated slump. It was one in the afternoon, but his breath reeked of liquor.

"We got more than fifty coloreds working for us here various times throughout the week," he explained to Bennett casually, as if the death of one of his workers was not completely unexpected. "I'm talking elevator operators, window washers, moppers and cleaners. Being completely truthful, I don't know any of them too well. For cleaners, I post an assignment list, which floors each of them will be responsible for, and they check it and go to work. I keep the supply closet stocked with mops and disinfectants, and when those get low, sometimes they tell me about it. Other times, they say," here his voice dipped into stereotypical slang, "Mistah Dubya, I ain't got no Lysol to scrub with, so can I go home early?"

He looked wistfully at his desk drawer, as if longing to sip from a concealed bottle. His eyes moved to the file spread before him. "This woman, Greene, looks like she just started here last March. I knew her name, but beyond that couldn't tell you much."

"She have any enemies?" Bennett wondered.

"Enemies? I have no idea."

"She ever have a run-in with anyone here at work?"

"Run-in? Don't think so."

"She didn't get into an argument with someone she worked with?"

"Detective, I would have no way of knowing that."

"You had any complaints about her job performance, anything like that?"

"Nothing. But let's be honest. Who would complain?"

*   *   *

Mark Bennett had already made one next-of-kin notification during his first week as a detective. It did not go well. Even before entering the academy, he had known it would be the least appealing component of his job. There was no adequate training for the task, no way to perform deftly. Bennett felt that he bungled his first time, behaving tentatively, exposing his own nervousness. Then, to compensate, he had tipped the scales too far towards comforting the victim's family, and felt his role became a counselor instead of an investigator. So he called his old partner, George Pope, a veteran copper who had once worked with his father, and asked how to overcome the awkwardness. Pope's advice was sage. Be respectful, be professional, and keep your eyes open to how people react in the face of horrible news.

Jermaine Greene, Rosa's oldest son, lived in a run-down clapboard house on the city's west side. Close to Bennett's age, he was short and stout, with blotchy black and purple skin along his neck and cheeks.

"I don't care what you say, no sir," he said. "My moms would never kill herself. This is a woman went to the Baptist service three times a week ever since I was knee high. Had a direct line to Jesus, yes sir. She was planning my boy's tenth birthday party this Saturday, and she loved him more than anything. Wouldn't go killing herself ever, but especially not before that."

17

The living room furniture was tattered, a remnant to past generations. Mark had been invited to sit on the couch. There were no longer springs within the frame. His bottom sagged to the floor, supported only by a lumpy parabola of cushion.

"Maybe it was an accidental death," Bennett suggested. "Maybe she stretched to clean some hard-to-reach area and lost her balance."

It was an improbable scenario, and Bennett knew it. In the hours he spent canvassing city hall, Rosa's broom and dustbin were discovered on the observation deck, and it appeared that was where she had been cleaning when the incident occurred. The railing there was stomach high, too tall to accidentally tumble over. But he had been taught to examine every possibility, no matter how far-fetched.

"My moms wasn't more than five-foot-three," Jermaine explained, sitting on a rickety wooden dining room chair. Despite their height difference, the chair had a plank seat, so the short man towered over Bennett. "She wouldn't be doing much stretching, no sir. She was careful, that woman. If you knew her, you'd know she didn't make no sudden movements."

Jermaine's eyes contained no tears, no blubbering emotions. He simply stated facts, as if resigned to a pain that was part of his daily routine.

"No officer, I can promise you this wasn't no suicide and this wasn't no accident. This was foul play. That woman came to a bad end, and while I don't expect no justice here on earth, somebody's gonna pay for this in the afterlife."

*   *   *

Bennett spent most of Monday at city hall, crisscrossing its marble floors, examining corridors and rooms of all twenty-eight stories. He was becoming familiar with its nooks and alcoves, its architectural subtleties. Now, sitting at his desk in the homicide squad, a toothache pattered his jaw. Would he have appreciated the building's design had he known it in another context? He could not get excited about the sandstone exterior or art deco design. To him it was neither beautiful nor majestic. It stood in the way of his case.

Across the room, one of the night guys with rolled-up sleeves puffed a cigar, keeping a sole angled against an adjacent chair, making follow-up calls from a list of names and numbers taken at the scene. No one else was around.

In the quiet squad room, Bennett wound down enough to consider the chief's words on the sidewalk.

"Where the hell is Connell? Fuck him, he's too slow. You'll have to be the primary."

You'll have to be the primary? Not exactly a ringing endorsement for a new detective. *We can't have the superstar, so we'll settle for you.*

Nine hours later, he was no closer to answers. Had a crime even been committed? It had all the makings of a suicide, but after spending the day assembling a timeline of Rosa Greene's last twenty-four hours, suicide did not appear likely. Her family and acquaintances painted a picture of a woman who displayed no signs of depression or anxiety. There was no note, but often there wasn't. Suppose the whole thing was an accident, and she just fell over the railing?

Bennett's desk phone rang.

"Marky, you're still there?" The caller was George Pope, his former partner. His voice scraped like he chewed nails. Mark's own father had mentored Pope when he was a rookie, just like George had done when Mark came on patrol. "I heard you caught that city hall jumper."

"Yeah."

"Welcome to homicide, here's a little doozy to start you out. Surprised they didn't give that to Connell."

"I was on the scene before him," Bennett admitted. "It was lunch hour. Half the administration was standing around looking up at the body."

"Chief figured if he foisted it onto one of his detectives it would take the heat off of him, huh?"

"Right place, right time."

"Don't kid yourself. You were a warm body who happened to be standing in front of him," Pope philosophized. "You know the commissioner is wondering why everyone was out to lunch when a call came in."

Bennett rolled a fresh carbon into the typewriter. Even without Pope's insight, he understood why he was assigned the case.

"So how's it going?" Pope wondered.

"Lousy. I got nothing. Just winding down for the day, about to type my activity report."

"Use the dictophone. That's why you've got secretaries. Be typed up, lying on your desk in the morning."

"This one is gonna be scrutinized pretty good, so I'd rather do it myself. Doesn't look like it's going to clear quickly."

"Keep plugging away, Marky. Wouldn't surprise me if when you're just about ready to close this, it gets yanked from you so somebody else can take the credit. This one is going to be dripping with politics. But you know what? You can't control that, so just work the case and follow your leads."

Sounds just like something my dad would have said, Bennett thought.

Chapter 3

Mark Bennett bounced along the rugged mountain. The car's shocks were destroyed; its chassis pounding up and down. Pivoting the steering wheel side to side, he tried to avoid boulders and uneven terrain, but hitting them was inevitable. Scrub brush whizzed by, twigs flicking against his windshield, some lodging under wiper blades. Ahead he spotted an incline, and pointed the nose toward it, removing his foot from the accelerator. Brakes did not work, and momentum was too fast. When he ascended the ramp, direction shifted. His heart plunged and he was airborne, arcing upward into sky, nothing but space and blue and washed horizon. Twisting, contorting, his left side sunk as free fall began. Flying without a safety net, he was terrified.

Then, like a magnet, he was pulled in another direction, bubbling toward the surface from a deep pool. A ringing interrupted the murkiness. Cold black enveloped him; his chest was damp with sweat. He leaned to the nightstand, fumbling for the phone.

"Bennett," he breathed with confusion.

"Mark?" An unfamiliar man's voice.

"Yeah."

"It's Lou." Background noises filtered into darkness. Talking, thumping music, scrapes, clinking.

"Who's Lou?"

"From Rendezvous. Did I wake you?"

Bennett squinted, too disoriented to locate the clock's glow. "Time is it?"

"After two. Hate to bother you, but you asked me to call if there was a problem."

Edges melted from the haze. Night air was frigid, unforgiving. "Yeah, right."

"Well, there's a problem."

Bennett stretched the phone cord then released it, exhaling and blinking in the dark. "Okay. I'll be there." The receiver missed its cradle and bounced on the floor, making a harsh thud.

"Dammit," he whispered.

Alison stirred, reaching for him, looping her ankle over his.

"What's going on?" she murmured, sounding as if her lips refused to move.

He kissed her hair and puffed his cheeks. "Nothing. I've got to run out. Go back to sleep."

He wiggled and slid from beneath the blanket.

*   *   *

Fifteen minutes later, Bennett parked along Niagara Street. The accordion grate was pulled back from Rendezvous' entrance. He pressed the buzzer and seconds later heard the muted click that unlocked its door. Inside was festive, despite the hour. The room was crowded, filled with smoke and noise. Behind the bar, Lou raised eyebrows in greeting, then shifted his head toward the back corner.

Bennett hesitated long enough to sense the evening. A pimp he busted two years ago was throwing darts, and three bikers averted their faces when they made Bennett for a cop. There were hookers and johns, drug dealers and drunks. These were west siders, many of whom were tough, mingling with some who were cowards but tried to act otherwise. At the far end, beneath the glow of a neon squiggle, were four men, with three skinny tramps in heels and miniskirts. Empty bottles were arrayed on the countertop. Bennett recognized two of the guys, one of whom was Angelo Battaglia. The girls he did not know, but could tell they made a living trading their strung out husks to score more dope.

No one noticed Mark's approach. Bobby, clad in jeans and a leather jacket, was facing the group, back toward the bar. Pink flesh beneath his brush cut gleamed in the colored light. Mark stepped forward quickly, laying a palm on Bobby's shoulder.

"C'mon," Mark said, crooking a thumb toward the door as Bobby turned. "It's time to go."

There was a momentary pause before recognition. "Hey! Look who's here!"

Bobby's smile turned wide, and Mark could smell his breath. "You know these guys? That's Angelo, and this is Carmen and Russell. These girls, we just met them, so I don't really remember their names, but—"

Bennett nodded with impatience and did not greet the men. At twenty-five, Bobby had acne scars on his cheeks. He was built low to the ground. An aura of restrained hostility radiated from his chin. Rub him the wrong way, and he might explode with the anger of King Kong. Eyes were deep set, lips perpetually swollen. Sleeves could not contain his bulging arms nor could pants mask his muscular legs.

"Okay, let's hit it," Mark said, laying a firm hand on Bobby's neck and twisting him from the group. Using force and momentum, they were halfway toward the door before Bobby objected to being hustled away.

"Hey, hey, hey. Slow down, turbo. What's the problem?"

"Outside," Bennett insisted, but Bobby did not hear him. Mark nodded thanks to Lou, who observed stoically, his disinterest worthy of an Oscar. Five feet from the door, Bobby tried to stop, but the decision came too late. Mark lowered his palm from Bobby's neck to the midpoint of his shoulders, pushing with authority.

On the sidewalk, night air was sobering. Bobby's face contracted in the cold.

"What the hell is this?"

"You can't hang out in places like this, Bobby. You gotta stay away from the bottom feeders. Trouble is a switchblade away. You gotta be smarter than this."

"Angelo and me were just having a beer after shift."

Sounds grumbled from the elevated highway on the far side of the building. Across Niagara Street was a darkened gas station. The road was deserted. Under the artificial glow of streetlights, Bobby's eyes flecked with growing anger.

"Wait... you came here to be a hall monitor?"

"I'm taking you home. You shouldn't leave Susie and the baby like this anyway."

Bobby's gaze narrowed. "Don't get all holy roller on me. We worked the four to midnight then came out for a drink. You've done that before, haven't you? Or you too busy polishing the halo?"

"I'll drive you home. You can get your car in the morning."

"I can drive myself."

There was a pause as Bobby exhaled and stepped back, shaking his head. He was annoyed, but Mark believed that a filament within him recognized worthy advice. The confrontation might have ended here, but Bobby's three friends opened the door and clustered onto the sidewalk. Bobby had been about to relent, but seeing them triggered the discomfort of a public scolding. Why should he be singled out when he wasn't doing anything wrong? Why should he be embarrassed before his buddies?

"What the fuck," Bobby spat with renewed vigor. "I know you think you're saving the world, Marky, but you can put the Superman cape away. You don't need to follow me every fucking place I go. I can make decisions on my own, you know."

"Yeah, you've done a great job so far."

"Everything okay, Bobby?" the one called Carmen asked, stopping a few feet from where the men squared off.

"Everything's fine," Mark growled through clenched teeth, keeping his gaze locked on Bobby. "Go back inside."

The audience energized Bobby. He stood taller, puffing out his chest.

"You're going to interrupt me with my friends and start preaching? Fuck off. Who do you think you are, my father?"

"Start moving to the goddamn car. If I was your father I'da kicked your ass a long time ago."

"Hey Bobby, if you need help with this cocksucker—" Carmen began.

Mark turned to him and aimed a finger. "Shut up."

The brief diversion was enough. Energy exploded and events shot into warp speed.

"Who the fuck—" Carmen began, at the same time that Bobby sprang and slammed his fist into Mark's jaw. He toppled backwards, elbow crashing on concrete. The angry man advanced, poised with gorilla-sized fists. Mark rolled left and kicked toward a wishbone of legs, connecting solidly with Bobby's groin. A yelp, then Bobby's knees turned rubbery. He hesitated, steadying himself, grasping a fire hydrant. It bought enough time for Mark to get to his feet.

Carmen surged forward, anxious to throw punches. Off balance, he lobbed a strike at Mark's shoulder. Mark expected him, parried the swing so it merely stung his bicep, and pushed the man's back, turning Carmen's momentum against him. Carmen collided hard into the pavement, where he remained face down, stunned by the sudden shift in fortune.

Mark seethed, blood roaring in his brain. He hadn't wanted to leave Alison in bed, hadn't wanted to venture out on a cold night. He sure as hell hadn't asked for any of this, but now that he was here, he might be bloodied by all four of them. That enraged him, making him want to fight.

Despite spiraling events, that didn't happen.

The one named Russell stepped back to avoid the fray and called ineffectually, "Hey, stop that. Oh, shit. Cut it out, guys!"

Mark planned to kick Carmen in the head. As he swung his leg back, Angelo leaped. Mark raised his hands, ready to parry. But Angelo did not approach him, instead pouncing to the sidewalk and planting himself on Carmen's prone figure.

"Stay down! Don't do nothing!" With annoyance, Angelo said, "You're going after a copper, you stupid son of a bitch."

Russell remained paralyzed near the accordion grate, so Mark turned his attention to Bobby, still crouching timidly and cupping his groin. Mark's jaw felt like it had collided with a cinderblock. His cheeks stung and his teeth were numb. He would be damned to let the punk bastard get away with snookering him. Compared to Mark's wiry frame, Bobby was strapping, but they had tangled before. Relying on muscles alone, it was no contest. But Mark was older, more experienced. If he stayed close and jabbed the doughy stomach, Bobby's strength would be negated because he couldn't put momentum into a roundhouse swing.

Without words, Mark crowded Bobby. He stabbed an uppercut to the chin and found the solar plexus with his left fist. Hunched over, Bobby had not anticipated another attack, so when it came, he crouched defensively. He laid a giant palm on Mark's shoulder and tried to twist away, but Mark kept moving forward, diminishing distance. With a wild cry of rage he jammed a knee into the groin again, and Bobby dropped to all fours. Mark cocked for a blow to the head, but arms wrapped around him from behind.

Russell's voice burned close to his ear. "It's over. It's over," he whispered urgently. "No more now." For a moment he struggled to free himself, but seeing Bobby's collapse, Mark

26

did not resist when he was dragged further up the sidewalk, twenty feet from where the three men were arrayed. "Bobby's down, Carmen's down. It's over."

When he let go, Russell raised his hands in a pacifying manner. Mark shook stinging knuckles and inhaled to steady his own breathing.

Sirens suddenly, then two cruisers came into view along Pennsylvania Street. Turning onto Niagara, they halted before the hydrant. Four cops spilled from the cars, all dark uniforms and caps covering short hair, palms flattened onto nightsticks as they assessed the scene.

Because he was away from the group, none of them recognized Mark. With everyone spread out and breathing exhaustion, one cop asked, "Everybody okay here?" He was blond, with chiseled features and a flattened nose.

"We're fine," Russell answered. "Everything's cool."

Mark curled his lip. His hands and jaw throbbed, frustration etched in his throat. "I'm on the job," he said, stepping forward. "Detective Mark Bennett."

"Oh shit," the uniform said. "All right, everybody stay where you are. I don't want to be swinging a bat, but I will if anyone moves."

Who the hell had called the cops? Mark wondered. The lot next to the bar was empty, and the lights of streetfront businesses were black. Even the apartments above these stores were dark. Then he noticed Lou's face pressed to the square pane of glass in the bar's door. He raised his eyebrows at Mark and disappeared.

The blond cop approached, studying Mark's disheveled hair, the welt raising on his chin.

"Which one hit you?"

Mark tilted his head to Bobby, who had shifted from all fours and was now sitting cross-legged on the sidewalk, rubbing a hand along his chin where he had been punched.

"He suckered me, then I clocked him back." Hearing this, another of the uniforms put a hand to his waist and removed handcuffs from his belt.

"Don't cuff him," Mark said. "He's a copper too."

The patrolmen looked to each other, shifting uncomfortably.

"This is not good." Skeptically, one of the uniforms asked, "You want to press charges?"

Mark shook his head. "No."

"Detective, if you think—"

"No, no charges. He's a pain in the ass, but he's my kid brother."

*   *   *

Back in his car, Mark felt the soreness that follows an altercation. Each time he flexed his jaw, he was stabbed again by Bobby's coldcock. His knuckles stung like a raw brush burn. The last hour had been stupid. Part of him wished that he had never given his phone number to Lou the bartender. He considered that maybe Bobby needed to learn responsibility on his own, even if that meant taking a fall. *I'm sure as hell not getting through to the kid*, he thought.

Bobby Bennett was a study in contrast. He could be charismatic, warming any room with laughter and good will. He was personable, the first to help someone in need. Yet there was a chasm in which Bobby's frustration accumulated then spilled over like a flash flood.

For many years, Mark could not understand his brother's anger, because he had no such feelings. Why were they so different? Were they not raised in the same house, composed of the same genetic makeup?

After their father's death, the family was lost. Bobby's anger grew more intense and frequent. Their mother retreated within the traditions of her church, distancing herself from her sons. Mark tried to maintain composure and support his brother, but Bobby wanted to kick at walls and challenge rules. More than ever, Bobby wanted to fight everything.

Past 3 a.m., streets were largely deserted. The police radio mounted to his dashboard crackled every few minutes with staccato reports, but quiet reigned across the city. Still, he kept his window down, and when a stray pair of headlights intersected his path, Mark examined the driver.

Being alone was comforting. Much like his lunch hours at the library, he found solace riding patrol. Constant movement conveyed accomplishment, protecting him from the vulnerability of standing still for too long.

He reached for the handheld, lifted the microphone, and stretched the cord toward his mouth. He did not depress the button on the side.

"Car fourteen to Mac," he said in a clear voice. "Come in Mac."

There was a pause before Mark heard, "Mac here. Go ahead, fourteen."

"How's it going, Pop?"

"Good, kid. How are you?" Genuine pleasure filled his words.

Mark paused. "Struggling a little bit. Things are tough."

"Bobby again?"

"Yeah, that's part of it."

"Tell me."

"The kid is twenty-five percent fuck up, Mac. I know you don't like to hear that, and I don't like to say it, but we gotta face reality. He's getting worse."

Silence became palpable, long enough that he wondered if his father was still connected. "You're right. I don't like to hear it."

"I know he needs looking after, but it's getting to be too much for me. I've spent my life tutoring him. Wasted time."

"What are you talking about? He's a copper now, just like you. Like his old man. You shaped him into that more than I did. He's a good boy."

"He can be, but he's not always."

The chuckle was sincere. "You're a meathead. Still an idealist, aren't you Marky? Nobody is good all the time."

You were, Mark wanted to say.

"Between you and George he's in the best hands," Mac said. "You couldn't ask for two better guys to look after him."

"I don't think it's enough."

"Have some faith, kid."

"Have some faith."

"That's right. An old sergeant always said, one shift at a time. If it gets to be too much, just take it slow. He's got Susie and the baby now. He can be a pain in the ass, I agree. He always could be. But he's coming around." Mac spoke with conviction, as if saying so made it true. "What else?"

"What else?"

"You said it's mostly Bobby. So what else?"

"Well, I got this case today. Black woman takes a dive off the top of city hall, gets impaled on a flagpole. Pretty gruesome. Right now I can't find a reason for it. I want it to be an accident or a suicide, but everyone who knew her said she wasn't depressed and was pretty careful. There's no evidence one way or the other."

"So you keep working it. Cases don't always solve on the first day. But something else is bothering you. I can tell."

Mark exhaled. "I don't know. Life. This woman I've been seeing, Alison. I like her, but there are some issues there."

"I gathered," Mac answered. "You don't really talk to me much about her."

"It's complicated."

"So simplify it for me."

"I can't. It's too complex to break into news clips."

"I don't care who she is. It's never easy with women. We're built differently from them. And being a cop makes it harder."

"I don't know how to put into words all the different aspects. I'm just struggling with it. And I'm scared because in addition to everything else, this one feels different from the others."

Mac hesitated, unsure what to say. "Different how?"

Mark reflected. "Like it could be for real. Long term."

Both men stopped speaking. Beneath streetlamps, a hunched figure pedaled a bicycle, flashing in and out of shadows as he rode along the curb. Mark slowed, but there was nothing unusual except the late hour.

"I'm sorry I can't explain," Mark resumed. "I'm not even sure I understand it all myself."

"You'll tell me when you're ready," Mac said.

"One shift at a time, huh?"

"You can scoff, kid, but it's good advice."

"Yeah."

"How's your mother?"

"She's a Jesus freak. We don't see her too much."

Mac began to speak, but halted before anything formulated. "Just look after her, okay?"

"Yeah. Right now she spends all her time at the rectory. I'm not sure I have anything she needs."

Mac's words were heavy. "That's how I felt a lot of times."

"I'm turning onto my road now, Mac, so I'm gonna sign off."

"Okay Marky. We'll talk again soon?"

"Soon," Mark said, then added, "I love you, Pop."

"Love you too, kid."

"Car fourteen out."

Mark laid the mic back in its cradle and exhaled. He spiraled the crank to raise the window. Before turning into his driveway, he switched off the headlights. A skunk or raccoon skittered from the concrete into the darkness of the yard. It was 3:20 and the neighborhood was tranquil.

Rather than slamming the car door, he closed it most of the way, then leaned with his hip and pushed until it clicked. Exhaustion had accumulated in Mark's neck. He needed to ice his jaw and swallow several aspirins, but wanted nothing more than to curl against Alison and encase himself in her warmth.

Chapter 4

Chippewa Street between Franklin and Delaware had been a good location for Sincere Malone. By nightfall, storefronts that weren't boarded up were mostly vacant. Pawnshops kept their neon signs illuminated overnight, with accordion-style mesh grates stretched across windows and glass doors. The deli was dark, the bail bond office forlorn. Only the liquor store remained open. Its owner, an old leathery man from Asia, was a son of a bitch, known to yell in a high-pitched rant, wield a broom handle and chase girls further down the sidewalk. For the past few months, however, he worked mostly days, having been replaced by a young Arab. Good looking, with dark hair and full eyes, he spoke little English, but grinned at the girls and didn't mind if they came inside for a few minutes to warm up on chilly nights. Sometimes, as a token of thanks, Sincere bought a small bottle from him and shared it with her friends.

Standing on a cracked sidewalk wearing three-inch heels and a short skirt was enough of a challenge, but when autumn nights turned frigid, it was disheartening. Sincere had never worked the streets in the cold. She turned her first trick in May, just as weather was warming. Alonzo told her it would be easy, a good way for her to earn fast cash. She could give a little to him for rent and food then keep the rest for herself. She liked sex anyway, so that wasn't such a big issue, and the money could be used to buy Alicia a new swingset. Grandma had enough space in her backyard that they could put a slide there, and then the two of them could play when Sincere visited. Alonzo told her to charge five bucks for a hand job, ten for a blow job, and twenty bucks a pop. At those prices, there would be enough left over to score dope once in a while. Maybe, if she saved up enough, she could get custody of Alicia and they could live together, like a mother and daughter should.

But the money went quicker than she expected. Sure, she could pull in close to one hundred dollars on a good night, but Alonzo insisted on a bigger cut for rent, and she splurged on high-end shoes and a purse last summer. Her mother had been a bitch about letting Sincere see her own daughter. The two times she visited, the old lady stood and glared while they spread out a blanket and tried to have a picnic in the backyard. When Sincere mentioned a swingset, her mother shook her head woefully, asking her not to bring up such farfetched ideas in front of Alicia. It would only raise the girl's hopes.

Now she stood along the curb, dwarfed by a giant hooker named Annette, and tried to push away the bad memories. She reached into her purse and withdrew a cloudy bottle, raising it to her lips, feeling the warmth coat her throat. Nights like these, she thought, will rip your insides out.

That's when Sincere noticed the tan car in a parking lot across the street. Someone was watching them with binoculars.

*   *   *

There were two niggers standing along the sidewalk, just outside the shadows. One was tall and gawky, with a blonde wig and leopard print skirt. She was bigger, muscular, almost masculine. Fuck that. He didn't need to wrestle with some amazon or get his ass kicked.

The other one, though, she was suited. Petite, with a mocha face and skinny legs, shivering nervously atop stilettos, tucking a flask into her vinyl purse. He could control her, pick her up and toss her over his shoulder if needed.

34

Fucking a black woman both excited and repulsed him. It was wrong to give his seed to them. Thinking of it caused bile to rise in his throat. But he loved the idea of lording over one, thrusting himself inside while it looked up and saw the rage in his eyes, the recognition that he was master. After penetration would come the payoff. He would beat the living shit out of it then stick it with a knife.

The hookers began their sidewalk shuffle, an aimless stroll from whores trying to stay warm. He watched their gait, then laid the binoculars on the floor behind his seat and started the car, crossing two lanes and pulling into an empty parking space along the curb.

He lowered the baseball cap low so it shielded most of his forehead. He tilted his neck back to see beyond its brim. As they approached, he checked the mirrors all around him. Besides the girls, there was no one around.

He leaned across the console and cranked down the passenger side window.

"Hi," he said meekly, keeping his eyes low. "You need a ride?"

"Hey Sugar," one of them said. He glanced up quickly to see the giant leaning elbows on his car. "You wanna have a party?"

"Not you. The other one."

"Not me?" She wondered with a teasing lilt in her voice. "My name is Annette. You ask me and I'll take you around the world."

He didn't answer and the silence became awkward.

"The other one," he repeated.

"What, you don't want to get caught in Annette?" She winked, laughing in falsetto at her pun.

Again, a delay. This fucking whore was dumb as concrete. From the corner of his vision, she stood waiting, lower lip ajar.

"Goddamn it, scram! I want the other one!"

Adjusting her blonde wig, she clucked her tongue and reversed direction, offended. "You don't need to be mean," she chided. Without breaking stride, she said, "Sincere, this cracker wants you."

"Good news," Sincere mumbled, and stepped off the curb and lowered her head toward the open window. "What do you need, handsome?"

He expected her voice to be guttural and ferocious. Instead, its pitch was feeble, almost childlike. He glanced at her, then lowered his chin. She was even skinnier up close. Thin, bony face, with sunken eyes. No muscle, just bone and flesh.

"How much for a party?" he asked.

"That depends. What kind of party you want?"

"Full party. Lights and fireworks."

He stared at his dashboard, not looking at her, hoping the amazon didn't turn around. *Come on, you fucking nigger whore,* he thought. *Strike a deal, get in the car, and we're in business.*

"Thirty."

"Going rate is twenty," he answered. "I'm not an idiot."

She sighed, looking over the top of his car. "Twenty-five. Believe me, Sticks, I'm worth an extra five."

He nodded and reached into his pocket. He planned on getting his money back anyway.

*   *   *

The man had been watching her for ten minutes, so Sincere knew that he was serious. He had scouted before choosing her, so she believed it was safe to ratchet up the price. This John wasn't looking for just anybody. He had selected her. That knowledge reassured Sincere, made her feel special, like she was the prom queen. She wasn't going to tell Alonzo that she earned extra on this job.

At the end of a long sleeved plaid shirt stretched a small hand with money spread into a fan: one twenty and a five. She reached through the window, but he pulled his arm back.

"How do I know you won't take this and run?" he wondered.

She attempted to charm him, lips parting with a smile. "Wouldn't do that. A little trust, Sticks."

So this was a businessman, Sincere thought. *Thinks I'm out to hustle him.* But he wasn't any suit and tie guy. His voice was smooth, with a country twang, like he grew up in cornfields somewhere. Big John Deere baseball cap covering his face. Why did he keep it concealed?

"I don't get in until I have the cash," she said.

The silence stretched several seconds. He extended his arm again and she took the bills, tucking them in her purse.

"Good boy," she said, opening the door and dropping into the passenger's seat. "Now tilt that hat back so I can see how handsome you are."

He kept the curve of the bill lowered, his eyes toward the driver's side door. "That kind of money should make me handsome enough."

Country music came from the radio, interrupted by muffins of static. Its volume left little space for chatter, which was fine with Sincere. But God, what awful music. She rested an elbow on the windowsill and positioned the heating vent towards her neck.

After several turns, the car eased into a deserted parking lot. There was one floodlight at the far corner, but most of the pavement was sheathed in darkness. When he turned off the ignition, Sincere noticed the absence of blowing heat. The car smelled greasy, like old French fries.

"Take off your clothes," he ordered. His voice brimmed with sudden anger.

Sincere felt incoming evil.

"Listen, Sticks," she began, but before she could say more, a steel vise gripped her windpipe. Her fingers shot up to his wrist, trying to pry it away. She had noticed that his hands were small, but they were still large enough to stifle oxygen in her throat. She flailed but was unable to escape.

Wordlessly, he mounted her, forcing her skirt above hips and thrusting himself inside her while she thrashed.

"You'll take this, whore, and you'll like it," he moaned. Hot breath rushed against her lobe. She tried to wedge her knees together, but his thighs were heavy iron skillets pressing on hers. As he penetrated, his grip relaxed enough that she could suck in a breath. Still his hand remained firmly around her neck.

With his other fist he punched her in the mouth.

Sincere saw a wobbly explosion of purple colors, and passed out. A prick at the hinge of her jaw jarred her back to consciousness. From the edge of her vision, the lone streetlight reflected off sharp metal. She couldn't tell how large the knife was, but its presence terrified her.

"Don't kill me," she whispered, clamping her eyes shut. "Please don't kill me. I've got a daughter."

The pinpoint pressure stopped. Its cold blade had already punctured her skin. Sincere felt blood pooling along her chin, its warmth dripping onto her bare sternum.

His face was inches from hers, lips twisted in exertion. A patchwork of stubble flecked his cheeks. He tilted his neck back and Sincere looked into his eyes, the first time she was really able to see him. Dark pupils, wide set, angry but restrained, as if his urges were schizophrenic, yanked in two separate directions.

Remember this face, she thought. *If I get out of here alive, I'll need to remember this face.*

"You're lucky," he panted. "I threw a monkey off the top of city hall today, so I've already met my quota for dead niggers."

Then, in a fast-forward of events, Sincere Malone was punched again, shoved from the car and tumbled to the blacktop, where she sprawled face up. After a moment, her purse thwacked the pavement beside her. The engine turned over and the car pulled away, sound vanishing into the night. Her neck was swollen, and she wondered whether her cheekbone was broken. Thighs and legs felt like they had been rubbed with a belt sander. She was afraid to move. *I'm alive*, she thought. *At least I'm alive.* Raising an arm to her throbbing neck and wiping the blood from her chin, Sincere inhaled a shallow breath, hoping to minimize pain.

What if he comes back?

She couldn't muster energy to sit up.

* * *

Blood had splattered onto his sleeve, so he removed the shirt and rolled it into a paper bag. The next day he would burn it in a metal can and discard the ashes in a dumpster. Or should he do it now? His brain turned somersaults, and he struggled to think clearly. There had been too much activity that day. Tomorrow would be better. All these jumpy thoughts would even out.

He had turned weak in his car, and an hour later, regret pounded his temples. What the fuck did he care if that monkey whore had a daughter? He was seconds away from shanking her, but that peeping confession in her little high-pitched voice made him stop.

Why?

He had thought of his own father, killed anonymously, and for a fleeting second, had wondered if it was right for another kid to grow up alone. But a nigger had killed his dad. Five days earlier, a pack had even beaten him up. He needed to kill them to even the score.

So why hadn't he? That was the whole point of this. He had missed his chance for justice.

"Aagghh!" he screamed, and thundered fists against his own skull, rocking back and forth before the bathroom mirror. He collapsed into a fetal position on the floor, shaking. His mind traveled to a faraway place, with pulsing strobes and roaring sounds. He lost all understanding of himself and the world.

The tremors stopped after a time, and once his stomach warmed again, he was able to prop to one knee, then stand and look at himself. It hurt to admit he was cowardly, but maybe he needed to let himself off the hook. He had only done his first killing earlier that day. Like anything else, it took time to become good. He planned to learn from each attack.

One thing was sure: he wouldn't leave any opportunities for sympathy. No more talking. Next time, he would simply kill, quick and sudden.

There would be no mercy.

Chapter 5

Just after 8 a.m., Mark Bennett stepped off the elevator onto the third floor, where the detective division was housed. Ken Connell idled in the hallway, hands in pockets, staring at tiled walls, waiting to take the elevator down. There were many reasons for Bennett to not like Connell, and their curt exchange was about to add another.

Lack of sleep plagued Bennett. For three hours after returning home, he straddled the line between frustration and restless dozing, mind tumbling with images of his brother and murky details of the Greene death. Seeing Connell look up as the doors creaked open, Bennett's throat constricted. He did not need another albatross.

"Heard you got the jumper from city hall," Connell muttered without greeting, entitlement radiating from his chest. "That should have been mine."

Bennett lowered his eyes and stepped into the hallway. His daily routine was to interact with his fellow detective as infrequently as possible. "Chief called for you, but you weren't around."

"Still open, huh?" Connell looked at his watch, tapping its face with his index finger. "Don't fuck it up," he threatened, then disappeared behind elevator doors.

Bennett knew Connell was an asshole, although everyone in the department, especially the commissioner, viewed him as a superstar. Three years ago he had closed an old homicide from the 1960s by re-interviewing witnesses and tracking down one promising suspect. Behind closed doors, the man had finally admitted to murder and revealed that he had kept the victim's blouse hidden in a secret drawer of his bedroom bureau. Rumor was the confession was coerced in a locked room and the bad guy had bruised cheeks afterward, but regardless of how it happened, evidence for the conviction was solid. The case garnered national attention, and suddenly Ken Connell became the personification of all that was right with the Buffalo Police.

It didn't hurt that he was handsome with a face that played well to TV cameras. At forty, age had loaned him a rugged appearance. Light hair was beginning to fleck gray near the temples; skin around his blue eyes remained tight. There was a two-inch knife scar along his jaw line, a remnant of his tour in the jungles of Vietnam. Rather than detract from his looks, the imperfections enhanced them. His tall body was still lean and straight and he appeared a decade younger.

The public, however, was not privy to his dark side. Mark was.

The cold elevator door slid shut, while Bennett stood watching the lighted numbers above drop from three to two to one. He saw no way this tension would end.

The detective bureau was a room the size of a tennis court, scattered with desks. As Bennett passed through the entryway, the chief barked from the far side.

"Bennett! My office!"

Bennett plopped his briefcase onto a metal rolling chair without breaking stride. The chief began ranting before he closed the office door.

"I thought this would be open and shut. The mayor has every colored organization in Erie County clamoring for answers, especially because there was a black power rally going on in the square below, so this is kind of personal to them. When the mayor isn't happy, he takes it out on the commissioner. When the commissioner isn't happy, he takes it out on me. You see where this is going? Now I read your activity report and know you were here late last night, but that doesn't mean shit until this is solved." He paused long enough for a breath. "Why is this still open?"

Bennett stood before his boss' desk. He waited for an invitation to sit, but after a beat, it was clear none was forthcoming.

"It isn't open and shut," he replied slowly, leaning against a radiator. "It doesn't appear to be suicide. There was no note, and no sign of depression. In fact, Rosa Greene seemed pretty happy with her life. Lab guys dusted the observation deck for prints, but even if we get results, that won't prove anything. There are hundreds of people who visit that deck each day. It's possible this was an accident, but... that doesn't seem right either."

"So you've got nothing."

"We canvassed city hall yesterday and we'll do follow-ups today. We couldn't secure the crime scene, obviously. There were thousands of people in the building. There are four elevators going to the top, but none of the operators remember anything out of the ordinary."

"The elevator doesn't go directly there, does it?"

"No, it stops on the twenty-fifth floor. You have to walk up another three flights."

"And nobody saw anything?"

"Haven't found anyone yet."

"What about the group from the rally?"

"They saw Greene after she was impaled, but not before then."

"Do we know for sure she was on the observation deck? Could she have fallen out a lower floor window?"

"It's possible," Bennett agreed. "She was responsible for cleaning the upper floors and the deck. She had only punched in twenty minutes before, so we think she began her shift on the deck. It would explain why her cleaning stuff was there. Plus, the deck is isolated, and nobody on the other floors saw her. It makes sense that's where she was."

"No fights with her boss?"

"No. He was too drunk to remember anything useful."

"No arguments at home?"

"Nothing. She was looking forward to her grandson's birthday party this weekend."

The chief chewed a thumbnail and leaned back. Although there were no leads, just talking about the case caused some of the tension to melt from his brow. "Son of a bitch."

"I know," Bennett sighed.

"Okay, topic two. You want to explain what you were doing causing a disturbance on Niagara Street at 2 a.m.?"

The chief's accusatory tone hung in the air, and Bennett remained frozen. He had hoped to keep mute about the events of last night. He did not want to implicate his brother or put him on the bosses' radar as a troubled cop.

"Yeah," the chief nodded angrily, as if agreeing with himself. "I got a call from a lieutenant telling me his blues rousted you and a couple other guys outside a bar and they looked the other way. I told the loot that didn't sound like the Mark Bennett who worked for me. He is a pretty straight arrow."

Bennett tilted his head back and stared at ceiling tiles. "I'm sorry, Chief. It was personal and I'm asking for some privacy. Isolated incident. It won't happen again."

"Dammit, Bennett, you don't have a long leash to play with. If you're awake in the middle of the night throwing punches, you can just as soon be awake and working this case. There is another factor at play here. The mayor wants to know why *you're* working this instead of Connell."

The avalanche kept tumbling on Bennett. He did not want to be replaced, especially by Ken Connell.

"I'm not saying this to threaten you," the chief continued, softening his tone, "but the orders may come down from above to switch investigators if this isn't closed in a timely fashion."

"What the hell, Chief," Bennett said steadily. "That's not the way this should work."

The big man lowered his voice. "I know. I'm against that idea, and I'll defend you like a junkyard dog. But you should know I don't win most of the fights I have with the commissioner."

Bennett ran a hand over his forehead and felt his hairline. "How long do I have?"

"There's no timeline. Close the damn thing today and this becomes a moot point. Right now I've got your back, but I can only take it for so long. You ready to get to work?"

"Yeah." Bennett opened the door to the squad room, retrieved his briefcase and headed to the far window, where his desk wedged against a row of filing cabinets. He picked up a ceramic cup filled with remnants of yesterday's coffee and went to the break room, emptying the muddy puddle and running the mug under a faucet.

Eric Lenehan entered through the far door and opened the refrigerator behind Bennett, leaning down to peer inside. Lenehan wanted their encounter to appear coincidental, but Bennett knew how calculating he was.

"Hey, I saw Connell piss down your leg," he said cheerfully. Lenehan had wrenched his back on the job two years ago, and had been relegated to squad duty since then, answering phones and doing in-house busywork. Most fellow officers understood he was milking the disability. His desk was placed behind a floor-to-ceiling glass divider that overlooked the elevator. Because he had nothing better to do, he watched everyone who entered or exited the hallway.

"Yeah," Bennett said noncommittally.

"He tell you he would have closed it by now?"

Not outright, Bennett thought, *but the implication was clear.* "No," he said simply.

Lenehan did not listen to the response. "Don't let it get you down. Connell's just steamed because he was banging a pross when the chief called him yesterday."

Lenehan grinned like a fraternity boy, as if delivering a punchline. His reputation was that of the office prankster, but his jokes didn't play to everyone. Although Bennett was new to the detective bureau, already the act had worn thin.

"Buried in a piece of tail when he could have scored this high profile case, made an even bigger name for himself." Lenehan shook his head. "He thinks you're gonna take his glory. Fucking jumper off the top of city hall. You couldn't make this one up. That's why he's all attitude around here this morning. Prima donna. Thinks he could have solved it."

Bennett poured fresh coffee then raised his chin in farewell. Lenehan dumbly watched him go.

Rounding the corner back to the detective division, Bennett nearly collided with Angelo Battaglia.

"Sorry," he muttered. His pupils narrowed when he realized it was Bennett. What he was doing in the detective bureau instead of his own precinct house was anyone's guess.

Battaglia didn't look any worse from the events of early morning. Cops knew that double-back shifts were a two-edged sword: great for blocks of free time to work a second job, but tough on the body's internal clock. Pulling a four to twelve and then going back on shift early the next morning made for a long twenty-four hours.

Bennett wondered if Battaglia even slept. He had been oiled up at 3 a.m. and here he was a few hours later back in uniform. Was he juiced on something now?

The patrolman appeared uncomfortable standing before Bennett, but did not step aside. His voice was soft, but lilted higher, with a challenging tone. "Detective, all due respect, I think you were out of line last night."

Bennett paused. "What?"

"You heard me. Your brother doesn't need a babysitter."

The hall had been empty until Lenehan came out of the break room and hesitated long enough to be nosy. Eavesdropping on snippets of gossip was his full time job, and Bennett did not want an audience.

"Come here," Bennett said, tilting his head to an interview room down the hall. The square space was empty. Bennett entered first and set his mug on the table, then unscrolled the door's shade. His temples pounded. In the past six hours, he had been a whipping boy for his brother, Ken Connell and the chief. He would be damned if some corrupt patrolman was going to join that list. When the handle latched shut, Bennett whirled on Battaglia and put his nose inches from the other man's.

"You're a piece of shit, Battaglia," Bennett said calmly, although his eyes burned with rage. "I'm telling you this to your face. You're a bad cop and a worse human being. I don't want my brother hanging out with you because the shit you pull stinks up everyone within a ten foot-radius. Stay away from Bobby and we won't have to hold another conversation like this. Are you hearing me?"

Battaglia bobbed his chin in a vague gesture.

"I don't know what that means, that little head wobble, but I'm serious. Bobby is a great kid, but he goes off track easily, and you're a bad influence. Don't invite him out drinking with you. If he asks you, make up some excuse why you can't go. You're a good enough liar that it shouldn't be a problem."

Bennett stepped back, picked up the coffee cup, and swung the door open, leaving Battaglia backed against the wall in a sparse cinder room. For several seconds the cop didn't move.

"Asshole," Battaglia muttered under his breath.

In the corridor, Lenehan walked by, pausing at the doorway. "Hey Angelo. Everything okay in here?"

*   *   *

After storming out of the precinct house and getting into his car, Battaglia rolled down the windows and lit a cigarette. His nerves fluttered. *That fucking Mark Bennett*, he thought. *So high and mighty now that he made detective.* Six months ago he had been a fellow patrolman, a skinny egghead without personality. Just buried his head in books all the time. No fun allowed around that asshole. Put in for a promotion and got it because his dead daddy used to drink with some politician.

Battaglia's heel tapped the floor mat, leg bouncing as he sat. He recognized his own nervous energy. What the fuck did that mean, you're a lousy cop and a worse human being? Did Mark know about his side project? How could he? No one knew.

He could sense the valley coming, and his faceoff with Bennett hadn't helped. Battaglia had woken at noon yesterday, but didn't sleep during his off hours overnight, which put him awake for twenty-one straight hours. He would be on shift until four this afternoon, and needed a bump to stay alert. Plus it wouldn't hurt to get some face time with Alonzo to be sure that fucker hadn't squealed.

Ten minutes later Battaglia parked the cruiser along a curb and climbed an outside wooden stairway that led to the upstairs apartment. He laid a fist against the sill and boomed, "Police!"

The black man who opened the door had an enormous girth, pudgy neck and bloated cheeks. Short hair spiraled tightly to his scalp. He wore a faded Hawaiian shirt unbuttoned to his navel.

"What's up, Officer?" he asked.

"You Alonzo Reed?"

"You know I am," the big man said calmly.

"Sir, I need to come in," the cop continued in his public voice.

Alonzo stepped back.

"What the hell you doing coming here in uniform?" Alonzo asked after he closed the door. "White cop here in broad daylight. Gawd almighty, is that your car parked on the street? Neighbors probably writing down your plate number right now."

"Cut the shit, Alonzo," Battaglia shot back. The black man might be right, but he was too deep to retreat now. "Anybody gives you grief, you tell them the cops were questioning you. Which is true. I wanna know who you been talking to."

"I ain't talked to nobody."

"Bullshit. I got a detective breathing down my neck, telling me he knows I'm a bad cop."

"You are a bad cop. Don't take brains to figure that out. He's a detective, so he probably put two and two together. But he didn't hear nothing from me."

Battaglia's eyes narrowed. The big man was mocking him, but Battaglia could not tell whether it was playful or malicious. How much tension did he want to raise? He still needed some product, and getting chesty would only diminish his chances for a score.

"What about your little slam piece?" Battaglia wondered. "What's her name? Charity?"

"Sincere."

"Yeah. She been babbling?"

"Hell no. She's sacked out in the back room. She don't know nothing about my business."

Battaglia surveyed the apartment. It was decorated in a jungle motif, with a leopard print sofa, zebra-striped chair and dark velvet wallpaper strung with twisting vines. Exactly the kind of place a pimp and drug dealer would occupy, he thought.

"I need some goods," Battaglia said.

"You sell out? We don't do another exchange til a week from Monday. Gotta keep a regular schedule."

"I don't mean that. I mean a little pick-me-up. I'm crashing and I need a jolt to get through the shift."

"Ah, hell, you tasting the shit you moving? That's a bad recipe, Officer. You can either sell it or use it, but you can't do both. Least not for long."

"You a minister now, too? I didn't come here for advice."

"Shouldn't have come here at all, specially not first thing in the morning. Next time you want some shit, you give me a courtesy call and we'll meet somewheres else. I don't want the neighbors seeing no cops around here."

"So give me a taste and I'll be on my way. I'm prepared to pay."

"Oh, you'll pay, one way or the other. No fear of that."

Alonzo waddled down the hall and unlatched a door, disappearing into a bedroom. Battaglia stared down at the shag carpet, thinking he just needed to hang on for another few minutes.

It sounded like Alonzo was rearranging cardboard boxes, but noise stopped when a little girl's voice asked, "What are you saying about what I don't know? You couldn't talk louder if you had a megaphone."

Alonzo's reply was so muted Battaglia barely heard it. "Go back to sleep," he mumbled. The puttering sound resumed.

"Get me some more ice?" she asked.

"Not now."

"Goddamn it, Lonzo, I got to do everything myself?"

Battaglia scratched his crotch and was looking toward the room when Sincere appeared, wearing a "Juice 32" t-shirt that stretched to her knees. Her legs and feet were bare, gait wobbly. Battaglia had met her before. She was a waif, such a contrast to the big man.

Her black hair was matted on the side. When she came near enough to pass, he noticed her face, riddled with bruises and contusions.

"What the hell happened to you?" Battaglia wondered. He turned to Alonzo, who had reappeared with a powder-filled baggie. "You do this to her?"

"Hell no. I ain't never laid hands on her. Treat my woman right."

"Treats me so right I gotta get my own icepack," Sincere grumbled, reaching into the freezer and twisting ice cubes into a dishtowel. "A john beat me up good last night. Cops in this city ever protect a working girl?"

Battaglia scoffed. "You don't like it, stay off the streets. You should know that going in, sweetie."

"Law enforcement to the rescue."

"Kind of an occupational hazard, isn't it? Stop hooking, these things stop happening."

"Oh, you think it's funny?" she asked, face hardening in response to his grin. "This guy talked about things cops might be interested in hearing."

"Yeah?" Battaglia wondered skeptically. "What would that be?"

"Said he killed a nigger yesterday. Threw her off of city hall."

"What?"

"Yeah, who's laughing now? I seen that on the news. Had a murderer pick me up last night. Beat the shit out of me, held a knife to my chin and said I was lucky cause he already met his quota for dead niggers on the day."

Battaglia hesitated. Could this little whore be making up a story to get attention? The jumper was high profile, all right, so he did not doubt she saw the story on TV. But most people believed it to be a suicide. A half hour earlier, at the detective bureau, Battaglia heard rumblings that perhaps it was not.

How would Sincere have known that?

"You going to investigate it?" she asked.

Between last night's booze and lack of sleep, Battaglia's senses were dulled. God, he just needed a boost to clear his head. Mark Bennett was the primary on the case, and he was in no hurry to help that bastard. Besides, even if he shared the information, Bennett would want to know the source. What would Battaglia say then? *I was at a drug dealer's apartment looking to score when his whore girlfriend with bruises up and down relayed some sad sack tale?*

"Maybe I could file a report with you," Sincere suggested. "Do some paperwork right now."

"Use some fucking judgment," Battaglia said. "It can't be on record that I was here. Wait til I leave and call it in you think it's so important. But you mention my name, so help me God-"

"Ain't nobody calling nothing in," Alonzo said, raising his hands to calm the situation. He was thinking straight. Sincere's agitation grew, and the cop's only concern was diving into his baggie. "Just cool it, both of you. We ain't about to go blabbing. What you gonna tell them, Sincere? You was out hooking last night and got a little beat up? They haul you in for solicitation cause you the one they got. Ain't got no bad guy, just some hooker's story about a man who probably don't even exist."

"Don't even exist?" Sincere repeated, her voice rising into fury. "The fuck does that mean? You think I put these bruises on myself, Lonzo? You think I like lying in a parking lot all beat up, fucking cracker stole my money?"

"I think you're a dumb whore who probably ought to keep her mouth shut, is what I think," Battaglia said.

Sincere whirled on him. "Fuck you, copper! And fuck you too, Lonzo!"

"You little bitch," Battaglia raised his palm from the door handle and stepped toward the center of the room. Alonzo positioned his girth between the officer and Sincere, keeping his hands upturned.

"Stay calm, everybody," he growled, and his raised voice was a blast of sobriety. "Sincere, get back in that bedroom. Officer, you on duty. You don't need this. Go inspect your product and do whatever it is you do on your shift. I'm throwing you that gratis, a one time gift, so let's all be reasonable."

Battaglia's aggression remained suspended in the air, but his movement had stopped. Although he wouldn't give the black man satisfaction by saying so, Alonzo was right. He adjusted his sleeves and turned back toward the door. He got what he had come for, so it was time to get the hell out before anyone noticed. Besides, his partner was probably waiting for him back at the station. Battaglia folded the baggie against itself and slid it deep into his right pocket.

"I'll be in touch," he said, before pulling the handle shut. His soles echoed as he trudged down the stairs.

*   *   *

Bennett was three hours deeper into the investigation, but no closer to results. A command post had been set up at city hall. With help from other officers, everyone who had walked through the revolving doors that morning was interviewed, all to no avail. No employees had an overnight revelation about Rosa Greene. In fact, no one ever recalled seeing her. She was a black cleaning lady in a bustling government building. It was a sad commentary, but Bennett realized the woman had been invisible to the hundreds of people she served every day.

His spirits sagged when the deputy police commissioner showed up in the staging area and began to shake hands, asking for the latest update. His chief appeared soon after and milled about without directly addressing him. Under the microscope of his bosses, Bennett had nothing to offer. He realized it was a matter of time before he would be yanked from the case.

"I'm gonna try a different track," he said, without explaining further. "Be back in an hour." He carried three manila folders filled with notes from the previous day's interviews. The plan was to grab a sandwich and read over the file. Maybe something in the paperwork would kick loose and trigger an idea.

The Thirsty Bison was a hole-in-the-wall bar three blocks from the homicide squad. Its owner had retired from the job, so cops had an inside connection to the place. Many gathered there for lunch or after a shift change, reveling in the safety of its dim lighting. With dark paneling and square tables, The Thirsty Bison's food was a little-known secret in downtown.

Bennett sat at a corner table by himself and nodded to Paulie, the owner's son. Paulie had done a stint in the army after high school, and returned home to tend bar. He planned to take the police exam and follow in his old man's footsteps. He liked to joke with patrons.

"What'll it be, Detective?"

"A Reuben and a 7-Up," Bennett said.

"You got it."

At eleven a.m. on Tuesday the place was nearly empty. Two white haired men sat talking over frosted drafts on the far side of the room. Bennett chose a table near the front window and immersed himself in the file, glancing up only when his drink was laid before him. When the bell on the outside door tinked, he looked toward the ring and scowled, raising a palm to his forehead.

Ken Connell entered with a skinny bleach blonde. They both smoked cigarettes, sitting on barstools and cozying up close. Neither noticed Bennett. Paulie laid napkins on the counter before them and took their orders. Although he couldn't hear what was said, Bennett watched as Paulie nodded toward his corner. Connell and the girl swiveled to see.

Bennett recognized her. She was a streetwalker named Valerie. Nearly half Connell's age, her tiny waist was overshadowed by hair that fell toward the small of her back. A plunging neckline revealed the rounded insides of small breasts. She had big doe eyes painted with purple eyeliner. They projected an innocence that belied her experiences.

Across the room, Bennett watched as Connell put his mouth close to Valerie's ear and whispered something only she could hear. Absently, she threw her head back and laughed, nodding in agreement.

He had encountered Valerie years ago, when she was just a teenager. Bennett found her wandering through Delaware Park at three a.m. on a Saturday. He put her in the backseat of the black and white and drove her to a narrow two-story house a few blocks away. A drunken father answered the door, and proceeded to glare at his daughter through an alcoholic haze. The man grabbed Valerie around the forearm, so tightly that the skin drained of all color. Her eyes went dead, resigned to pain. Backing out of the driveway that night, Bennett wondered if he had helped or hurt the girl by returning her home.

Now Connell brushed a strand of hair away from her forehead and whispered again. Their body language was comfortable and familiar. Maybe this was the girl he had been with when the chief called for him yesterday.

"That is one primo piece of ass," Paulie said, dropping a plate with a Reuben and fries onto the table. "I know she's been around the block, but holy shit. Banging her would be a good tradeoff for the getting the clap. I could fit both her ass cheeks in one hand and grab her waist while she bounced on top of me."

"How about you just bring me my sandwich, Paulie? I don't need the commentary."

Paulie looked away from the girl and focused on Bennett, grinning a harmless smile. "What, no verbal banter today, Detective? Got a bug up your ass?"

"Clock's ticking on my case."

"Oh yeah, the colored jumper. Connell was bitching about it. Seriously, I don't understand that guy. I heard he's got a grade-A wife, we're talking thoroughbred, and I know for a fact he bangs three times as many broads as me."

Mark hesitated at the assessment. "That's not saying much."

"Detective, be real. Look at me. I'm an Adonis. I'm younger and more handsome. I'm betting that guy's got a ten-inch dong, what do you think?"

"I think your old man is calling you from the kitchen. I can just about hear him."

"He's not in today. Geno's back there."

"You better go check, just in case."

"Okay, I can take a hint. But you know I'm right." Paulie spread his hands apart, as if measuring an invisible fish. "Ten inches."

As Paulie walked away, Bennett chewed his sandwich and re-read notes from the day before. He had hoped to get a clue from one of the elevator operators, but neither remembered anything unusual about the morning. One asked to look at a picture of Rosa Greene, but couldn't identify her for sure, much less confirm she had been in his car that day. The pages before him were an accumulation of useless observations.

Connell's voice interrupted him from across the room.

"Hey Bennett, you clear that yet?" he boomed. "No? That case still isn't closed, and you got time to sit in a corner and eat a sandwich? That was me, I'd be working round the clock. Citizens of Buffalo deserve the best, don't you think?"

The two white haired men raised their eyes, then looked back at their plates. Paulie shook his head and went through a swinging door toward the kitchen.

Mark scratched his nose and stood. He stepped forward, nodded to Valerie, who showed no sign of recognition, and leaned down to Connell.

"Can I have a word privately?"

"No," Connell glared at him. "This is a public establishment, and I got nothing to hide."

Valerie realized there was little value in sitting adjacent to two bickering cops, so she squiggled away and disappeared toward the restroom. Mark kept his voice low so no one else could hear.

"All right, then let me make this clear. Taunting me isn't helping anyone. I haven't closed this because there were no witnesses, so it's pretty much a guessing game. I could write it up as a suicide and probably get away with it, but no evidence suggests suicide, so that doesn't strike me as ethical. You know what that word means, ethical?"

"You gutless little puke," Connell said.

"Yeah, I didn't think so. It doesn't really matter though, because by the end of the shift, this case is probably going to be reassigned to you."

"Good. Make sure your notes are legible."

"Yeah. You can flap your lip and act like a big man all you want, but unless you produce some magical witness, this is going to be you spinning your wheels in a few hours. And don't you try to clear it by claiming it was a suicide, because I'm not going to let you do that."

"Let me?" Connell leaned back and let out a deep belly laugh. "You don't let me do anything. I been a detective thirteen years, and you've been here three months. I remember a time — I guess it was about four months ago — when new detectives sat on the bench until they learned the job. If I think it's a suicide, that's how I'll write it up. I actually have a record to stand on." He reached up quickly and touched the back of Mark's ear. "See? My fingers are wet."

"You happy now?" Bennett moved out of arm's reach. "You had your big moment where you try to embarrass the new guy in front of a young girl and a bartender. Congratulations. That's why you're a superstar. If you need me, I'll be out working. And hey, Ken, I really appreciate the feeling of brotherhood you infuse into the squad."

"Infuse?"

"Yeah, infuse. You need a definition?"

"Go waste a few more hours, Bennett. Looking forward to reading your file this afternoon."

*   *   *

None of the bar's windows overlooked the parking lot. Bennett sat in his car, exhaling. He did not ask for the encounter, nor had he sought conflict, but he held his own in a verbal joust with Ken Connell. It was a small victory. Still, he quivered. He never liked talking to the guy. Shoulders and hands felt shaky, stomach clenched. The back of his throat was raw as sandpaper.

Although he did not want to add to Alison's stress, she would be the only one to understand his feelings. He would detour to the library for ten minutes before heading back to city hall. Unless some break developed, he did not know what else to do. He started the engine and drove up Ellicott Street.

He parked, rode an escalator to the third floor, and weaved through a series of thick wooden doors and bland corridors. He knocked on the metal frame of her office.

"Hey," she said, looking up from behind her desk.

"Hey yourself." As he entered the room, she stood. They kissed, wrapping arms around each other, holding the embrace longer than needed. She moved her mouth toward his ear and spoke softly.

"Did you come for that nooner?" she wondered.

He grinned, feeling desire spring below his stomach. "No, but it's a hell of an idea. I'm glad you're coming around, but I need a raincheck. I can't stay."

"Okay," she leaned back. "I probably would be too timid anyway. What's up?"

"This case is kicking my ass. I wanted to tell you that I just had another run-in with your husband."

Chapter 6

One of the reasons Mark Bennett loved road patrol was that movement and motion were regular components of the job. Yet after being promoted to detective three months earlier, he felt rooted to his desk too often. When he spent long blocks of time in the office, days dragged. The homicide squad was six blocks from the library. He began walking there during lunch hour just to break up the day.

He observed everyone he passed on the sidewalks. Once inside the library, Mark found a solitary contoured vinyl chair where he propped open a book, alternately reading words and watching people stroll past.

The dark-haired woman was pretty, but he thought nothing of her until she passed by again the following afternoon.

Sharp features made her distinctive. Eyes were the color of milk chocolate, brows shaped into a prominent arch. The nose was bigger than it should have been, sporting a bump in the middle like a fading peach welt. A mole dotted the center of her neck. In heels she was taller than most men.

On one pass, she tucked three paperbacks into the crook of her elbow. Another time she lugged records in an oversized brown traveling envelope. Still again she carried nothing, arms swinging with a singular purpose. Watching for her became habit-forming.

Their meeting was a fluke. Nearing the end of his break, he was leaving the library when a gray-haired woman lost her footing on the tiles and staggered, trying to right herself. No sound came from her lips, but in slow-motion delay Mark witnessed her fall, his own body tensing for the collision. A chuffing sound filled the room, like air being sucked away. Books splayed around her, and a snapping— either dust jackets smacking the floor or bones breaking — buried the white noise. Mark was already in motion.

Dazed and shaken, the woman sat up. He knelt by her side, insisting she remain seated to catch her breath. A crowd assembled. The cute librarian wedged into their space and bent down, wondering what had happened. That afternoon she wore a black skirt and ribbed turtleneck sweater whose blue intensified her hair. As Mark explained, an older man appeared, claiming to be the library director. Then an off-duty nurse happened by. Within minutes, the fallen woman stood, wincing, and hobbled a few tentative steps, with no apparent long-term damage. She promised to head home and apply a hot-pack to her aches.

The assembly scattered, and Mark left without speaking to anyone further.

Two days later, however, back in his familiar nook, his favorite librarian walked past, glancing absently in his direction. Confusion clouded her face, followed by recognition.

"You helped the woman who fell the other day," she said, stopping to retreat two steps toward him.

"That's me."

"I didn't get a chance to thank you," she said. Her voice sounded like coffee, steaming and sonorous.

"You didn't need to."

The response seemed to puzzle her, and she paused. "I work here," she explained.

"I figured. I've seen you a couple times."

She smiled and leaned forward, extending her hand. "Alison Keane."

Mark stood and shook. He was taller, but not by much. "I'm Mark Bennett."

"I never noticed you before the other day. Are you a regular?"

He shrugged. "When it's not too busy at work I come during lunch hour. Feel like I'm improving my mind." He held up the paperback in his palm. "Reading calms me."

"Me too," she smiled, studying the spine. "And Gatsby's a classic. I adored that book in college. I really should re-read it."

"I was forced to in high school, but I'm enjoying it more this time. Books are better when there's no essay requirement."

"No kidding. You like the classics?"

"All different types of books, really."

She stepped back with narrowed eyes. Playfully, she said, "Okay, what's your favorite novel of all time?"

Mark blew out a breath and searched his memory.

"Tough to answer. There are so many good ones that I wouldn't want to limit myself."

"Coward."

"Coward, huh? Okay, what about you?"

Her lips pursed. "I like the classics too, but I also like quiet little books that I discover on my own. Novels that don't win any awards or make anyone's top one hundred list. A book that I pick up with no expectations and it pulls me in and makes me sorry when it's over."

He nodded. "That's great, but you really didn't answer the question."

"You're perceptive." Her laugh was slinky.

"So?"

"So I guess I need time to think before I can give you a good answer."

Mark smiled. Sometimes he was intimidated around attractive women, concerned about saying the wrong thing. But she had initiated their flirting, and already, after just a few seconds, he had slipped into an easy comfort with Alison.

"It's nice to meet you, Mark," she said, face open as if she shared his instinct. "I appreciate your help the other day. I'll be seeing you around, right?"

"I'll be here." She turned to walk away, but he called to her. "Hey Alison? You're not off the hook. Next time I expect an answer."

Mark noticed she did not wear a ring on either hand.

* * *

With the morning newspaper spread before him, Mark perched on an elevated stool in the library's new coffee shop when a silky voice said, "The Heart is a Lonely Hunter."

It had been five days, and he had forgotten the intricacies of her face. She was pretty, he had known that, but not until she stood before him did he remember her exotic appeal. Today her eyes were a rich carmel, cheeks thin and high set. She nodded, a combination greeting and acknowledgement that she was proud to have reached a decision after pondering the question.

"Good choice," he admitted.

"I just re-read it last month, and it's even better than I remember."

"Want to sit for a minute?" he asked.

Sipping from a styrofoam cup, she pulled the adjacent stool from its nesting spot under the table. A minute turned into twenty, and by the time they parted, Mark was more than intrigued — he developed a fast crush on Alison Keane. Maybe he was being optimistic, but conversation with her could stretch deep into the afternoon without any effort.

* * *

"Last time I saw you, you said same time tomorrow," Alison mused. "That was four days ago."

63

He smiled. Today she was wearing a black scoop-neck blouse and gold necklace with matching earrings.

"Yeah, I did say that. But the last few days have been crazy. I caught a case."

"A case?" Her welcoming eyes hardened. Shoulders tensed as she stepped back. "You're a cop?"

"Yeah, a detective," he said.

"Oh," she paused, concern creasing her forehead. "I didn't know that." She pushed hair away from her temples and tucked a long tendril behind her ear.

"You okay?" Mark wondered.

"Sure," she said, shaking her head as if she had just stepped through a cobweb. Straightening, her arms loosened. "I'm just surprised."

"Is that a problem? Are you wanted on a felony or something?"

"No, of course not." She grinned tepidly.

He shrugged. "Because that's not my department. I work homicides."

She nodded as if a secret had been revealed. "A homicide cop. Wow. I'll bet you know all sorts of interesting people."

"Yeah."

"Who's worse, the cops or the killers?"

Mark clucked, unsure what she meant. "What did you think I did for a living?" he asked.

"I... I guess I didn't know. I wouldn't have guessed a detective. You don't see many detectives who read Fitzgerald on lunch hour. For some reason I envisioned you at a law firm."

"A law firm? Wouldn't I have to dress a little nicer?"

"You always wear a coat and tie."

"Yeah, a sport coat off the discount rack. Not a suit. I dress too shabby to be a lawyer."

"It doesn't mean anything. Some lawyers dress like bums."

"And I look just as good as them? Thanks."

"You could have been a lawyer. You're good at twisting words." She grinned. "How long have you been a detective?"

"Just a few weeks. I worked patrol before that."

She looked over his head, through the wide plate glass window, and stared at a faraway spot as if a hidden truth might be discovered there.

"I was wondering if maybe sometime this week you wanted to grab lunch," he suggested. "Maybe we go off campus."

Her gaze focused, coming back to him. "Are you asking me out?"

Until then, he hadn't felt nervous. But with her hesitation, he inhaled and locked onto her eyes. "Yeah."

Alison's lips pursed and she hesitated five seconds before speaking. Mark felt time turn elastic. "Okay, I accept. But I need to tell you some things first, and if you change your mind I'll understand."

*   *   *

She was only twenty when she met Ken Connell. Six weeks later they married. He was a few years older, handsome and funny and experienced in a way unlike other boys who paid attention to her. The first few months were a whirlwind. They spent every moment together, laughing, joking, discovering each other's foibles. He was stunning in his uniform, a rookie patrolman set on advancing his career. She pushed ahead in school, determined to earn an English degree. Penniless, with no savings, their parallel goals lent them a common interest.

For all his ruggedness, Alison soon learned that there was a part of her husband that was walled off. He rarely talked about hours canvassing city streets, or the fellow officers he spent his days with. His silence, she thought, was meant to protect her. Maybe it was better that she not grapple with the perils of his job. Nor did he ever mention the years in Vietnam. She wondered what he had been like before traveling to Southeast Asia. Had he once been outgoing and gregarious? Had part of his personality been lost forever in those jungles?

Soon the initial burst of affection evaporated. He was promoted to detective at twenty-seven, the youngest in the squad. While he logged unconventional hours, she was bored. With wide blocks of time, she spent evenings in darkened movie theaters alone, listening to concerts at churches or Kleinhan's Music Hall, sometimes sharing dinner with friends. It drove him crazy when he called home and no one answered. He didn't think Alison should be out, because that suggested that she was available to other men.

Ken did not want Alison to work. He held the traditional notion that a husband should provide for his wife. Her job was to manage the house and be supportive when he arrived home. They talked of having children, but Alison hoped to delay that until her thirties. Without consulting him, she continued taking birth control pills. He grew frustrated with her inability to become pregnant.

She wanted to take a job, even part time, but he rejected the idea. "The timing isn't right," he said. "We'll have a baby soon and you'll just have to quit anyway." As seasons passed and spring turned to summer, the question began to nag her. Why did I marry so young?

While doing laundry, she emptied the pockets of his work trousers and found a scrap of paper. The name "Betsy" and a phone number were scrawled in cursive. She asked him about it that night, and he turned angry, claiming Betsy was a witness who had vital information about a suspect. *Why the hell are you always so suspicious?* he demanded.

Until that point, Alison had not been suspicious. Maybe Betsy was a witness, but Ken had protested too much. Soon she was sniffing his shirt collars, curious about the scent of unfamiliar women. It would be easy for him be unfaithful and never be caught.

She sought a marriage counselor, but he refused to go. Nothing was wrong with their marriage, he insisted. Soon she would have a baby and there would be a focus to her life. She tried to explain that she felt boxed in, jailed within the walls of their home. It didn't even feel like a home. It felt like a detention center. She wanted something to fill her days, something with which to define herself more than simply "Mrs. Ken Connell."

He could not understand. "I'm not abusive," he said. "You've got a roof, a clean home, a good healthy life. I go into places on the job where women don't have it half as good as you and they're happy."

It wasn't enough. He did not understand.

When she told Ken she wanted to move out, the quiet tension exploded into firebursts.

"You're cheating on me," he said, tipping over a kitchen chair. "There's another man!"

"There's not."

"Then why?" Rage leapt in his eyes.

"I've told you why."

"Dammit, those aren't good reasons!"

"They are for me," she pleaded. "I have nothing that is my own. I have no reason to wake up each day except to serve you. I know that you don't think this is a problem, but to me it is."

Ken heard the words, but could not form them into blocks of understanding. Empathy was never one of his traits. His frustration grew, and he lashed out at her. This was her fault, he had been happy in the marriage, they had been a good team, but now she was bent on destroying it.

"You're a selfish whore," he told her. Alison marveled that he could be so contradictory. He wanted to remain married yet

peppered her with insults and derision. Did he think that might
lure her back?

*   *   *

When he heard her history, Mark felt divided. Part of him
screamed to hightail himself away. Get involved with a woman
who wasn't even divorced yet? And worse, her husband was a
superstar detective who worked two desks away at his new job?
There was no way this was a good idea.

He vowed that these romantic notions needed to put under a
lid. When he wasn't around her, it was easy to play the role.

But the attraction was unlike anything he had felt. When
they were together he spiraled deeper into her life. Alison was
smart and funny and sexy and they could talk about anything.
When they were apart, he wanted to share snippets from his day
that he knew would make her laugh. Their relationship remained
a secret, and they both clung to it with desperation.

*   *   *

Now, just minutes after his verbal sparring with Ken Connell
in the bar, they sat on opposite sides of her office desk.

"He's been unbearable," Alison admitted. "Called here this
morning and wondered how late I was out last night. He knows
it was after midnight, because that's when he gave up calling.
Said I'm a harpy."

"What did you tell him?"

"It's none of his goddamn business and that he has no reason
to be checking up on me."

Mark shook his head. "This is bad. We need to be more
careful. If we're seen together..."

"Mark, we are careful. I park around the corner when I come to your house. We hardly ever go out in public. But you have to realize we have nothing to apologize for."

Mark felt confused. He wanted to slow things down without ending the romance. It was morphing into something bigger than him. He was having nightmares about the loss of control. There was no way to predict the outcome. If their affair was discovered...

"How's the divorce coming? I'll feel so much better when that's done."

She exhaled. "Slow. He's doing everything he can to delay. Different lawyers, adjournments. I love when people tell me that divorce is the easy way out. There's nothing easy about this. The easy thing would be to shut my mouth and stay with him. But if I do that, I lose everything I ever have a chance to be. I'm too young to just give up on life."

Chapter 7

His body unwound from its curl, eyes opening suddenly then snapping closed as afternoon light flooded the room. The window was open, and a breeze fluttered through pale curtains. Soreness permeated his shoulders and hips. He flopped onto his back and pried his lids open. The ceiling came into focus, and he studied its fault line. Like his emotions, the crack zagged and turned against itself, splintered rivulets that vanished into paint.

Had yesterday really happened? Did he really throw a jig from the balcony? Was that him who picked up a hooker, forced himself inside her, beat her and stole her money?

Who was this new man?

He was both frightened and emboldened by the last twenty-four hours. He was, after all, the boy to whom nobody had ever paid attention. He had always been the kid who sat on the grass at the playground, the student stuck to the back of the classroom who was ignored by both his teachers and peers. Little Joey was an odd one, everyone said. He never learned how to fit in.

Those niggers never should have messed with him.

Five nights ago his beater was in the shop so he rode the bus to work. Even in this realm he didn't feel comfortable. Confused about procedure, he had to ask the driver how much it cost to board, and the old man quoted a figure and showed him how to drop coins into the slot. Then he paused to count out the proper amount. He sensed the glare of other riders, their eyes boring into him, telling him without words that his ignorance was slowing them down. Again, he felt inadequate.

On a night after his shift ended, past midnight, he waited for the bus, sitting on a bench with hands pressed under his knees. All around him was pavement, and he felt weary, mind numb from eight hours of factory work. Around the corner came three blacks, young turks with a swagger for trouble. They were drunk. It was dark. A late summer rustle swept through the oak leaves above.

"Curtis, look here. We got us a white boy waiting for da bus."

His throat clenched. He would not run. Avoid eye contact, he told himself. Don't acknowledge them.

"We gonna to need borrow somea you money, son. Those whiskeys was goin down smoove, but den we run outta funds."

He said nothing, staring straight ahead. The one called Curtis used a toe to stab at his leg.

"You heard da man."

His eyes shifted quickly to their sooty faces, then looked away. "Sorry. I only have enough for one fare."

"Then it looks like you gonna be walking, don't it?"

"Huh?"

Before he knew it, two of them laid their paws on him, securing his arms and shoulders from behind. They grabbed for his back pocket and ripped out his billfold, finding a crisp ten-dollar bill and guffawing with glee. While he squirmed, the other one remained in front and balled a fist into his belly. As he fell, they began to stomp on his cheeks and fingers and legs. He tucked into himself, heard their hyena laughs and jungle hoots. As their shoes pattered in a primitive tribal dance, warm spittle landed against his cheek.

He staggered home, penniless and battered, with a reawakened hatred. His father had been right. They were useless, taking up good oxygen that should be reserved for the whites. That's when he decided to launch a new apocalypse.

His blood felt charged, and he awakened to reality.

He would kill again. Today. This time at a bus stop.

*　　　*　　　*

"You want me to top that off, sweetie?" Joanie asked, poised with a clear pyrex coffeepot hovering above his cup.

"No thank you," Jerry Deck answered. "I gotta shove off."

"Second shift today?"

"Logging as many shifts as the boss lets me. We're on deadline and I like the overtime."

"Don't weld your fingers together, you hear?" she teased.

He watched her turn away and stared at her hips as she rounded the row of booths. Jerry had discovered the diner by accident but had been coming here for several weeks because the job site was around the corner. He would load up with a big meal beforehand, or sometimes wander in afterwards to wind down from hours wielding a steady blue flame.

Joanie was the reason he kept coming back. Her personality glistened. She was nearly forty, with fading auburn hair and freckled cheeks, and there was still a swagger there, a reluctance to slip gracefully into middle age. She gave him little snippets about her kids, and he spoke in sound bites about pipe welds and elbow joints. It wasn't a crush, because he was engaged to Marie, but it was fun and harmless to flirt, a pleasant diversion to the monotony of work.

Ten years ago, Jerry thought, before squeezing out those two kids, Joanie would have been a stunner. But back then he was still in high school, and would have been too young for her anyway.

Jerry checked his watch and folded the newspaper against its crease. Within a week, the job would be finished and inspected, and he would move to another site. Round-the-clock urgency would slow. With that would come relief. Odd hours of the past month strained his body, and he needed to log a regular pattern of sleep. But he would also stop coming to this diner. It was too far from his neighborhood, distant from any new job site, and returning would smack of desperation.

With his palms around a coffee cup, looking through the diner's plate glass window, Jerry felt a teenage glumness. He didn't want the playful banter to end.

That's when he noticed movement at the bus stop across the street.

A young black guy hunched over, collapsing to his knees, holding his mid-section. A steady stream of crimson spilled from his stomach, puddling onto concrete.

Standing above him was a short white man in a baseball cap. He made no move to help the bleeder. In fact, for a moment he studied the tableau, as if trying to memorize its chaos. When he turned, a large knife glistened in his right hand. With no sense of urgency, he strode away and rounded a corner, vanishing without ever looking back.

"Oh," Jerry said, getting to his feet. "Oh my."

At the bus stop, two men seated on a bench noticed the blood now, their faces registering shock. One stood and backed away, while the other leaned down and touched the neck of the man on all fours.

"Joanie," Jerry yelled, urgency filling his voice. He hurried toward the door. Her head appeared in the opening between the serving room and kitchen, brows furrowed in confusion.

"Yeah sweetie?"

"Call an ambulance, right now. There's been a stabbing across the street."

*　　　*　　　*

Patrolmen had strung yellow crime tape to secure the scene. The victim was gone by the time Ken Connell arrived. Standing on the sidewalk, he examined the layout of the bus stop, looking up and down the city street, taking in exhaust smells, aware of the noise level. A drying crepe of blood had baked into concrete, hardening into rivulets along the gutter.

To the right, a patrolman stood with a witness, a laborer in his twenties with moppy hair and a jutting chin. Connell removed a thin spiral notebook from his back pocket and approached.

"Detective, this is Jerry Deck," the uniform said.

"Hi Jerry," Connell said. "I guess you called this in?"

"Well, actually Joanie did. She's the waitress at the diner there." He pointed across the street. "But I told her to call. I watched the dead guy fall then noticed the dude next to him had a knife."

"You saw the guy who stabbed him?"

"Oh yeah. He wasn't jumpy or jittery or anything. He moved in slow motion, almost like he was calculating. He watched the brother drop, paused for a while, then strolled up the block and turned at the corner." Jerry raised a hand to signal direction.

"What did he look like?"

"White guy. Short, maybe five-six."

"How old?"

"Hard to tell cause he was wearing a baseball cap pulled low. I didn't see much of his face. Maybe thirty, but that's mostly a guess."

"What color was the cap?"

"Blue maybe?"

"Maybe?"

"I think it was blue, maybe green, but I'm not sure."

"Did it have anything written on the front? A logo of the Bills or Sabres or anything?"

Deck curled a lip in concentration, exhaling. "I don't remember that."

"Okay. How about his clothes? What was he wearing?"

"Plaid shirt, I think it was red and black plaid. Tucked the shirt into blue jeans. I couldn't tell the shoes, but I think the toes were pointed, like cowboy boots. But the blue jeans were over top of them, so I can't be sure."

"All right."

"You know, the thing is, detective, I only watched the dude for maybe ten seconds. I wish I remembered more details, but I was a bit dazed wondering if I had really just seen this."

"No, that's great Jerry. You're a big help. You go home and think about it and maybe something else will spring up. The officer here took your contact info?"

"Yeah."

"All right, so we may be in touch. And if you remember anything more — "

"Oh, one other thing. The guy who got stabbed, he said something to me when I ran over here. But it doesn't really make sense. Maybe he was in shock or something."

"What'd he say?"

"Well, he was gurgling blood, really struggling to talk. I asked him what happened, you know, and if he knew the dude."

"The guy who stabbed him, you mean?"

"Yeah. But he didn't. The brother said he got poked, then the dude looked at him and said, *This is better than a flagpole in your stomach.* What the heck could that mean?"

*   *   *

"What it means is that we've got a connection between the two cases," the chief explained. "It's thin and may prove to be nothing, but you need to combine your efforts on this."

The chief looked to the two men standing across from him. Connell edged a toothpick around his lips, appearing bored. He rested against the same radiator where Bennett leaned that morning. Bennett did not appear so casual. His shoulders remained rigid while he stood at full height.

"Talk to each other," the chief ordered. "Keep the other guy informed about what you're doing and what you find. Odds are good if we find this stabber there's a link to the jumper."

When summoned to the office two minutes earlier, Bennett had expected he was being yanked from the case, not to learn about another death. Still, he was unprepared for what Connell proposed.

"Chief, if you want I could take over both cases. That way there's only one chef in the kitchen instead of two."

Bennett glared at him, seething beneath the calm. *The fucking nerve. He wanted to pop this motherfucker in the jaw.* Then he thought, *Now we'll see if the boss' loyalty is all an act.*

The chief stared for too long, but Bennett couldn't read his expression. He was either annoyed or truly considering it.

"Work your case, Connell. Bennett will work his," he said, nodding. His eyes narrowed. "I'm sensing that you two don't like each other. Is that accurate?"

Both men were silent, their faces blank.

"Well, I don't give a shit. You two are the primaries on parallel cases where a black victim got impaled. Today's killer makes reference to yesterday. That's not an accident. Go out and prove it. I'm not asking you to like each other, but I am ordering you to cooperate. If you can't do that, tell me now and I'll bump both your asses off this. I don't like petty personal shit and I like it even less in my squad room. This is not the time to figure out who's got the bigger johnson. Got it?"

Bennett studied the floor while Connell smirked. There was a space before both detectives muttered, "Yes sir."

"I want hourly updates. When the colored groups get ahold of news that one of theirs was killed, they're going to start ranting like Son of Sam is back."

The chief nodded dismissively toward the squadroom. Bennett, adjacent to the door, left first and headed to his desk. Connell vanished into the break room.

Wonderful, Bennett thought to himself. *Now I'm going to be side by side with this asshole.* He tilted his head back and rubbed his temples. How could he work with this guy? How could he sleep next to Alison under these conditions?

He considered coming clean to the chief. Confess that personal differences were too deep to overcome, that partnering with Connell was not an option. Maybe the old man would understand. But it was more likely that he would be bumped back to patrol. His career would skid into a brick wall.

"Bennett," Connell called across the room, crooking two fingers toward the break room.

There were no options here. He had to do it. Bennett pushed away from his desk and crossed the floor, wishing his father was still alive to offer advice.

"Shut the door," Connell commanded, but Bennett ignored the request, folded his arms, and waited for the veteran to speak.

"Okay, let's put our cards on the table," Connell said. "It's no secret that I think you're a snot-nose college boy who doesn't know his ass from a hole in the ground. This coffeepot knows more about homicides than you do. There's things you can't learn from books. You need experience. And truthfully, I wanted that fucking jumper case, so the fact that you got it pisses me off. But the chief's right. We gotta look beyond all that and work together to close these two. If this is one guy murdering blacks, he's not gonna stop until we get him."

Bennett scowled. "Maybe side by side you could teach me everything you know. Be my mentor."

Annoyance crept into Connell's eyes. "You say shit like that and then wonder why I don't like you."

"Don't jerk me off. That's not why you don't like me. You didn't like me from the moment I got transferred here. Maybe you see a college degree and feel threatened. Maybe you're so insecure that you foam at the mouth whenever a new dog comes onto your lawn. Maybe you see me as someone with principles and know that you'll never be that guy. As for the sarcasm, that's only to amuse myself."

The two men stared at each other, frustration quivering like maggots beneath their flesh.

You have every reason to hate me, Mark thought, *and I have even more reason to hate you. You are manipulative and controlling and you treated Alison like a plantation slave. If you had any idea the things I know about you... If you knew that this morning I woke up next to your ex-wife...*

"Okay, so we'll never do backyard barbeques together," Connell admitted quietly. "But if you're so fucking principled, let's close these cases. Then I can get back to the business of thinking you're a little prick. Fair enough?"

"A little suspension of the tension?" a voice chirped from the doorway. Both men turned to see Eric Lenehan leaning against the metal frame, grinning like he had just delivered a punchline. Neither detective knew how long he had been there.

"Get the fuck out of here, Lenehan, and mind your own business," Connell growled.

Lenehan's smile fell flat. He scurried away like a gerbil.

Connell shook his head with disdain. "Fucking floater. Sometimes I want to give that cocksucker a real disability."

Bennett nodded. *There's one thing we can agree on,* he thought. He looked at his fellow detective, aware of the crow's feet etched around his eyes. *Not long ago, Alison shared everything with this man. And he has no idea that I love her.*

"Come on," Connell said. "I'm willing to trade files and I'll run my case for you if you'll do the same."

Bennett ran his hands along the flat countertop. He didn't have a choice.

Chapter 8

George Pope carried himself with the swagger of someone who worked patrol for twenty-four years and understood its rhythms and complexities. There had been opportunities for advancement, but he liked the independence that came from riding the streets. His first partner, Mac Bennett, had been promoted several times, but over the years warned Pope of the pitfalls.

"When you become a detective, you have to go downtown," Mac said. "That's where you see bosses. The more you're seen, the more chance somebody's gonna get some bright idea about how you're supposed to act. Believe me, there's days I wish I had stayed on patrol."

Pope took the words to heart, electing to remain in his comfort zone. He knew neighborhoods all over the city, exuding a sense of authority when he stepped out of his car. He wasn't tall, but was a big man whose waistline had expanded over the years. His hair was a crew cut, a reminder of the day in 1955 that he was discharged from the army. His eyes were different sizes — the right was wide and alert, the left perpetually narrowed into a questioning slit. His chin and neck were thick with flab, his voice crushed stone.

Pope had deep ties to the Bennett clan. Mac had been a veteran cop who mentored George when he was a rookie, teaching him about the streets. Years later, when Mark became a cop, Pope did the same thing for him. Mac had pulled strings to set them up as partners. Then, around the time Mark was promoted to detective, Bobby graduated from the academy and joined the force. Pope requested that the youngest Bennett ride patrol with him. He felt like a surrogate parent to the boys, happy to repay the debt he owed their father.

On Bobby's first day, George shook his hand and led him the passenger's seat of the patrol car. Bobby knew Pope because he had visited their house when Bobby was growing up, and stories about him were part of the family's history. Last time they had seen each other was at Mac's funeral.

"I heard you had other plans for a partner, kid," Pope said, giving voice to a rumor circulating among rookies.

Bobby rubbed his forehead and turned to face the veteran.

"It's nothing personal. I met this guy in the academy, Antonio, and we got to be friends. We made a deal that if we got into the same house, we'd request to work together."

Pope grinned smugly, like he watched an infant who struggled to reach food on the countertop.

"I realize it seemed like a long shot," Bobby admitted, uncomfortable with the other man's silence. "But we both thought..."

"You both thought with shit for brains," Pope finished. "You two don't know thing one about how this department works. Bosses aren't going to put two rookies together. Ain't gonna happen. Ever."

"Oh."

Bobby felt reluctance. His dad and George had been partners years ago, and this made him nervous because he and his old man had disagreed about everything, right down to how to describe the color of paint on the kitchen wall. Was Pope hoping to rekindle some long-lost days of his youth, expecting Bobby to act just like Mac had back in the 1960s?

Mark had told him that George was a great partner, a guy with a treasure chest of knowledge. But Bobby and Mark didn't always see eye to eye either. Bobby believed he learned best when discovering things on his own.

He figured Pope was a dinosaur who thought he knew everything about the job, that all the snot-nosed kids coming up couldn't hold their own with his generation. He was going to be pompous and arrogant and a pain in the ass. First chance he got, Bobby was going to switch to a new partner.

"So whatever big plans you had, amend them," Pope ordered. "You're stuck with me."

For now, Bobby thought. He absently clicked the pen attached to the duty clipboard, then realized it might betray nervousness. He didn't want Pope to see his jitters, especially not in their first few minutes together. He laid the clipboard on the console in front of him.

"Don't put that there," Pope said. "Set it on the floor between your legs. Otherwise it slides back and forth across the dashboard. It's gonna end up in my lap."

Bobby did as his partner asked and stared out the window at passing houses. Many Buffalo homes were built early in the century, before cars became the centerpiece of daily life. As a result, there were few attached garages. Houses were clustered close together, with space enough for a narrow driveway that led past the side door. If there was a garage at all, it was detached and often filled the backyard.

Five minutes into his first shift, the tips of Bobby's ears felt cold. For an autumn day, weather was unseasonably cool. He opened his mouth, but Pope spoke first, dispensing advice without invitation.

"I'm going to tell you right now there's three B's that will wreck you for this job: booze, broads and bribes. You want to be a good copper, you stay away from all three."

Bobby sighed. *Here we go.*

"Don't roll your eyes at me, kid."

"I didn't."

"You were thinking about it. You take a drink after work, that's fine, but stop after two. Never on the job. Far as broads go, you got a wife, right?"

"Yeah. Just had our first baby."

"All right. Congratulations. So keep your pecker in your pants, stay away from the floozies you bust. They'll offer you things to get out of trouble. It will be easy and tempting and no one will ever know if you accept. But don't accept."

"Okay." Bobby picked up the clipboard from the floor and ran his fingers across its metal arch.

"All my years on the job I never took a bribe and I never lied on the witness stand. You tell the truth, even if it means the asshole might walk. If he's guilty, he'll slip up again and the next copper'll get him. You'll go to sleep at night with a clean conscience."

Bobby waited for more. He knew that this was monologue, not dialogue, and to interrupt would be unwise. But the old cop paused, as if extra silence would allow his words to marinate.

"My ears are cold," Bobby said. "Could you roll up the window?"

Pope glanced at his new partner, shaking his head. "I could. I choose not to."

"It's like thirty-five degrees out. Some fucking September."

"Watch your mouth." Pope pointed to the dashboard. "You're so cold, turn up the heater."

"Isn't that kind of a waste? The president says we need to conserve."

"Jimmy Carter is an idiot," Pope scoffed. "He's a peanut farmer who got elected because he wasn't the one who pardoned Nixon."

"Yeah, well, I don't know much about politics. I don't see why you don't just roll it up."

"I know you don't see. That's why I'm here. With the window down, you can listen."

"Listen for what?"

"For everything. You're stopped, you might hear breaking glass. Or when someone sees your cop car, they might call out for help. A good cop is prepared and ready to act. So you keep the window down all the time, even if it's snowing. That's one thing I taught your brother."

Great, Bobby thought. *Here we go with the comparisons to Marky. First fucking thing I do when I get a different partner is crank up the window. Gonna freeze my ass off with this crackpot.* Thoughtlessly, he tossed the clipboard onto the dash.

Rolling through the quiet Buffalo night, George Pope realized he had his work cut out for him. The new kid was a handful, just bursting at the seams with rebellion. Didn't want to listen. Somewhere up in heaven, Mac was gazing down and shaking his head. There had always been tension between Mac and Bobby, even when he was a little boy. Pope understood why. He remembered how Mac had struggled with the kid's stubbornness. Over a sandwich one night, Mac vowed to break Bobby's spirit, just like they do in the military, really teach him who's boss. Only then could the kid be built into the man Mac wanted him to be. The project had been long-term, ongoing at the time of his death.

Pope turned left onto a side street. The clipboard slid across the dash, changed trajectory at the dimpled center console, and tumbled into Pope's lap.

"Sorry," Bobby offered, but before he could say more, Pope wrapped his meaty hand around the clipboard and threw it out the window.

*　　　*　　　*

Purple mimeograph ink smeared onto Alison's fingertips as she flipped pages of the quarterly budget report. She brushed back hair and scratched absently at her nose, wondering if the county legislature would try paring more money away from the library system. Last year's budget had been a disaster, even though numbers of checked items had grown steadily throughout the 1970s. Politicians, however, saw the library system as a pawn to the altar of politics.

She laid the pages back into a manila folder. Rolling a piece of stationary into her typewriter, she flipped the on switch and heard a steady drone of power. Before she could peck at keys, the phone rang.

"Alison Keane," she answered.

"Ally, this is Marissa," a nervous voice fluttered. "I'm in section seven. You better get over here now."

"Why?"

"Just get here. Trust me, it's bad. I'm freaking out."

"Marissa? What's wrong?"

"There's a heart."

"What?"

"There is a heart," she repeated, a little less confidently. "Sitting on an empty shelf."

"A heart? Like, a cutout valentine?"

"No, Alison. An actual heart. It's bloody and browning, the size of my fist. I have no idea if it's human."

*   *   *

On a torn sheet of lined paper, the note said, "Give from the heart to the KKK." The printing was crude and blocky, almost like it had been written by a grade-schooler.

In a little-used aisle tucked against a wall, Marissa had been reshelving books when she came upon the scene. At eye level, on the middle of an empty metal plank, sat a pulpy heart. Drops of blood dribbled the shelf then splattered the tile floor. The girl dropped the two hardcovers she carried, screamed, and rushed to a phone to call her supervisor.

When she saw it, Alison felt an oozing in her stomach. Could this heart be human? The note suggested that some "white power" wacko was running around loose in the city. Was it connected to Mark's case? Why had this nut chosen the public library for his display?

"And this was found where?" the older cop asked. With his bulbous nose and fleshy jowls, he was a battleship, but the younger one unnerved Alison. Short and muscular, with a crew cut, he had introduced himself as Officer Bennett. With mottled cheeks and a bullet-shaped head, he didn't look anything like Mark. She didn't imagine that Mark would have mentioned her to his brother, and Bobby's indifferent behavior seemed to confirm that. But what if a detective was called into the case? Under the watchful eyes of his colleagues, would she and Mark pretend they were meeting for the first time? Worse, what if it wasn't Mark? What if the detective who came was Ken?

"Right next to it," Alison explained. She talked with the police rather than Marissa, who had been sobbing for the past half hour. Marissa was a twenty-year old college student whose nerves were frayed on ordinary days. She might have to go into therapy after this.

"So you didn't see anyone suspicious around here, is that right?"

"I didn't see anything. I was in my office when Marissa called me. I came right away, saw this, then phoned you guys."

"Yeah, we get that," Bobby said. "But I mean earlier. When you were out of your office, walking the floor. See anyone unusual in the building today?"

Pope sighed. The kid was still green, phrasing stupid questions, ignorant of his surroundings. *Was there anyone unusual in the building today?* It was a goddamn public library, people shuffled in and out by the hundreds. Of course some were unusual. The building was a haven for the homeless, particularly when the weather turned chilly. What did Bobby hope to learn from his question? This pretty librarian would have a different definition of the word *unusual* than Bobby's. Whatever her reply, it would not add to their body of information.

"Well, I guess..." Alison began.

Pope interrupted. "Does the building have security cameras?"

"Uh... yes."

"Everywhere, or just at the entrances and exits?"

"Just the main doors, as far as I know."

"Okay," Pope nodded, glancing at his partner with some sort of buried meaning. "We're going to need to find one of those video tape machines and review what you've got."

*   *   *

He chose his current apartment because his father was buried two blocks away.

A gray slab dimpled into earth was the only grave marking. When he was younger, its simplicity bothered him. Maybe he hadn't discovered plutonium or been president or written the great American novel. But he had raised a son under difficult circumstances and taught the boy important things.

Then during his teen years, he refused to think about his dad. What was the point? The guy was gone, and all the wishing in the world wouldn't bring him back. There was no time for emotions. Survival filled his days. Foster homes took him in only so a string of skeezy tightwads could make some extra cash. There was no caring or tenderness on those threadbare sheets. School wasn't the answer either. He couldn't concentrate, teachers ignored him and his grades were always low. No one gave a shit.

At eighteen he joined the army, and during the sweltering days of basic training, thoughts about his dad boiled back. His pop had been the only one to care, the only one who ever taught him about the world. How would his life have been different if the old man lived? What would they both be doing now? He realized he had neglected that part of his history. His dad deserved more than a pauper's grave in a little rinky dink cemetery. With that epiphany, he promised himself that one day he would gather up a stake and buy his dad an upright tombstone. It would be straight and distinguished, polished granite, flecked with sparkling stones, engraved with his full name. Below his birth and death dates would be etched "loving father to Joseph."

After his discharge and return to Buffalo, he priced tombstones and realized this dream would take some time.

Now, standing over his father's grave at dusk, he shuffled his feet. Night was clear and the only sound within the iron fence was the gentle swish of branches. He stared down at the weathered marker. An upper corner had been chiseled away, perhaps rutted by a lawnmower blade years ago.

"I killed another one today, pop," he said anxiously, the pitch in his voice high. "Fucking monkey standing at a bus stop, staring off into space, and I shanked him good and deep, right in the guts. Never knew what hit him. He dropped to all fours, then looked up at me with these big saucer eyes, like he was saying *why*? And I watched those eyes get real scared, and it made me think of you."

He nodded to himself and thrust his hands deep into pockets of his dungarees.

"So that's two in two days. I figure one killed you, and then three kicked the shit out of me, so I owe them at least four. But I'm not gonna stop there. This is gonna be the fucking apocalypse. They're gonna be slammed into a brick fucking wall."

His voice burrowed deeper, breaths coming fast. *Slow down*, he told himself. He was getting too excited. His dad was always calm in the face of danger. What would he think if his son behaved like a woman?

Pulling hands from his pockets, he stroked the tattoo at the top of his shoulder, the one that read "MAD DOG." *Should get some memorial ink*, he thought. *One for each killing.*

"Anyway," he resumed with level speech, "I think the revolution might be underway. My job led off the six o'clock news, and then they said someone cut out a heart and left it in the library with a note about white power. News fucker said was only a cow's heart, but still, I wish I had thought of that. Either way, I'm inspiring people. Giving them ideas about our supremacy, about terror and extermination."

His mouth tasted gritty. The past two days had been exhilarating, but there was a price to pay for such peaks. He surged now, like he was racing a go-cart without brakes. A good bender usually brought him down, but then a valley could last for days, and he didn't want to crash completely. At home there was a six-pack in his refrigerator. Three beers would soften the harshness. He didn't want to puncture the high, just level it out.

"I gotta go, pop. But trust me, there's gonna be more. You know that. This is just a start. Another one tomorrow, okay?"

*　　*　　*

Mark crooked a finger behind the curtain, slivering it from the wall so he could observe the front yard. His neighbors' handicapped teenage daughter stood near the curb wearing headphones that snaked to a fist-sized tape player. Becky swayed in time to music that only she could hear. The girl was pear-shaped, with fleshy arms and sagging breasts. Her flab bounced as she shifted from side to side, clapping. When she wasn't in school, she was on this narrow strip of lawn nearly every day, dancing inside her own private universe, eyes scanning happenings along the road.

Alison appeared from around the corner, crossing the sidewalk in long strides. She waved to Becky, who spoke loudly over the din of music.

"Happy Tuesday, Miss Alison."

Mark dropped the drape and opened the door. He met Becky's gaze, raising a hand. With Alison inside, he snapped the dead bolt and wrapped arms around her, kissing her.

"What a day," she sighed.

"You okay?"

"Yeah," she shook her head as if the afternoon's events were inexplicable. "What's up with your case?"

"No closer, but we've got a new direction." He replayed information about the bus stop stabbing and how Connell was assigned that investigation.

"Oh hell, I need to call him," Alison interrupted. "He left a message for me at work, but with all the excitement I never called back." She laid her purse on the counter and stepped toward the phone. "You've still got the jumper, though, right?"

"For now."

"Good. I'm glad he didn't take that from you. Mind if I call him quickly?"

"I'll pour us some drinks while you do."

Alison flicked the rotary and said "Hi" into the phone.

"Why didn't you call me back?" Connell demanded.

"I'm doing it now."

"I left a message five hours ago."

"I didn't get it until later. We had an incident at work and things were crazy."

"The cow heart?"

"Yeah."

"What happened?"

"This little mousy college girl found it and called me right away. So I phoned the police and spent the afternoon talking to them."

His voice flattened as he asked, "You're okay?"

"Sure. It was a bit chaotic, that's all."

"Where are you now?"

"Home," she lied.

"I called your house ten minutes ago and no one answered."

Alison exhaled, shaking her head.

"Why didn't you answer?" he wondered.

"I was running the vacuum. I didn't hear the phone."

"Are you with another man?"

"Ken…"

"Because if you are, I can find out. I will find out."

"Really, Ken? Does that even matter? We're getting divorced."

"There's no reason for a divorce unless you're a lying, cheating whore—"

She cut him off. "What do you need from me, Ken? Why did you call?"

"If I come over there, am I going to find you home?"

"If you come over here, I'm calling your chief to tell him you're harassing me. You're not welcome here now. There's no need for you to check up on me."

"Well, I don't understand why you wouldn't answer the phone."

"I told you, I couldn't hear it with the vacuum running."

"You're driving me crazy. If there's another guy, Alison, I swear—"

"Ken, you need to stop this."

"Don't you understand that I love you?"

He loves me so much that he sleeps with a parade of women, Alison thought, *then feeds me these bullshit double standards.* But she didn't want to string out their argument, so she inhaled deeply. "How can you say that?"

"Because it's true. No one will ever love you the way I do."

God, I hope not, she thought.

"And we were happy together, for a lot of years, before you just—"

"We weren't happy. You were happy. Why wouldn't you be? I did everything you told me to. There was no room for me to learn or grow—"

"Things changed when you started working. That was a bad idea. What the hell does the library give you that I didn't?"

"How many times do you want to have the same fight? I needed something more."

"Ally, if you would only—"

"Please don't call me that. I'm too tired to do this all the time. I'm trying to figure out the reason for your call. If you don't need anything, I'm hanging up."

"You dirty bitch," he cursed, then disconnected.

Alison laid the phone onto its cradle and exhaled. Weary from the fight that never ended, she felt embarrassed to argue from Mark's house, where he heard their meanness.

Mark sat on the couch, clutching the tumbler with two hands, watching ice clink as he swirled the glass. He had listened to Alison's side of the conversation before, feeling helpless at her frustration. He wished she would scream "fuck off" then hang up. He wanted Ken Connell gone from both their lives. But Alison kept engaging him in a directionless dance instead of ignoring his requests to talk.

She walked slowly to the couch, as if sore or repentant.

"I think Ken wants me to commit suicide," Alison said.

Mark looked up as she sat.

"His plan is to push me until I'm so exhausted that I just say, screw it, I can't do this anymore. He's trying to create a situation where I'll kill myself. He wants me broken so I'll just give up."

The words hung between them.

"You can't let him do that," Mark said with resolve.

Alison stared at the far wall, tears pooling in her eyes. "It's so hard to fight with him every single day. The only break I get is when I'm at work, or with you. Whenever he talks to me, it's just a mind fuck."

"What do you mean?"

"He makes up lies about me. Earlier he said I stole from him. Accused me of having an extra set of keys and sneaking into his house when I know he's not there. He always wants to know where I am. He claims I'm sleeping with strange men I've picked up at a bar. Says I'm a selfish whore who ruined his life."

Mark's anger smoldered, but he struggled to remain stoic in front of Alison. *What kind of a man would say such things to a woman he claimed to love?*

"If it was once a week, or even every few days, I could get by," Alison continued. "But every day is wearing me down. I think he's close to driving me insane."

Mark laid his drink on the end table and adjusted himself, enfolding her in his arms. Her shoulders trembled. She felt small and vulnerable.

"I don't know how to tell you this," he said, "but while we're working these parallel cases, Connell is my new partner."

Chapter 9

Angelo Battaglia had crested the hill and approached its lee decline. After the sweet exhaustion that came from juicing while staying conscious for twenty-eight hours, relief was close by. The end of two long shifts blurred his edges, nerves tingling with euphoric confusion. He planned to shed his uniform, stand under a shower that alternated between scalding and frigid, then rub against Lisa. When he rolled over on the satin sheets, he would descend the dark hole of sleep and languish there for twelve hours.

Battaglia clopped up the stairs, unafraid of waking her. It would be better if Lisa had some inkling he was home. He preferred she at least be conscious when he humped her. She was probably passed out, though, and even sober that girl could sleep through a thunderstorm. Opening the bedroom door, a shaft of light from the hall erased the dimness. Her prone lump angled across the middle of the mattress. He slapped the doorframe with his palm.

"Wake up, beauty queen," he boomed. "I gotta take a shower then you're gonna make some room for me."

"Fuck off, Angelo," she mumbled without opening her eyes.

He grinned and nodded. "Nice mouth. You starkers under there?"

She didn't reply, so he swatted the wood trim three times. "Hey!"

"Stop, you asshole," she whispered, cracking an eyelid. "You bring me something?"

"Maybe."

"Then maybe I'm naked."

He unfastened his belt and slid it off. Stepping forward, he grabbed the blanket's corner and flicked, arching covers toward the ceiling. Lisa laid on her stomach, breasts flattened against the sheet, their rounded sides squeezing out. Her bare bottom looked saggy, like kneeded dough that failed to rise.

"What the fuck?" she said, tucking herself into a fetal ball. The dark rims of her nipples were visible as she rolled.

"Good girl." He retrieved a clear plastic baggie from his pocket and tossed it onto the pillow. "Get yourself ready. I got the itch."

Crossing the hall to the bathroom, he stripped, dropping his clothes on the floor. He stood before the mirror, leaning forward and studying himself. Scruff darkened his chin, hair was disheveled and his eyelids twitched. He was twenty-nine, but after a double-back shift, he felt twice that. Battaglia understood he looked like hell and was overtired, but something still felt off. He couldn't explain why, but a thumb-sized spot in his brain left a troubling shadow.

That fucking hooker Sincere had made reference to the flagpole jumper that was getting airplay on every radio channel. "I met my quota for dead niggers at city hall," or something like that, he told her. Could that have been a murder and not suicide? Battaglia knew that whores were notorious liars who adjusted their stories to align with reality. There was no denying she was beat up good. But dammit, was the little piece of snatch telling the truth? After hearing her and seeing the bruises, he couldn't shake the notion that maybe she was.

The right thing would have been to tell somebody about it. But that led to uncomfortable questions.

Where did you encounter this prostitute, officer?

In her living room.

What were you doing there?

Well, her boyfriend is my dealer. I move his product, pocket a shitload of cash, and in return for my discount Alonzo gets the inside skinny if the narcotics boys inch too close.

That would not work. Plus the case belonged to Mark Bennett. That son of a bitch was a holy roller who acted superior to everyone. His zinger that morning had plagued Battaglia for the rest of his shift. "You're a bad cop." Who the fuck was Bennett to judge him?

He twisted both handles in the shower, waiting until the temperature warmed. Stepping under the water, he let the perils of the day slide from his shoulders. What he needed was sleep. Sex and sleep would clear away cobwebs. Battaglia washed his neck and armpits so Lisa couldn't complain he was stinky, then lathered his groin, feeling desire spring to life.

*   *   *

Connell drove the unmarked sedan while Bennett sat in the passenger's seat.

"I'm going to assume that nobody gave you training in how to investigate a homicide," Connell said.

Bennett exhaled. He had stewed about Connell's treatment of Alison overnight, wondering how he could partner with a man who would treat any woman, let alone one he claimed to love, with such disrespect. And now the asshole was needling him?

"You really are a bottom feeder," Bennett spat. "Is everything out of your mouth going to be a slam? Cause I can't work like this. My father was an inspector who came up through the ranks and my old partner is a twenty-five year vet. Family dinners were like a how-to course about being a cop. So while I'm not a self-involved superstar, I do know a little bit about the job."

An amused look curled Connell's lips. "Cool it, college boy," he said softly, keeping his eyes on the road. "I probably phrased that wrong. I know who your pop was. And I know your partner was George Pope, right?"

Bennett nodded.

"Stand-up guy, but he rides patrol. He doesn't investigate murders. So just calm yourself down. What I was trying to say was that I'm almost certain you didn't receive any homicide training because the department doesn't do any. Ain't that a kick? Here, solve a murder, but we're not going to teach you how. There's funds for diversity training, because God forbid we offend a minority. But there's no classroom for how to close a case. I know because I've lobbied the chief about it, for all the good it's done me."

Bennett did not respond. Connell was right. There had been no training once he was promoted. New detectives were supposed to learn from guys in the squad. Perhaps wondering if his pedigree outweighed his abilities, none of the current crop had taken Bennett under their wing.

"So I'm not trying to patronize you or talk down, even if you are a douchebag," Connell continued. "Got it? I'm going to show you the way the veterans taught me. Now you can be a smart-ass if you want, but at least I'll know you've been exposed to the right methods. What you do after that is up to you. Okay?"

Bennett mused silently, then nodded.

"Murder is the most heinous crime there is," Connell's voice assumed a somber tone. "Any good detective takes pride in catching the guy who does it. The money isn't great, but comp time is a nice benefit. Problem with comp time is that you don't want to be out of the office too much. You gotta be around to catch the case initially."

Connell paused, reflecting that his untimely lunch two days earlier allowed Bennett to be assigned the murder at city hall. He inclined his head and continued.

"Anyway, it takes about two years to learn how to investigate a homicide by yourself. That's why I'm stunned that you were handed this one so early. To get good at it takes anywhere from three to five years. By then, you'll know what you're doing." Connell eyed Bennett with an ironic smile. "You're lucky you got me to show you the way."

"Big honor," he said dryly.

"Guys who are good at solving murders work round the clock. Your mind is going night and day. Right now we're working two cases, but sometimes it's more like six or seven at the same time. We've all stayed up until dawn reading files, hoping to shake loose another clue. Once you land a suspect, the biggest thing is you gotta work the case backwards."

"Backwards?"

"Yeah. Start reading the most recent files and go backwards, examining every little detail. Re-interview witnesses. Double and triple check facts. Visit crime scenes again with a fresh set of eyes, around the time of day when the murder occurred. You go all the way back, just looking for some mistake that you or some other cop made, anything that will prove the suspect's not guilty. You're looking to find that he's innocent."

"Innocent?"

"Absolutely. Explore every angle you can think of, no matter how far-fetched. If there is any possibility that your guy didn't do it, you need to pursue that. If you reach the front of the file, and you think he's still your guy, you're halfway there."

"Halfway?"

"Yeah, because now you're going to work the file again, only this time going forward. If you can reach the end and there are no other possibilities, then more than ninety-nine percent of the time, the fucker you got in your sights is guilty."

"So you're saying every case gets investigated three times."

"If it's done right. The original one, then backwards, then forwards. You won't have anything bite you in the ass if you're that thorough. It's when detectives start taking shortcuts, making leaps of logic, when problems come up. Defense attorneys drool when we cut corners. I hate defense attorneys, so part of the motivation is to give them nothing. Put all those bastards out of a job."

"First we kill all the lawyers," Bennett said softly.

"Huh?"

"Shakespeare."

Connell rolled his eyes. "Whatever. I heard he was a fucking fruit."

"Where are we going, anyway?" Ten minutes earlier, after Bennett walked into the squad room but before he had a chance to pour coffee, Connell insisted they sign out a car and take a ride.

"This is one of the things I wanted to tell you. Our cases don't seem to be connected."

"Really?"

"This woman from city hall, this Rosa Greene, she had no enemies. That's why you're hitting a dead end. But my guy that got shanked, Calvin Richie, is one bad dude. I did some work last night, and it seems there's a lot of people wanted him dead. This is the second time he was stabbed."

Connell shared his investigation. Although he was only twenty-three, Calvin Richie had been on the radar of the Buffalo police for nearly a decade. He had been popped for a series of low-grade stuff throughout his teens — petty theft, shoplifting, marijuana possession — and after leaving school, bounced between a series of minimum wage jobs.

Three months earlier Calvin had been stabbed while playing poker in an east side apartment. According to police reports, the perp had been Phillip Dunphy, another low life with a rap sheet of his own. Calvin had been insulting him all night, and after a particularly heated hand — in the incident report, Dunphy insisted that triple queens were on the board — Calvin had flapped his lip one too many times. Dunphy brandished a carving knife, threatened to gut the bastard if he didn't shut up, and then lunged across the table when the scrawny twerp spit at him. Adding to Dunphy's anger was the fact that Richie continued to laugh like a rabid hyena, even after he was cut.

"So we're gonna chase down this Dunphy, see where he was yesterday afternoon. Maybe they had a poker rematch and it triggered something."

Bennett nodded. "Okay. But if these cases aren't related, why don't we explain to the chief there's no reason for us to work together?"

"We need more info. Listen, I don't like this situation any more than you, but we go to him now, he's gonna blow a gasket. Claim we're both looking for an out."

God knows I am, Bennett thought. Then he felt excitement. If Dunphy was involved in the Richie stabbing and they closed it today, there would be no reason to partner with Connell any longer. The flip side, however, is that the chief might just pull Bennett from the jumper case and hand it to Connell.

Dunphy, who they located sleeping on a couch in an apartment on Richmond Avenue, remained unapologetic for his actions three months earlier.

"Fucking-A right I stabbed him," he boasted, once he rubbed the sleep from his face and slid on a t-shirt. He had wide, alert eyes and thin lips. "He was sitting 'cross the table proud as a peacock, talking shit all night. Amazing one of them other guys didn't beat me to it. They all called me afterward and congratulated me. I even got a new nickname. The poker of poker. Get it?"

Dunphy grinned, a big man, twenty-eight, with curly hair trimmed close to the scalp. In the car, Bennett had read the criminal record from the manila folder. Sitting before him, however, Bennett sensed the black man's jocular personality.

His eyes had a sparkle that contrasted with the hollowness of criminals that he had witnessed as a patrolman.

"Yeah, that's great," Connell scowled without amusement. He opened the folder and leafed through several typed sheets. "According the arresting officer, you said, *the nigger stays away from me, we ain't gonna have no problems. He comes around, I can't promise it's not gonna happen again.*" The detective looked up. "That sound about right?"

Dunphy nodded. "Sounds exactly right."

"Did he? Stay away?"

"Yeah."

"When did you see him last?" Bennett asked.

"Ain't seen him since that night."

"Did you see him yesterday?"

"Yesterday? Naw. Not since that night." Richie's eyes narrowed and he sat up straight. "Say, what's all this about?"

"Where were you yesterday afternoon?"

"Working. Did a noon to eight shift."

Bennett observed the body language of both men. Connell did not avert his gaze from the suspect.

"Where you working?"

"Curtis Screw."

"Over on Niagara Street?"

"That's it. Got me a good job, they paying eight-fifty an hour. Been on the straight and narrow two months now. Ain't gonna do nothing to louse up a job pays that good."

"And you were there all day?"

"Punched the time clock to prove it."

"You got a boss who can vouch that he saw you there?"

"Sure can." He paused. "Lemme guess. That bottom feeder trying to get me in more trouble. Telling you I assaulted him yesterday, right?"

Connell spoke like a hardened cop. "Actually, he's not saying much."

"Why, somebody clock him in the jaw?"

"No, somebody shanked him in the gut. He's lying in the county morgue."

Dunphy's eyes arched and he bit his lip. His lips pancaked into a grin. "Well, I'm not gonna lie to you, this is a happy day. Guess you might say I'm one to hold a grudge. Have to get me a drink after work."

"We're gonna need to talk to your boss, Phillip."

"I give you his number."

Connell copied the digits into a notebook, exhaling. "Present company excluded, you think of anybody that might want Calvin Richie dead?"

"How many blank pages you got there?" he chuckled. "He didn't exactly give you the old warm and fuzzy feeling. Bet even his momma didn't like him. Eight other guys at poker that night. Each one might just have a celebration when they find out the news."

"We're gonna need all their names."

"Not a problem. Let me spell it out for you like this, detectives. If they was giving medals at Lake Placid for assholes, Calvin Richie would be wearing a neck full of gold."

*   *   *

"So what's your read on that?" Connell asked Bennett once they were in the car.

"He didn't do it," Bennett said, tucking the folder between his seat and the center console. "Why are you asking? Do you think he did?"

"No, he didn't do it," Connell agreed. "But we still check with his boss and co-workers to confirm Dunphy's story. I'll drop you back at the house and you can get a car and go do that. I want to be sure he was seen at work all afternoon. If he took a long lunch, that's gonna be a problem."

"We gonna check the other guys from poker?"

"Yeah, start calling guys on that list. I'll look for his mom and dad and brothers and sisters and any broads he might have been banging. If this guy's as hated as Dunphy would have us believe, we could be interviewing half the blacks in the city."

Bennett rolled down his window and stared at the passing homes. "I'm with you. I don't see any connection to the city hall jumper."

"Chief thinks there is. We got that witness, that Jerry Deck, who gave a pretty clear statement from the dying man." Connell hesitated. "Right now we got two dead end homicides. We're due for a break here."

Chapter 10

It was almost noon, and ambition coursed through him. When he first considered the holy war, he envisioned killing at night. Darkness would afford a cloak of protection. But after the flagpole at city hall, and yesterday's stabbing, he knew that murdering at mid-day, in the open sunshine, held the brazen promise of terror. They could not feel safe in daylight or crowded spaces. Word would spread and they would cower in fear, shackled by invisible chains, like the way they were brought to this country, like the way it should be.

He parked along a side street off Hertel Avenue, running a thumb across the flat-edged blade in his jacket pocket. Temperature was cool, so there was no fear that his canvas army coat might draw suspicion. He wore a t-shirt and jeans, both comfortable and loose fitting for easy movement. Checking himself in the mirror the night before, the blade's handle had peeked out of his jacket pocket. He would prefer it did not, but realized no one would notice unless they were studying him, and who would do that? He was accustomed to being ignored.

At a supermarket he had picked up a photocopied map of city bus routes. In the dim light of his bedroom, he studied its crisscrossing lines and intersecting streets. Armed with knowledge he had memorized, he drove along avenues and scouted neighborhoods, alert for pickup points, scanning overhangs where they might loiter. Within a three-block radius he noticed several "bus stop" signs, two of which fronted plastic shelters. There a collection of them ate away time, waiting with slackened eyes for busses to transport them nowhere.

His gait remained constant as he strode closer, but fingertips tingled. This would be like a military strike deep behind enemy lines. Anticipation grew like a bubble in his brain.

Two stood near the curb. They looked like scumbags, boys in their early twenties who suckled from the welfare state. One wore a tank top, skinny arms contrasting with white ribbed cotton covering a concave chest. The other was a blackened bowling pin, topped by a mop of unruly hair. They did not notice him approach as voices pitched higher. They argued over cigarettes.

"Them's my fucking smokes," the chunky one yelled, trying to snatch a pack from the other man's hand.

Waving it like a baton, he twisted and spiraled away. "The fuck they is. We was gonna split this, but you never gave me the cash."

"That's cause I ain't got the cash here. You gotta wait til I get home."

"You ain't got the cash, then you ain't got the smokes," the thin man taunted. "When I get my green, you can have your half, if there's any left."

"I'm good for it man, you know that."

"I don't know that. Tyrone's still waitin on his cut from that lawnmower you was supposed to sell."

The big man stopped and stared down his partner.

"Aw, man, why you gotta bring up the lawnmower? That lawnmower a craw in my side."

"You talking bout a craw and Tyrone's still waiting."

"You a motherfucker, you know that? Just want me a smoke, and you bringing up shit from the past."

Their talk was so animated that he heard each word. He honed onto the thin man. Although wiry, he appeared harder, meaner, more likely than the butterball to wrong a white man. Besides, the tubby one would be too obese to chase.

He exhaled a calming breath and stepped into the nigger, who was still engaged, ignorant of the stranger's approach.

"You call me a motherfucker, but at least I'm square with Tyrone," he declared smugly.

It was the last sentence he said. Joe locked his elbow and extended his arm, ripping through cotton, skin, blood and stomach. The target felt firm and tense, softening as it split.

There was a pause of recognition as the nigger realized he had been stuck in the gut. He grunted an exhale. His eyes never widened or pleaded, just remained hard, examining the crimson stain and gashed shirt. He glanced up to meet the attacker's face. It was almost like he expected to die this way, and was simply curious to know who had fulfilled his premonition.

As he spread hands across his stomach, trying to contain the blood, his knees buckled and he collapsed to the sidewalk. The tubby one staggered in confusion, slow to process what had just occurred, stuck in a three-second delay. A moment ago he had been lobbying for a cigarette, arguing about a lawnmower deal gone south. With wrinkled brow he turned toward the attacker, his face flattening in fright when he saw the knife.

"Hey, hey, hey," he muttered, raising pudgy palms and backing away. "What the fuck just happened here?"

"Tell all your nigger buddies this won't be the last," Joe hissed. He lorded over the skinny one, whose blood leaked from a creased and withering body. "City hall on Monday. Elmwood Avenue yesterday. Spread the word, Sambo." Then he nodded, turned, and continued along the sidewalk at the same brisk pace he had used to approach.

A nearby church bell tolled twelve times.

*   *   *

TV crews were already on the scene when Bennett pulled up and got out of his car. Simultaneously, from the opposite side of

105

yellow police tape, Connell parked and emerged from a sedan. Their eyes met across the chaos, flashing recognition.

"I want all cameras out of here," Connell barked to one of the uniforms. "We need the area secure. Move 'em back then put up some tarps to block their view. I sure as hell don't want to be looking at pictures of a body on the six o'clock news."

"You heard the detective," the officer said, spreading his arms into a fan. "Back it up, folks. A little respect for the dead." Another patrolman trotted up with a blue vinyl dropcloth he retrieved from the trunk of his car.

"Detective," a lumpy reporter called out, "Anything you can tell us about this?"

Connell did not break stride or turn toward the questioner. "Scratch your itch somewhere else. I'm not saying anything."

Taking in details of the scene, Bennett's tie felt tight against his neck. Connell's hung an inch below the collar, like it had been twisted in haste, so Bennett loosened his own and fingered open the shirt's top button. Connell, he noticed, looked the part of a homicide cop, with his military haircut, steel blue eyes and open trenchcoat flapping like a superhero's cape. He strode with purpose. TV cameramen, now shielded from the corpse, turned their lenses toward Connell's motion, where the detective flexed his jaw and radiated a tangible feeling of confidence.

Bennett studied the crime scene, where he noted the position of the body and the split stomach, sliced deep enough to reveal bloody innards. He looked up and down the street, trying to envision where the killer came from and the route he used for escape.

"Bennett," Connell called, "C'mere."

A chunky black kid, in his early twenties, stood before Connell.

"Last thing I told him was he was a motherfucker," the boy said, words emerging slowly like they were mired in liquid tar. Tears bubbled along his lower lids. "But shit, I was just squeezing him. We been friends for years. I just wanted a smoke was all."

Both detectives listened. They hadn't even seen the white man approach, the witness continued, but suddenly he was there and Arthur had been stabbed and the skinny dude muttered something about city hall then casually walked away.

"What'd he look like?" Bennett wondered.

"A good head shorter than botha you. Like a runt. Stringy hair, baseball cap, blue jeans. Walked like a crab. He was in then he was out, zap, like that. Happened too quick to notice much more."

"He didn't run?" Bennett asked.

"Run? No sir, he just walked away real calm. I was in shock, saying what's going on here. None of it seemed real."

Two patrolmen led the kid away as groups rubbernecked outside the police tape.

"Son of a bitch," Connell said. "Exact same description from yesterday. Him mentioning city hall pretty much removes any doubt that he did your victim too."

"Three days, three murders," Bennett mused. "But I'm not sold on the pattern. Two men stabbed and one woman thrown from a tall building? Your two are connected, no question, but mine—"

"Come on, Bennett, get with it. It's the same guy. He killed your broad then did two more and mentioned city hall both times."

"A killer doesn't change M.O.s like that."

"This guy does."

Bennett bit his lip thoughtfully. Maybe the first killing was to make a splash, get everyone's attention, then he switched into a steady routine. It wasn't probable, but it was possible.

"Are we looking at a serial killer?"

The gravity of those words halted Connell, who turned to face Bennett.

"This is Buffalo. We don't have serial killers in Buffalo. That's Hollywood stuff. But he's doing a murder each day. Right now our job is to stop tomorrow's murder."

*   *   *

"Bus stops," Bennett said, standing before the chief in his office. "If we could blanket bus stops with patrols tomorrow around lunch time—"

"You know how many bus stops there are in this city?" Connell countered. "Hell, there's one every block. We can't even narrow his activity to a neighborhood. Today's killing was in North Buffalo, yesterday's was near the west side, and city hall is the heart of downtown."

"North, west, central. He's covering the compass. Maybe tomorrow he goes for South Buffalo or the east side."

"You're playing a guessing game," Connell said.

"That's right. You got any better ideas?"

The chief interrupted. "You found nobody in the canvas who got a partial plate?"

"We went up and down Hertel for blocks," Bennett said. "We didn't even find a witness who remembered him, let alone saw him get into a car."

"Our descriptions have him as ordinary looking," Connell added. "Nothing about him sends up any flags. Not the kind of toadstool little gray-haired ladies call the cops about."

The chief exhaled, shaking his head. "All right, let's put together a team of uniforms and plainclothes guys and blanket Elmwood and Hertel tomorrow before lunch hour. We'll put a man within sight of every bus stop. Maybe we catch him, maybe we scare him off."

"What if he doesn't go back to Elmwood or Hertel?" Connell offered. "He's picked a different spot every day."

The chief's hands went up with exasperation. "It's a crapshoot. We don't know shit, other than he's some white dude in cowboy boots."

"We gotta have something about this guy in our files," Connell said. "He's been arrested before, I can promise you. You don't just start killing people. You work up to it with little petty shit first."

"Maybe we spend some time pulling old arrest reports," Bennett suggested. "Find any white guys matching that description who were popped within a two or three block radius of our crime scenes. Go back, maybe what, three years?"

Connell nodded reluctantly. "It's as good an idea as anything else we got. Put out a notice to patrols to keep their eyes open. We get that sketch artist with the kid from this morning to update yesterday's composite. I'll go back out and re-canvas this afternoon."

"He's like a goddamn ghost, this guy," the chief spat in frustration. "Does he even go back to the same spot? Does he pick a new street? I don't have a goddamn clue."

"Well, at least we're all on the same page about that," Connell said. "Right now we don't have a clue either."

Chapter 11

Along Washington Street, near its intersection with Goodell, weeds sprouted between cracked sidewalks, tattered newsprint clogged drain grates and glass shards clustered against brick facades. A few blocks north of Shea's, the regal 1920's era theater, were two industrial giants. One was the Trico plant, which manufactured windshield wipers; the other was a stout red building housing the Courier Express, one of Buffalo's two daily newspapers. Although vibrant during the day, people walking the neighborhood at dusk seemed weighted by decline, burdened with slumped shoulders and suspicious gazes.

The patrol car plodded through the autumn night. George Pope did not instruct his partner to remain observant because there was no need. Bobby Bennett studied the scenes with rapt attention.

"Get a load of that pross," he said. "Frigging amazon. You think guys are afraid of her or do some like 'em big like that?"

Pope watched the black woman in a bright pink miniskirt cut just below her ass, wide shoulders and dark fishnet stockings. Stiletto heels stretched into a long stride. She towered over the derelict she passed, standing close to six-three.

"Haven't seen her around before," Pope mused.

Against traffic, he pulled to the left curb and called out the window as she strolled alongside.

"C'mere, you," he ordered.

The prostitute slowed, then looked up the street, as if considering escape options were she to dash away.

"Officer, I haven't done anything wrong," she protested in a falsetto voice, head turning sideways with suspicion. "Just walking down the street."

Pope and Bennett got out of the car, and the woman stepped back, eyes widening with fear.

"Relax," Pope said in a soothing voice, keeping his hands on his belt. "We're not looking to hassle you. You're not in trouble. We just want to know your name."

Distrust filled the pause. "Annette." When she spoke, the name stretched to four distinct syllables.

Bennett marveled at her smooth mocha cheeks. She was striking, although much of her was phony. Long blonde hair was a wig, nails were glued on, and heels thrust her taller than both men. With wide brown eyes, she was attractive, but in an odd way. Something struck Bennett as wrong.

"What's your real name, Annette?" Pope asked. "Anthony? Antonio?"

She clucked nervously. "What you mean?"

"You're no woman," Pope said.

She blew out a breath. "How can you tell?"

"Because your adam's apple is bigger than mine, and I'm old and fat," Pope admitted.

Bennett stood shocked, fighting to keep his jaw closed. He felt stupid, naïve that Pope had recognized what he did not. She was a man, but if not for the protrusion along her throat, he never would have known.

"Annette is my stage name," she said, her falsetto voice dropping several octaves. "My real name is Henry."

"Okay Henry," Pope said. "Ever been arrested?"

"Once. Shoplifting."

"Nothing violent? No assaults?"

"No officer, nothing like that."

"How long you been on the streets?"

She shrugged and bit her lower lip. "Coupla weeks now."

Pope nodded toward the car's backseat. "Get in. We need to have a conversation."

Again, Annette looked up and down Washington Street. "You looking for a freebie? I respect the cops, but I ain't so—"

"No," Pope interrupted. "We're looking to make you an employment proposition, and we're trying to be discreet. If you want, we can continue to talk here in front of potential customers, and then they'll know you're about to become a police informant. I don't imagine that will help your business."

Annette shut her mouth, opened the door and sat in the backseat. Pope and Bennett got in, and the black and white pulled away from the curb. As they zigzagged onto Main Street, Bobby pivoted so he could watch both his partner and the prostitute behind him. He was aware that Annette studied his face.

"What's your name?" she asked.

Bennett turned to look at her with a mixture of hesitation and intrigue.

"Officer Bennett."

"What's your first name?"

Before Pope could stop him, he replied, "Bobby."

"You're cute," she offered in a singsong voice.

"Cute?"

"That's right. I like muscles and a brush cut. You short, but you built powerfully. Whole lotta man, ain't you?"

Pope chuckled. "Excuse me, Annette, what about me? Aren't I cute?"

"You a little old for me, pops. But Bobby here, I like him."

Pope shook his head and spoke playfully. "Ah, twenty years ago I was damn good looking. Fifty pounds lighter too. You woulda fallen head over heels for me then, Annette, believe me."

"I'm sure that's true, pops, but I'm living in the now. This is the eighties and I'm one of the ladies."

They pulled into the parking lot of the Anchor Bar, a restaurant famous for inventing chicken wings. Pope shifted into park but kept the engine running, craning his neck to face the backseat.

"Here's the deal, Annette. Prostitutes make good informants. You know the streets, so you can help us, and we can help you. You're going to turn tricks whether we like it or not. You're not mugging people, right?"

"Told you no."

"Good. Don't mug people, don't get crazy, just do what you gotta do. You'll need to turn in some information once in a while."

"What kinda information?"

"Anything that'll help us. You get a john that you know is wrong, you tell us, and we'll get him off the streets."

"And in return?"

"In return you get some cash. And some leeway if you get into scrapes with the law. Just so long as you're not violent."

"Oh no, I'm not violent. Not at all."

"Good. We got a deal?"

"How much cash we talking?"

Pope inflated a figure, knowing that would whet her interest.

Annette took the bait, nodding with enthusiasm. "Give you all the information you want," she agreed, batting false eyelashes. "Specially to Bobby."

Shaking his head, Pope put the car in gear and looped back to Washington Street, where he paralleled the curb and got out to open the back door.

"We'll be seeing you around," he said.

"Okay." She leaned down and called through the slamming rear door, "Bye Bobby!"

Bennett raised his eyebrows in farewell. He supposed it was harmless, but didn't like the fact that a transvestite had taken such an interest in him. Perhaps Annette had sensed his discomfort and played up the flirtation.

Pope plopped his bulk into the driver's seat and pulled away.

"My mom and her church friends think we ought to be taking freaks like that off the street," Bobby said. "One of the few times I agree with her."

"First off, we got nothing to hold Annette on. We didn't catch her soliciting. You don't look the other way, but hookers are going to be out doing their trade anyway. One hand washes the other, so long as they don't mug anybody. If some idiot is stupid enough to spend his money on that, that's his business. A lot of good info comes from hookers if you treat 'em right."

"What about quality of life? Get rid of hookers and this neighborhood cleans up pretty nice."

"She's only been on the streets a few weeks. I'm betting half the Trico plant has already gotten blow jobs from her. Listen, kid, I'm one of those cops that thinks prostitution should be legalized, like they do in Europe. You make sure the hookers have a clean card, and then you can control diseases. I don't know if it's a victimless crime, but most of the time both parties involved are making their own choices."

Bobby watched his partner's profile, and wondered how much of Pope's opinion had been influenced by his own father. What had been Mac's stance on prostitution? Was Pope offering values that trickled down from his own father?

*   *   *

Later that night, near the end of their shift, Pope and Bennett found Annette trolling the sidewalk on Pearl Street. When they pulled alongside her, she offered an exaggerated wink at Bobby.

"You ever let Bobby drive?" Annette asked Pope, leaning down and resting her elbows on the open window's ledge. "Like to see a handsome man in uniform behind the wheel."

"Again, Annette, you're insulting me," Pope teased. "Overlooking how striking I am for an older man."

"Annette, you taking hormone pills or something?" Bobby wondered, winking to his partner.

Annette enjoyed the banter, but stepped back and pretended to be offended.

"Oh Bobby, Bobby, Bobby," she warbled. "Why you being mean to me?"

Bobby ran a hand over his brush cut. "I'm telling you, Annette, your titties look bigger from this afternoon."

"Bought me some grapefruits 'stead of oranges. Went up two cup sizes." Using upper arms to squeeze her breasts together, she leaned forward again, lowering her voice. "See that guy at seven o'clock? Dude in the green jacket? This is me helping you out, like our arrangement was. He got a gun."

"All right, Annette, thanks."

Pope merged into traffic and circled the block, giving Annette a chance to stroll away. The patrol car came back around, remaining double parked for several minutes while they observed the man she had pointed out. In his early twenties, with a Beatles mop of hair, he idled, smoking a cigarette, leaning against a brick façade with one knee crooked. Upon noticing the cop car, his shoulders tensed. He tried to appear unaffected, but the bobbing head belied nervousness. He pushed his weight off the wall and walked in the opposite direction.

"Let's go," Pope said.

As the car pulled alongside him, Pope gave the siren a blast. The suspect winced with anticipation. Bobby got to the sidewalk, palm pressed to his pistol.

"You there," he said. "Hands up! Face that wall."

The kid stopped and stretched, like he was being mugged in a dark alley. He did not speak. Bennett cuffed arms behind him, kicked his feet so they were spread wide, and searched. Sure enough, tucked into the front of his waistband, was a tiny .22-caliber pistol.

Annette, you might just become a gold mine for us, Pope said to himself.

Chapter 12

Their father, Mackenzie Bennett, had been a hardnosed
Buffalo cop who once patrolled the streets with an equal measure
of wisdom and compassion. He was thin, with narrow hands and
fingers and blanched hair that began turning gray in his thirties.
His slender build often deceived suspects into thinking he was
fragile, when in fact, he was strong as iron.

For nearly a month that spring, Mac felt fatigue. He spoke
in brief bursts then gulped mouthfuls of air to regain his
shortened breath. Walking more than a few steps became a
chore, so he was relegated to home. Climbing stairs turned into
a challenge. He slept away most of the day on the living room
sofa. By the time it was detected by the doctor, the tumor had
expanded in Mac's colon so rapidly that treatment would have
little effect.

Diagnosis was bleak. Mac had between three and six
months to live.

The news hit Mark unprepared. His dad was a rock, healthy
and fit, working out with dumbbells as recently as six weeks
earlier. Now he sprawled on the couch, struggled to sit up,
requested help to stand. He felt wobbly on his legs, reaching for
support along countertops and kitchen chairs when he shuffled to
the bathroom. His soft groans scraped like steel threads being
pulled through Mark's veins.

His mother remained distant, praying for Mac's recovery
with her rosary group. There was little tenderness, no overt
concern as she waited for the miracle. God would solve this, one
way or another.

On an overcast afternoon, Mark drove by Bobby's house, where his brother hosed his new car in the driveway. He pulled to the curb and walked along the concrete, hands thrust in his pockets. Bobby nodded in acknowledgement, as if Mark's rare visit had been expected.

"Pops is bad. You need to get over there, Bobby."

"I know," he said, soap bubbles clinging to his meaty hands. "I plan to."

"Sooner, not later. I mean it. I'll go with you if that'll make it easier."

Bobby slid the sponge across the contoured hood. He wore an olive-colored tank top that revealed chiseled forearms and biceps. His glare turned combative. "Can I finish washing the car, or should I just go like this?"

"You're really going to be sarcastic?"

"I been busy, man," Bobby continued. "You know, we got a baby on the way, so I'm caring for Susie, and the academy is tough. This sergeant trained at Auschwitz, I'm not kidding. It's not like I'm lying in a hammock eating bons bons with all my free time."

"Hey, you might not want to face it, but this is the end for our dad. I know you guys never had a good relationship, but—"

Bobby squeezed the nozzle and a burst of water drenched the hood, drowning out the sentence. After ten seconds, he lowered the hose and turned to face his brother.

"So Marky, what the hell am I supposed to say to the guy? I wanted his attention for years, but never got it. The job always got more of his time than we did. You were the golden boy, and I was the outcast. Now I'm supposed to go running to him and kneel at his altar and hope he'll bless me with a ray of kindness? Can that just wash away twenty-five years of neglect? I sense you want me to apologize, but what for? He ought to apologize to me."

Mark studied Bobby's restrained fury. He would never understand the anger, the entitlement he felt as a perpetual victim. "You're a shithead," Mark muttered, pivoting away.

"Hey Marky, I'm giving it to you straight," Bobby called after him. He shot a snake of water onto the sidewalk. Mark did not break stride when droplets bounced onto his legs.

"Sorry if it leaves you feeling bitter, but I'm dealing with my own reality here," Bobby said.

Mark turned his head but kept moving. "Maybe it's time to stop thinking about you. Maybe Pop just needs you there."

*   *   *

Mac's last days were spent curled in a hospital bed, where he slipped into a coma and wheezed deep, irregular breaths. Mark kept a solitary bedside vigil, not expecting his mom or brother to appear.

Nurses advised him that coma patients, while unresponsive, likely retained their hearing. Talk to him, Mark was told. Tell him what you need to say.

At first the one-sided conversation was difficult. Before illness overtook him, Mac knew Bobby had joined the academy and was planning to become a patrolman. Mark expected promotion to detective soon, but title changes like that occurred at the whim of the mayor and police commissioner, so everything was a waiting game.

Whenever it happens, Pop, I'll make you proud, he said.

Looking out the dirty window, he noticed a yellow finch resting on the concrete sill.

A little canary is just outside. Wish you could watch him with me. Two days ago I saw the first robin of the season, with a big fat red belly. Looked like Pope after a full plate of ravioli. So I guess spring is unofficially here.

119

Mac's breathing was strained, and Mark clenched in terror when the next inhalation fell a fraction of a second off its rhythm. He dreaded the moment when the last breath would come, but knew it was imminent. Mark pulled his chair close to the bed and laid a palm against his father's frail shoulder.

Don't know how I'm gonna make it without you, Pop. But if I'm half as tough as you, I'll be okay. Just half as tough.

Mark had stepped away for a sandwich when his father passed away. Part of him felt he should have been by Mac's side, but the greater emotion was relief that he was not. *Am I selfish?* he wondered. That memory would have replayed itself in his mind for years, and it would have been unbearable.

*   *   *

After his dad died, Mark reflected on his life in ways he had never before considered. While growing up, he knew that his parents' marriage was aloof. In all his years living under their roof, not once did Mac and Judy ever raise voices to one another. They never disagreed or feuded. But neither did they laugh or spend time together. They shared the same space but occupied separate worlds. Dad worked odd hours, shift times constantly changing. When he arrived home, he ate the meal his wife prepared, then vanished into the basement, where he fiddled at his workshop, woodworking or assembling transistor radios. Most of his time away from the job was spent with his sons or in solitude beneath a fluorescent light.

After Mac's death, Mark's mother requested that he be the one to clean out the workshop. It would not be a pleasant job, and Mark procrastinated for several weeks. He began slowly, reluctantly, venturing downstairs to survey his dad's tools during a Sunday visit. Old metal files and chisels, many handed down from his father's father, rested on hooks protruding from particleboard. The weathered workbench was a slab of varnished wood with years of accumulated scrapes and nicks. Plastic trays with sliding drawers held screws, nuts and washers. The process of dismantling his father's life was overwhelming and heart rending. Mark considered it his cross to bear.

It took time, but after most of the tools had been removed, Mark made an unexpected find. Hidden against the underside of a metal drawer beneath the workbench he discovered a cloth bound notebook. In all their years together, Mark never knew his dad kept a diary. It contained dated entries spanning nearly thirty-five years, beginning in 1944. The musings were infrequent, brief and irregular — at most a few lines. Tucked inside the back cover were two black and white candid photographs of an attractive blonde in her twenties. He did not recognize the woman.

He slid it quietly into a paper bag and smuggled it from his mother's home. If Mac had taken such steps to conceal it from his wife, there must be a reason, so Mark did not inform her of its existence. That night, sitting at his own kitchen table, he felt otherworldly when he read his dad's angular cursive. As Mark's fingertips brushed against the fading ink, he transported to another era, and his focus shrank to the confines of those lined pages.

Here was his father, little more than a boy, single, stumbling through his twenties, trying to find a path in the world. He had yet to meet his wife or consider his future sons. A few sentences about joining the police force. An excited entry about his first basement apartment on Delaware Avenue. While Mark was fascinated by these bursts of words, they were too brief. Always, he wanted to know more.

As he continued chronologically, the absence of key events grew puzzling. There was no mention of meeting Judy, falling in love, their wedding day. During a two-year block the entries ceased altogether. As the winter of 1949 flipped to the new decade, they resumed. This was when Mac learned Judy was pregnant.

On July 2, 1950, he wrote: "Today my son was born. At the hospital he was wrinkly and swaddled in cotton. Looked like an alien. I now know complete love. Never experienced such pure happiness. Judy is okay."

Mark felt a pang of emotion, and slid the notebook to the far side of the table so his tears would not patter its pages. For several days, the journal remained closed, perched on the counter's edge. Its silent presence became the focal point of the room. He avoided the kitchen, instead eating meals on the couch while he watched TV. When he had to pass along the linoleum floor, he curled a path away from the ominous diary. Emotions contained there were too raw.

*   *   *

That was to be the easy part.

When he mustered the courage to resume reading, Mark learned dark secrets about his family and came to understand, perhaps, why Bobby had always brimmed with anger.

By 1953, his dad's scribblings became even more brief, short bursts singed by frustration, like someone held a flame against the edges of comfort. A one-line entry in March read, "Judy lost the baby."

Mark's heart felt encased in plaster. He read the sentence several times, trying to shape some explanation.

Mac's brevity rolled into April: "Depressed. We are fighting a lot." Two months passed before he wrote, "Judy wants to try again. I'm not sure." The next day: "E. helping me inch back into life. Another kid would NOT be a solution but a setback."

He had only been a baby himself, but had no memory of his mother being pregnant. Did she carry a child to full term? Was it stillborn? A boy or girl? Why did he not know about such a seminal event in their family's history? What were the devastating effects on his parents?

In a psychedelic haze, sounds and shapes bounced off the walls of his kitchen, yet he could not look away from the yellowing paper.

Who was E.? Was Bobby an accident, or had his mother convinced Mac to have another baby against his will? Continuing the thought seemed logical: had Mac ever really loved Bobby, or had he been a reluctant father, secretly resenting the child because it strapped him tighter into a loveless marriage? Did the subconscious rejection fuel Bobby's anger?

Mark felt as if he had been confined to invisible gallows. Eviscerated and exhausted, he resented his father's reflections. He wrapped the notebook tightly in a paper bag and placed it in a fireproof strongbox on his closet floor. He understood why Mac had taken such pains to bury the journal in a secret cache. His deepest thoughts should not have been shared with his family. Mark made a promise to himself that neither Bobby nor his mother would ever read these words.

*   *   *

But he had read them, and resentment smoldered.

For several days, he was unable to sleep, often distracted while performing the most mundane tasks. Within a week, Mark recognized that idle time was an enemy, allowing his brain to tumble over the minutia of this revelation, so he volunteered for double shifts and logged as much overtime as possible — anything to prevent him from reflecting on the tumult which spiraled through his father's life.

He kept himself busy that summer, building a new back porch, and during that time, his promotion was approved. He earned his shield and reported to the detective squad. The change helped his outlook, yet he still refused his mother's offers to come to the house for Sunday dinner. She did not appear to notice the pattern.

After a month in a new job, his sense of betrayal fizzled. Summer progressed into September, leaves began to change colors, and as time passed, his acceptance grew.

What should his dad have done, burdened his son with the problems of his marriage? The issues between Mac and Judy were not his business.

Still, questions smoldered in his stomach like hot rocks. Mark wanted to ask his mother about the lost baby. But how could he bring the subject to discussion? His parents had kept it from him for more than a quarter century. Were he to ask now, Judy's first question would be "how did you know?" Probing would all but announce the presence of some murky remnant that his father left behind.

The entire saga remained frustrating. While the diary illuminated part of Mac's life, it also raised questions to which answers would never appear. Why had he and Bobby never known of another sibling? Who was the mysterious "E" that helped Mac inch back into life?

So Mark carried the burden of knowledge alone. He recognized that he knew more about his father than anyone, including his mother. That provided him with an uncommon connection to his dad.

*   *   *

Mark spent the afternoon combing through cardboard boxes crammed with old arrest reports. It was tedious and labor intensive, but as darkness fell, he had assembled an expansive list of one hundred sixty-three suspects who matched witness descriptions and had been arrested within blocks of the murder sites during the past three years.

The chief laid the report flat on his desktop and ran a finger down the page.

"Holy shit, that's a lot of names," the boss growled. "Can't track all those yourself. Make copies and get the night shift to help you. Call in as many suspects as you can and conduct your interviews here. The ones you can't reach or who won't come in, we'll go to them, probably tomorrow." He looked at an arched clock propped on the corner of his blotter. "You planning on getting any sleep tonight?"

Bennett lips turned downward. "Hadn't thought much about it."

"Listen, kid, keep working this, but grab a few hours when you need it. Don't be a hero. Too long without sleep, you're a zombie. Then you're no good to anyone. Where's Connell?"

"Not sure. He said he was going out to work things on his end."

The chief leaned back in his chair. "So far we've been lucky. But the clock keeps ticking."

"Lucky? We're anything but lucky. We don't have a single lead. Even this list is grasping for straws."

"Yeah, but we've been flying under the radar. Three murders in three days? The black community is upset, but they haven't caught on yet that they're connected. The media was all over that city hall flier, but they haven't linked these stabbings to Rosa Greene. Someone will, it's just a matter of time. You thought Monday was bad? Watch out, because then you're really gonna see it. Round-the-clock sit-ins, blacks marching down Delaware Avenue. We could be looking at a race riot. Media is going to be unbearable. Reporters might follow you into the urinal when you unzip to take a piss."

Lovely image, Bennett thought. *It can't really get that bad, can it?*

"The point is this," the chief continued. "You and Connell gotta solve this thing before that happens."

"We're trying, Chief, believe me."

*   *   *

Three of the men on Bennett's list had agreed to come in that evening, so he conducted a series of ten-minute interviews. None were legitimate suspects. Too tall, too fat, and all had alibis for at least two of the three murders.

Connell sauntered in after ten-thirty, expression serious and intense, frayed from a long day.

"What do you got?" he asked.

Bennett's mind had fogged and his lids felt heavy. He showed Connell the list, explained the chief's plan to track down each man, and summarized the three suspects he had eliminated that night.

"But I'd guess the odds of our killer coming in here are long," Bennett suggested. "He's not going to agree to a voluntarily interview."

"You'd be surprised," Connell shook his head. "You would think that if a guy is guilty, he'll stay away, but sometimes it's just the opposite. Killers are curious. They want information. They talk to cops, they can figure out how much we know. Plus, they get arrogant. Think they're smarter than us. They like to match wits."

"Huh," Bennett said.

"Yeah, don't get caught up in that line of thinking. Our guy might very well walk through that door and meet us face to face, act all innocent like he's granting us a big favor."

"Good to know," Bennett said. "What were you doing?"

"Working the streets. I put the word out to keep an eye open. I got snitches all over watching for any suspicious white guy who's scoping out blacks. Lots of legwork, a few long promises, but maybe it'll pay off."

.

Bennett's phone rang. He cradled the receiver against his ear while Connell went to his own desk fifteen feet away.

"Hey, it's me," Alison said.

Bennett's eyes immediately shot to Connell, who lowered himself onto a wooden chair, leafing through the list.

"Hi," Bennett said neutrally. He had phoned Alison earlier, told her he would be working late and could not see her that night. She said okay, but he could hear disappointment permeate her voice. How many times had she taken a similar call from Connell during their marriage?

"Can you talk?" she asked.

Connell ran a hand across his chin and studied the names before him. Bennett moved the mouthpiece close to his lips but did not turn away.

"Not really."

"Oh, okay. Well, I just wanted to say that I hope you catch this sick bastard. I miss talking to you. I miss seeing you for lunch. I miss holding you at night."

"Me too," Bennett said.

"Have a good night, okay Mark?"

"Yeah. You do the same. I'll try to catch up with you tomorrow."

"I'd like that."

He laid the phone into its cradle and picked up a yellow marker, drawing a streak of color across names he had already contacted. The rest would wait until the next morning. Connell set his own list aside and made notes in a spiral-topped pad.

Bennett felt fatigue deep in his shoulders. When he was tired, he was prone to mistakes, and this investigation could not afford a screw up. *Call it,* he thought. *Nothing more is getting done tonight.* It took another thirty minutes to type his activity report, and when he finished, uniforms were just ending the four to twelve shift. Connell remained seated but his head lilted to the right, lids closed. Bennett stood, arched his back, and slid into his sport coat. The scrape of chair against floor tiles caused Connell's eyes to open.

"Heading out?" he asked.

"Yeah. Big day tomorrow."

"Right. I'm gonna leave soon, too."

"Don't stay too long." Bennett hesitated. "Chief told me that getting sleep is important."

"It's more important to get this asshole off the street. If that costs me an hour or two of sleep, so be it."

Bennett waved a goodbye and exited the hallway, where two patrolmen muttered goodnight as he walked down three flights. Outside, the night was cool, and its crisp air reawakened his senses. Bennett's car was parked around the corner, and he cranked down the window, then traveled two blocks before he stretched the cord on his radio.

"Long day, Mac," he said, raising the mic to his lips. His thumb hovered over the "talk" button. "I'd like to say we're closer to catching this guy, but I'm not sure it's true."

Since her phone call, Bennett found himself thinking about Alison. There was the physical aspect of her: tall figure, her vanilla scent, that tender spot at the base of her neck where hair gave way to smooth skin. Then there was her personality, a charm that filled a room, soothing his uncertainties, making him laugh, rounding away his loneliness.

Still, could this relationship really work, considering the circumstances?

He loved her, but could not bring himself to voice that.

"Three simple words, Mac," he said into the mic. "That's all it is. But I'll be damned if I can say them."

"Ah, the three little words," came the response.

"Why is it so hard to say? We probably don't say it enough in this world. I wish I'd said it more to you. I tried saying it to mom, but I stuttered and stopped, and she didn't notice that I was being serious. I don't think it registered with her."

"You say it to Bobby?"

Mark paused while guilt pooled in his belly. "No."

"I'm probably the wrong guy to talk to about this," Mac sighed. "I can count on one hand the times I told either of you boys that I love you."

Christmas morning, Mark remembered. Sometimes on birthdays. The day he graduated the academy, his father sat in the second row in full uniform, watching stoically. When Mark caught his dad's eye, a subtle nod conveyed more than three little words ever could.

"This about Alison?" Mac wondered.

"Yeah."

"So this mystery woman you won't tell me about, you want to say you love her, but you're struggling, is that it?"

"I could say the words. That's not the problem. It's the meaning behind them. How will she interpret them? What does that phrase even mean?"

"I worked with a guy, Charlie Connors. We used to call him Charlie Knuckles because it was like there were giant golf balls imbedded under his skin. He was a lousy cop, but funny as hell. Used to crack us up in the break room, then we'd all try to avoid riding patrol with him. He said you know you've found love when you can lie under the covers with a girl, rip a juicy fart and not be embarrassed."

Mark grinned. "Something to aspire to, huh?"

"Yeah. Charlie Knuckles was a comedian, but he was a meathead."

In the silence, Mark heard his own breathing, despite the open window. "So what do you want it to mean?" Mac asked.

Mark struggled to voice his thoughts. "Girls have told me they've loved me before. I've even said it a few times myself. It was awkward and I felt constrained afterward. None of that love ever lasted. So if I say it to Alison, does it imply that I'll love her forever? Because that's a hell of a thing to promise. I can't guarantee that. Who knows how we'll both feel in six months, or a year?"

"So you want it to mean, I love you right now, with no strings?"

"I love you now, but can't guarantee how I'll feel tomorrow."

"I don't think she'd go for that."

"I don't think so either. But saying anything else is untrue, and I don't want to overstep myself."

Mac hesitated. "I never knew a whole lot about women, Marky. Your mom and I had a couple good years, then drifted apart. This might hurt you to hear, but we never really came back to one another. So my advice is that it's better to keep your mouth shut than say something half-assed to Alison. Doing this half-assed will only make it harder later on."

"Harder?" Mark asked. "It's already as hard as I want it to be."

Chapter 13

Autumn always ambushed him with a head cold. Days were warm and sunny, but at night, when temperatures dropped, germs crept through the narrow slit between window and jamb, attaching themselves to his pillow. As he dozed, openmouthed, viruses wormed into his nostrils and took refuge on his tongue.

A ringing phone pulled him from deep sleep. His throat was swollen and scratchy, skin around his eyes inflated like pufferfish. Stretching off the mattress, he picked up the receiver and mumbled a greeting.

"Joe?" the man asked. "Is that you?"

Hearing the voice, he dropped the receiver back onto the cradle, then curled into a fetal pose, rubbing his eyes. The next ring came ten seconds later. He struggled to swallow, lifted the phone and held it to his ear without speaking.

The voice was angry this time. "If it is you, you dumb bastard, consider yourself fired!"

Big shock, he thought. *Can't believe the stupid fucker hadn't figured out that I quit.*

He had stopped showing up at the job site six days ago. After a long summer on the assembly line, nearly five hundred dollars had been banked, so there was no need to break his back again until the account ran down. His killing spree would fill much of the next month, and that transcended the need for cash. Right now, the concept of money was an October mist, just outside the edges of reach. When the account plunged into double digits, then he would start to worry. Would he even be around by then? Or will he become a martyr for his crusade?

This boss was an asshole, just like everyone at work. They made fun of him. He heard their snickers as he turned away. Once, when he spoke, a fat bitch rolled her eyes at the other cow next to her. Sometimes they teased him openly, calling him "mad dog" in a sarcastic tone after someone asked about the tattoo peeking beneath the sleeve of his t-shirt. Another joker dubbed him "triple K" after he tried to give a history lesson on the KKK during a coffee break. They wouldn't miss him, weasely little drones, and he sure as hell wouldn't miss them. Too bad they were all white, he thought, because he would be doing the world a favor to shank some of those doozies.

He creased the pillow and tucked it under his skull, hoping elevation would clear his nostrils. His hips were sore again this morning, and a knot burned in his calf like a coal brick. The mattress springs were loose, and he had never gotten used to sleeping in that slingshot. Woke up everyday with a new ache. It took a good half hour of moving around before he started to feel right again. He was twenty-five, too young for these kind of hassles. He wondered if he would be better off sleeping on the floor, but there were mice droppings in the kitchen corners, and he didn't need a fucking rodent gnawing on his nose each night.

He coughed, bones creaking as he stretched. A dough of phlegm balled in his throat, and he cursed silently, sitting up. He was too stiff to dash to the bathroom, but there was a half-filled water glass on the wooden crate next to the bed. He grabbed it and spat with relief.

It would be hard to kill today. He didn't feel up to par. Could he take a day off? He supposed there were no set rules to this cleansing, but he had hoped to complete one purge each day for an entire week. That would get them good and scared.

But as he rubbed his leg, he thought maybe if he went on hiatus, they would all exhale, consider that the worst was over. A short break might lull them into false security, and then he could resume with ruthlessness.

"This day is going to suck," he said out loud.

*   *   *

Eric Lenehan's eye level was equivalent to other men's shoulders. He had stout little legs and a compact trunk. When he grumbled about his back injury, his cousin had teased him by saying, "Why don't you just have the doctor remove the vertebrae you tweaked? It's not like anyone is going to notice that you're shorter." Since puberty, he had been sensitive about his height, so Lenehan kept his adjustable chair at its uppermost setting. Behind his desk, he sat higher, providing a false feeling of authority even though his feet dangled, unable to touch ground.

Lately, however — since going on disability, in fact — every morning when he entered the squad, his chair had been reset to its lowest point. At first he suspected someone from the night cleaning crew sat down while emptying the wastebasket, and tinkered with the adjustable lever underneath the seat. After months of ruminating, he abandoned that theory. Cleaning people had come and gone during that time, and every morning revealed the same thing. Now he suspected his fellow officers were playing a prank. Lenehan became annoyed each day when he absently plopped down and realized that the setting was wrong. He stood, reached below the pad and pushed the crooked handle, watching the seat ascend several inches. Often he scanned the room, searching for malicious glee in other cops' eyes. As yet no one had betrayed himself.

On Thursday morning, he had just sat back down when the elevator door opened to reveal five large, well-dressed black men entering the squad room with stone-faced venom in their eyes. Without hesitation they marched to Lenehan's desk, precise as a military drill, and stopped.

133

"I am Reverend Willis T. Brown," the largest man proclaimed in a baritone preacher's voice, with the other four assembled in a wedge behind him. "I am here to speak to the chief of detectives with regard to the brutal injustice being perpetrated on Negroes in this community."

"Have an appointment?" Lenehan asked.

"No. The police work for the general population. We are taxpayers and citizens. We should not need an appointment to see someone who serves the public."

Lenehan's brow furrowed, and he appeared confused. "I'm not sure the chief will see you without an appointment," he cautioned.

"We, sir, are prepared to wait." None of the Negroes backed away. As if on cue, five men widened their stances, folding arms across chests so they resembled ebony statues. Their position this close to the desk was intended to make Lenehan uncomfortable.

Despite Lenehan's stoic mask, his cheeks concealed a secret smile. Although he did not care for blacks, this had potential to be the most exciting event at the office all week. It might enliven an otherwise drab morning. The chief would not want to see them, but at the same time could not allow five well-dressed Negroes to idle in his squad for the day. Rumors about the sit-in would race up and down the corridors. He would be caught in a shitstorm, and Lenehan had a VIP seat to witness the chaos.

"I'll let the chief know you're here. And I can rustle up some chairs so you can have a seat," Lenehan suggested.

"We will not sit," Brown declared loudly, as if speaking to a rally. "We will not rest while innocent Negroes are being slain in our community."

Lenehan shrugged. "Suit yourself. But I'm going to need you to step to one side so I can watch who gets on and off the elevator."

*   *   *

The shotgun was old, its metal tarnished from years of disuse. It was stored in a trunk beneath his bed. He hadn't thought much about the weapon until they had beaten the shit out of him. If he had access to it that night, there would have been three corpses at the bus stop, that was for damn sure.

In the days that followed, he inspected the barrel for rust and considered its usefulness. Using a wood-handled hacksaw he swiped from a neighbor's shed, he spread newspapers across the linoleum floor and slid the blade back and forth, sawing off nine inches. The metal, hard and unforgiving, made the process grueling, but after several starts and stops, above a scattering of filed shavings, he had a shotgun stubby enough to be concealed.

Now, he knelt next to the spongy mattress, pulled out the bin and unlatched the clasp. He held the modified weapon with the tenderness of a newborn, cradling the grip in one palm, the barrel in the other. The gun felt heavy, awkward. Shells clanked in an old jelly jar. Would they even fire after all these years?

One way to find out. Today would be perfect to experiment, because he was feeling off. Stabbing was violent and forceful and required strength from his arms and chest, a power he lacked this morning. There was no way to muster that energy.

The plan was taking shape. And if for some reason it didn't work, then so what? Take a day off and maybe the stupid niggers would start to feel safe again. He could resume with the knife tomorrow.

If he was successful, the terror would be even greater.

*   *   *

Gerald Harold was having one of those days. It began that morning when he feuded with his wife over the toothpaste cap, and here he was ruminating about it six hours later. Their argument was stupid, he knew that, but was it too much to ask the woman to screw the cap back on instead of leaving it on the countertop? My God, this wasn't their first go-around with the issue. Each time she answered "yes" with disinterest in her voice. Repeated incidents left him more frustrated.

"Just screw the fucking cap on," he had finally barked this morning. Michelle hadn't cared for his use of the expletive, nor his snarky tone. Well that was too damn bad, he thought, because he didn't care to keep replacing the top every time she walked out of the bathroom.

Because of their tiff, he had arrived late to work. Only five minutes, but his boss made eye contact as he came through the glass door. It was no big deal on the surface. He would simply comp an extra five at the end of the day, but the company was talking about abolishing the time clock and converting to an honor system. Shuffling in late didn't help anyone's cause.

Then Frankie from the shop had approached for clarification about one of Gerald's designs. Frankie was an old codger who made a full time job out of annoying people. He refused to say, "Gerry," or "Gerald." Instead he used both names, always addressing him as "Gerald Harold." He did not do that to anyone else in the plant, and each time he said it, he let the rhyme linger like he was sniffing the air for offensive smells. At first Gerald thought it might be a racial issue, a way to keep a black man subservient to the whites. But in the lunchroom, Russ suggested that Frankie wasn't racist, just an asshole, equal opportunity notwithstanding. Still, he didn't like being called "Gerald Harold" in a demeaning tone by some shop jockey. Gerald had an engineering degree. He doubted if Frankie had a high school equivalency diploma.

The topper was that he had stormed out of the house this morning without his lunch. Packed the night before, it consisted of a roast beef sandwich on a Kaiser roll, with a Bartlett pear and Oreo cookies. He had heard the whispers of "Oreo" his whole life — black on the outside but white on the inside — a not-so-subtle put-down suggesting a black man could not attend college and be successful while still honoring his race. Gerald considered the cookies a treat, but also a personal protest, an affirmation of both his blackness and his advanced education.

So he punched out at 12:05 and drove his Impala down Union Road toward Burger King. After buying a whopper, fries and root beer, he pulled across the street into the parking lot of the Como Mall. The plaza's front bustled. Little old women and workers on lunch break streamed through the glass doors of Sears. Gerald drove around the rear, near the movie theaters, where the pavement backed up to a grove of maple and pine trees. He eased under their shade and turned off the ignition, unwrapping his burger. The day was warm enough that he could sit in the car with the windows open and smell the autumn air.

*   *   *

Once out of bed and moving, he swallowed an Old Milwaukee and crunched a stalk of browning celery. He needed to get out of the apartment. Its rooms felt small; his aches throbbed. He checked yesterday's Courier-Express for movie listings, hoping to see Private Benjamin, because Goldie Hawn was sexy, even if she was flat as a skillet. A matinee played in Cheektowaga at 12:30. Sitting in a darkened theater, he could eliminate the interference, clear his mind of clutter, decide whether to go on the attack today.

Now, fifteen minutes before the movie was to start, he waited in his parked car with windows cranked down. Indian summer had dawned, sunshine warming the day, and most of the cobwebs evaporated from his brain. Maybe he was well enough to do a stabbing after all.

That's when he noticed the coffee-colored Impala looping around the far edge of the lot, braking to a halt then turning into an isolated patch of shade. The nigger driving was seventy yards away, but his afro was visible through the open window.

Joe checked his mirrors. A green van passed and turned left on the road, but there was no one else around. He was early for the screening, and besides, how many people came to the movies on a Thursday afternoon? His heart beat faster. This would be perfect.

Before leaving his house, he had placed the sawed-off shotgun in a grocery bag then carried it out to the car. He wanted to travel to the country this afternoon and fire test rounds, but this was more brazen. Keeping his windows rolled down, he removed keys from the ignition and walked around to the trunk, unlatching it and hefting the brown bag. He did not glance around to eliminate distractions. Maintain focus, he told himself. A guy carrying a bag won't draw attention until after the blast.

Leg muscles remained tight. Each step felt like razors cutting into his tendons, but with a singular purpose he plodded forward.

*   *   *

The radio station was playing a song by the Commodores, and Gerald Harold hummed along absently. That stupid spat with Michelle. Why didn't he just screw the cap on and keep his mouth shut? Was it worth a big fight? Meanwhile, licking his lips and sipping root beer, he wondered why Burger King sprinkled too much salt on their fries.

The man walking toward the woods caught his eye. What was this guy doing, strolling through a parking lot? Was there a path back there? Gerald observed that his arms and legs shifted awkwardly, out of synch, like an upright crab stumbling across uneven coral.

A dollop of mayonnaise squeezed out from the far side of the bun, dropping to his lap, lettuce fragments tumbling beyond and hitting the floorboard. Gerald reached his left hand between his legs toward the mat, bending his neck low. A clicking sound was faint above melodies from the speaker, and when he sat up, a silhouette filled his side-view mirror. Although he did not see a face, he noticed dungarees, an olive t-shirt, and a brown paper bag swinging upward.

Before Gerald could turn his head, an explosion filled the car.

*   *   *

Intrigued by the splattering that dripped across the dashboard and steering wheel, he hesitated long enough to commit the scene to memory, to inhale the humid smell of death.

"Shells worked," he said out loud.

He turned and strolled casually, pain in his legs less distinct on the return trip to his car.

*   *   *

"Side of his head was blown off," Connell said, dropping his scribbled notes onto Bennett's desk. "Victim was an electronic engineer, worked up the road. Gerald Harold. There was blood, brains and Burger King plastered inside his windshield. Pretty gory. Cheektowaga cops phoned us as a courtesy."

Bennett squinted at Connell's illegible handwriting. "Why?"

"The guy's black. They figure he might be related to our cases."

They had spent the morning tracking down names from Bennett's list. With help from fellow detectives, they had interviewed more than seventy people and were pursuing others. The team planned to convene that afternoon to share their findings, but so far, Bennett had not found any solid suspects among the men he spoke with. He felt he was spinning wheels in vain.

Bennett looked up skeptically. "Do you think our guy did this?"

Connell eased into the adjacent chair and looped fingers behind his neck. "Why not?"

"Our guy doesn't use a gun. He uses a knife. He's a stabber, not a shooter."

"On Monday he threw a woman off a tall building before switching to stabbing on Tuesday and Wednesday. I don't think he's too worried about the weapon he uses. He's already shown us he's not afraid to change."

"Only reason Cheektowaga called us is cause the victim is black, right?"

Connell nodded.

"Big whoop. How many black vics do we see every week in the city? Besides, our guy only works in Buffalo."

"Until now. You think he gives a good goddamn about city boundaries? All he cares is that there's another dead Negro."

Bennett hesitated, staring at his desk blotter while Connell remained still. "Maybe," he conceded.

"You're not convinced?"

"Not sure."

"Fair enough. Cheektowaga is going to keep us updated on the investigation. Maybe it's not related at all. Maybe Gerald Harold's got an angry wife or he pissed somebody off at work or he's trading drugs on the side. Maybe somebody doesn't like the fact that his name rhymes. But you didn't think the Monday and Tuesday killings were linked either," Connell reminded him. "It took that fat witness yesterday to change your mind."

Bennett nodded. Connell's arguments were compelling.

"Our Tuesday and Wednesday witnesses both said he did the stabbing, then didn't rush away," Bennett reflected. "Just

140

walked on casually, like he was out for a weekend stroll. This guy is calculating. It's like he wants to stick around and see his handiwork. If he did this, he'd have to run away because a gunshot draws attention. If he stuck around, he would have been caught."

"Whoever it is, how the fuck does nobody see him in a mall parking lot?"

*   *   *

Too many details of these cases did not fall into a pattern. Bennett struggled to understand the intricacies of each murder. The two stabbings were linked and the bad guy made reference to the city hall flier, so that connected as well. But were the dead people all targets, or simply random victims? Could a different person be responsible for the parking lot shooting? The killer had never used a gun before, never acted outside of Buffalo's jurisdiction.

Sitting at his desk, Bennett doodled notes. But when the loose leaf became too cluttered, he used a ruler to divide a sheet of typing paper into four columns. At the top he wrote the date, time and location of each murder. He continued downward, listing the victims' names, ages, and method of death.

Bennett stood and leaned against his blotter, examining the chart from a further distance. He didn't like that the killer used different weapons, because it suggested a break in the pattern. Serial murderers took refuge in familiarity. Still, laid out visually, common elements were clear: murder of a black victim, middle of the day, public setting, high risk for being seen.

When would it end? If this was the same guy, would he only stop when caught, or would he reach some magic quota and feel satisfied?

Bennett called to Connell, emerging from the break room while twisting a paper towel through his hands. Connell approached Bennett's desk and studied the chart.

"I think when you see it like this, there is little doubt," Connell said after reading it twice. "Throw out the weapon, and the M.O. is consistent. It's brutal and brazen, done right around noon in a wide-open space. That fits. Based on this, I'm leaning toward the idea that our guy did today's shooting."

"You might be right," Bennett agreed. "Evidence is pretty compelling."

"We need to take a ride and check out the scene."

*   *   *

Ninety minutes later, after returning to the squad room, Bennett and Connell were summoned into the chief's office. Approaching three o'clock, it had already been a long day.

"I got good news and I got bad news," the chief explained once the door was shut. "Black leaders started screaming today at anybody who would listen. I tried to calm them, but they got the ear of the mayor. With election day just around the corner, he's taking their complaints seriously enough that he wants the commissioner to give him hourly updates."

Connell rolled his eyes. "What's the good news?"

"The good news is this: the mayor supports the idea of a task force. We're ramping up our efforts and our resources. You two are going to be in charge. A press conference is scheduled for five o'clock. The three TV stations and both newspapers will be there."

Connell snorted and massaged his forehead. "Hell, chief, I don't want to be paraded in front of the media. I hate those bastards. It prevents us from doing our work. TV people are morons."

"I'm not so sure it's a bad thing," Bennett said. "Publicity might help. Somebody out there has to know something about our killer. He's somebody's son or brother or neighbor, and he's behaving oddly. Maybe a good citizen sees this on TV and thinks to call us."

"You just want to be on TV," Connell said.

"No, I just want us to catch some kind of break."

"If we don't get something soon," the chief explained, "the next step is to bring in the Feds."

"No way," Connell objected. "Huge mistake."

"The idea came up at a meeting of the minds."

"The mindless, you mean," Connell said. "If the mayor thinks the Feds can solve this but we can't..." He let the sentence trail, then began again. "We've covered every goddamn base, Chief. Unless the Feds come up with some miracle witness who followed the killer home and can tell us where he lives, they're going to be in our way. You've never worked with the Feds, have you, Bennett? Adds another level of bureaucracy to everything. Bringing them in would be a boot to the balls."

"I'm with you," the chief agreed. "I want you two to close this so it stays in house. I don't like when the Feds swoop in here and glom onto our cases any more than you do. Makes it look like we can't control our own city. But let's be honest. The mayor is a politician who's trying to get re-elected. If this thing stays open a few more days, and the blacks ramp up their protests, it's gonna happen. He wants to say he's doing everything he can."

"Can you explain this task force?" Bennett asked.

"You two are the point men. You're getting six more detectives at your disposal, full time. None of them work anything else until this is closed. They're going to coordinate their activities through you. Now you've got more resources to track down any lead, no matter how remote. It's important that we talk to everyone on Bennett's list. Re-interview witnesses. Maybe they remember something a day or two later. Oh, and I just got this."

The chief opened a manila folder and slid two sheets across his desk. The department's artist had assembled a composite drawing.

Bennett studied the black and white sketch. An Anglo face filled the page. The killer was depicted with dark, close-set eyes, a narrow head funneled toward a distinctive chin. Hair parted along the right side, sweeping across his forehead. Ears were barely noticeable, pressed flat and buried under hair. Lips turned down at their edges, and there were creases of flesh in the neck. The artist had given him a collared shirt, buttoned to the top, below a dark sweater vest.

Bennett thought the killer looked like a dignified, forty-year-old business-school dropout. "This isn't really how I pictured him," he said.

"Our artist isn't real happy with it either," the chief admitted. "Said he was getting conflicting statements from the two witnesses. The black kid thought one thing, that white construction worker said the complete opposite."

"The black kid was two feet away when his pal got shanked," Connell said. "That white dude, Dunphy, saw him across the street and through traffic. I'd put more stock in the kid's memory."

"Just because he was closer doesn't mean he's a better witness," Bennett said. "He saw his pal get knifed, but he was in shock. Dunphy watched our killer do the stabbing, then hang around before leaving. He was further away, but I think he's more reliable."

"Well, I don't know how much weight was given to each, but this is what we've got," the chief said dismissively. "This is what we're going to release to the public. Maybe some component will ring true and jog somebody's conscience." He closed the folder and leaned forward. "Now listen, by five, I want you both cleaned up, shaved, and wearing a fresh shirt. Connell, tighten your tie before you go on camera. You're both representing the Buffalo police."

"I hate TV people and I hate jumping through hoops," Connell grumbled.

"This isn't about your likes and dislikes," the chief said. "It's an order."

He sighed. "All right."

Bennett had not looked away from the sketch. "I've never seen the guy, so this is just a gut feeling," he said, laying the single page on the chief's desk, "but I don't think this drawing is right."

Chapter 14

The six o'clock news led with stories about his crusade. He held the antennae's rabbit ears to keep the black and white picture from turning to snow. The anchor was a Jew, his two-syllable surname a rhyming cadence that played well across airwaves. This channel was good, because unlike the other two, there were no coon reporters at the station.

"Topping tonight's Eyewitness News," the Jew intoned, and the next several minutes were a blur. Another killing had happened that day, and nigger community activists were outraged at the crime spree, convinced that Buffalo police had put the issue onto the back burner because blacks were second-class citizens.

"Fucking-A right they are," he agreed with the TV.

As a montage of cops and crime scenes flashed before him, his heart somersaulted. In his excitement, he wiped his forehead, quickly wrapping fingertips back around the antennae's point when images turned fuzzy.

"Police claim to have several promising leads…" the Jew continued.

He listened intently, wishing the words would slow down. But that part was bullshit. If the cops had anything, they would be here by now, knocking on his door, or more likely, knocking down his door. Pictures flashed of the bus stop from Tuesday. He wished the camera would pan lower so he could know if someone hosed down the blood.

The screen filled with a composite sketch. He leaned back and studied it, then barked a laugh. The eyes looked like his, but the rest was flat out wrong. They drew his chin almost to a point, ears flat, and the shape of his jaw and cheeks were not even close. If their plan to catch him relied on that, he could roam free for a long time.

Another reporter stood behind the Como Mall holding a microphone, a dark-haired bitch who enunciated every word like she was British while directing the cameraman to zoom on the location of this afternoon's shooting. Her teeth were perfect, dark eyes sultry, hair falling to her shoulders. Was the same person involved? she asked rhetorically.

Cut to film from a press conference earlier in the day.

"There are strong similarities," a middle-aged police boss said from behind a podium. His metal buttons shone under the glare of bright lights. "Each attack appears motiveless. We are unable to find a connection between any of the victims, other than the fact they are black. The bold manner of each attack, the time of day and geography makes us believe they are linked."

A full seven minutes were devoted to the issue, and when it ended, he was sweating and giggly, unable to contain enthusiasm. The dream was coming true.

He stepped away from the TV and began jumping jacks to calm his nerves, but pain in his legs forced him to stop after two hops. He flopped onto the couch, massaging his calves, contemplating how to celebrate. The image of the dark-haired reporter was strong. He would love to give her an interview, let her wave that microphone like a wand and ask probing questions about his mind. Then he would knock her down and climb on top of her, shredding her expensive clothes to tatters while he fucked her, pounding her so hard that she would forget her phony professional demeanor and cry out in pain, wailing for mercy.

If only she was one of them so he could kill her too. He needed to find another whore to release his aggression.

But first he wanted to make these memories permanent.

When the call came about a liquor store robbery on West Tupper Street, Angelo Battaglia and Jason Markham were riding patrol three blocks away. While Battaglia pressed the accelerator, Markham, in the passenger's seat, turned on the light bar before he picked up the mic to respond.

"Two white males, early twenties," the dispatcher said. "No weapon displayed. One punched the clerk when he turned his head and did a grab into the cash drawer. Suspects fled eastbound in a cream-colored Ford Pinto, partial license G16."

At nine p.m., traffic was sparse, and after a fast left turn, the black and white raced up Washington toward Tupper. A car with only one headlight rounded the corner towards them, hesitated, then banked a hard right into a parking lot. Markham called excitedly, "Go Angelo, that's them! Cream colored Pinto!"

The cruiser gave chase, and after losing sight momentarily behind a brick building, found the car nestled with headlights off in a narrow space between two warehouses. Battaglia blocked them in. With the searchlight turned onto the Pinto, both officers emerged with guns drawn, barking orders for the passengers to show their hands outside the window.

Although their adrenaline surged, as fast as it began the conflict was over. Within a minute the pair of scruffy young whites were out of the car and cuffed. Clad in denim coats, with stringy hair and foul breath, they confessed to the robbery before they were even advised of their rights, admitting they intended to use the sixty-dollar booty to score drugs that night.

It was a quick, successful arrest, and Markham thought they should all be this easy. Within five minutes of the crime, both bad guys were captured and en route to the Holding Center. When they had calmed, Battaglia and Markham drove by the liquor store to survey the crime scene. The patrol car nudged to the curb and both men got out with a swagger that results from a successful shift. Battaglia's chest inflated with pride, filling out the blue uniform.

Behind the counter was a middle-aged man with skin the color of faded parchment. When he spoke there was a drizzle of accent, and he used precise words, as if trying to impress with his second language. Battaglia could not determine his nationality.

"I thank you, officers," he said, holding an ice-wrapped towel to the welt on his temple. "They are very bad men who would hit and rob me. You do the city proud to have captured them so hastily."

"Good timing for us," Markham said. "We were only a few blocks away when the call came."

"Impressive nevertheless. I will speak highly of the police from this day forward."

Battaglia surveyed the shelves of different colored bottles. As a teen he had been excited by alcohol, but as years passed, drinking took a toll on his body the following day. The dry mouth, the hangover, the heavy-tongued feeling that lingered until noon... Pills were more convenient, leaving a mellow feeling without nasty after-effects. Seeing the bottles, however, brought back recollections of youth. Memories of cool gin slithered up the aisle and leaped toward his lips, expanding along the crease of his tongue like an old friend.

"I would like to offer you a small token of thanks," the clerk continued. "I am proprietor of this store and would be honored for each of you to select a case of beer. Your choice of label."

Markham smiled humbly. "Sir, that's not necessary."

Battaglia shot him a shut-the-hell-up look. Markham had been born again the following spring, and as part of his conversion he chose to abstain from alcohol. Finding Jesus morphed him from a fun hell-raiser into a dull partner, and also blinded him to the ways of the world. Battaglia, however, clung to no such convictions. If this Green Card was going to offer free beer, he sure as shit was going to take it. One of the best things about his job was a perk like this.

"It would be my great pleasure," the owner insisted. "I feel indebted to such kind officers who ensured that two hooligans are removed from the street."

"Sir, we're not all—" Markham began, but Battaglia interrupted.

"We're not always witness to such a generous gesture," he said. "I'd take a case of Heinekin myself."

"Excellent choice," smiled the owner. "And you sir?"

Markham looked at his partner, hesitating, so Battaglia answered before he could start preaching. "He's a Labatts man."

Emerging from behind the counter, the proprietor shuffled to a floor-to-ceiling refrigerator and swung open the glass door, removing two cases, stacking them atop one another, and moved toward the entrance.

"Shall I put these in your trunk?" he wondered.

"That'd be great," Battaglia said, bell jingling as he opened the front door and held it ajar so the man could pass.

After a round of handshakes and a suggestion to keep icing his bruised temple, the officers climbed back in the car. As Battaglia pulled away, Markham shook his head.

"You know we're not supposed to accept—"

"Save it, Markham. It's a case of beer. Before you got into bed with Christ we did shit like this all the time. I'm gonna call some of the fun coppers and host a little party after the shift ends. I'd invite you, but I know what you're gonna say."

"I'm gonna say you're an asshole." Hostility filled the space. Finding God had changed Markham's life, and often his past behavior embarrassed him, especially when Battaglia continually brought it up. He wondered how he had ever gotten along with his partner before. Had he really been blind to this snake?

"You allowed to talk that way?" Battaglia asked.

Markham glared.

"I mean, being a new convert to Christ and all, I wouldn't think that sort of hedonistic language is really appropriate," Battaglia needled.

"You bring out the best in me."

"So you're allowed to say asshole?"

"About you, yeah, I am."

Battaglia chuckled. "Well if that's the case, maybe I can get behind this born again stuff. You got any literature to share with me?"

*   *   *

Back at the squad, Battaglia dialed the black phone.

"Bennett," the voice answered.

"Bobby, it's Angelo."

"Hey. What's up, man?"

"Markham and I busted these two low-lifes who did a smash and grab at a convenient store. Rag-head owner took a bump on the noggin, but he was so grateful we caught the bastards he gave us two free cases of beer. We just stumbled over these guys by accident. Right place at the right time. Talk about a good shift."

"Nice going."

"You doing a four to twelve?"

"Yeah," Bennett answered.

"Good. Me and the boys are gonna tip a few after shift, two free cases and all. Meet us at the cemetery like last time."

Background noise from Bennett's squad room filled the phone line. Scraping chairs, low-toned chatter, the clack of a distant typewriter. He didn't respond.

"You hear me?" Battaglia asked.

"Yeah, I hear you," Bennett's tone sounded reluctant. "I'm gonna have to take a flier on this one."

"What? Are you kidding?"

"No, not tonight."

"How come?"

Another hesitation. Although he would not concede it aloud, Bobby considered his brother's words. He couldn't very well tell Battaglia that Mark had warned him to stay away because bad cops were like a virus. Any excuse would only be temporary, but at least it would buy tonight. Later he could figure out a better way to elude Battaglia for good.

"I'm in the doghouse with Susie," Bobby lied.

"So?"

"I better get home."

"Don't let her wear the pants. Be a man."

"Well, being out late the other night, stumbling in after that scrap with my brother, I just think I better lay low for a while. Anyway, my sack is still sore from where he kicked me."

"We're drinking, not fucking. I don't care how sore your scrotes are."

"Yeah, well, you'll change your tune when you try walking around with two swollen balls."

"I'm not sure you have balls. I think it's a goddamn pussy," Battaglia said, and hung up the phone. *Mark Bennett didn't just corner me,* he thought. *He sprinkled a guilt trip on his brother too.*

*   *   *

Daylight had faded, and the shop's interior was dim, its stale air thick with patchouli and rubbing alcohol. An electric buzz hummed from somewhere outside the cones of light. The guy behind the counter had the girth of a hippopotamus, long hair

152

restrained by an American flag bandana, stringy beard tickling his chest. Taped to the wall next to him were hundreds of patterns drawn onto square white paper.

"Help you?" he grunted.

"I want four chef's hats," Joe said. "About an inch high, all going down my left arm."

"Chef's hats?"

"That's right."

Joe had considered the best way to commemorate his killings. At first wanted a cross tattoo to represent each victim, but didn't like the religious parallels. There was nothing sacred about dead niggers. Then he considered an X, like a crossed-out mistake. But that was too simple. No, he considered himself an artist, a poet, a chef who skewered his meat and served it to the world. That was it: he was a chef.

The big man wedged a fingernail into his teeth. "Got lotsa other designs here," he said, pointing out barbed wire, motorcycles and naked women whose large breasts were disproportional. "You sure about this? Nobody asks for tattoos of a chef's hat."

"It's what I want."

The big man studied him for a moment, then shrugged. "You in cooking school or something?"

"Yeah," he smiled meekly. "Cooking school."

A nod. "All right, that's what you want, I can ink you up. How about I sketch one out by hand, you can tell me if you like it."

He lit a cigarette, produced a pen and pad, and drew the bottom third of a rectangle with an arching squiggly line on top to close the box.

"Looks good," Joe said. "Start at my shoulder and work down. Space 'em maybe an inch apart. Leave room for more."

"More?"

"You do a good job with these, I might be back."

"Need more than four?"

He hesitated. "I plan to get one each time I perfect a new dish."

The big man flicked his cigarette ash onto the floor, adding to the soot underfoot. "Get to be a gourmet chef, you could have ink all over you."

"Wouldn't that be nice?"

*   *   *

Fuck Bobby Bennett, Battaglia thought. *If he wants to go all holy roller like his brother, that's his problem. I can still celebrate with the boys while he's home jacking off cause his wife just had a baby and is too sore to give him a good lay.*

Still, it bothered Battaglia that his circle of friends seemed to be shrinking. First his partner had found Jesus, now Bennett was pulling away under the influence of Reverend Mark. *If this keeps up, I'll have to start hanging out with Alonzo and his little live-in whore.*

He wondered what she'd be like in bed. Looked like a twelve year-old, that little Integrity bitch, or whatever her name was. No tits at all, with a high squeaky voice, but she had a banging ass and lots of practice sucking cock. Alonzo probably washed his big black dick in her mouth every night after she came home from trolling the streets.

What about her story? Was it possible that the city hall killer beat her up? Or was that just a big act to get attention? He wanted to confide in someone about her claims, solicit a second opinion, but didn't know who to tell without revealing his side business. He wasn't about to stop moving product, because that was some lucrative cash, and he needed it. When he retired from the job after twenty he was going down to Florida to buy a giant fucking yacht and live like a beach bum, staring at the little co-eds with their big hair and teeny bikinis.

154

Before his shift ended, Battaglia rounded up a group of guys from the four to twelve who agreed to drink with him that night. The lure of free beer, he thought. Everyone promised to rally at their usual spot, a secluded cemetery, with few houses scattered between factories. The boys could be loud and raucous and no one was going to complain.

"Meet you there soon," he told them in the locker room after clocking out. "Gotta make a detour."

Alonzo's house was dark as Battaglia ascended the outside steps. Through lace curtains, he saw flickering lights of a TV. Johnny Carson was interviewing some old-timer. Battaglia rapped softly on the square pane.

Like a bear coming out of hibernation, Alonzo's bulk hefted itself from the sofa and shuffled toward the door. He frowned when he recognized Battaglia in street clothes.

"You ain't getting no more until Monday, officer," he said through the closed door. "This becoming a real issue now."

"No, no," Battaglia shook his head. "I'm here to talk to your girl. I wanna know more about the creep that beat her up."

Alonzo's eyes narrowed with suspicion. Reluctantly he unbolted the lock and swung the door open.

"For real?"

"If she's telling the truth, her info might be useful. Let me sit down with her for five minutes. We don't have many leads on that case."

The black man snorted. He recognized what Battaglia could not: because of their connection, it was impossible for this cop to share Sincere's information with fellow investigators, because it would link him to a dealer.

"So you all about truth and justice now, huh?" Alonzo deadpanned.

Battaglia glared at him, thinking, *you fat fucker. If I didn't need you, I'd kick your lard ass right here on the stoop. You're*

*going to give me shit when I'm a respected cop and you're a
low-life pusher?*

"Well, Sincere ain't here. She's a working girl, you know?
This her time to earn."

"Out on the streets, even with those bruises? No john is
gonna pay for that. She looked like walking death two days
ago."

Alonzo appeared disinterested. "Girl gotta make a living,"
he shrugged. "She laid on some pancake makeup. Anyway,
she's feeling better."

"You're a real humanitarian, sending her out on the streets
like that."

Alonzo's fleshy cheeks inflated in and out, like he was
chewing carrots without moving his jaw. He didn't like being on
the receiving end of sarcasm any more than Battaglia.

"Maybe it's time for you to leave, officer," he suggested.
"Pleasant as your visits are, don't come back here unless it's part
of our regular schedule, you hear?"

Battaglia nodded, descending the steps. At the bottom, he
turned to see Alonzo on the stoop with arms crossed, overseeing
his retreat.

Lousy fucking gorilla, he thought. *Good thing we need each
other or one of us would seriously unburden the other.*

What now? Should he wait in his car for the little whore?
He checked his watch. The boys would be en route to the
cemetery, and who knew what time a hooker finished her work?
She might not stumble home until dawn. No, he would find her
tomorrow. He just hoped there would be no killings overnight.

*   *   *

His first tattoo, a growling pit bull with the words "MAD
DOG" on the right shoulder, had faded after nine years, green
edges leaking into nearby pores like water absorbed by a paper

156

towel. It was a rush job back then, and he only paid a few bucks to a guy who worked out of his parents' basement.

He hoped the chef's hats would last longer, maintain their shape as years went by.

Hell, he thought, *it might not even matter. I probably won't live through this crusade.*

He stopped at a corner liquor store for a bottle of Jim Beam, gulping down two healthy swallows in the car. The drink, he hoped, would round the edges off. Half an hour afterward, he could still feel needles puncturing his arm. The lard ass had given him some gooey Vaseline gel that was supposed to prevent infection, but fuck that, he didn't have time to be rubbing jiz all over himself. He never saw that shit when he got the MAD DOG.

Alcohol burned his throat, but its heat numbed the stinging arm. Life is a matter of redirecting pain, he told himself.

He parked on his street but didn't go toward the apartment. Instead, he walked two blocks to the cemetery, zipping his jacket to ward off the chilly night air. Clusters of leaves gathered along the sidewalk. His boots made a swishing sound as he shuffled through the dry piles. Every few strides he would break his gait to step on them, crunching stems. Once inside the wrought-iron fence, he raised the bottle to his lips, letting its warmth coat his throat.

The cloudless sky revealed a scattering of stars. The graveyard felt tranquil tonight. Maybe it was the new ink, or the autumn air, or the Jim Beam, but he felt less hostile. Earlier aggression had faded. He wouldn't mind finding a hooker tonight, but she wouldn't be a nigger and he wouldn't beat her, just do his business and go home to sleep.

He knelt, ignoring his creaking knees, and wrapped knuckles against his father's marker.

"I'm back, Dad. Two more since I was here last. It's leading the evening news now, if you can believe that. Your boy turned out okay, huh? They're talking about me on TV. It's my tribute to you."

Silence stretched and he felt overwhelmed. What would his dad say if he could respond? Would he wrap arms around his son, pull him close and nuzzle the boy in the crook of his neck? Pupils grew watery. Joe dabbed at gathering tears along his lids.

Across darkness, sound carried. A slamming car door, the camaraderie of approaching voices. What the hell? It was after midnight in a neighborhood cemetery. Who would be coming now? Footfalls grew louder, coarse masculine sounds mingled with laughter. He pushed himself up and scampered behind a tree, its rough trunk shielding his body.

There were five of them. In silhouette, he could not see their uniforms, but from the way they walked, he knew they were cops. His throat constricted, anxiety stabbing his chest. How had they found him? The police boss on TV had been telling the truth. Were they coming after him here because there would be no observers, no witnesses to the beating and torture he would suffer while they sought a confession?

He didn't want to be hit. He knew he was cowardly at heart, the opposite of brave, petrified by physical pain. Soreness and dull aches he could tolerate, but the threat of being struck by a wooden baton consumed him with terror.

Fuck it, he thought, *I'll tell them everything. Yes, the one at city hall got skewered like a kabob, but it was a lucky break. Only wish I had planned it that perfectly. Hell yeah, I stabbed them. And yes, I blew out that one's brains in the mall parking lot. Fucker was chewing his burger and never even saw me coming! I also beat the shit out of a tiny hooker with a little girl voice. In a moment of weakness I let her go. I regret not doing her too.*

In a brief flash he contemplated future glories that might come his way. He could be a celebrity prisoner. Broads all over the country might write letters, sending marriage proposals.

Finally, someone might pay attention to him. And his dad would achieve fame, because he would tell every reporter that his crusade was a means to avenge his father's murder.

If only he could be that courageous, one of those Navy Seals whose mind is so strong he can harden himself to ignore physical pain.

But that wasn't him. He couldn't live in prison. He couldn't exist confined to a cell with niggers. That wasn't an option.

Cops were coming. How could it be? They hadn't even gotten the composite sketch correct.

And yet, here they were.

He shuffled left, concealing himself behind a wider tree. For an awful moment all movement stopped and he knew they had pinpointed his location.

He turned and ran.

*   *   *

When Battaglia parked on the edge of the cemetery's lawn, two other cars were already waiting. He flashed headlights, then turned off the ignition and opened his truck to retrieve the beer. The guys slammed their car doors and came to help.

"Thought you stood us up," one of them said. "I got ice and an empty cooler."

"I brought a six pack," another guy chimed.

"Nolan, you're a fucking meathead," Battaglia spat, shaking his head. "Why would you bring a six pack when I got two free cases?"

"Well, I just thought—"

"You didn't think. Let's leave it at that."

"Fuck you, Battaglia, My beers are chilled. Yours been sitting in a trunk for three hours. While we ice down yours, we can each start with a cold one. Drinking warm beer is like swallowing goat piss."

"That's a good idea," one of them agreed.

"Maybe you'da preferred I brought caviar and brie, Angelo?" Nolan persisted.

Starting with chilled beers made sense, but Battaglia wasn't about to relent. "I'd prefer it you shut your mouth."

The rest of the crew chuckled, falling silent as they crested a hill. Trudging past tombstones, moonlight was the only illumination. They followed a path toward the center of the cemetery, where a grove of evergreens offered the buffer of privacy. Arching tree limbs absorbed most of their voices.

Battaglia, lugging one of the cases, heard a shuffling to the left and thought he spied movement in the shadows. The dark form was big, larger than a rabbit or skunk. "Hold it," he said, and put out a hand to stop the others. Could it be a deer or coyote? After two steps and another harsh shush, the cops paused, all senses springing alert. For several seconds there was no sound except wind through the branches.

Then a snapping sound, footfalls pounding over twigs and fallen leaves. Something or someone was running.

"There!" Nolan pointed, and began to sprint, but the six-pack he carried impeded his progress, and he gave up after ten yards. Battaglia laid the case onto the lawn and took a few tentative steps himself, but by then the runner had a jump on them and he wondered why he was giving chase. The other three cops were uninterested in the fleeing figure, remaining rooted like the surrounding pines.

"Should we check it out?" one asked doubtfully as the figure vanished down the lee side of a hill.

"I'm here to guzzle beer, not go chasing shadows in a graveyard," another replied.

"Probably just some kid smoking pot," Battaglia concluded. His mind turned to the task at hand. "Let's chill these bottles."

"Good idea."

Battaglia's sarcasm reared itself again.

"Nolan, if I didn't make my feelings clear, you're a genius for bringing some cold ones," he said, and although his words were complimentary, his fellow cops were certain they lacked sincerity.

Chapter 15

Mark Bennett did not intend to stop at the bar, but had been so exhausted when he left the squad that he neglected to phone Alison. He wanted to confirm that she planned to sleep over at his house. Paralleling the curb, he locked the car door, fishing in his pocket for a dime. There was a pay phone inside.

The jukebox was playing a guitar riff from Boston, smoke curling through the evening shadows. Ken Connell perched on a swivel stool before the bar. In his hand was a tumbler of amber liquid, with an empty resting before him. A cigarette smoldered in an ash tray, its tip sparkling orange. As the bartender engaged in conversation at the far end of the room, Connell appeared to be alone. His short hair shone paler under the dim light, but his reflection in the mirror revealed pupils that were clear and steady.

Three steps across the threshold, Bennett recognized the scene and turned around when Connell called to him.

"Bennett, you son of a bitch," Connell said, "get over here and share a bourbon with me."

Mark raised his chin but maintained distance, hooking a thumb toward the door. "I'm on my way out."

"Bullshit. You just came in. I've been on this stool for twenty minutes and I would have seen you before now." Connell tapped the empty seat next to him, crooking his neck toward the space. "Sit down," he ordered.

Bennett hesitated before stepping forward. He kept a wide arc of distance between them. "The thing is, Connell, we don't like each other," Bennett reminded him.

"That's true. But we're partners now. It's like that little floater Lenehan said: a suspension of the tension. Come on. I was meeting a broad here, but she's late. I don't mind drinking alone, but do it for too long and it becomes oppressive."

Bennett glanced longingly at the door. A smell like boiled cabbage filled his nostrils. It was bad enough to work with the guy; he had no desire to spend his free time with him as well. Five minutes, he told himself. No more than that. Reluctantly, he fitted the stool under his legs.

"Besides," Connell said, once he recognized Bennett was going to stay, "didn't you want me to teach you everything I know about being a good person?"

"Why don't we just stick with what you know?"

Connell ignored the insult, narrowing an eye and focusing on Bennett. "Sometimes I think the chief partnered us on purpose. Light the fire, stir the stew, and see what comes of it. He knew I'd mentor you, even if it's against my will. I love my job and I'm a good cop. For me, solving cases takes precedence over everything. I got my reservations about you, but that's irrelevant when we're a team."

"You're one hell of a motivational speaker."

"Win one for the Gipper, right?" Connell pumped a jovial rah-rah fist, caught the bartender's attention and raised two fingers in a peace sign. A pair of shot glasses materialized on the counter before them.

"Let's toast the chief for manipulating me into being your mentor," Connell suggested, raising the smoky liquid. "That's why he's a boss. Once this case is over it'll be a different story."

Bennett downed the brandy in a swallow, warmth expanding in his throat, wiping lips with the back of his hand. "I may just stick by my convictions if it's all the same."

Connell grinned. "Sarcastic son of a bitch, aren't you?"

Bennett did not smile. He studied the rugged face, tiny moles and indentations along Connell's jawline. The image of

Ken shaving, maneuvering the razor cautiously around those bumps, made him seem more vulnerable. He envisioned Alison running hands over his chin, pressing her mouth against his nose, fingertips massaging short hair with a gentle touch. She had loved him once, he knew, but now, in the dim bar, those emotions felt to Bennett like they had existed in another dimension.

Connell noticed his partner's downturned lips. "You're a dreamer, aren't you, Bennett?"

"What do you mean?"

Connell's grin turned wolf-like. "You read books. You stare at the stars. You contemplate bubbles in your drink. I'm betting you go for long walks on the beach on rainy August mornings. Your head is always somewhere else, am I right?"

"I have an ability to formulate thoughts, if that's what you mean."

"And you don't think that I do."

"I think you're a hell of a cop. I'm just not sure what kind of a man you are."

Connell reflected on the compliment, then said, "And how would you have any idea what kind of a man I am?"

Because I'm sleeping with your wife and she tells me what an asshole you are. "I hear things. I see things too, around the squad. I see suspects locked in an interview room who come out singing a different story from when they went in, shaken and a little bruised. I see you jump on every new case, trying to gleam credit from others."

Connell nodded as if the truth had inconveniently escaped from beneath its metal lid. "Part of being a detective is making arrests, and sometimes you have to play dirty because the bad guy will too. Clearly you don't understand the subtleties of securing a confession."

"Treating people like objects, like they are a stepping stone to your needs, is morally offensive."

The two men locked eyes, each inspecting the other with disdain.

"Aren't you glad you invited me to stay?" Bennett wondered with irony.

"Hell yeah," Connell sat up straight, his eyes showing no effects from the alcohol. "I enjoy this intellectual exchange of ideas. See, I never sat in a college classroom. That would have been a luxury. I was too busy trying not to get my ass shot off in Vietnam."

"I thought you enlisted."

Connell paused, then nodded. "I did."

"So how can you play the poor-me-I-didn't-get-to-go-to-college routine? You made a choice."

"How did you know I enlisted? I never told you that."

Alison, he thought, but simply shrugged. "I don't know. Heard it somewhere."

"I don't recall telling anyone at work."

"I'm a detective. It's my job to find out things."

Connell swallowed and kept his gaze on Bennett. "You're a detective? Oh right, I must've forgot. I look at you and still see Mac's little boy on patrol."

Bennett absorbed the insult, fearing that if the issue was pushed, Connell might ruminate further, connecting him with Alison.

"So you've been investigating me, huh?" Connell asked. "What have people said?"

"It's not so much what's been said as what I've seen. You hate me for no reason. I bet you're not even sure why. You're just naturally miserable and suspicious of anyone who comes onto your turf, am I right?"

"You have no frigging idea, do you, Bennett?"

"Why don't you tell me your story? Did you turn your back on a college scholarship or something? Is that why you're so mad at me? Why did you enlist?"

For the first time, Connell looked away and mucked his lips. There were several long seconds of contemplation before his tale burst out. "My old man and me didn't get along. He wasn't any hero like yours, he was a mean son of a bitch. I went to the recruiter's office the day I turned eighteen and shipped out a week later. Never finished high school. I had to get the hell away. He died of kidney failure while I was over there, and it was one of the few times that I smiled in country."

Bennett ran his hands across the lacquered bartop. He had never learned any of this through Alison. "I heard you did two tours."

"Yeah. After the first, I wasn't ready to come back, so I stayed on. By then I'd gotten used to the fucking jungle and heat and insects and those goddamn slanty eyed gooks. One of the reasons I stayed alive is because I never trusted any of them, even the ones who claimed to be on our side. I've carried that mentality to this job. You never know who'll turn out to be an enemy."

A burst of raised voices caused both men to swivel toward a booth behind them. There, a small man argued with a woman who towered over him. With the wide shoulders of a linebacker, she looked comfortable with her anger, like it was a familiar smock. Their body language suggested she was accustomed to crushing him. Although words were mumbled, too distant to be distinct, the henpecked man lowered his head in defeat, submitting to her.

"Holy shit, I thought I had it bad," Connell muttered. "I got a wife and I'm juggling two other broads on the side."

Bennett's throat constricted and his senses sprang alert.

"That poor bastard is way worse off than me. That she-monster has his balls in a vise. What about you, Bennett? You got a woman?"

Bennett's gaze remained blank as he stared at Connell. How should he answer? Yes, I have a woman, and she's your ex, and we both know you're a son of a bitch. A surge of taboo coursed through him. This was the conversation he had wanted to avoid forever.

"What are you, a fucking mute?" Connell pressed. "You don't wear a wedding ring, so I figure you aren't married, but are you banging some broads or not?"

"I'm dating," he said quietly.

"It's a woman, right? You're not some goddamn queer?"

Bennett was so stunned he did not take offense. "It's a woman. I don't like to talk about it."

"What, is she a dog? Six fingers and a hare lip?" Connell winked.

"No, but it's personal. I like to keep personal stuff personal, you know, out of the office."

Connell nodded, his expression turning cruel. The effects of alcohol were beginning to creep into his cheeks. "She must be a mutt. Or a porker. That's it, I bet she's fat. Big rolls of jelly bouncing over her waistband, am I right? So you like them tubby. Nothing to be ashamed about. Sometimes the fat ones have the biggest rack. You must be a tit man." His eyes flamed with mischief, gleaming expectantly, like he hoped Bennett would smile and join his crude antics. But the younger detective ignored him, keeping his face averted toward the empty shot glass.

"All right, Connell, let's move on," Bennett suggested soberly.

"Maybe I ought to do a little investigation of you. Look into your penchant for the portly."

Bennett pushed his empty shot glass away with anger. "Don't."

The older man's smile faded. "You're a weird bastard, you know that? What guy doesn't like to talk about women?"

"Not in this context."

"I love women. Love everything about them. I love the way they smell. I love the way they walk. I love how they get all bent out of shape over some innocent comment and cling to it for six months. I love when they lean over to pick something up and a fart squeaks out. They're beautiful and sexy and mysterious and sublime. I've never been so happy as when a broad is bouncing on my lap and I've got her tits in my hands. That's when it's great to be a man."

"Is that how you define being a man? By taking a woman to bed?"

"Jesus, Bennett, you really are far out. You gonna start talking about women's lib shit? Do you march with the dykes who burn their bras? The best way to treat a woman is show her who's boss."

The bartender approached and swept aside their empty glasses. Connell requested two bottles of beer.

"Not for me," Bennett said, pointing at the pay phone in the corner. "I really only stopped in to make a call."

"Where you going?" Connell asked. "I'm just having fun yanking your chain."

"No you aren't. This is who you are. I'm not sure I want to hang around with a man like you." Bennett thought about his father, how Mac had little patience for nasty and cruel cops. Maybe Connell acted this way because his own dad had set a bad example for living.

"I'm hitting the road, but anyway, I'm sorry about your dad," he said.

Connell's posture shifted. "I'm not. I wish he woulda kicked sooner. Life might have been a whole lot easier."

"I don't care how bad your relationship was. It's hard to lose a father."

Connell exhaled. "Harder on you, I'll bet. Your pop was a good man. We only crossed paths a few times, but there was an aura around him. Were you two close?"

"Yeah. Been a tough year."

Connell studied his face and Bennett looked away, feeling discomfort that comes from being examined.

"Part of life, right?" Connell finally mused. "We're all gonna go sooner or later."

Bennett slid off the stool, sobered by the realization he had exposed so much of himself. His guard was down, and that was a mistake around Ken Connell, because sometime later this knowledge would be used to further his own ends. How had he slipped into a conversation about paternal love?

Connell still hadn't taken his gaze off Bennett. "You know, kid, we come from separate worlds," he said. "And I enjoy razzing you, but maybe we aren't so different after all."

God, Bennett thought, I hope you're wrong.

*   *   *

After Mark Bennett left the bar, he stopped at a pay phone in a plaza parking lot and phoned Alison. Her warm voice soothed his frustrations. She needed to change and wash her face, but would arrive at his house in twenty minutes.

It was nearly nine o'clock, and he hadn't eaten, so he stopped at a pizza shop and ordered two subs. By the time he rounded the corner toward his house, Alison's car was parked a block away, under an elm tree. He flashed headlights to her and pulled alongside, leaning over to unlatch the passenger's door.

"Hi," she said, twisting herself into the seat and leaning across the center console to kiss him.

"Boy, did I miss you," he said.

"Saw you on TV. Long day, huh?"

"Felt like a hundred years," Mark said. "There was another murder, and now there's a task force, and then a stupid press conference. And to top it off, I just shared a drink with Ken Connell. He thinks we're buddies now."

Pulling into the driveway, Mark slipped the car into park, got out and unlocked the garage door, rolling it open and snapping on the overhead light. He returned to the driver's seat to nose the Buick inside, rolling up the window as he did.

Alison did not say anything until they were inside and she had kissed him again.

"Explain to me about this drink with Ken. He likes you all of a sudden?" she asked.

"No, not really. He's being civil. We've been working together. Maybe he's warmed to my charming personality, but I doubt it. He openly admits to not liking me, then demands I sit with him and tells crude stories, winking and nudging. At one point, he turned all serious about what a punk I am. If he hates me so much, why does he want my company?"

"Because the boss probably told him to look out for you."

Unwrapping the sub from its butcher paper, Mark paused. Alison's explanation made sense. Had the chief pulled Connell aside and directed him to act this way?

"The thing about Ken is that he respects rank," Alison said.

"What does that mean?"

"Just what I said. He spent time in the military. When someone has a chief or a lieutenant in front of their name, he follows orders that those people give. It's a form of respect. He always talked about the chain of command the way my Italian grandmother talked about the Catholic Church. That's why he's partnering with you. He sets aside his personal feelings to follow orders."

Mark sighed and ran a hand through his hair. "I feel like a hypocrite. He doesn't know that he has a reason to hate me. He does, but it's completely arbitrary. He's treated me like dog shit ever since I walked into the squad room. Now we're getting friendlier, and all I can think about is what he's done to you."

Alison nodded. "He likes to dominate people. He's a bully. If he thinks he can control you, he will. It's why he likes whores and young girls on the fringes of society. I'm guessing he looks at you and sees a rookie. He senses you possess some quality he lacks, and that's why he doesn't like you."

"Integrity?"

"No, not integrity. Ken has integrity, in his own unique way. He's all about law and order and rules. I think his problem with you is more about compassion. He has zero. He lacks empathy. Everything with him is black and white. I read once that there are a lot of good cops around. Guys who are inflexible and tough. But it would be better if there were more good guys who were cops. You distinguish shades of gray. That makes him uncomfortable. It forces him to see things in a new way, and it illuminates his own shortcomings."

Mark bit into the ham sub. He had not eaten since that morning; his stomach ached. He planned to sleep for a few hours, then head back to the squad before sunrise.

"When I'm around him, I feel two-faced, like that Roman god, Janus," he said. "Maybe he's got some sixth sense. Maybe he's smelled your scent on my clothes. Is there any way he knows?"

"No. Not possible. First off, we've been discreet, but more telling is that he would force a confrontation. He couldn't keep quiet about it. If he finds out about us, we're going to know it."

What in hell am I doing in this relationship? Mark wondered, staring into Alison's cocoa eyes. *If he finds out. There is no if — he's going to eventually. Is there any way this can have a happy ending?*

"Let's not talk about Ken for the rest of the night," she said, hugging him as he stood chewing, laying her head against his shoulder.

"Fair enough. Want to watch TV before I crash?"

"Yeah. The debate is tonight."

Alison settled onto the couch while Mark went toward the bathroom, changing into a t-shirt and sliding off his pleated pants. He brushed teeth and splashed cold water on his face, staring into his own eyes. They looked old, he admitted, with droopy pouches under his lids. Those half moons had been etched there since his teens. Sometimes, before the mirror, he would stretch his cheeks, tightening the skin, just to see how a different appearance might look.

Hell with it, he thought. *It's the face I was given. Wasn't enrolled in any beauty contests anyway.*

He clicked off the light, moving to the living room wearing boxer shorts. Alison had adjusted the antenna, but reception was still fuzzy. The two candidates wore dark suits and stood behind podiums with a pair of microphones before each man.

"I was always a Democrat, but how can anybody support Carter?" Alison asked, legs stretching the length of the couch. "He's like the captain of the Titanic. Double-digit inflation, gas prices, and we've got to bring home the hostages. We need a change."

"So we're both Reagan Democrats."

"Thus it must be love," she said softly, resting her head on Mark's chest, as he slid down beside her. She crooked a knee over his legs.

TV provided the only light in the room. Carter's fair hair and southern drawl was a marked contrast to Reagan's steely gaze before the camera. Carter dubbed his opponent "dangerous" and Reagan coolly rebutted about the worsening economy under Carter's watch.

"Reagan's old, though," Alison said. "I worry about his age."

"My father would kick my ass up and down the sidewalk if he thought I favored a Republican," Mark said. "Glad he's not alive to see me vote."

Reagan's voice was a soothing, grandfatherly cadence.

"This is the first time I've heard you mention your dad in a long while," Alison said, brushing a hand against his cheek.

"I've been thinking about him the last few days. Wondering how he'd handle this case. Wish I could ask for his advice."

"You can talk to me about your dad, you know," she offered. "Sometimes it helps to talk."

"No point burdening you. You've got enough on your plate."

"Sharing your feelings with me isn't a burden, Mark. I want you to. One of the reasons I left my marriage is because Ken never would. Are all cops so closed up?"

"Thought we weren't going to talk about Ken."

"Oops. You're right."

"I don't know if it's being a cop as much as a personality trait." Mark inhaled.

"Great," she rolled her eyes. "So tell me."

Mark breathed deeply, and his words came out measured. "The thing is, when you're growing up, you take for granted that your dad will always be around. Now I'm thirty-three, and he's not anymore. It doesn't seem fair. I can't get my head around the fact that he's not going to be tinkering in his basement or sitting next to me at Thanksgiving dinner. I know more about him than anyone on earth, so I don't think I'll ever get used to his being gone."

They fell silent while candidates' voices dueled in two-minute intervals.

Pressing a palm against the middle of her back, his lids felt droopy. She ran fingers over his waist and slid the flat of her hand up toward his chest. A hollow expanded across his stomach, the cooldown before sleep overwhelmed the day.

After a time, she whispered, "Since we're opening up, I want to tell you something. But this may sound stupid."

His eyes pried open; he became aware of her scent and inhaled, trying to trap it in his throat. The debate had ended; the anchor reminded voters that Election Day was less than two weeks away.

"What?" he asked.

She raised herself onto an elbow and peered intently into his eyes. Their brown edged toward ebony, dark as a bottomless well.

"For the last few years, I've felt like driftwood, lost in the middle of the ocean, just flailing and trying to keep myself above water. There were nights when I went to sleep and hoped I wouldn't wake up in the morning. But when I'm with you, I can see land. You give me hope."

Her soft tone added to the gravity. Then she exhaled. "I told you, it would sound dumb."

Mark lifted his lips to hers, cupping her head and smoothing the falling hair.

"It's not dumb. It's beautiful. I don't know what to say."

Is this the moment? he wondered. *Should I tell her I love her?*

She leaned into the hand that stroked her neck. "You don't have to say anything. I just wanted to tell you." Her fingers moved to his forehead and tussled his hair.

Chapter 16

Get the fuck outta here, he repeated the phrase like a mantra, legs burning with pain and fear as he sprinted through the cemetery. They know where I am, so get the fuck out of here.

He ducked behind a warehouse, doubling over to catch his breath, eyes fixed on the corner around which he came. When his breathing steadied, he crept forward, peering around the cinderblock wall. No sign of anyone. He checked pockets. The tattoos, still throbbing, had been more expensive than he hoped, but he still had forty-seven dollars and change. That was a nice chunk of money, brought along because he had been planning to pay for a blow job that night. Would it be enough to get out of town? There was more at home, but he couldn't go there, not if they knew where he lived and followed him to the cemetery.

Get the fuck outta here, he told himself, and continued to move along the back of the factory, keeping his body in shadows. How the fuck did they find me?

He zigzagged through streets and residential yards, hopping fences, concealing himself against clipped hedges, clinging to darkness while avoiding lighted corridors. On a front lawn he discovered an unlocked bicycle, so he hopped on and began pedaling toward downtown. The bus station was always open, with Greyhounds pulling away from its hub every few minutes, final destinations spread across the country.

Get the fuck out of here.

They were breathing down his back now, sensing him, on high alert for the genius who purged the city of low lifes. Pretty clever to trick him by showing the false composite on TV, making him think they were trotting down the wrong path, when in fact they had tracked his every step. Had they watched him go into the tattoo parlor? Had they let him suffer the dirty, dingy needle pricks as a way to accumulate more evidence against him? Maybe the fat hippie hippopotamus was really an uncover pig, the green ink injected beneath his flesh a truth serum that would force a confession against his will.

Get the fuck out of here, he shivered.

"When does the next bus leave?" he asked meekly at the ticket window.

The old man behind the glass looked like a scarecrow, with a withered neck and flaps of skin dangling from his chin. He turned to a wall clock and said with disinterest, "Three minutes. Off to Erie, Pennsylvania."

"I'll get a one way." He slid several crumpled bills onto the dimpled tray between them. The scarecrow handed him a ticket and pointed through a plate glass window toward a long bus angled against the curb. He slogged there, without luggage, and kept his face averted from the driver as he ascended two steps, moving to the very last seat. Keep my enemies in front of me, he thought. Any cops try to board, I'll... well, what can I do?

Just get the fuck out of here.

Peering over the high-backed bench before him, he felt trapped. If a pig did walk up the steps right now, he was done. There was no rear escape door like in the school buses of his youth. He might duck under the seats, or maybe kick out the window and dive, but both those options required bravery and fast thinking, traits he lacked. He slid down into the seat, deep enough that his eyes just cleared the bottom ledge of the window. Were cops smart enough to stake out the bus station?

Hurry up and start this fucking rectangle, he thought. Nobody will stop us once we're on the road.

*   *   *

Traveling west along interstate 90, the trip to Erie lasted an hour and forty minutes. It was approaching three in the morning when he descended the stairs and stepped atop the curb in an asphalt lot. As the bus rolled away, he stood alone. Night air was warmer here. Vibrations from the ride had lessened the pain of his new tattoos, shaking away the itchiness. He breathed deeply, infused with a sense of optimism. He had escaped his fate, at least temporarily.

Now what? he wondered.

There wasn't much around. A grove of low evergreens crouched to his left, near a scarred picnic table, while a dark and lonely street stretched toward either horizon. Tucking hands into his pockets, he began walking along the road. Having been here all of three minutes, he decided Erie was a bleak little town. Dreary Erie. Two fellow passengers on the bus had talked loudly, saying it was the halfway point between Buffalo and Cleveland, a thumbprint unlucky enough to be stuck between two dying steel cities.

He wondered where the niggers lived. If he found a neighborhood overflowing with them, he could renew the crusade. Take out a few here, then shuffle off down the highway again, maybe even south to Pittsburgh, spreading fear all over the map so that truth would reign across the country.

But now he was tired. It was middle-of-the-night quiet, nearing dawn, and he had been awake for more than nineteen hours. He needed a spot to call home base, a cheap room or flophouse where he could crash for a few days. Someplace with a decent mattress so he wouldn't wake up sore. With rest, he could get his mind straight and sketch out a plan.

After another half hour of walking, he crested a hill and came upon a lighted neon sign with a letter burned out: MO EL.

Like me, he thought. I'm a mole who's burrowed out of Buffalo, away from danger. And part of me is burned out too.

He signed in using the name Boyd Ardee, admiring himself for how clever he could be despite the exhaustion. Who would recognize the similarity with the famous chef? He paid cash — that was all he carried — but this was good because there was no way anyone could track him. He had heard about cops going through banks or credit card companies to review recent purchases. The fucking government was always manufacturing new ways to screw the little guy. His father taught him that. What did it matter? He didn't have a checking account or a credit card anyway.

The room was stale and outdated, small enough to hold a single bed and nightstand. He slid out of his shirt, dropped his jeans on the stained carpet, and shuffled to the bathroom wearing only ragged briefs and socks with a hole near the big toe. He lifted the toilet seat, exhaled, and leaned against the wall in a three-point stance, releasing a powerful stream. It feels great to piss, he thought. Feels great to stiff the cops and finally leave a mark on the world. The past four days had been... well, nearly perfect. After a good night's rest I'll get back that focus.

Water from the tap smelled like the bottom of a well. Splashing a handful against his face, he flopped down and burrowed under the scratchy sheet. Although the mattress was thin and lumpy, he was too tired to protest, dropping into sleep like a skylark plunging into a dark tunnel.

*   *   *

Ninety miles away, Mark Bennett lay on his back listening to the night. Curtains were open, allowing dim illumination to filter within the room. Alison curled next to him, turned with knees tucked close to her stomach, each exhale releasing the softest hint of snore.

A black man is asleep right now, not knowing that when he wakes, today will be his last day alive. This sicko is going to keep killing until we stop him.

Bennett was overtired and he knew it, but he couldn't stop thinking. Tonight he missed his dad more than ever, the void stretching deep into his stomach. He wished they could talk; he knew his father would provide sage advice. Mac taught him that a good partner was vital to success. A partner listened, kept an open mind and confirmed or refuted the other's theories. Connell displayed flashes of those traits, but how far could he trust the guy?

He touched Alison's dark hair, smoothing it off her forehead and stroking so it conformed to her neck. The rhythm of her breathing remained steady. Mark stared at the ceiling and moved his lips, whispering softly enough that he could barely hear his own voice.

"You there, Mac?"

Quiet reigned in the bedroom. The rest of the house had stilled; no creaks or groans penetrated hardwood floors. After ten seconds, the response was equally as faint.

"How you doing, Marky?"

He smiled with relief. "It's two-thirty in the morning and I can't sleep. How do you think I'm doing?"

"You're home, huh? Not driving?"

"I'm home."

"So what's the problem?"

Mark snorted. "Where to start."

"Okay, this about the woman or the killer?"

Mark looked at Alison, beautiful in slumber. "The killer. I'm turning it over in my head and wondering if my inexperience is a factor. This guy has done four murders in four days. Maybe a better cop would have caught him by now."

"Doubt it," Mac said. "You're new to the job, but don't think you're a liability. You come from a family of cops. You have a pedigree. You bring enthusiasm and a fresh set of eyes to the squad. There was a reason you were promoted and it's more than just being my boy."

"I keep thinking there's something we missed. Is the key so obvious that it's being overlooked?"

"No," his father told him. "I don't know details of your case, but I promise you the answer is no. Both the chief and Connell have seen the exact same evidence as you. They each have a lot more years on the job, and they're stumped too. So this isn't you. You're dealing with a cunning killer."

"Chief formed a task force today. Ken Connell and I are spearheading and we've got six more cops working for us. Top priority, round the clock stuff until this bastard is caught."

"That means the brass is taking this seriously, and they've got your back. That's a good thing."

Mark exhaled. "Connell told me that a good homicide investigator is thinking about his cases all the time. I guess he's right, because this thing is always on my mind. I wish I could turn it off for a few hours, you know, to get a break. No one told me it would be like this. This job might be a curse."

"It's good you're taking it seriously. This frustration will be a memory once you catch him."

"Yeah, well, right now it sucks. I need to sleep, Pop. There's going to be another killing tomorrow. And one the next day. And the next, until we get him. But we can't predict what he's going to do because he changes tactics just about every day. He's pushed a woman off a tall building, done two stabbings and now a shooting. What's next, a syringe of cyanide?"

"No way to know."

"I'm thinking if I study the crimes enough I should be able to get inside his head. That way I can extrapolate what he'll do tomorrow."

"The best indicator of future behavior is past behavior."

"That makes sense," Mark nodded. "You think he'll go back to pushing someone off a ledge?"

"I don't know. But you're being diligent. That's good. You have to learn to strike a balance or this job will consume you. Take a few deep breaths, relax your mind, and drift off. You'll hit it hard tomorrow and give it everything you've got. You are going to get this guy, Marky."

As Mark's lids felt heavy, Mac's soothing voice evaporated into the night.

Chapter 17

There had to be some in this sad little town. *Shouldn't be too hard to find,* he thought. *They live in slums and sit on porches sipping cheap beer out of paper sacks.* He rose from bed, feeling a creak in his shoulders, moving tentatively to test flexibility in his back. Still sore, but not as bad today. This mattress must be better than that slingshot he had at home. He pulled back the curtain and looked through a metal window frame flecked by rust. The morning was overcast, and he realized in daylight why his room was so cheap. He was smack in the middle of a run-down neighborhood. Ought to be able to find one here real easily.

His stomach churned. He could smell himself, his odor overpowering the stale scent that clung to muslin drapes. The tattoos tingled, all of fourteen hours old, their green edges dark and crisp and fresh. He was hungry. It had been nearly twenty-four hours since he ate.

On the way to the bathroom he stepped out of his briefs and left them on the floor. Sitting on the toilet, he took note of the tattered shorts. Elastic had lost its spring, and holes appeared below the waistband like moths had gnawed through cotton. They needed to be washed, but how could he do that here? He might use the sink, but there was no way to dry them, and he had no desire to walk around in wet underwear. Maybe there was a store nearby, a K-Mart or Twin Fair where he could buy a cheap three-pack. He could slide them on in a men's room.

Shit. He would have to buy food and underwear. He hadn't brought much money to begin with, and at this rate it wouldn't last long. How could he stretch it further without going home? Should he shoplift a pack of briefs? *Hell no*, he decided. *I'm no thief.*

The ceramic shower was cloudy with caked-on soot. Spiderweb cracks ran along its base. There was no complimentary soap or shampoo, so he simply scrubbed himself under the stinky spray. It wasn't the best method of bathing, he knew, but at least he washed away the dried sweat from last night. For that matter, he had no toothbrush or toothpaste, and the idea of gargling with this rancid water stopped his hunger pangs. His breath must be foul.

He left the underwear in the bathroom garbage can and slid into his jeans and shirt, then went to the motel office. The same old man from last night emerged from behind a paneled door, chewing a plug of jerky.

"How's yer room?" he asked.

"Fine," Joe said, dropping the key with its giant plastic diamond onto the counter. "Gonna check out, though. Running low on funds and I gotta grab a bite."

"Ya sure? We got weekly rates, might save ya a few bucks."

"Right now food's the priority."

"Okay," the man said. "Yer looking for some cheap swill, you might wanna try Wanda's, little café two blocks that way." He waved the jerky like a baton, winking conspiratorially. "Tell her Earl sent cha, she might not jack the price up that much."

He nodded goodbye. As the left, the man called, "Hey kid, didn't ya bring any luggage?"

After crossing a gravel field, he wandered through a used car lot with colorful flags strung between light posts. It was a pathetic little dealership, with only twenty-five or thirty cars on display, all of their windshields painted in foot-high digits advertising mileages above seventy thousand. *Having wheels would be nice. If I wasn't against stealing, I could boost a car, hit the road and no one would ever find me.*

It didn't matter, really. No cops knew where he was. Hell, he didn't even know where he was, other than to say it was Erie. He couldn't recite street names or directions, and had not provided his real name to anyone since leaving Buffalo. If nothing else, he was isolated.

How the fuck had the cops found him? For them to track him to his dad's cemetery, they must have been doing round-the-clock surveillance. They could not have known he was going there ahead of time because he hadn't planned it. Seeing his father's grave had been an impulse. If he hadn't known where he was going to be, how could they?

He stopped walking and pulled at his lip. Maybe they didn't. Could it have been coincidence? Probably not. Nothing with cops is coincidence. But he realized in retrospect that none of them gave chase. No one tried following him as he scampered down the hill. He would be easy to catch. With his sore legs, he didn't run that fast. Maybe he simply intersected with a posse of cops on a different mission, corrupt pigs determined to exhume a corpse or something.

Could it be he had fled for no reason?

The café's sign was a flaking red banner advertising "FOOD." No mention was made of Wanda, but breakfast was cheap, as old Earl had promised. Joe chose a swivel stool at the counter and kept his head low. The bubble-bottomed waitress knew the other three customers, so she chatted them up, but after taking his order she left him alone. *Fucking her big cushy ass would be like pounding a bouncy ball*, he thought. Pressure built inside him. He had planned to get a hooker last night, just to release the poison inside. Now the build-up was ten times worse.

Think, he told himself. Ignore the semen issue and think about how much or how little those fucking cops knew.

Once the husky taste of bacon and scrambled eggs hit his stomach, the fog began to lift. He savored the feeling. He wanted to go home, if only to get money. He wouldn't last long in Erie, not unless he began to steal, and he hadn't robbed anything since he was a teenager. No, those days were past. He was a man now, and the reality was this: the crusade was sacred, and he was willing to trade his life for it. He fully expected to die. A man who believes in the sanctity of his mission does not flee at the first hint of trouble. A man who responds to a higher calling tightens his resolve in the face of danger.

Leaving Buffalo was the act of a coward, a frightened boy trying to avoid his destiny.

Taking a deep swallow of orange juice, he studied the waitress's ample ass. Desire swelled. He wanted to kill again then find a nigger hooker to fuck. Once he ruminated on the possibilities, it was really the only option.

He needed to return home.

*   *   *

Elevator doors closed behind Mark Bennett as he turned into the squad room. He sensed Eric Lenehan's mischievous grin before looking down at his face. Sure enough, perched as high as his chair would rise, stubby little Lenehan nodded and licked thin lips. He couldn't wait to share a secret.

"Chief's got a whack job in there," he whispered conspiratorially, nodding toward the glass divider. "Fucking psychic. Withered old broad with love beads and a head scarf. Says she's having visions of your killer, it's her civic duty to tell a detective all about it. I'm betting the hippies kicked her out of the yurt she's so crazy."

Bennett looked across the room. The door was closed, horizontal blinds angled just enough to expose two outlines — the chief's bulky silhouette behind his desk and a petite shadow in the chair across from him.

"I was you, I'd hightail it outta here," Lenehan suggested. "Come back in an hour, hope the old bag is gone. I warned Connell and he sped out like there was a fireball up his ass."

Bennett hesitated. "Why is the chief talking to her?"

"Cause neither you nor Connell was here. I'm telling you, get the hell out. He sees you standing there, he's going to rope you into this. I been on this job seventeen years and I never seen a psychic contribute to solving anything."

Bennett did not believe in other world experiences, but knew that psychics often intersected with the detective bureau. Their advice was unsolicited and ineffective, but that never stopped them from phoning or stopping in to share their self-proclaimed knowledge or special gift.

"Screw it," Bennett mumbled, moving across the floor toward his desk. "I got work to do."

"You're gonna regret it," Lenehan warned.

But Bennett was not summoned into the chief's office. Sitting at his desk, he skimmed an activity report, known as a P73, from a fellow detective written the day before, searching for any connection to his cases. After twenty minutes, the chief's door opened and he ushered out a gray-haired woman, shaking her hand and expressing thanks for the information. Bennett could tell he was as phony as a politician, but the woman apparently did not.

Once the psychic was gone, the chief crossed back to Bennett and leaned on the edge of his desk. From his swivel chair, Lenehan followed the boss's every step with curious eyes.

"You're welcome," the chief said, leaning back and looping hands across his ample belly.

"Anything I need to know?"

"According to Madame Kreskin, our killer's name is Allen. She insists it's spelled A-L-L-E-N. When his presence appears, she sees images of penguins, so Allen either lives near the zoo or has some connection to the South Pole. His house is up the road from a graveyard where an important family member is buried. He selected that house because of its proximity to the cemetery."

Bennett offered an amused nod.

"I asked her to write it all up for me in a very detailed report. Told her we'd take it under advisement, that the department appreciated her help. I think she bought it."

"You want me to start pulling files we got on people named Allen?"

"Of course not. It's all horseshit, Bennett. I don't believe in that voodoo nonsense, but usually it's easier to listen to the nuts than turn them away. I saw Connell stand in the doorway then fly out of here. He knows when to make himself scarce. You're either really green or you have some secret desire to talk with this hag."

"Or I've actually got work to do and I'm not going to be spooked out of my office by a fortune-teller."

The chief nodded. "Good answer. You read the P73s?"

"Yeah. We just met with the team and we're going to do some background work on yesterday's victim, Gerald Harold. We're not completely convinced our killer did him, so a few guys are going to check him out."

"Okay. Keep me updated. Good news is that overnight crime was practically non-existent," the chief said. "Black neighborhoods were deserted. A little media attention is a good thing sometimes. Even low-level scumbags must've been afraid to go out. Quite a turnabout, huh? Usually the whites are nervous, but this killer's got the blacks trembling. City streets have never been safer, if you can believe it."

Chapter 18

Zack Mavrakis and Nick Spanos had been on the road for four hours, pausing long enough to buy sandwiches, chips and bottles of cola in a roadside deli along the way. Their only stop had been an hour into the trip, back when the eight-track was cranked to full volume and sounded good. But now the tinny notes had dulled their enthusiasm, and the caffeine edge had ground down into paste.

By Zack's estimate, Rochester was another two hours away and they were sinking into a lull. He tried to push away the discomfort that came with admitting his old man might have been right.

"Dad, we're seniors in high school," he had pleaded after being told no. "This is a once-in-a-lifetime thing. This band is like royalty. They're progressive rock gods. This could be our last chance to see them. You never know how much longer they're going to be around. The Beatles broke up in their prime. Besides, we're good kids. We aren't going to be drinking or doing drugs."

It had taken some convincing, but his dad had relented and let him borrow the car. It cost Zack two weeks of extra chores and the promise to clean the garage sometime before the month was out. Hard work, considering all the accumulated crap there, but well worth the trade-off.

Nick reclined in the passenger's seat, eyes narrowing to slits. He was not asleep yet, but his open mouth suggested it wouldn't be long. Zack socked him on the shoulder.

"You look like you're catching flies."

"What the hell," Nick complained, startled into coherence.

"We gotta get some petrol."

"You had to wake me up for that?"

"You weren't asleep."

"I was getting there. Did you say petrol? What are you, British?"

"At's right, mate."

Nick scowled and shifted the seat upright. "Sounds more Australian."

"Ah, as long as the fair lovely queen's our sovereign, what's the difference, laddy?"

"Now you sound Scottish." His friend did not laugh, but Zack was unconcerned. He was amusing himself, punchy from the long ride. Nearing the New York State line, the expanse of Lake Erie was visible on their left, stretching to the horizon's edge. A square sign advertising GAS rose high from the ground so truckers had plenty of time to slow and exit along the steep ramp.

They pulled into the crushed gravel lot and Zack topped off the tank. When Nick returned from the bathroom, he warned, "Not a pleasant smell in there. Take a deep breath before you go in to pee." Zack grinned and went inside.

"I'll get us to Rochester," Zack said when he returned, "but don't fall asleep on me, man. I need you to keep me company."

"Shit, I'm wracked," Nick complained. "I'm only on a couple hours of sleep. The tunes aren't keeping me juiced anymore. Let me doze."

"Liven yourself up. Keep the window down. Deep breaths."

"Hey," Nick said, pointing toward a figure at parking lot's curb. "Let's pick up that hitchhiker."

"Are you crazy?"

"No, seriously. He'll keep us awake. We'd talk to him, learn about his life."

"My dad would kill me."

"Like he's ever going to find out. Besides, if this hitcher is an asshole, we'll just pull over and tell him to scram."

"I don't know," Zack mused.

"We need a jolt of excitement here. I don't want to be the douchebag who keeps falling asleep on you."

"You're gonna be the douchebag whether you fall asleep or not."

Along the roadside a slight man stood idly with a tiny thumb extended. He wore black jeans and a fading army jacket. The boys looked at each other with doubt, then the brakes exhaled a reluctant groan. The hitchhiker's work boots plodded against blacktop. As he trotted, Zack saw the guy was only a few years older than them. He had stringy sandy-colored hair, dark eyes set wide against the corners of his face, with a patchy beard clinging to his chin.

He trotted past the hood and opened the rear door on Nick's side, squatting into the seat.

"Thanks guys," he said. Soft-spoken, his voice was smooth and polished.

"Where you headed?" Nick asked, pivoting his shoulders to see behind him. Zack turned onto the road toward the highway on-ramp.

"Buffalo. I had a bus ticket, but I lost the fucking thing when I got out to take a leak. Must've left it on the goddamn seat or something."

Nick nodded. "That's rough."

"Where you guys headed?"

"Stopping in Rochester," Nick answered, and Zack shot him an angry glance. He didn't want this vagabond to know their route, because he could call their bullshit if they tried to drop him off too soon.

"We're picking up my cousin but then we're going on to see a concert," Nick continued, oblivious to Zack's concern. "You a fan of Yes?"

"Yes? Naw."

"They're really good. British lads. Kings of progressive rock. Well, King Crimson and Emerson, Lake and Palmer are right up there too, but Yes is the best in my opinion. Everybody thought the band broke up after their last record but they got two new members now, the guys from the Buggles." He bent his head toward Zack. "This clown thinks the new version is going to become too bubble gum, because that's what the Buggles are, but their new album came out in August and it's pretty solid. The first track is almost like heavy metal."

Zack was embarrassed by his friend's exuberance. Where was all this energy five minutes ago?

"For God's sakes, shut the hell up," he said. "The guy doesn't care about all this."

The man in the backseat squeezed a smile, revealing tiny chipmunk teeth. "Naw, it's cool." In the rearview mirror, Zack watched him itch his chin.

Nick remained undaunted. "I'm Nick, by the way, and this is Zack."

There was a tenuous pause. "Hey guys. I'm Joe." He thrust his hand over the bench seat. Nick shook it, but Zack left his palms on the steering wheel and raised his eyebrows in greeting.

"Where you guys from?"

"Meridian."

"Meridian?" Joe repeated. "Where the hell's that?"

"Rinky-dink town north of Pittsburgh," Nick said. "About three hours from here. Nobody's ever heard of it. Hell, movies don't even come to the theater until like eight months after they're released."

"That sucks."

"What about you? Where you from?"

Another pause, this one wider — long enough for Zack to glance away from the road into the mirror to see if his passenger had heard the question. Joe stared ahead with a vacant look, like he spaced out. Coherence returned after a long five seconds.

"All over, really. I go three months here, six months there, another four somewhere else. The road is my home."

"That's cool," Nick nodded. "You're like Jack Kerouac."

"What about originally?" Zack wondered. "Where were you born?"

Joe's head did not move, but Zack watched a tick cross the stranger's cheek. The man in the backseat avoided looking in the mirror, staring instead at the back of Zack's neck.

"I don't like to talk about it."

"That's odd," Nick said.

"What's so odd about it?"

"He's only asking where you were born."

Suddenly Joe's tone changed, like a cornered animal lashing out. "I had a lousy fucking childhood, okay? Talking about it brings up bad shit, and what's the point? I'm an adult now."

Nick recoiled, raising palms in contrition. "Hey, easy."

"I mean, what the fuck?" Joe exhaled.

Zack glanced at Nick, whose mouth hung open. He wanted to say, *This picking up a hitchhiker — is this looking like a good idea now?*

Nick shook off his concern. "All right. We won't talk about it. What would you like to talk about?"

"Any other fucking thing," he replied slowly, a pulse pounding in the side of his neck.

"You like music? I'll try to find us a radio station."

Static erupted when Nick pushed the console button. He spun the dial slowly, passing over a news channel and settling on a song from the Temptations. In smooth melody they were "…talking 'bout my girl, my girl, my girl."

"Seriously?" Joe wondered from the backseat. "You listen to this nigger music?"

192

"It's the Temptations, man. They're an American institution."

"I can't stand listening to jig's sing. It's like they're fucking slaves trying to impress the master. How about dialing up some country station?"

"Country?" Nick argued. "Uh uh. We sit in class with kids who ride to school on tractors. This weekend we're trying to get away from that shit."

Joe's agitation grew. "Well then turn it off."

In his head, Zack was formulating how to get this psycho out of his car. The guy was touchy and abrasive. You sneeze the wrong way, and his fuse might ignite. How would he say it? *Hey Joe, at this next exit here, we're going to let you out. I'm not feeling well, and we might just pull over to rest, so you'll probably want to keep moving.* Or what? What other excuse could he use? Suppose this nut-job refused to leave their backseat?

His thoughts were interrupted when Joe asked, "You guys hear about them niggers that were killed up in Buffalo?"

For the first time, Nick's head turned toward Zack. "Uh... no."

"You didn't hear about them?" Joe asked with a grin.

"Uh uh," Zack said.

"That's too bad. This fucking cleaning lady was tossed from the top of city hall, one of the tallest buildings in the city. Then these two other monkeys got shanked at a fucking bus stop. Another one took a shell in the brain while he was eating lunch in a parking lot."

The boys in the front seat said nothing. They both anticipated there was more to the story.

"Anyway, you fellas might want to read the papers a bit more," Joe said. "Stay on top of the news. Although, hell, maybe news doesn't travel to Meridian. See, the fact is, you're in the presence of someone famous."

193

"Famous?" Nick wondered.

"Yeah, famous. People know my work. But nobody knows my name, which is how I like it. You see, I killed those fucking niggers."

Zack's fingers remained paralyzed on the wheel. With his back to the drifter, he felt vulnerable. He looked in the mirror, where Joe grinned an obsessive smile. Was he kidding? He didn't look like he was kidding. Is this something a person would even joke about?

My God, he thought. *What if my dad was right? I never should have left home to go to some stupid concert.*

"And I'll tell you something else," Joe continued, warbling with anticipation. "It's a holy war and I'm just getting started."

*　　*　　*

Friday was when the crazies came out.

Media attention brought the murders to the front of everyone's mind. The morning paper's headline read "Task Force Hopes to Snag Killer." TV cameramen converged on the squad room until the chief instructed Lenehan to turn them away at the door. Still they set up tripods and filmed live shots outside headquarters.

In addition to the psychic's visit, dozens of calls filtered into the squad room about suspicious and irregular behavior. Wives implicated husbands who had been out late the night before, although the murders had occurred at mid-day. Neighbors tattled on one another, describing perverted scenes witnessed through sheer drapes. Disgruntled employees tried to convince police that their boss was the culprit because he was so demanding and precise that there must be something obsessive about him, in addition to which, he told an off-color joke about Negroes last week. Anyone with an ax to grind tried to pin the murders on the object of their displeasure.

Bennett and Connell listened in the conference room as their team of detectives briefed them on each bizarre tip. A few seemed intriguing, so further investigation was delegated to the other cops. That day's plan was launched for the city, with cooperation from police in first-ring suburbs: during a two-hour block, from eleven to one, every available officer should make himself visible on a busy street, particularly within view of a bus stop. Even if it did not lead to immediate capture, it was hoped that the sight of a uniform would frighten away the killer and thwart his plans.

"We want to catch the guy, sure," Connell explained. "But we also want to stop today's murder. If we can do that, then this is a good shift."

Everyone shuffled out of the room, and Bennett returned to his desk. He was going to follow up calls from his list of former arrestees within blocks of the two stabbings. Part of him wondered if he should bother following up the tip from that psychic. Combing through old files for suspects named Allen would be labor intensive because there was no way to search first names without skimming the tag on each folder.

It was too much of a long shot, he decided, and he didn't want to spend the day chasing rainbows. But really, that was as good a lead as any. When his desk phone rang, Bennett spoke to a trooper from a State Police barrack in Fredonia, who relayed the story that Zack Mavrakis and Nick Spanos had told them in his office.

"Anyway, these boys got off the Thruway here, said they were stopping for food. When this Joe fellow got out of the car, they squealed the tires and booked the hell out of there. Left him standing in the parking lot slack jawed. Kids were so damn scared they were afraid to get back on the highway. Drove around town a few times until they stumbled into our station. But we had a pileup out down on route 60, so by the time we got wind of it, a good two hours had passed. We looked around for him, but who knows where this guy made off to."

"The kids were heading towards Buffalo, huh?" Bennett asked.

"Affirmative. Listen, they're young and shaken. Trying to do the right thing, but green around the gills. I'm pretty sure one of them shit his pants cause he smelled like my baby's diaper. Anyway, who the hell knows if this is serious or not."

"Well, that description sounds similar to what our witnesses gave. And they said his name was Joe?"

"Right."

"Not Allen?"

"Allen? No, the hitchhiker used the name Joe. But shit, Bennett, the guy they picked up might have been some kook trying to impress a couple teenagers, you know, dazzle them with stories of the macabre. I don't believe these kids are fibbing me, but there ain't much to go on here. Good luck tracing somebody named Joe."

"Yeah, first names aren't doing me any good," Bennett said.

Chapter 19

Despite having been on the streets for only a few weeks, Annette discovered that mid-day Friday was a lucrative time to make money. Most guys had paychecks burning a hole in their pockets, and if they weren't taking an extended lunch, had already punched out early to get a jump on the weekend. A few customers had even said that the blow job from her was a warm-up for doing their wives or girlfriends later in the evening, an overture that kick-started their willies into gear.

Whatever works for you, baby, Annette said to herself. *Just so long as I get my green.*

The man who summoned her towards the Chrysler had hands like cinderblocks, fingers thick as sausages. Wide shoulders filled the front seat. He wore a blond mustache and bushy eyebrows. He appeared Nordic, a hero from Scandinavian mythology. *A big man to handle a big woman*, Annette thought. A pale-skinned giant contrasting with her mocha hue.

"Need a ride?" he asked.

She put a little extra shake in her hips, sauntering to his rolled-down window.

"What you looking for, sugar?"

"You're a big one, aren't you?" he asked.

"Whole lotta woman," she agreed.

"What are you, about six-two?"

"Taller in heels," she winked.

"I'm six-four" he said, "and I like tall ladies. Maybe we have a little party."

"Ooh, I'd like that too," she cooed. "What kind of party you thinking?"

"Kissing party. I'd like your lips and my dick need to meet."

She smiled coyly. "Gonna cost you twenty bucks."

"Twenty? More like five."

"What do I look like to you, the discount bin?" She stood to full height, adjusted the bangs on her blonde wig, and began to walk away, maintaining the sway in her hips.

He honked to stop her. "Here's ten," he called.

She hesitated, turning to look at his rugged face through the windshield. He held the bill in his outstretched arm. She stepped back and leaned down again.

"Only cause you're so handsome that I'm agreeing to this price," she smiled, accepting the cash and folding it into her purse. "But this is highway robbery right here on Pearl Street."

She got into the passenger's seat and he slid the car into gear.

"Where should I go?" he asked. "I'm not from around here."

Adjusting the stuffing in her bra, she directed him to turn right. "I got just the spot," she said. "Where you from?"

"Idaho," he said, and he grinned like he had let her in on a secret. "The Pacific Northwest. I'm on a freighter that lugged coal to the steel mill. Got off shift an hour ago, have a layover until tomorrow morning, and I thought, what the heck? Why not sample Buffalo's finest?"

"A man has needs," Annette nodded. "Turn here. Gonna take you to a little park along the waterfront, nice and private." She reached a hand across the console and touched his leg. "I'm gonna suck your dick while you stare across the river at Canada, how's that sound?"

His smile grew wider. "Never cared much for Canada, but I like the dick sucking part."

*   *   *

Despite Annette's claims, their trysting location was neither nice nor so private that it eluded the police. George Pope knew that corner of the park was a hotbed of hookers, dope dealers and petty criminals. He drove along the access road once or twice each shift, pointing out illicit behavior to Bobby Bennett, hoping to catch someone breaking the law.

Overhanging branches of a weeping willow dwarfed a chocolate-colored Chrysler. Its bumper sticker advertised a rental car company. The driver's side window was down and exhaust stuttered from the tailpipe. The figure behind the steering wheel had leaned back, remaining motionless while the black and white approached and stopped behind him.

"Why would the engine be running?" Bennett wondered. "Should we check it out?"

"Might be waiting for a drug deal," Pope offered, angling the cruiser so the sedan was blocked in.

The officers stood, sliding nightsticks into their belts. As they slammed car doors, another figure emerged from beneath the window line, sitting up quickly in the passenger's seat. Movements of both occupants seemed jerky, scrambled.

"Okay, folks, hands where we can see them," Pope said, resting his palm on the butt of his gun as he approached the driver's side.

"Let's see those hands," Bennett echoed.

"What do we got going on here?" Pope asked the driver.

Big knuckles curled around the top of the doorframe. A mop of blond hair protruded through the opening and pivoted to look at the cop.

"The girlfriend and I are just having a talk," he said. "No problem here, officer."

"Okay, good." Pope leaned down to peer into the car. "What's your name?"

"Dave."

The woman in the passenger's seat was leaned over, face hidden, as if she was tying a shoe. "And what's your girlfriend's name?"

The man answered immediately. "Phyllis."

Bennett tapped on the closed passenger's window. Bobby saw blonde hair before the woman looked up to face him. They recognized each other at the same moment. Her lipstick split into a smile and through the glass, she yelled, "Bobby!"

"Oh boy," Bennett said. Then, across the top of the car to Pope, "Our friend Annette is adjusting her wig."

"Out of the car, Dave," Pope said. "Nice and slow. Keep those hands where I can see 'em."

The heavy door swung open and Dave stood to full height. He had failed to latch his belt through one of the front loops. Blue jeans rode up his waist, and a flap of shirt was untucked. This guy was a giant, with square shoulders that looked like he was wearing football pads. Pope's hand moved from the pistol to his nightstick. If Dave had a temper, he could do some damage.

"What's the problem, officer?" he wondered, and Dave's posture turned defensive. "I'm just having a chat with my girlfriend here. There's no law against that, is there?"

"And your girlfriend is named Phyllis?"

"That's right."

Pope nodded to Bobby. "Bring her over here, will you?"

Annette, now out of the car, looped her elbow through Bennett's as they walked around the trunk side. She strutted like a southern belle being led to the cotillion.

"Where do you live, Dave?" Pope asked.

He hesitated. "Out of town."

"So you and this lady have a long-distance relationship?"

"That's right."

"Okay." He nodded to Annette, who stood beside Bennett. She had buttoned her collar above the protrusion in her neck.

The four of them formed a loose circle, with only Bennett and Annette close enough to touch.

"Sweetheart, what's your name?"

Dave shot her an angry glance. *You better fucking say Phyllis*, his eyes commanded. But Annette had been hastily assembling herself when Dave spoke with Pope, and then was so excited to see Bobby Bennett that she had not listened to any of their conversation.

"Come on, officer, don't pretend we not friends," she said coyly. "It's me, Annette."

"God damn it!" Dave mumbled, and tossed up his hands in exasperation. His shoulders drooped and he turned away.

"Now, Annette, this man isn't really your boyfriend, is he? This man gave you money to engage in a sexual act, isn't that right?"

"Said he was from Idaho," Annette shrugged. "I wanted to show him a good time away from home. See, I like to consider myself a welcome wagon for the city of Buffalo."

"The wheels are coming off the wagon," Bennett said.

"Bobby, Bobby, Bobby. How come you so mean to me?" Annette's smile did not disappear. "Beginning to think you don't like me, and that's not possible. We got ourselves a special relationship." She blew an exaggerated kiss.

"Okay, Dave, so you're from Idaho," Pope said. "What are you doing in Buffalo?"

"Delivering coal. Freighter docked this morning. Tomorrow we head up the St. Lawrence."

Pope exhaled. Dave's fingers drummed against the denim jeans, his mouth stretched in strange contortions, and he flicked his forehead back to keep locks of hair from falling across his brow. He was beginning to recognize his predicament.

"Dave, you're looking at bad news," Pope told him. "You got some legal issues with us, but you're going to have even bigger problems if I get you back to that ship."

"What do you mean?"

"How are the guys going to like it when they find out you're a fag?"

Muscles in Dave's forearm clenched. Pope was standing six feet back, out of reach, but remained alert. If this bull charged, he could end up flat on his back.

"I'm not a fag," Dave spat.

"You're with a guy, so you must be a fag. Your buddies aren't going to let you on deck when they find out you just got a hummer from a dude."

Skin on his face tightened. "Why you keep talking about my girlfriend like that?"

"Because she's not a girl."

His agitation grew. "She's beautiful, and she's my girlfriend, goddamn it!"

"Still sticking with that girlfriend story, huh?" Pope shook his head. "All right. I didn't want to do this. Why don't you show him, Annette?"

"Really?"

"Yup. Take it off."

Annette shrugged again, unbuttoned the overshirt, and slid it from her shoulders. Underneath was a neon pink tube top. She looped thumbs at the edges of her chest, just inside the armpits, and yanked down. Two fist-sized oranges rolled down the curve of her stomach and bounced onto the pavement. Her chest was broad, flat and hairy.

"Holy shit," Dave stuttered, staring at the thick fuzz.

Annette turned to Bennett and winked at him, her voice still a high falsetto. "You know, Bobby, I always say a day without oranges is like a day without sunshine."

Pope chuckled, rolling his eyes. *This one is a trip*, he thought. Bennett studied Annette's bare torso, curious as to how a man could transform himself into a woman and pull it off well enough to fool just about everyone.

While the cops looked at Annette, Dave cocked brick-sized fists and leaped forward, knocking the nightstick from Pope's grip so it clattered on the ground, then landed a single punch on Annette's jaw. The sound of flesh against bone made a sickening thud. Her head snapped back, legs crumbling beneath her and she dropped like a wet sack onto the blacktop.

"You fucking whore," he wailed. "You just turned me into a faggot!"

He paused, heaving, arms spread, and Pope sprang for his baton, crouching low to avoid a blow should the shipper turn and swing blindly. Knees creaking, he bent and scrambled. Bobby watched open mouthed, unmoving despite the sudden burst of action.

Pope corralled the wooden stick, gripped it like a tennis racket, and swung at Dave's shin. Its crack sounded like a bat connecting with a fastball, and the man collapsed, howling with pain and humiliation. Pope snapped cuffs onto one wrist, twisting arms, and secured them behind his back.

Bobby moved now, stepping ahead and standing over the prone shipper. "That was a stupid fucking thing to do," he said.

Dave released a primal cry. Tears gathered in his eyes; color drained from his face. "Go ahead and arrest me. Shoot me while you're at it. A guy just sucked my cock!" He tried to writhe away, but Bobby laid a heel against his neck to secure him. Dave stopped wiggling, then heaved enormous shoulders before releasing a milky stream of vomit. Its pasty spittle arced and landed with a splat, pooling, flecks of digested food clinging to Bobby's pants.

"Aw man," he whined.

Pope knelt beside Annette, who had been knocked out cold. He pressed fingers against her forehead and massaged her temples.

"Oh my," she mumbled, eyes fluttering open.

"Come on back, Annette," Pope said. "It's okay. Sorry we let him sucker you."

Still woozy, she sat up, locking elbows, leaning back on her hands. Her eyes were dilated and unfocused.

Pope glared at his partner.

"This guy is bigger than the two of us put together. What the hell were you standing there for?"

Bobby's expression was disgust as he studied chunks clinging to his pleated pants. "I didn't expect that."

"The vomit or him punching the shit out of Annette?"

He exhaled, looking around. "Either, I guess."

"You gotta be ready all the time," Pope scolded. "Did you learn anything in the academy? You freeze like that when there's a weapon drawn, one of us gets our head blown off."

Annette's brows arched. Edges of understanding sharpened her gaze. She saw Dave cuffed on the ground, inhaling deep breaths, choking back futile sobs. With soiled trousers, Bennett loomed over him.

"You got him under control, Bobby?" she asked, quivering.

"Yeah," he said absently. "He ain't going anywhere."

Her lips, smeared with rouge, had already started to fatten. Within minutes, she would look like a balloon.

"Bobby, Bobby, Bobby. You're my guardian angel, aren't you?"

*   *   *

Annette refused a ride to an emergency room.

"I'll be fine," she said, voice plunging several octaves. "Used to box when I was a kid, so this is nothing new."

How do you go from being a boxer to a cross-dresser? Pope wondered. "You're gonna have a swollen mug tonight and tomorrow," he predicted. "Gonna hurt every time you move your face."

204

Her pitch climbed again. "Some guys like full lips on a girl, don't they Bobby?" she wondered.

"Beats me," he shrugged. "I like my women to be women."

With that damper on her flirtation, she touched her jaw and winced. She wanted to go home and make an icepack.

The shipper was transported to the precinct house and hustled upstairs in cuffs, where paperwork was processed. As Pope and Bennett idled before the desk sergeant, Bobby recounted the burst of action when Dave's meaty fists thudded against Annette's face.

"Part of me thinks that Annette could have given Dave a fair fight," Pope said. "But none of us knew it was coming. Annette might dress like a dame, but she's no wallflower."

As he spoke, the veteran cop felt reticent. Here was Bobby, describing the sucker punch in exacting detail with the enthusiasm of a boy who has just witnessed playground justice. But rather than partake, Bobby had stayed anchored in place, content to watch. He had failed to mention his inactivity to the sergeant. If Mac's kid was going to remain an observer, then Pope needed to put in for a new partner before he wound up dead.

"I'll be back," he said, starting to walk away.

"Where you going?" Bobby wondered.

"Taking a piss, Bennett."

Bobby watched Pope's squatty frame waddle away. He turned to the sergeant. "I never know how to read that guy. You think Pope is mad at me?"

"I dunno."

When Pope disappeared around the corner, Dave the shipper strolled down the hall towards Bobby, arms swinging freely.

"What the hell?" Bobby said, raising a hand to stop him. "What are you doing out here?"

Dave shrugged. "They told me to go," he said.

"Who did?"

"That cop in there. Unchained me and told me to scram."

Bobby scratched his head. The solicitation charge was negotiable, he knew, but Dave should certainly be booked on assault. You don't cold cock somebody in front of two cops and get a freebie.

Ken Connell strolled down the hall following the path Dave had taken seconds before.

"Hey you, c'mere," Connell called. He approached the big shipper and cuffed his hands. "You're under arrest for assault."

"What?" Dave asked. "You just let me go."

Connell spun Dave around and marched him back from where he came.

Bobby looked at the empty hallway with confusion.

"What just happened?" he wondered. "Did that detective make a mistake? What's going on?"

The sergeant watched the antics with a weary eye. "You and your partner just got played, kid. Ken Connell is going to take credit for that one. You bring in the guy, he cuts him loose, then grabs him a few minutes later and gets to claim the arrest."

"Are you kidding me?" Bobby asked.

The sarge exhaled. "Sadly, no. It's dirty pool, but it happens sometimes."

Pope emerged from around the corner, hands still damp from having washed. "What's going on?" he wondered when he saw the long faces.

Bobby filled him in, and Pope's expression changed, eyes turning to stone.

"Wait here," he ordered Bobby.

*   *   *

George Pope stormed into the detective squad like a charging rhinoceros, fire brimming in his eyes.

"Connell," he barked.

206

The detective turned, pausing, face breaking into a grin. His tone was friendly. "Hey, Pope, what's going on?"

Pope snarled and raised a finger. "Don't you fucking do that again."

Connell's smile melted away. "What?"

"You heard me. You know damn well what. You stole that arrest from my partner and me."

"Hey man—" Connell looked over Pope's head.

"No, don't give me any fucking excuses. You stole it. I don't give a shit about me — I been on this job long enough that I ain't going anywhere. But you're robbing a rookie of a good arrest that can build his career. That's the trick of a goddamn bottom feeder and I've got half a mind to clock you right here."

Connell's body stiffened into defiance. From his perch near the door, Lenehan stared with greedy anticipation.

"Let's talk in there," Connell said, pointing toward the break room.

"Fuck that. We'll talk right here, out in the open. I want everybody in your squad to know what a thief looks like."

Connell's cheek twitched. "Back off," he cautioned.

The two glared at each other, a short, fat patrolman with his face angled up toward the lean detective whose rugged features could be used in a magazine advertisement.

"We've all done it before," Connell said with a lowered voice, hoping Lenehan couldn't hear. "It's a numbers game, and you know it."

"Why are your numbers more important than ours? In your mind, you're probably thinking, hey, I missed out on arrests this week because I've been chasing that Negro killer. You saw our case was a slam-dunk so you jumped all over it to inflate your stats. It's sickening."

"Happens all the time," Connell countered. "You and Bobby Bennett are still going to get your names on the report for bringing that guy in. There's enough credit to go around."

Pope's cheeks ticked with agitation. He despised injustice. Connell's only contribution to their case was that he walked by a room when the suspect was being processed. Unless Pope wanted to make trouble with a boss — which he wasn't about to do — there was little recourse, and that frustrated him even more.

"Stay the fuck away from me and partner or I'm gonna kick your ass," he said. "And don't you try pulling a stunt like that again, on me or anybody else."

Pope turned and hurried away, leaving Connell humiliated in the room where everyone had considered him a star.

Chapter 20

Because of the General Mills factory, when the wind blew, Buffalo's waterfront carried the scent of his favorite cereal. Joe inhaled deeply, trapping the odor of cheerios in the back of his throat. Despite overcast skies and his physical pains, he felt spiritually reborn. What a difference an aroma makes, he thought. Things shouldn't have been too foreign in Pennsylvania. Erie was on the same shore, after all. But the neighborhood where he stayed smelled like a rat hole, and he had been too hasty to leave home in the first place. Being back brought him contentment.

Although it lasted only twelve hours, the trip had taken its toll on him. His legs were on fire and stiffness spread into his lower back. Maybe it was the walking, maybe it was being cramped in that teenager's puny backseat. More likely it was a combination of those things and the stress of the past few days, but either way, his muscles throbbed. He felt like a puppet master had been stringing wire around his arms and legs.

And now he was off schedule. It had only been yesterday since the last one died, but so much had happened... the tattoos, the road trip, the decision to return and continue the crusade. Should he try to get in a killing before sunset or resume tomorrow?

Shuffling along the cracking sidewalk, he leaned over the railing above the corrugated breakwall rising out of Lake Erie. This might be a good place for an offering, he thought. Find one of those shines who pretends to fish but really sucks beer all day while sitting on an overturned bucket. Jam the knife blade in deep, and while he flopped like a bass, toss him over the railing. Would a dead one sink or float? Would fish naturally shy away from eating their sooty corpses?

He looked up and down the walkway. There were two spic teenagers holding hands, and a bunch of wrinkly old dudes with lines bobbing in the shallow waves, but no monkeys. As drops of rain began dotting the sidewalk, those people packed up and left the shore.

If there was going to be a killing today, it would not happen here.

*   *   *

The worst part of Derrick Stroud's paper route was the nasty old Polish lady whose house was in the middle of the block. She didn't actually address him as "Little Sambo," but even at fourteen, Derrick could tell she wanted to. Once each week, when he knocked on her door to collect, she griped about his incompetence. An edge of the paper was left in the rain, and water absorbed, soaking the entire spine. The paper should be placed inside the storm door, with the crease on the bottom, and make sure the aluminum frame closed tightly behind him, otherwise there were drafts and the newspaper might fall out onto her driveway. She never invited him into her vestibule when he went to collect, even during the most inclement weather. His second week on the job, he realized no tips would be forthcoming either. The old lady just let him stand on the stoop and glared at him through narrowed eyes, angling her head with derision. It was as if she expected him to pull a switchblade or something.

Derrick's mother counseled him to be nice. "You're not going to change that old lady's opinion," she said. "She's going to be watching you like it's her full-time job, waiting for you to slip up, so you be flawless and don't give her any ammunition. Just kill her with kindness."

I'd rather kill her with a steak knife, Derrick thought, but then regretted such a sentiment. That was the sort of comment that would get him in trouble with his pastor.

On a late afternoon Friday, he trudged through the wetness into her driveway. Rain was soft and steady, the type that falls gently and absorbs sound, making the neighborhood unnaturally quiet. Passing cars were barely audible, like a skiffle of ghosts. Derrick kept his head tucked low, careful to avoid lawns and puddles. He tried to flare his pant legs wide to protect new leather-top shoes. It hadn't been raining when he began the route, and he was upset that they were getting wet. Temperature had been in the fifties, but now it fell. Because he had not worn a hat, his ears were cold, so he compressed his neck like a turtle and pulled the denim jacket over his head.

At the old lady's storm door, he caught sight of his reflection in the glass. Raindrops had landed atop his short curls, their transparent beads catching the light like gems, lending him an aura of an old man with salt and pepper hair. Derrick paused, staring into his own face. Seeing a glimpse of what he might look like in fifty years was time travel straight out of *Star Trek*. Where would he be in 2030? How much will the world have changed?

He grasped the aluminum door handle and pulled, but it remained shut, locked from the inside. Damn. God forbid he couldn't put the paper where the old lady wanted it. She'd call the circulation department and insist he be fired. He gave the handle a good shake, but it remained welded to the frame. Its glass pane rattled, however, and he looked up at the kitchen window, where a lace curtain fluttered and her wrinkly face appeared, frowning with scorn.

"What are you doing there?" she harped, yelling through the glass. Her voice was thin and inconstant.

"I can't get the door open," he said, jiggling it for her benefit. "It's locked."

"How am I going to take my paper then?"

"You could unlock it."

"I hurt my hip. I don't have a walker to get down the stairs."

"I could bring it to your front door," he suggested.

Again she shook her head. "I don't open my front door until spring. My son put a plastic sheet of weatherstripping around it."

Derrick shrugged. "I don't know then. You want to open a window and I'll slide it through?"

"These things have been painted shut so many times that I'm not strong enough to open any window."

"I guess I could tuck it in the mailbox." He folded the newspaper and flipped open the black box attached to the side of her house. She reacted as if he was spraying graffiti.

"No! That's not where it goes!"

Derrick shrugged, enjoying the fact he was upsetting her. But he heeded his mother's advice and remained polite.

"There aren't a whole lot of options here, ma'am. You get that door unlocked and tomorrow I'll put it right back in there like I always do."

He smiled and offered a farewell wave. Pressed to the pane, her face remained curdled with distaste. This, he thought, might end up being the highlight of my week.

Derrick backtracked down her driveway. The shower seemed to be letting up. He turned onto the sidewalk and saw a car waiting at the next house. It was a tan four-door, with a white stripe along the side. Its engine was running, the tailpipe sputtering fumes whose sound was muted by rain.

The driver's door opened and a slim white man stood, wearing cowboy boots, a denim jacket similar to his own, and blue jeans with a patch on the knee.

Fifteen feet away, Derrick slowed.

"What's up?" the man asked, one hand thrust in his pocket and the other on the car door's edge.

Derrick halted before answering. "Nothing."

"Lousy day for delivering papers. You want a ride?"

Derrick's eyes narrowed. Why would this stranger offer to help him? Why would a white man want to help a black kid? And why was he wearing cowboy boots in a rainstorm?

"No thanks."

"C'mon fella. Get in the car."

As he stepped forward, Derrick backed up, sensing a blanket of evil. From reading the front page of the papers he delivered, Derrick knew there had been a rash of killings this week. All the victims had been black. That pocketed hand concealed something. This situation is bad, Derrick thought, and it's about to get worse.

Pressing the canvas sack against his waist, Derrick turned and began to sprint, looking behind him to see if the man was following. He remained rooted before the open car door, rain pattering the shoulders of his jacket. It was only a glance, and visibility was limited, but Derrick thought the man held a knife. Derrick turned into a driveway and scampered through several backyards before he ducked under the low canopy of an evergreen tree, shivering, hoping the man would not be able to track his indentations in the wet grass.

His new leather-tops were soaked and splattered with mud, a thick brown film clinging to the soles. Tears welled in his eyes, both from fear and the recognition that his mother had spent good money on the shoes and he had ruined them already.

*   *   *

That is one smart little monkey, Joe thought. *If the old legs weren't throbbing I could chase the bastard. They are on high alert now. Have to be sneakier in my approach.*

213

He wondered if he should try for another kill or simply admit it wasn't going to happen today and buy himself a hooker.

*   *   *

An hour later, nearing the end of the workday, Lenehan hung up his desk phone and bounded toward Bennett and Connell.

"You two are gonna wanna sit down," he chirped, ignoring the fact that the detectives were already seated side by side. He approached their desks, movements jerky and birdlike, as if summoned onstage to accept a lifetime achievement award. Restrained excitement rippled through his voice.

"You ready for this?"

"What is it, Lenehan?" Bennett asked, failing to disguise annoyance.

"Big news. The biggest." His grin was rigid as a mockingbird's beak.

"You gonna enlighten us?" Connell asked without looking up from the file he read.

"Sure. If you're going to be so casual, I'll just spit it out. Two uniforms are bringing in your guy."

"Huh?"

"That's right. We got him."

"Your jokes aren't funny," Connell growled.

"No joke. Jacubzak and Parnell just called," he said, shoulders bobbing with enthusiasm. "Wanted to be sure you were here and have you to stay put. They're bringing in a guy they just arrested. Half hour ago he did a stabbing in broad daylight at a bus stop and they saw the whole thing."

He had their attention now. Bennett and Connell looked at Lenehan, then toward each other.

The two patrolmen, Lenehan explained, had parked along Elmwood Avenue near Summer, thirty yards from a bus stop, and kept the windshield wipers going. Around four-thirty, a lone

214

man approached the overhang, finger pointing angrily at a black youth there. Words were exchanged, voices raised, and before the cops could intervene, the man brandished a long carving knife like you see at Thanksgiving, thrusting it toward the other. The victim leaped back and parried the assault, suffering a lacerated forearm. He was transported to the hospital for stitches. Within seconds, cops had cuffed the stabber, who snarled and spit and acted like a madman.

"He may have a welt or two from resisting arrest," Lenehan confided with a wink, "but they got him. Caught your guy in the act! And the black guy survived, so he can give testimony. You two been holding your johnsons all week, and out of the blue, two flat-foots knock home a slam-dunk!"

A burst of adrenaline rushed through Bennett's neck. He sprang to his feet, addressing Connell. "I'll find a tape recorder and get the interview room ready. We better keep this bastard cuffed to the chair."

Connell did not match the enthusiasm. "All right," he said.

Lenehan stood idle, grinning with pride as if he had been the one to capture the guy. By relaying the news, he believed he was an important component in the case, a feeling he rarely experienced since becoming a desk jockey.

Bennett hustled down the hall. Connell closed the manila folder he had been reading and slid it into the center drawer, locking it there after he noticed Lenehan straining to read the tag. He yawned, stretched, then pushed back the chair, leaving Lenehan like a sculpted faun in the middle of the room.

Bennett was pulling open slatted blinds in the interview room when Connell entered.

"Do you believe it?" Bennett asked. "I hoped it might happen this way. Couple of uniforms stumble over him by accident. We needed a break and we got it! See, these criminals get arrogant, keep doing the same thing and figure we're not smart enough to understand their pattern, but we had those bus stops under surveillance."

"Calm down, Bennett."

"Why aren't you excited? Oh, I get it. You're pissed we didn't get him so we could take credit."

"That's not it," Connell said softly. "Just take a breath."

"Hey man, I been up nights all week thinking about his bastard. Maybe now I got a shot at some sleep."

"There's something you need to consider," Connell said. "This might not be him."

"What do you mean?"

"You heard me."

"A dude stabs a black guy at a bus stop in the middle of the day? How many of those do we get a year? Believe me, that's him. That's his whole M.O."

"I don't think so."

"Why not?"

"Because our guy didn't approach with any fanfare. You know that. Think for a second. He certainly didn't yell and point fingers at his victim. That would have warned everybody what he was about to do. He walked up quietly, stabbed, watched the blood spill out, then strolled away just as cool as the autumn morning. Our earlier witnesses agreed on that."

Bennett hesitated. He had not considered this. Reluctance clung to the end of his voice.

"Still... it would be a hell of a coincidence if this wasn't our guy. Three bus stop stabbings in a week? We got matches on location and time of day."

"If it's him and I'm wrong, then great. But I got a feeling about this one. Don't get jazzed until we're sure."

Connell went to the window, removed a toothpick wrapped in cellophane from his shirt pocket, and poked its point through the plastic sleeve. He stuck it into the end of his mouth and raised a sole to an adjacent chair, staring outside.

Bennett sat, blew out his breath and checked that the tape was set to record. He drummed a pen against the yellow legal pad on the table. Impatience brewed.

"I'm chewing toothpicks as a way to quit smoking," Connell said absently.

Bennett glanced to the older detective but said nothing. He was too wired to engage in small talk.

"I was hoping to duck out of here soon," Connell continued. "Got some personal business."

Free time was an enemy, so Bennett wrote a list of questions to ask the arresting officers, Jacubzak and Parnell. He had accumulated five when they heard a commotion in the hall. A short patrolman stood in the doorway with hair cropped so close its color melted into the flesh of his scalp.

"Connell and Bennett?" he asked. "Lenehan told me you guys were chomping at the bit for this one. Pretty big arrest, huh?"

"Spare us the chit-chat," Connell said. "Bring him in here."

The officer's lips turned down. He knew he was being chided, but after a moment's disappointment, he pressed ahead, turning to signal something down the hall, outside the detectives' range of sight.

Following the shuffling of feet, in his best Ed McMahon voice, the patrolman said, "Gentlemen, I give you Marcus Duquesne."

The prisoner, thrust through the doorway by a tall, lanky cop, was cuffed behind his back, wearing thick corduroy pants and a wool sweater whose neck had been stretched too wide. His eyes were wild, pupils moving independently of one another, hair frizzed and swept away from his forehead. The side of his face sported a purple welt, and he favored his left leg.

Bennett's heart, having been anxious for the past ten minutes, plunged to his knees. Marcus Duquesne was black.

Connell spat his toothpick to the floor. "Are you fucking kidding me?" he said.

"Is this one of Lenehan's lame jokes?" Bennett asked.

The two uniforms had stood behind the prisoner proudly, but their faces turned flat when they saw the detectives' reaction.

"What's the matter?" the taller one asked.

"This isn't our guy."

"What do you mean?"

"This isn't our guy."

"Yeah it is," the shorter one insisted. "Frankie and me watched him do the stabbing."

"You might have watched him stab somebody, but this isn't our guy. Our guy is white."

"You tell him I'm from Xanadu and I'll take you to the moon," Marcus Duquesne shouted. His deep baritone tenor was like the wrath of God, startling the men as it echoed off tile walls.

"What the fuck is he talking about?" Connell wondered.

"Not sure. He's been babbling like this since we grabbed him. Won't shut up either."

"Mercy mercy mercy!" he yelled, eyes as intense as a prophet's.

"He's on LSD or something," Bennett said. "He's tripping."

"Got a voice like James Earl Jones," the tall one said.

"Yeah, it sounds rich and regal, but we've been listening to this gobblygook for a half hour," the short one added. "I'd like to put a goddamn muzzle on the guy."

Connell waved a hand like he was dismissing a servant. "Shit, get this hophead out of here. Throw him in the tank until he sobers up. He's not our guy. I doubt he's even going to remember that he tried to stab somebody."

"I stabbed because he was putting ants in my food!"

"Ants, huh?" Connell complained, pressing his thumb to the bridge of his nose. "That's fucking great."

"But we saw him do it," the short cop insisted.

*   *   *

Two things annoyed Bennett: he had jumped the gun without examining facts, and Ken Connell had been right.

Getting excited and working himself into a frenzy had been a rookie mistake. Overanxiousness was the mark of a bad cop, and Bennett did not want that label weighing him down. In his enthusiasm to catch a bad guy, he hadn't paid attention to facts. Connell had, knowing that this suspect's M.O. did not match their killer's. So now what? Would Connell turn this incident against him? Would he walk through the halls and malign Bennett to their fellow coppers? Would he sit on bar stools and whisper about Bennett's incompetence to anyone within earshot? *The snot-nosed kid had been ready to arrest and close the case before even laying eyes on the dude. Turned out to be two patrolmens' wet dreams.*

Bennett was embarrassed. He stared at himself in the bathroom mirror, searching for answers within his own sad eyes. Friday, five days into the case, and still no solid clues. Splashing water onto his cheeks, he used a cupped hand to swallow and wet his tongue.

Mac would counsel him to write off the last hour, re-group, and get back out there. He pursed his lips and tweaked air through them like he was blowing an oboe, then opened the bathroom door.

At his desk, Connell ignored everything around him, directing all his energy into the conversation on the other end of his phone. Unlike Bennett's chair, Connell's swiveled, and he pivoted with agitation, like he was trying to elude logic. His back was to Bennett when he spoke.

"Hey, dummy, I'm telling you, it shouldn't be this way," he snapped. "I want you to move back, but that offer isn't going to be on the table forever."

Bennett's jaw tightened; shoulders turned stiff. He knew Connell was scolding Alison. He could not hear her response, but Connell slammed his hand onto the desk blotter. A ceramic mug holding pens and pencils rattled.

"I'm tired of it. The Wonder Woman fantasy is over. It's time to give it up. If there's another man, tell me, because I'm going to find out. The more you deny it, the more I think you're a two-bit whore."

Bennett pushed back his chair and hastened out of the squad room.

"So it wasn't your guy, huh?" Lenehan asked, arms upturned in an apology. "I just gave you the information that came my way." As Bennett brushed past into the hallway, Lenehan raised his voice. "Hey Mark, what's your big hurry?"

*　　*　　*

He felt like a goddamn criminal, casing his own house. He had safely grabbed his car earlier that day, but it had been parked a block away. Who figured he would have to sneak home like a cat burglar? Odds were long that the pigs were onto him — he had reasoned all that out down in Erie — but he was smart enough to recognize that he wasn't all that smart. There may have been angles and combinations he failed to comprehend. He did not see how those cops at the cemetery could know he was there, but there was always that slim chance that they did. And if they knew his location, then they knew his name and where he lived. Could it be? Were they staking out his apartment?

If so, he thought, they've been lulled into boredom.

After nightfall he parked three blocks away and slinked home. Rain and humidity combined into a cool mist; air hinted toward winter. The chill cut through his jacket, brushing his skin. He was anxious to be back in familiar rooms, to get out of his dirty clothes and stand under a warm shower.

With the elusiveness of that little paperboy, he shifted through neighborhoods while clinging to shadows, avoiding streetlights and the sweep of headlight beams. Turning onto his road, he scouted the scene from behind a thick hedge three doors away.

In the darkness, quiet reigned.

There were no cop cars idling in the drive, no unmarked sedans waiting within sight. Maybe they had binoculars trained on his apartment from a nearby window, but that was a long shot. Cutting through two backyards, he pressed his toes into the empty squares of the cyclone fence. Leg muscles throbbed when he shifted up, but he took the weight along his arms and hoisted himself over, inching closer until he could touch his house. Wooden siding smelled musty, caked with time. Layers of paint had settled into a neglected chocolate stain.

He had lived there for nearly three years. The butch landlady, Mrs. Boyd, occupied the lower floor. After her husband died and the kids moved out, she installed a lock at the top of the stairs, converting it to an upper apartment. She heard everything, but it didn't matter because he was quiet. He never had visitors, paid the rent on time, and only saw the old lady every few weeks. There was never any trouble.

Number ninety-two had been constructed around the turn of the century, with a high gable peaking above an enclosed sunroom that fronted the house. It was a long, thin structure, stretching in length three times its width. A single-lane driveway passed the side entrance, the fence rimming the lawn's perimeter.

Sneaking along the left flank, he avoided pipes and valves and hose connections protruding from the block foundation. He paused before stepping across a pair of sunken window wells.

The latch to the basement doors was broken. Without letting Mrs. Boyd know, he had removed the lock, providing a ready-made entry or exit point if he needed a fast break. The basement was filled with decades of accumulated junk. Maneuvering around shelves and mildewed boxes required dexterity that the old lady lacked, so she rarely ventured down there.

The metal door squeaked as it unfolded. He cringed at the sharp noise. He had always meant to dab oil on the hinges, but never got around to it. Was it truly loud, or was he over-sensitive? If cops were on a stakeout, they would be alerted now.

He scurried into the basement, pulling the door behind him. In the dark, he kicked at a plank of wood angled against the wall, but reached up a steadying hand to prevent its tumble. Using his sense of touch, he probed his way into a nest of boxes that were arranged into a fort. Ducking low, there was no sound of movement, no brushing treads along the interior stairs. His hand reached into a cubby and felt the cold shotgun barrel which he had hidden after yesterday's killing. Its presence calmed him. If the pigs had been here, they would have searched top to bottom and confiscated this. It never would have been left behind.

Finally, Joe knew he was safe. There was relief at being home again.

The killings would resume tomorrow.

Chapter 21

"No murder today," Ken Connell said when they left the squad Friday night. "We must be doing something right."

"Don't pat yourself too hard," Mark Bennett answered. "He's not done yet."

"I know. But at least we won today."

Still, Bennett had not slept well. He could not find a comfortable position, flipping from stomach to back to side while ruminating on the cases, wondering what had prevented the killer from acting. Had posting cops at bus stops been a deterrent? It had yielded a slam-dunk murder arrest, but it wasn't the man they hoped to catch. After four straight days of murder, the bad guy broke the pattern. Where had he been today?

Saturday morning, the doorbell roused him from the edges of sleep. Dazed, with tousled hair, he stumbled through the house wearing a t-shirt and boxers to find Alison standing on his stoop. Puffy cheeks were tear stained. She tried to restrain shaking shoulders.

There's been an accident, he thought.

"What's wrong?" He stepped toward her with arms extended. His bare feet pressed into the cold concrete porch.

She shook her head, jaw quivering. Words came softly. "Ken is such an asshole," she whispered.

"That's not a news flash," he said, folding her to his chest. "Are you hurt?"

"Not physically."

"Come in, settle down, and you'll tell me."

She brushed hair back from her forehead. Her breaths were shallow and uneven. Kicking off shoes, she stepped into the living room and went directly to the box of tissues on an end table.

If it wasn't so early, Mark might have insisted she swallow a shot of liquor. Instead, while she sat on the couch and dabbed her eyes, he went to the kitchen, puttering with a teapot, waiting for water to boil, pouring it into two mugs. His languid pace was intentional, a ploy to settle her nerves. He poured a teaspoon of honey into each cup and allowed the tea to steep. With five minutes elapsed, her panting had eased into regularity.

"I got a call this morning at six-thirty," she explained, wrapping palms around the ceramic mug. "He tells me my stuff is at the curb. He's tired of waiting around for me, so he's moved it there to clear out my junk. If I want anything, I better get over there now before scavenger trucks roll up. Do you realize the planning that must have taken?"

"He mentioned yesterday that he had something going on," Mark reflected. "Had he told you he was going to do this?"

"No, never. But he said that because I've moved out, he needed to unload all my crap. That was his word, *crap*, but I think he was talking more about me than my stuff. He's thinking of selling the house so he wants to pare down."

"I doubt he used the words *pare down*," Mark said. "That vocabulary is too advanced for him."

Alison showed the first glint of a smile. "So I went over there right away, and Mark, I've never seen such a sight. The front lawn is filled with everything I left behind when I moved out. It was like a branding iron on my heart. I never went back to get it because he changed the locks and wouldn't let me in the house, so I always figured we'd work it out later. The entire eleven years we spent together is kicked to the curb, on display for strangers. He must have spent weeks preparing for this, sorting everything from the basement, filling the empty garage space where my car used to go."

"Shit."

"Yeah. I wasn't ready to see that. Here's my crumbled marriage, the biggest failure of my life, scattered before my eyes, for everyone to see."

Mark exhaled.

"I fell apart," she continued. "I don't like to show him any weakness, but I broke down, sobbing right in front of him. I mean, he was tossing out the Christmas ornaments that we picked out together every year. We'd shop the Friday after Thanksgiving, wake up real early, you know, to get the good bargains. And every year we'd stop at AM & A's and pick up that season's annual design. There they were, lined up chronologically. None of that meant anything to him. This wall of sadness just slammed into me and I couldn't pull myself together."

Tears came again, the crumpled tissue frayed at its edges. Mark got up and carried the Kleenex box to her, laying it on the cushion between them and resting his palm on her knee.

"I know we're not going to be together anymore, but there was no respect for our past. If he wants to move to a new house, that's fine. Couldn't he have said, *hey Alison, come on over some time when I'm at work. I'll leave the key under the doormat and you can take what you want? Or we can decide together what we should keep and what should go.*"

"That would be mature thinking. Too advanced for him."

"But none of that was the worst," Alison said, tears beading along the rims of her eyes. "While I stood there shrinking into myself, he laughed at me. It was like he had choreographed the moment and it was playing out exactly like he wanted it to."

Mark's adrenaline raced. *How could Connell call himself a man?* he wondered. *How could he sleep at night, taking sadistic pleasure from the agony of his ex-wife? And what kind of man am I to work with him every day and not knock his fucking teeth out?*

*   *   *

Ken Connell struggled to accept the changes his wife had undergone. When she took a job — against his recommendation, he recalled — it was the beginning of their downhill slide. Soon after, she stopped wearing her wedding ring, reverted to her maiden name, and told people she was separated even though they still lived together. Last April, on a bright spring day while he was working, she had taken her clothes and a few kitchen items and moved out, using money she had earned to rent a downtown studio apartment. Furious, he felt blindsided. In a short time, Alison became a different woman than the one he married.

Initially, he had not thought that she had a boyfriend, but as time passed he wondered what else it could be. Her conscience must have nagged, forcing her move. Connell himself had no such qualms. He had temporarily stopped sleeping with others during his courtship of Alison, but a few months into their marriage, he felt the limitations of sex with only one person. While single, he had always dated a stable of girls, so becoming monogamous felt confining. While with Alison, he learned it was easy and convenient to date whores or married women, because they did not expect commitment and could be brushed off easily.

Connell was adamant that he and Alison should remain together. He wouldn't sign any separation agreement or divorce paper. Despite the fact that she had lived on her own for half a year, he believed she would come to her senses, returning home one day, meekly seeking forgiveness. After a little taste of freedom, she would recognize that it was a tough world out there and a pretty girl would get swallowed alive unless her husband could protect her.

The longer she stayed away, however, the longer the odds of her return.

At first he fought the arrangement, insisting each night on the phone that she needed to come back. But as spring morphed to summer, he tried a different track and backed off. With space would come clarity, he thought. Six months passed before he realized no resolution was on the horizon.

The little skank Valerie had forced the issue one day, probing him as to why he wasn't making an effort to please her. "Other guys buy me gifts," she whined, purple mascara glowing like a circus clown. "Jewelry, makeup. You just treat me like a piece of shit."

"I got one wife already," he said without feeling. "Don't need another."

"Fuck you," Valerie shot back. "You said your old lady left you. From where I stand you ain't doing much to get her back."

Rage exploded. He grabbed her neck and thick fingers dug into her tendons. "Don't ever mention my wife again," he breathed. Her doe eyes dilated and she knew she had crossed a line.

He steamed for several days. If a little high school dropout coke whore saw the truth, then it must be plain for the world to see. Were people laughing at him? Something needed to change, because waiting it out was not working.

Now, as he thought about Alison on chilly autumn nights, he sensed her unfaithfulness more than ever. Why else would she have stayed away so long? It was one thing for a man to have an affair. All cops did it, and hell, all guys did it too, unless they were too priggish for a little adventure. But Alison wasn't the disloyal type.

This shouldn't be too hard to figure out, he realized. *I'm a detective.*

But Alison was smart and knew what kind of car he drove. She would recognize a department sedan if he signed one out to follow her. So he devised creative ways around that. He could borrow personal cars from young patrolmen, promising to owe them a favor. He could rent a beater for the day and crouch low behind the steering wheel, staking out her apartment.

He intended to ratchet up the pressure on his wife. He would move her stuff to the curb, use free time to tail her, learn where she spent her days and nights.

But then the Negro killer struck and twisted his plans into orbit.

Although there was no attack on Friday, Connell agreed with Mark Bennett. The bad guy wasn't about to stop. He would keep up the slaughter until they caught him. How long would that take? Days? Weeks? Months?

He could not wait on either front, so Connell spread himself parchment-thin. He wanted to be in two places at once. Could he simultaneously catch a killer and keep the pressure on Alison?

In spite of that day's corpse, Thursday had been his night to follow Alison.

*   *   *

"You don't look so good," Bobby Bennett told his brother, standing on Mark's front stoop wearing a bomber jacket, jeans and wraparound sunglasses. "Bags under your eyes."

Mark opened the storm door and shook his brother's hand, stepping back to allow him to pass. "There's always bags under my eyes."

"Yeah, but today they look saggier."

He closed the door and latched the deadbolt, a habit he had fallen into once Alison started coming over. How might he explain this to his brother? *I'm having an affair with Ken Connell's ex, and he's making her life a living hell?*

"I been logging a lot of hours," Mark admitted. "This detective work is kicking my ass."

Like Alison several hours earlier, Bobby slid off his shoes. They thudded into the baseboard with a clunk. "First big homicide, huh?"

"Yeah."

"Heard you've partnered with Connell."

Mark grimaced, but Bobby had stepped onto the kitchen's linoleum floor so did not see the reaction. "It's true."

"He's supposed to be the best."

"He's a good cop," Mark conceded, "but a lousy son of a bitch. You want a beer?"

Bobby checked his watch. "I'm on duty at four, but what the hell, one won't kill me."

"No, we'll have Pepsi instead." Mark retrieved two glass bottles from the refrigerator and pried open the caps. Bobby pulled out a chair and sat at the kitchen table.

"So why was it so important I come by, Marky? We gonna re-hash the other night outside of Rendevous?"

Mark blew out his breath. That had not been his plan, but this was his impetuous brother, tackling an uncomfortable issue head on, even if the fallout was sure to be damaging.

"We can if you want," Mark answered, reaching toward the counter, where an envelope leaned against the backsplash. "But that wasn't what I had in mind. I asked you over because I thought you might want this."

"What is it?" Bobby asked, taking it from his brother. Mark did not reply.

The protruding photo was too large for its holster, so the top flap remained unsealed. Bobby slid the picture out and laid it flat on the table, studying intently. Mark had already committed the scene to memory. Framed by blanched edges, in hues of black and white, a thick man wearing a pale t-shirt cradled a newborn in his arms. The baby was swaddled, cheeks scrunched with discontent. In the frozen moment, the man's upturned lips suggested the beginnings of a smile.

"Who is this?" Bobby wondered.

"The baby is you."

"I thought so. That's the living room couch. But that's not Pop, right? Who is it?"

"Look closely. Take away fifty pounds. Peel back twenty-five years."

Bobby's focus narrowed. He ran a thick hand across his head while he concentrated. Although the man's features were chubby, his nose was not, yet one eye appeared more dilated than the other.

"Holy shit," Bobby muttered. "George Pope?"

Mark laughed. "Can you believe it? Pop must have invited him over when you were born and taken the picture. George was a rookie then, just like you are now."

Bobby grinned. "Oh man, look at Pope. He practically smells like salami. My partner held me when I was a baby. This is shameful. Pop probably made him change my diapers. Where did you find this?"

"In some of Pop's things."

"What things?"

"Stuff mom asked me to clean out."

Bobby looked up with happiness. "Can I keep it?"

"Sure."

"I don't want this falling into Pope's hands. He'll make copies and post it around the station. My reputation will swirl down the shithole." Bobby's eyes gleamed as he tucked the photo back into the ill-fitting envelope, then slid it into his shirt pocket. He swallowed and looked at his brother.

"I gotta tell you, Marky, even though we didn't get along that good, I miss the old man."

Mark was surprised at his brother's admission. "Me too."

"And I don't want you to get smug or say I told you so, but... uh... I wish I had been with you at the hospital."

Mark's jaw tightened. He studied the contours of his cola bottle, recalling the sterile smell of intensive care. He saw the angled bed, white linens, tubes and wires snaking between Mac and imposing machines. He sensed the quiet impending doom, like death had unfurled a blanket as it made a slow descent. His eyes inflated.

"Me too," Mark repeated.

"He and I always butted heads, but I miss it in a way I can't explain. We never had the kind of relationship that you and he did. The three of us could be in the same room, but you two were always together, you know?"

Mark kept his eyes toward the floor.

"Anyway, I've been trying to look after mom a little more," Bobby continued. "I've been stopping over there a couple times each week."

"Really? When?"

"Before shift, or if I'm doing a day tour, afterwards. Sometimes Pope and I zip in for ten minutes."

"How's she doing?"

Bobby shrugged. "You know Ma. Tough nut to crack. She's got rosaries draped over the armchair and doilies on every table. Seems like there's more statues in the living room than I remember. I could never keep track of all those damn saints. How she and Mac stayed together, I'll never know. They were from two different worlds."

Mark thought of Alison, about her desperate need to get away from Connell's controlling personality. Unlike his girlfriend, neither of his parents ever acted on their desires to escape.

"In the fifties and sixties husbands and wives stayed together," he said. "They took those vows to heart. Through good times and bad."

"So is it better or worse that they stuck it out?" Bobby asked.

"I don't know."

The brothers fell silent, considering the distance between their parents, how it affected their childhood years. Mark wondered what their lives would have been like if their parents had split. Would he have stayed with his mother or would Mac have lobbied for custody? Considering his irregular hours on the force, could his dad really have raised two boys on his own?

"Hey, I don't mean to stir this up again, but I gotta ask you something about the other night," Bobby said, interrupting Mark's reverie. "What do you have against Battaglia?"

"He's a douchebag."

"I know you think that, Marky, but why? You're hardheaded and stubborn, but you don't pass judgment for no reason."

"He's a bad guy and a bad cop. Not the kind of person you should be hanging out with."

"I'm old enough to make my own decisions about that."

"You don't know him like I do."

Bobby nodded and twirled his bottle on its ring of condensation. "There's a side to this you're not telling me."

Mark watched his brother, the careless posture reclined far back in the chair, big bulky hands alternately grasping the glass and drumming against the table's edge.

"Am I right?" Bobby asked.

"Yeah."

"So tell me."

"I've never told this story. Only three people know it, and I don't want it out there, cause it's too late and will look like sour grapes. So if I tell it, can you keep it to yourself?"

Bobby met his brother's gaze, nodding. "Sure."

"It goes back a few years. We were both young cops. I never partnered with Battaglia, but I knew him. Sometimes we worked the same shift, and he's about my age, so we had friends in common.

"One night, just about this time of year, a drunk driver t-bones a pickup. No one is hurt, just a few scrapes and bruises, but the cars are blocking a side street off Richmond. I had already clocked out and was on my way home when the call squawks across my radio. It's four blocks away, so I detour toward the scene. Battaglia and his partner are already there.

"I see this guy Lefty standing under a streetlight wearing a silver jacket, one of those silky things. He's moving like a chimp, arms flailing all over, and the light is catching on his shoulders. I'm wondering what the hell kind of fashion statement Lefty is after, because when he turns a certain way, I see the jacket's back is sparkled with sequins. I'm thinking maybe he's trying to become popular in disco parlors or something.

"All the cops knew Lefty. He's a notorious drunk, he's arrested for public intoxication about once a month, but he's not violent or harmful in any way. In fact, he's usually good for a laugh, he's so blotto most of the time. He likes to get loaded and wander through streets at four in the morning belting out show tunes at top volume. Imagine a drunk slurring the words to *the guy's only doing it for some doll*.

"I get out of my car and hear Lefty saying, *all I'm asking for is a ride downtown. My ve-hickle is parked on Tupper*. He's over-enunciating every word.

"*You're in no shape to drive, Lefty*, Battaglia tells him. He stands to the right of the drunk, while his partner, a troll called Kowalski, waits a few feet away to the left. I thought it odd that they spread out and kept Lefty between them. He was no threat to their safety.

"*I wasn't driving here*, Lefty says. *I was only a passenger, so you can't arrest me*.

"*Why would we arrest you?* Kowalski says.

"As Lefty turns to face him, Battaglia leans forward, and his jaw juts toward the drunk's back.

"You're not in any trouble. But we're cops, not a taxi service. You're going to have to hoof it or call yourself a cab.

"Call a cab? Lefty echoes. *With what money am I going to pay a cabbie? I'm flat broke.*

"So now I can see these patrolmen are having fun at Lefty's expense. You know we're not a taxi service, but we have a responsibility to be sure that citizens aren't abandoned at an accident scene. They should be returned to a situation of safety. It would be unethical to leave him there, and they both knew it. The clowns should have offered him a ride without putting him through the ringer, but that's the kind of assholes they are.

"Your lack of funds is not our problem, Lefty, Battaglia says.

"I suppose you want us to front you some change, Kowalski adds, and he lays his palms on Lefty's shoulders so Lefty spins toward him. Again, Battaglia angles forward, thrusting his head at Lefty's back.

"When I realized what was happening my stomach tightened. As Lefty looked toward his partner, Battaglia would spit on his back. The sequins reflecting under the streetlight weren't sequins at all — they were little gobs of saliva clinging to shiny fabric."

Bennett's eyes gleamed with passion as he paused in the narrative.

"That's when I knew the kind of cop Battaglia was. More importantly, I knew what kind of man he was. He's a vermin that makes a mockery of anyone he considers below him on the social scale. Our job as public servants is to help everybody, not just the rich or well educated. We owe something to guys like Lefty, too."

"So what happened?" Bobby wondered.

"I approach and walk into their light. Both cops stand up straighter, you know, like they're trying to flush away a memory.

They pretend they are all serious. Turned on their professional act the second they noticed me on the scene."

"Did you confront them?"

"No. Doing that would only embarrass Lefty. Besides, these were fellow cops, and we were all new to the force. But they knew I was Mac's kid. I wasn't about to blow them in. So I got Lefty out of there. Told him he should come with me and I'd drive him home. Of course, I made him take off his jacket before he got in my car."

"You never said anything to Battaglia or Kowalski?" Bobby asked.

"I didn't need to. As I led Lefty away, I turned around and met eyes with Battaglia. One look said it all. It was clear to both of us that I knew the kind of cop he is. I saw his underbelly. There's a saying that character is what you do when nobody's watching. Since then I've never trusted him. We've stayed away from each other."

Bobby drank a swallow and leaned forward.

"Saint Mark," Bobby exhaled, shaking his head. "So the copper did a boneheaded thing. You're taking it way too seriously. Seeing you probably kick-started his conscience. He probably regretted it and made sure it didn't happen again."

"I doubt it. You might think it's harmless fun, but it's not. You need to recognize that, Bobby. Battaglia treated a citizen worse than an animal. You wouldn't spit on your dog and laugh about it, would you?"

Bobby frowned. "No."

"That's not the sort of thing normal people do for kicks. This was sadistic. He's a scumbag. I never told Pop, because I didn't want him to bring the wrath down on Battaglia, but I wonder what he would have done in my situation."

"Something heroic, I'm sure," Bobby grinned.

"Yeah, probably. He'd use the wisdom of Solomon." Mark turned the bottle upside down, draining it over his lips. He laid it

235

on the table and aimed a finger at his brother. "My point is this. You just mentioned your reputation. You're a rookie, and you're going to get a reputation on this job real quick. It's going to be based on what you do, but also by the people you hang out with. You got to think about these things. Battaglia is not a great character reference. We're cops, so we've got to behave with integrity. As if that wasn't enough, Mac set the bar pretty high for us."

Bobby finished his soda, wiped the ring of condensation with his hand, and slid it across formica so it touched Mark's.

"Point taken. Sermon over for today?"

*   *   *

Outside the house, under the spanning branches of an elm tree, a Ford Pinto nestled against the curb fifty yards away. Ken Connell surveyed the quiet street, focusing on the happenings before him and in the rear-view mirror.

Thursday night, when he tailed Alison, she had parked the next block over and rounded the corner on foot. By the time Connell believed he could pursue without being spotted, she was out of sight, having vanished into one of these houses.

He intended to use a variety of cars to avoid suspicious neighbors. He would come by at odd hours and wait. Just what the hell had Alison been doing here?

Saturday afternoon was uneventful. There wasn't much to see in this neighborhood. In twenty minutes of surveillance, he watched a retired man push a lawnmower in what would likely be the final cut of the season. A mailman wove between houses, emptying the contents of his shoulder bag one envelope at a time into door slots and aluminum boxes. Three kids played street hockey with a tennis ball, and a fat teenage girl stood on a front lawn, swaying to music heard through flimsy earphones.

Connell knew that hours logged on a watch job were tedious, rarely leading to valuable information despite the time commitment. Patience was key.

So he gasped in surprise when a familiar face opened the front door, descended three concrete steps, and unlocked the Monte Carlo in the driveway of a pale-bricked ranch.

"Holy shit," Connell muttered in the quiet of his borrowed car. He did not believe in coincidences. This guy? He was short and built like a pit bull, bald with scarred cheeks. Connell had just seen him in the squad room yesterday when he arrested that shipper. Wasn't this Mark Bennett's little brother?

He swallowed, vortex raging in his brain. She was having an affair, he knew that, but he never considered it would be someone so young. Yet evidence was clear, right before his face.

Alison was banging a rookie patrolman.

Chapter 22

In his mind, Joe called it "Resumption Day."

A night's sleep had rejuvenated him. Soreness wasn't exactly gone when he woke, but everything hurt less. Lying on the bowed bed, his back was still spongy, but legs no longer burned. Being home made all the difference.

The clock stopped at 3:12, but already there was sunshine in the room. It couldn't be afternoon, so the batteries must have died overnight. The red second hand's sweep was frozen just beyond the number six.

It didn't matter. Time no longer held sway.

He would not flee from here again. Even if the cops found him, he wouldn't scurry off like a startled squirrel. The crusade was a commitment now, and he felt the call of a zealot, the sort of passion for which he was willing to die. His own death was imminent; he understood and accepted it was a fate he could not escape. This empowered him, filled his mind with courage. His behavior now would be bold, even more decisive. Let the pigs bull-rush upstairs and batter down his door. He would remain in the room's center, defiant, arms raised heavenward like a prophet, inflating his chest as a target for their bullets. Perhaps his death would inspire others to take up the call.

Bedsprings squeaked as he shifted. He sat on the edge of his saggy mattress, looking down at his soiled t-shirt on the floor. For a moment he simply stood, letting his equilibrium adjust to the vertical. He shuffled to the bathroom, relieved his legs felt looser. Moving slowly, he could endure the tenderness if he pre-planned each step. Waiting before the toilet, his bladder was full, his scrotum heavy. He needed release. After killing he would troll for a hooker, maybe another little nigger. He would fuck her then beat her good. He flushed, catching sight of his haggard face in the mirror.

Turning his shoulder towards the reflection, muscles tightened in his skinny arm. Tattoos were still fresh and crisp. He grinned, beady eyes narrowing to slits, teeth predatory. The concept of becoming a martyr inflated him with confidence. He would add another chef's hat today. And one tomorrow. Then the day after that.

One a day for the rest of his life, however short that might be.

He showered, donned fresh clothes and bought a ninety-nine cent breakfast at the corner counter. It was a sunny day, cool with a strong wind. He drove to the waterfront, parallel parked along Niagara Street, and approached the river, stepping over scattered weeds, broken bottles and crumbled papers before shuffling along the walkway. Its concrete bubbled with inlaid pebbles, edges chipped by time.

The trunk of a maple tree angled toward water, its spanning branches like human hands stretching above the current. At the crest of a knoll, he sat on a bench and faced west, staring across the water toward the low-lying ridge of Canada.

Autumn was a magnificent time. Trees had morphed to orange and yellow and fire-red, vibrant colors like dancing flames whose bursts contrasted against the teal blue mouth of Lake Erie. *Everything had color*, he thought, *except black. Those people infected what was otherwise a beautiful world.*

Just beyond his line of vision, the lake narrowed into the Niagara River. Before him waves thundered by in a fast chop. A sign hooked to the metal railing cautioned, "SWIFT WATER — NO SWIMMING." That didn't stop a stray duck from barreling along eddies, twisting and swirling and diving underwater, only to emerge thirty yards downriver.

If he stabbed one here and dropped the body into the river, no one would ever know. Without witnesses, he could carry on his crusade in secret. He savored the thought for a while, drawn to the comic book fantasy of an undercover assassin. While that had advantages, it also missed the point. These killings needed to be public and brutal, cold-blooded enough to make them quiver in fear.

Maybe he should work his way closer to Niagara Falls. He imagined all the tourists standing on the platform, watching water pound over the escarpment, gasping in shock as a floating corpse bobbed downstream. Wire brush hair would bounce and vanish beneath the rapids, tourists would point to the area and ask one another, "did I really see that?" Then the body would float toward the brink, hover for a heartbeat, and crash down the high cascading falls, submerging into the vortex below.

It would make international news, spreading across Asia and Europe, word traveling as far as remote villages in China.

Joe snapped from his reverie, stiffening when he noticed a black man walking along the path wearing heavy boots, lugging a fishing pole and plastic pail. The man hiked alone.

He did not make eye contact trudging past. A hundred yards away, the man stopped, emptied the bucket and turned it over, sitting on its bottom. From that position he baited the hook and tossed a line into the water.

Joe looked up and down the empty path. No one was within view. Cars zoomed by on the highway, moving metal swishing behind him, exhaust fumes settling into the dimpled river.

His heart beat faster, that rush of euphoria that had intensified in the past week. Again, this was fate, just like Monday when that cleaning woman came into sight at city hall.

Joe approached from behind, neither sneaking nor disguising his intent. This killing was his destiny, and he had no desire to slink about. It didn't matter if anyone saw him. He was not about to alter the plan.

He had heard them called shines, but had never understood why until now. This one was entirely without hair, head polished glossy like a new kettle. Noontime light reflected off his skull. The glow was a beacon, an invitation to sink the knife into the soft dimple under his ear lobe. He anticipated the blade slipping into ebony flesh, emerging as a dark puddle. The bald head was a summons to kill.

The man's fishing pole angled toward the lake, its invisible line vanishing into lapping water. He sat, both hands wrapped around the flimsy rod, starting absently at the wave where his sinker disappeared. A dark brown bottle rested on gravel near the crook of his knee.

Joe could not estimate the nigger's age. There were a few wrinkles in the back of his neck, where the hairline would be if he had one, but they didn't age like whites. Their charcoal skin just absorbed living, and years spent roaming the slums and drinking and smoking and sucking in drugs made them age faster. This one might be anywhere between thirty-five and fifty-five.

Walking along the cracked pathway, aware of his own calves tightening, Joe knew one thing: the shine wouldn't get any older than he was now.

The black man did not turn as Joe approached, did not seem to notice the cars or the wind or anything around him. He was focused solely on a small patch of water. Without breaking stride, Joe pulled the bowie knife from its sheath, clutched hard and swung underhanded at the fleshy neck. The blade slipped into the skin like warm cheese.

There was a brief delay before the muscles seized up, shoulders tensing. Joe watched the progression of emotions on the face with fascination and disdain. His eyes filled with confusion, then grew wide with pain. He never shouted or screamed, but stared at Joe with helpless agony. Joe watched the lips flutter. He withdrew the blade when pupils went blank.

He was amazed that their blood was crimson. Each time he stabbed, he had expected soupy mud to ooze out and dribble down the body like liquid shit.

The dying man slumped and started to tip off his bucket.

"No, no, no," Joe spoke his first words. "Get up, get up, come on stand up."

He grabbed the man's shoulders and encouraged him to straighten his legs, but the nigger was not cooperating. Joe reached under his arms and lifted, repulsed by the smell of hair lotion, the sooty scent that clung to his skin.

He grabbed at Joe's thigh, unable to get traction around the waist. A hand rose to Joe's scrotum, clenching weakly.

"You fucking nigger faggot," Joe spat, and raised a knee to the man's chin. His consciousness was fading. He let go before incurring any damage. Taking him by the shoulders, Joe heaved the torso so it bent over the railing. A guttural groan scraped the throat. Blood drizzled out of the neck, dripping into the current like colored rain.

Joe noticed a dark splotch on his knee. He looked left and right, turned in a three-hundred-sixty degree pivot. No one noticed his conquest. He had hoped for some sign of encouragement, some congratulations for ridding the world of one more welfare sucker. None of the cars along the Thruway beeped, stopped or even slowed.

Silently, he crouched low, wrapped his arms around the man's knees, and heaved. Using the railing as a fulcrum, the legs tipped up like a teeter-totter and shifted momentum. The splash hardly made a sound.

Free of the body, Joe shook out his arms and brushed debris from his pants legs. He kicked at the overturned pail and stepped on the fishing pole, cracking its plastic and unspooling nylon wire. Then he leaned over the railing. The corpse floated, drifting slowly from its entry point, just a foot every few seconds. The current was faster away from shore, and the man's

242

shirt seemed to lodge against an underwater rock. It was soothing to watch the baptism, but part of him wanted the fucking nigger faggot to be sucked away and forgotten forever.

He would have to get rid of his jeans because of the blood stain.

Have to get another tattoo.

He was proud to repay them for what they had done to his father.

*　　　*　　　*

The knowledge was profane, like a glowing metal stake pressed against his brain. That fucking whore. That fucking woman who vowed to be his wife and stay with him forever. Suddenly, her beauty was irrelevant. Her virtue spun away like a memory. She was false, cold and uncaring.

This was not the same Alison Keane.

How long had the affair gone on? Connell knew the bullet-headed patrolman was a rookie, because Mark Bennett had mentioned his brother just got out of the academy, and when Pope scolded him in the squad there had been some comment about robbing a young officer of a good arrest.

Unbelievable.

Connell was experienced at juggling different and complex interests. He usually worked more than one case at a time, employing a flashbulb memory to remember specifics from each, shaping that knowledge to execute justice. Sometimes he wrote things down, but more often he didn't. His mind was able to compartmentalize. He juggled women as well, from his wife to call girls to broads he met in bars that slept with him. There was no need for any of them to know about the others.

So he should not have been surprised that Alison was able to maneuver into secret relationships as deftly as he did. In spite of his suspicions, however, facing the reality was difficult.

She was banging a fucking flatfoot. Worse, it was his partner's brother.

He phoned Bobby Bennett's precinct and identified himself to the sergeant.

"Tell me about this rookie," Connell said.

"Well, he's Mac Bennett's little boy," the sarge confirmed, voice hoarse from decades of whiskey and cigars. "And you must know his brother, Mark. Just got promoted to homicide."

"Yeah, I don't need the family tree. I want to know about this kid."

The sergeant paused. When he spoke again his tone was harder. "Well, he's twenty-four or five, pretty green. My impression is that he's full of piss and vinegar, thinking he knows more than everyone else. George Pope requested the kid for a partner. Nobody's said anything, but I sense that Pope is trying to break him down, you know, like they do in the army. Get rid of that me-first attitude and he might develop into a good cop."

"How long has he been there?"

"I dunno. A month?"

"You asking me?" Connell wondered.

"Hey, detective, why the attitude?"

Connell ignored the comment. "You get him right out of the academy?"

"Yeah. With Pope's seniority he can pick any partner he wants. Guess he's trying to pay back the old man. They teamed up back in the fifties or something."

"Bennett been any trouble so far?"

"Not yet."

"Is he a good cop?"

"He's a rookie. Too soon to tell."

"He married or anything?"

"I don't know too much about his personal life."

Connell's lip curled, knuckles around the receiver clenching tighter. The boss was stonewalling.

"What's this all about, detective?"

Connell drummed a pencil against his knee. "Ongoing investigation," he replied absently.

"You're working on those blacks getting killed, right? You looking into one of my cops?"

"I'm looking into a lot of things. There's a murderer on the loose and I'm trying to cover every angle I can think of. Keep this conversation between us, okay?"

Again, hesitation. "Mmmm."

"When is this kid back on shift?"

There was a ruffling of papers in the background. "Works a four to twelve tonight and another tomorrow."

*   *   *

Bobby Bennett's sergeant knew a hell of a lot more than he let on, but fuck Ken Connell. The sarge had no use for what the mayor thought. Connell was an asshole, a hotshot detective who stole cases from guys in uniform and paraded around downtown like his shit didn't stink.

When Connell said, "Keep this conversation between us, okay?" the sarge simply groaned. He didn't owe this guy any favors. Behind his own desk, he hung up, then raised a middle index finger and saluted the phone. Sliding open his top drawer, he reached for the worn address book he had kept for years. Opening its cracked leather cover, he thumbed through pages. It took a few seconds to locate Mark Bennett's home number.

Mark had worked in this precinct for seven years. He was a solid cop. Being Mac's boy had gotten his foot in the door, but once in uniform, he earned accolades on his own. A promotion to detective was always mired in politics, but Mark deserved to climb the blue ladder.

The sarge understood that the younger Bennett was a bit of a project. At this point in his career, he needed people looking out for him, and Mark was a stand-up guy.

He dialed the phone.

*   *   *

By Saturday afternoon, things had calmed around Mark Bennett's house. After her emotions leveled, Alison left for her office to review a grant proposal. Bobby had come and gone, so Mark showered and dressed, preparing to head to work as well. The killer had been quiet since Thursday, but he was still loose. In the mudroom, Bennett was knotting the lace on one shoe when the phone rang. With the other untied, he trotted to the kitchen, picking up the wall receiver.

"We got another one," the chief said. "Black victim down at the waterfront. Somehow ended up in the river."

"Son of a bitch," Bennett exhaled.

The chief told him the location then signed off.

Before he took three steps, the phone jingled again. He was expecting to hear some forgotten bit of information, but was surprised by the raspy voice of his former sergeant. After two minutes, he hung up and stared down at the squiggled ends of the untied shoelace.

His house was empty, but he asked out loud, "Why the hell is Connell asking about my brother?"

*   *   *

He felt control slipping away. *That fucking whore*, he raged.

What was she thinking? She married a detective, whose full-time job involved uncovering secrets. Did she imagine she could keep this from him?

And with a fellow copper? He had a brush cut, pockmarks on his pug face, and stood like a fire hydrant. Connell was the star of the homicide bureau and she rummaged around the barrel for Bobby fucking Bennett?

He couldn't understand why.

Where had they met? Did she visit his house regularly? Is that where their obscene intercourse took place? Did he ever sneak over to her apartment, or was this a one-sided, you-come-to-me thing?

Connell poked a wrapped toothpick through its plastic sleeve, crunched its sliver between his molars, and pounded his fist against the dashboard. What did Bobby fucking Bennett's house look like inside? Did he have a striped sofa? Did his rooms hold the musky smell of a gym locker bay? Connell pictured a collection of mismatched plates, hand-me-downs from a stuffy old aunt who bought used dishes at garage sales. The kid was so young, Connell suspected there was a Farrah Fawcett poster tacked to his bedroom wall. Did Alison slither into his den, lie on her back, spread legs and moan "Oh Bobby" while staring up at Farrah's hard nipples and perfect teeth?

Had Alison recognized she was being followed? He was careful and crafty, so he doubted she could have known. Yet why had she parked around the corner?

Years of interviewing witnesses left Connell with a sharpened sense when someone withheld information. He knew he didn't receive full disclosure from Bobby's sergeant, but at least he learned the little prick's schedule for the next two days. He could run surveillance, both on Bobby's house and Alison's apartment, catch them during his off hours either coming or going.

Connell's mind was so jumbled with rage that he had not formulated a plan beyond that.

Everything was tilted off kilter when he entered the squad room. Stopping by the station to return the Pinto he borrowed from a young uniform, he learned about another murder.

*   *   *

Standing opposite the chief's desk, the flaps of Ken Connell's trench coat hung open. The office door was ajar. The squad fell quiet on Saturday afternoon. No Lenehan lurking around, poking into everyone's business, no clattering typewriters or perking coffee. The only sound was a hissing radiator on the far wall.

Mark Bennett's footsteps pattered against the tile floor. Connell and the chief both turned to face him.

"Get in here," the chief commanded.

Bennett unzipped his leather jacket as he entered the office. He did not acknowledge Connell, nor did the veteran nod to him.

"I just started the briefing," the chief said. "Two hours ago a Puerto Rican from the west side walks down to the river with his fishing pole. He's got a bottle of Pepsi and a couple sandwiches. Casts his line into the current and sits down to pass the time. He's three bites into the ham and cheese when he sees a body floating past his bobber. Looks like a black man, and the guy ain't moving. Sees it snag on a rock, then runs to the corner store and calls us. Uniforms say the witness still has mustard on his lips when they get there, only the body's gone. Must've shaken loose, floated downriver. Takes another half hour of scanning the shore before they spot the body a few hundred yards away. They get a rope and a winch and it pull out. Sure enough, dead black man, deep stab wound puncturing the neck."

"Estimate a time of death?" Connell wondered.

"Recent. Within the last few hours. Tough to tell after having been in the cold water."

"So we're thinking it's our guy, huh?" Bennett asked.

"No shit, genius," Connell turned to him with a curled lip. "Of course we think it's our guy. Why else would the chief call us in?"

Bennett shot him a glare.

"We don't know if this is our guy or not," the chief said. "But the M.O. is the same, and I want you two on the scene. They've taped off the area and the body is headed toward the morgue. Maybe if you work backwards you can find where the body was dumped into the river. Maybe there's blood splatters somewhere."

"If this vic has been in the water twenty-four hours, maybe our guy did do a killing yesterday." Bennett shook his head. "I told you we shouldn't be too quick to pat ourselves on the back."

"Score one for the rookie." Connell's sarcasm hung in the air. "Yippee."

Bennett's lips tightened. It was bad enough that Ken Connell had abused Alison, but now he was investigating Bobby. Why was he so short-tempered?

"What's up your ass?"

"The stuff you're saying is pretty obvious to anyone who's investigated a murder. Only reason your lips are moving is so you can hear yourself talk."

Before Bennett could respond, the chief said, "Relax, Connell. What's your problem?"

"I'm thinking he sprinkled an extra helping of douchebag onto his cereal," Bennett answered. "Kick any puppies yet today?"

Connell stood straighter. "Fuck off, Bennett," he replied.

The chief slammed a fist on his desk. Fury rose in his voice.

"What am I, a goddamn hall monitor?" the chief yelled. "I got five bodies and no killer in custody. You two want to have petty little arguments? You want to sit here and play word games? I'm looking for detectives who are going to wrap up this bastard before another body appears! Neither one of you is getting the job done, so maybe you both oughta be bounced from this case."

Although he remained stoic, Bennett's anger seethed. He wanted to slam his fist against Connell's jaw and shout, *You're abusing Alison! You've made her life a living hell! She finally recognized what a controlling, manipulative bastard you are, and you can't handle it!*

He wanted to demand an answer to why his brother was being investigated. He wanted relief, some way to uncover this muted tension.

But he stood frozen and accepted the scolding from his boss.

"Are you two willing to work, or just piss on each other's toes?"

Ten seconds stretched, but Bennett spoke first.

"I'm willing to work, sir," he said.

Connell snorted, shook his head, then brushed past Bennett, leaving the office, and depositing himself at his own desk, where he opened a folder and hunched over his blotter, back toward the window.

"I'll head down to the scene," Bennett said. The chief's glare moved beyond Bennett through the glass divider. He did not speak.

Bennett didn't stop at his desk or idle to see if Connell wanted to ride with him. He strode directly across the floor, into the stairwell and outside toward his car.

He squelched the urge to storm back into the office. He could explain to the chief what was going on and hope there would be no repercussions to his job, yet there was the very real possibility he would be demoted back to patrol. Plus, it would feel like tattling. He could corner Connell, demand to know the angle being played on his brother, then take a swing at the asshole's jaw. Immediate relief, yes, but that would lead to a suspension. The time had passed to get in Connell's face and scream.

Any of those options would betray the secret relationship he shared with Alison.

Bennett sat down and turned the ignition key. Before putting the car in gear, he checked up and down the street. He didn't want Connell to come out of the building then, but no one was watching. He grabbed the mic and raised it to his mouth.

"It's getting to be too much, Mac. I have no fucking clue what comes next."

Chapter 23

Sincere Malone did not look healthy. Her eyes were still swollen, pupils hardly visible behind narrow slits, purple bruises penetrated deep into her cheeks. She didn't want to work the street, especially on a cold windy night like this, but Alonzo had insisted she go. *He was a stupid lousy bastard,* she realized, *and I'm even stupider for staying with him. Get the shit kicked out of me and a few nights later I'm back out here just waiting for the next beating.*

During the past few days, mist melted away and her life sharpened into focus. This was the time to make changes. She was going to start saving money for her daughter. The maroon vinyl purse had a false bottom, perfect to conceal flattened bills, and Alonzo didn't know about it. She planned to stop doing drugs, skim a little from customers. Alonzo was so caught up in moving product that he wouldn't miss twenty bucks a week. Money would accumulate then she could secretly empty the stash of cash into a cigar box during visits to her mom. It would take some time to build up a nest egg. Changes wouldn't happen overnight, but they would happen.

She remained angry at how she was treated, both by the cracker who beat her and by Alonzo. Now she was working with a purpose.

These October nights turned cold. Sincere balanced atop stilettos, careful to avoid cracks in the sidewalk when she placed tiny heels. Most of the evening was idle time, a pointless stroll up and down the block, not much action for a weekend. Where were all the big spenders?

As she stood wondering, a fellow hooker named Annette rounded the corner, wearing a skirt that masked her muscular thighs and a frilly blouse that was buttoned to the neck. In heels, she towered over everyone else, with a powerful chest and strong arms. She had a reputation for keeping a bottle tucked in her oversized purse.

Some of the girls didn't care for Annette, who had only appeared on the scene near the end of summer. Annette was a cross-dresser, really a man posing as a woman, and many voiced their suspicions about her true motives. Maybe, someone suggested, Annette was working some ploy and her real goal was to get laid by all the working girls. Others saw any new face as competition. Guys got tired of the same ass all the time, that was part of human nature, so fresh legs translated into less money for the veterans — even if those legs looked like a linebacker's.

Sincere didn't care about that. She didn't plan to be on the streets much longer anyway. Besides, Annette was nearly six feet tall, a good ten inches above her. Annette wasn't going to steal her business. If a guy wanted a she-man, Annette was on deck, but if he wanted a girly-girl, someone to fulfill the teenage fantasy, he was coming to Sincere, that was obvious. No one would ever confuse the two.

When Annette noticed Sincere shivering, she plunged into her bag for the amber bottle, extending it at arm's length. Sincere hesitated. From high school health class she knew that alcohol was a drug, and since the beating she had vowed to quit drugs to keep her mind clear. But a belt of booze on a frigid night wouldn't fog her brain as much as it would keep the rest of her warm. It was survival, she told herself, a plain and simple need. The contoured glass looked huge when she took it in her tiny palm, tipping back to gulp.

"Thanks," Sincere muttered.

"Child, looks like you needed it," Annette answered in an alto pitch. "Your man beat you up like that?"

"No. Crazy customer. Real bad seed. But my man sent me back out here tonight when I oughta be home with an ice pack."

"I got smacked the other day, too," Annette admitted with solidarity, pointing at her own swollen face. Gently she used a finger to pull down her lower lip, exposing gleaming teeth and lacerations along the moist pink skin inside her mouth. "Guy pays me for a blow job, then freaks out when he finds out I've got a johnson. Like it makes any difference, right, sugar? I mean, I sucked him good either way."

"Yeah, guys get touchy about stuff like that," Sincere said. *What a crazy world*, she thought. *How could a transvestite not understand that normal guys don't want a hummer from another dude?*

"Amen," Annette said. "So what happened with this guy that beat you? Who was he?"

Sincere folded wrists across herself, tucking fingers beneath her narrow arms to conserve warmth. "White farm boy with a baseball cap pulled low. I called him Sticks. Didn't even notice how crazy his eyes looked til after he picked me up and we was driving. He stops the car, next thing I know he's got his hand around my throat and my eyes are popping out. Figured I was about to die."

"My, my," Annette shook her head. "Where'd you pick this guy up?"

"Chippewa. He was watching me in that parking lot across from the liquor store. Jacked up the price, thinking I could get me a little extra, but it didn't make a damn bit of difference because he robbed me after."

"He rape you?"

"Oh yeah."

Annette's memory triggered. She remembered walking near Sincere the other night when a guy in a ball cap shooed her away.

"Honey, when did this happen?" Annette wondered.

Sincere shrugged. "Couple nights ago. Monday, it was."

"Monday," Annette repeated, thinking it must have been one hell of a beating if Sincere still looked so bad. "Was I with you when he called you over?"

Sincere tried to remember. The drugs had clouded her recollections, leaving hazy edges around days and times. But everything snapped into focus when he laid the knife against her throat, when she saw the hate spilling from his marble eyes.

"You mighta been. I'm not sure."

"Yeah, I strolled up to a dude like you described but he was asking for you. Remember?"

Warmth coursed through Sincere's arms and legs. She had returned the bottle to Annette, but now that the liquor settled in her stomach, she craved another swallow. "I guess."

"Your man say he gonna take care of this?" Annette asked.

"My man don't say shit. Tells me he's not even sure there was a guy beat me up. Like I'd do this to myself."

Annette ticked. "You need a new man."

"You're damn straight I need a new man," Sincere agreed.

"I got some friends in the police," Annette said. "You wanna talk to them?"

"Police? Woman, you crazy?"

"Met some nice officers who helped when my face got smashed up. This one cop, Bobby, he's real nice to me when he don't have to be. Cute, too, like one of those little pug dogs. If he wasn't there, I'da been dead. This shipper guy come at me with fists like sides of beef."

"I ain't talking to no police."

"You got nothing to lose."

Sincere stepped back, shaking her head at this she-man's ignorance. "I work the streets and my man runs a pharmacy outta our apartment. I got a lot to lose. They put me in jail. I'm saving money so I can be with my daughter again. Can't do that from jail. Ain't nothing good coming out of meeting with no cops, that's for damn sure."

"So what are you gonna do? You were raped."

"Ain't gonna do nothing. Nobody gives two shits for little Sincere." She thought of that crooked cop who did business with Alonzo. "Cops is gonna say, you don't want to be raped, quit taking money for sex. Got a switchblade in my purse now, and I'm gonna keep a lookout for Sticks. I see him again, he's gonna know what it feels like to have a knife jammed up to his throat, that's for damn sure. I get done with him, he gonna look a lot worse than I look now."

"Ooh, that's a bad idea, honey," Annette said.

This phony woman didn't get it. She was going to preach at Sincere, keep yapping and blabbing until everything shifted around to her way of thinking. *You either agree with her, or she keeps the motor running*, Sincere thought. *I live with a man like this. Don't need to be friends with one too. Least my man knows he's a man.*

"You'd be better off going to Bobby," Annette continued.

"I'd be better off not talking to you," Sincere spat. She waved Annette away, like she was shooing a gnat, then turned on wobbly heels and teetered down the sidewalk, clacking sounds fading as she moved.

The sudden shift in mood caught Annette off guard. She didn't know that Sincere could anger so quickly. Watching the waif, she felt compassion for a wayward child. She was half girl, half woman, all messed up, a person who had nowhere to turn. *Still*, she thought, *that's the last time I share my bottle with you, you crazy little bitch.*

* * *

Pressure inside his loins felt like an inflating balloon. Poison accumulated inside his scrotum, filling incrementally until it

256

needed release. Since he had lived on the streets, masturbation was a last resort, a filthy and messy habit he tried to avoid. Better that the whore take his seed than fling a sticky mess into some wadded tissues. Hookers were cheap, and because he didn't mind clocking them afterward, he almost always got his money back.

Besides, nothing could stop him now.

This was his calling. It had taken him twenty-five years to discover it, but the act itself was pure euphoria. He felt untouchable. By living in the moment, he had become invincible. Let the cops find him. Stupid pigs hadn't yet. When they did, he might die, maybe even tonight. But he didn't care, because his reign would continue after death.

He had parked in the cone of darkness between two streetlights. From the shadows he watched hookers troll the sidewalks. All shapes and sizes strolled by: skinny and plump, tall and short, Hispanic, white and mudpie. These girls looked vacant, a world-weary tired expression. Life had kicked them hard, so now they went through the motions. Sure, I'll fuck you. Just give me money.

I used to be that way, he thought. *Once I was a zombie, stumbling through days without purpose. Now I am a holy man.*

He spotted one idling before a newsstand. Dressed in a cotton jumper, she had big dark eyes and a big dark gut. She was either really fat or really pregnant. Maybe both. He couldn't imagine anyone paying for her. With her flabby belly and fleshy shoulders, nothing about her was attractive.

But inside her was a little nigger just waiting to be squeezed out. This, he thought, was perfect.

The plan revealed itself instantly. Give this fat whore ten bucks, fuck the bitch to release his semen, then beat the holy hell out of her and kick her stomach until she bled. Two birds with one stone: he would experience ejaculation, and prevent another little one of them from polluting this earth.

Checking that his baseball cap was pulled low on his forehead, he started the engine and pulled up fifty feet, angling toward the curb. Rolling down the driver's side window, he called at the fat ox.

"Need a ride?"

She was smacking gum with the aggression of a chainsaw but didn't move for several seconds.

"Cost you twenty," she said lazily.

Twenty? Was this bitch serious? He wouldn't have looked at her twice if she hadn't carried a bun in her pouch.

"Ten," he countered.

"Ten?" Her voice dripped with disdain. "Go back to the barn and bang your sheep for ten. You ain't getting no piece of this chocolate for less than a Jackson."

This whore was speaking in tongues. Chocolate? Jackson? His rage bubbled, yet its only evidence was a subtle twitch along his nostrils. Why did every one of them think he was a farmer? He had never plowed a field. He lived in the city.

"Come on, momma. You and the bundle of joy could use the ten."

Get those fat ankles shuffling and get into the car.

"You might as well move it along," she drawled. "I'm trying ta work here."

They stared each other down in silence for a long five seconds. Then Joe relented and upped the offer. He knew these bitches liked to haggle, and the price they settled on would not matter. She wasn't leaving with the money.

"Fifteen," he suggested.

"See, now you just insulting me."

He kept his palms on the steering wheel and inhaled through his nose. The fat monkey would settle for fifteen, he knew that, but this stupid ritual dance that hookers always went through could be exhausting.

"It's fifteen or goodbye," he said.

"Then goodbye."

He released his foot from the brake. Before the car traveled two feet, she shouted, "Wait!"

*   *   *

When Sincere Malone got mad, clashing cymbals and echoing brass performed a private firestorm in her head. It had been this way for as long as she remembered. She didn't hear sounds around her, nor did she see or smell anything either. All senses funneled into one. She turned apoplectic with frustration.

That she-man Annette had backed her into a corner. *Call my friend Bobby. He's a cop and he'll help.* Only thing he's going to help was to put her ass in jail.

It took three blocks of speed walking before the anger began to evaporate. There was a frigid bite in the gathering wind. She had to turn her head away from its chill. She rounded a corner and adjusted a bang of hair that creased her forehead. Someone yelled, "Wait!"

A pregnant hooker who called herself Jazz stood before a storefront that peddled newspapers and smutty magazines. She pushed off the wall and her fat legs waddled toward the street.

A man wearing a John Deere cap had nudged his tan sedan to the curb. His window was rolled down, the elbow of a denim coat angled along its open frame.

Sincere felt the explosion of a head-on collision.

This was him. This was the cracker who nearly killed her.

Reflexively, her throat grew tight. Antennae raised along her neck. She stepped back, hoping to blend into the night. Plunging a tiny hand into her purse, she shifted aside makeup and cigarettes, then pried her fingers under the false bottom and cupped the switchblade into her palm.

Ain't calling no Bobby. Gonna teach this motherfucker a lesson. Reclaiming my life starts now.

She snapped open the blade, the force of its thwack lending comfort. The symphony of anger stirred again. She released a primal howl and started running.

*   *   *

The fat bitch had taken the money and loped around the hood of his car with the urgency of a lazy elephant.

Blood coursed through him. He was fully erect now, mouth dry with anticipation. His temples pounded. He yearned for sweet release and thought about how afterward, in just a few minutes, he would punch this oversized mouth, throw her on the ground and stomp her big fat gut with his boots. There would be one less little nigger in the world.

Fleetingly, he wondered how to incorporate this into the tattoo. If he snuffed a fetus, should he get ink for half a chef's hat? He moistened his lips while her jelly belly bounced.

A wounded wail pierced the night.

On the sidewalk, a tiny elf was staggering in five-inch heels, trying to run toward him, knife extended before her like a signal flare. She was awkward and uncoordinated, making slow progress. Ankles folded crookedly against themselves, so she didn't sprint as much as hop. What she lacked in athleticism, however, she compensated with spirit. Her dark face was angry and intense.

She had started screaming from fifty yards away. Joe's car was running, but the fat pregnant hooker bitch had stopped to watch the commotion.

"Get in, get in, get in," he shouted to the far side, but she just stood there, slack jawed, observing the spectacle.

There was no time to think.

When she was ten feet away he gunned the gas pedal, running over the fat hooker's foot. He hated to leave, but it was impulse, simple fight or flight. What else could he do? The engine drowned out the screams of two whores. Anyone within earshot must have been aghast.

Two blocks away, his hands were so tight on the steering wheel that he couldn't feel his fingers. Who was that little cunt, and why was she so intent on cutting him? What had he ever done to her?

The immediate rage was missing out on the pregnant hooker. He needed the release, plus it was a one-time chance to abort a little monkey. Should he circle back and try to find her?

Motherfucker. That opportunity is gone.

The capper was that she had taken his fifteen dollars.

Chapter 24

"In your down time, study maps of the city," George Pope told Bobby Bennett. "Just from living here you know the main roads already, but now start learning the side streets, where things intersect, which directions are one-way. When we're in the car, you pay attention to the signs we pass."

I can read a map, Bennett thought. *Why should I have to memorize it?*

"The extra fifteen or twenty seconds it takes you to unfold a map might make the difference between somebody living or dying," Pope said, as if reading his young partner's thoughts. "You get a call, you don't waste time running your fingers along the grid of letters and numbers."

"Okay," Bennett said, looking beyond Pope with an elastic voice that was far away. Pope recognized that he hadn't taken the message seriously, and clenched his jaw in silence. *From the afterlife you owe me a big one, Mac*, he thought. *This kid of yours is a pig-headed, stubborn little prick. It's awfully hard to teach a twenty-five year-old who thinks he knows everything.*

They drove in silence for a time, Pope's window open to absorb neighborhood sounds. His eyes were constantly on the move, scanning people and porches and yards they passed.

From the passenger's seat, Bobby leaned his cheek against a hand, gazing out at the night, drumming his foot absently against the floormat. He reflected on the conversation with Mark earlier that day. This fat irascible old man sitting next to him had once been a young turk who partnered with his father. Pope had actually cradled Bobby when he was a newborn. Sometimes, Bobby thought, these lost years were too much.

Pope broke the silence. "What street did we just pass?"

"Huh?"

"What was the name of the street we just passed?"

Bennett pivoted in his seat and squinted through the rear glass. "Why, don't you know?" he wondered.

"Yeah, I know. I want to see if you're paying attention."

"I'm paying attention."

"Good. Then tell me the name of that street."

Bennett exhaled. *Would this zealot ever let up, just rest for a moment?* "I don't frigging know."

Pope nodded sagely and plunged his arm between their seats. He came up with Bobby's nightstick and tossed it out the window, where it twisted end over end like a boomerang before clattering against asphalt.

"What the hell?" Bobby spat.

Pope drove two more blocks in silence, then pulled to the curb.

"Walk back and get your nightstick," he said. "And while you're there, find out the name of that street we passed the block before."

Bobby's cheeks burned with humiliation. "Are you kidding me? Are you fucking crazy?"

Pope glowered at him. "I'm gonna teach you this job, whether you like it or not. No coddling. I got too much respect for your family to let you get lazy. If you're this careless as a rookie, you're either gonna turn into a bad cop or get shot before you're thirty. Neither is something I want any part of. So get off your ass and go!"

Bennett exhaled with disdain, but got out of the car, leaving the door open as he trudged away. Pope watched in the rearview mirror as the young man stormed off with determination, head tucked low. It took four minutes before he returned, boiling with restrained anger.

"You ever do that again," Bennett threatened, "I'm gonna retrieve that nightstick, walk back to the car and swing it at your head."

Pope's expression didn't change, but inside his heart danced. He hesitated long enough to be sure his voice remained even. He turned his wide eye in Bobby's direction, and said in a whispered voice, "Kid, that'd be the worst mistake of your life. I'm old enough to be your pop, but I didn't last twenty-six years on the streets being soft. You talk like that to me again and I might just have to kick your ass, because you aren't listening to a damn thing I say."

The radio squawked before Bobby spoke: report of a domestic disturbance five blocks away. Pope had the car moving before Bennett latched his door.

*   *   *

It was windy as Bobby Bennett climbed the outside stairwell, pausing at the top landing, shielding the reflected glare with cupped hands as he peered through the window. Living room curtains on the opposite side were closed. Hunched over, eyes adjusting to dimness, he saw the apartment had black jungle themed wallpaper with twisting velvet vines. TV tables were overturned and an array of chips and cheetos scattered across the floor and leopard print sofa.

The breeze drowned out any sounds that might be heard inside. Before he could knock, a large black man materialized and threw open the door.

"Help you?"

There was a gash in his temple and a crepe of blood caked along his cheek. His breath sounded like a deep whistle.

Bennett stepped back on the porch and laid a hand to his baton. This guy was built like cement blocks. Two stories up, the last thing he needed was to be pushed off the porch. Pope had instructed him to wait while the car was parked, but screw that know-it-all. Bobby rushed upstairs, concerned someone's safety might be in jeopardy.

"We had a call that there was some fighting going on here," he said. "Sir, are you okay?"

"Who the fuck called? That nosy bitch next door?" His gaze went past Bennett to the tall narrow house whose walls were only a few feet away. A high watt bulb illuminated the doorframe. Over the banister was draped a brown t-shirt. Its sleeves flapped against the wooden rail, making a rhythmic thwack. "Whatchu getting into our business for?" he yelled. "Ain't none of this concern you!"

"Sir, sir, look at me," Bennett ordered, waiting for the big man's attention to return. "Take a breath and stay calm. Who else is in this house with you?"

On command, he inhaled deeply, but his words remained sharp. "My pain in the ass girlfriend. Comes home ragging, then when I tell her shut up she swings a frying pan at my head." He aimed a finger toward his wound. "You believe this? Cast iron collided with my skull. Sounded like a wrecking ball on a rock pile."

"What's her name?"

"Who?"

"Your girlfriend."

"My pain in the ass girlfriend?" he asked, as if to eliminate confusion stemming from other possible girlfriends. "Her name is Sincere."

"And yours?"

"Alonzo."

Bobby nodded and waited a beat. "Okay, Alonzo. I need you to remain calm. Can you do that for me?"

Another beat passed. "Yeah."

"We gonna have any trouble here?" Bobby wondered.

The man let out a sigh and his shoulders slumped. Pulling the door closed behind him, he stepped onto the wooden landing, facing the wind. His voice fell to passive. "Naw. I'm just steamed, is all."

"Where is Sincere now?"

"Locked herself in the bathroom. She's afraid I'm gonna beat her ass, but you look at this" — again he pointed to the gash in his face — "and tell me I'm the one ought to be afraid of her."

"Did you strike her?"

"Hell no. I don't hit women. Didn't go to Nam cause I'm a pacifist."

Pope's shoes clomped on the wooden stairs, and both men turned to the sound. His wide body climbed steadily, but Bennett would have preferred if he bounded up. His partner, he feared, was too old and slow for the job. It had taken a good minute for him to park the car and follow. Pope paused on a step below the landing, exhaling in strained bursts. In spite of the cold, droplets of sweat beaded against his neck. His eyes were glued to the black man.

"Officer, this is Alonzo," Bobby explained. "He and his girlfriend had a little domestic, but he's calm now and she's locked herself in the bathroom. There doesn't appear to be any danger."

Without looking at him, Pope aimed his comment at Bobby. "No danger? His face is a bloody pulp."

"No immediate danger," Bobby amended. "Different story five minutes ago, but everybody's calm now, right?"

"It smarts, I'm not gonna lie," Alonzo conceded. "But the worst is over."

Pope ascended the final step to the platform.

"Alonzo, why don't you step down to the foot of the stairs with Officer Bennett and I'll go and speak to the lady. What did you say her name was?"

"Her name is Sincere," Bobby said.

Alonzo's muscles tensed and eyes turned hard. "There is no call for you to enter this apartment," he said with an edgy baritone. He leaned back, blocking the door with his bulk. With those words, a sudden tension erupted between the three men. Everyone's senses heightened; shoulders flexed rigid. Suspicion crowded their space.

"We had a report of violence and we need to be sure your lady is okay."

"She is okay," Alonzo pivoted his neck, shielding the battered side of his face. Narrowed eyes watched the cops. "I'm telling you."

"And we need to confirm that."

"I do not give you permission to enter this apartment."

"That's not really an option for you, sir," Pope said.

There's a reason he doesn't want us inside, Pope thought. *Maybe the girl is dead. Or there are guns or drugs.* Alonzo used his rear to push open the door and stepped back, thrusting palms into his bathrobe pockets. Pope's sixth sense triggered. Without forethought, he lobbed himself through the threshold and wrapped his own thick hands around the black man's wrists.

Grunts and yells exploded in firebursts.

"Keep your hands where we can see them!"

"What the fuck? Get offa me!"

"Hands out! Get down! Get down!"

When his wrists wriggled away, Pope wrapped arms around Alzono's torso, restraining any movement. Bennett, following his partner's lead, surged through the doorway like a linebacker, knocking the men over. All three tumbled to the floor.

"Stay down!"

With a fluid motion spanning two seconds, Pope disentangled himself, removed handcuffs from his belt and strapped Alonzo's hands behind him. The big man lolled on the floor, rolling with the confusion of a tranquilized bear. Pope, breathing heavily, got to one knee, surveyed the apartment, then stood and stepped back. To his left was the kitchen. Behind him was the hallway to the bedrooms. Alonzo appeared stunned by his sudden change in fortune. After a moment to realize his fate, he settled reluctantly into laziness.

"What the fuck was that?" Bobby asked, standing and brushing cheetos dust from the chest of his uniform.

"Bad feeling," Pope explained, neck tense from the scuffle. "He made for the door and plunged those hands in his pockets. I didn't want to be staring down the barrel of a pistol."

"Holy shit, you could have fucking warned me," Bobby said with annoyance, shaking out his arms.

Pope aimed a finger at his partner. "You should have waited until I got here. You don't rush up and question somebody on your own. What in God's name did you learn at the academy?" He leaned down and frisked Alonzo's terrycloth robe. The hem stopped at the knees, revealing freckled legs. Pope ran the backs of his hands over Alonzo's thighs to ensure no weapons were concealed there. "If he pulled a gun when you came up here alone, I'd be arranging your funeral right now."

"Ain't got no gun," Alonzo protested from the floor.

"But we didn't know that, did we?" He looked at Bobby. "You see a suspect go for his pockets, you assume there's a weapon. Control the situation or you won't last—"

From out of the jungle vines came a banshee's wail. Pope pivoted, expecting to see a howler monkey swinging across the living room. Without warning, his torso lurched and he slammed against the wall. Off balance, he collapsed, skull thwacking the baseboard. A bolt of adrenaline dilated Pope's pupils. Bobby, a ball of muscles, pressed his forearms atop Pope's shoulders. As he turned away, his heel caught the veteran's knee, sending a surge of pain up his leg.

Pope's mind raced, draped in disbelief. His little shit rookie partner had just lunged at him because Pope called him out for procedure.

The old cop surged forward, fists balled and stretching toward Bobby's head. Half his age or not, Mac's boy notwithstanding, he would not tolerate this. The kid was out of control, borderline incompetent, and should be removed from duty. But first he deserved an ass kicking. Sprawled on his back, Pope's punch didn't connect, but he cocked his arm again, stopping only when he recognized Bobby was not alone.

Having turned and sprung to his feet with agility, Bennett was crouched, wrestling with a black girl whose shrieks rose above the wind, lending an evil air. The waif wiggled a carving knife before her like a flamethrower, thrusting it toward Bennett. Her screams contracted Pope's muscles. He rolled away from their scuffle and scrambled to stand.

Between her bursts, Alonzo turned aggressive too, struggling against his restraints. "You crazy fucking bitch," he yelled from the floor, "what are you doing?"

Her wails were punctured with a shout. "Fuck you, Lonzo!"

"You dumb ass bitch!" he countered.

Pope steadied himself and unholstered his gun, but their space was too narrow to aim effectively. Bennett and the girl spiraled around, Bobby shifting toward the far wall to place her between the two cops. For a moment, Pope had a clear shooting lane, but if he missed, his partner would be wounded.

"Hey!" Pope yelled.

The girl turned at the sudden clap of sound. With a frenzied look, their eyes met. She waved the knife wildly, unconcerned with the gun barrel aimed at her chest. Before Pope could pull the trigger, Bobby's forearms collapsed around her knees, tackling her from behind. As they dropped to the floor, the knife skittered away. Her face thudded inches from Pope's toe. She lifted her jaw and buried teeth into his ankle. Her wailing stopped, but a new sound of pain filled the room.

"Son of a bitch!" he cried.

"Sincere, you fucking whore!" Alonzo threatened. "You're gonna get us killed!"

Pope shook his leg loose, shin cracking the girl's jaw. "Cuff her! Cuff her!" he ordered, struggling to press his sole against the top of her bobbing head. "My cuffs are on the guy!"

The girl slithered like a constrictor, kicking at Bennett with her lower half, lunging towards Pope with her torso.

He leaped backwards but a wall hindered his movement. She bared fangs again and stretched for his leg.

Do it, Pope thought. Harking back to his days of high school football, he imagined her twisted face on a kicking tee, and kept focus on her mouth. Flicking his leg forward, he connected solidly with Sincere's jaw. Shoe collided with bone, freezing her movements. Blood erupted and Pope saw a tooth tinkle to the carpet. Lacking the fluidity Pope had exhibited on Alonzo, Bennett grabbed Sincere's wrists, crossed them behind her back and locked them into handcuffs. Only then did the veteran lower his gun.

Pope and Bennett paused in the living room, strained from exertion. Sincere's raw energy swirled away. Screams gave way to a vortex of sobs. She rolled like a bloody sausage, making no effort to stand. Alonzo bounced his bulk toward the cops, affording her extra space.

Bent at the waist, Bennett's face contorted as he inhaled. He wiped perspiration from his pock-marked cheeks, looking toward his partner, where Pope caressed his ankle. No one spoke for what seemed like a long time.

Sincere's crying gradually ebbed, and she asked, "You gonna let Alonzo go? You two working with that other cop?"

"Let him go?" Pope wondered.

"Shut the fuck up, Sincere," Alonzo said calmly.

"You ain't with that one what came here yesterday? The Nazi who got an arrangement with Alonzo, he told me I deserved to get hit cause I turned tricks. Well fuck that. Ain't nobody deserve the kind of beatin' I got. That fucking cracker is still on the street! Saw him an hour ago."

"What is she talking about?" Pope asked. "You have an arrangement with a cop? What does that mean?"

"Don't listen to her," Alonzo cautioned. "She's probably high."

Realization dawned on Sincere. "Now you done, Lonzo. These two ain't crooked. They gonna find your shit." She sniffled, then tears gave way to determination. "He got drugs in the other room, officers. He a big time dealer." She dragged out the last three words. "Won't even stand up for his woman when she gets her ass kicked by a stranger."

"You stupid bitch," he sighed, then looked up at Bennett. "You see what I'm dealing with? My pain in the ass girlfriend." He turned back to Sincere. "Cause of you, we're both going to jail."

"Jail be nicer than this place," Sincere screeched. "What I got to lose? I get beat up working the streets. My mouth is bloody, all because you trying to protect your stash. Look over there. You see my teeth lying there? We done, Lonzo. Can't live like this no more." Altering her tone to address the officers, she said, "I got lotsa things to tell you guys about. You offer me a deal and I can get you at least one arrest. You won't even have to leave the station."

*   *   *

Alison lay on her back, feet dangling over the bed's side, hair fanned into a pillow behind her. She raised her legs to

271

Mark's waist, pressing the pads of her feet against his rough skin.

Mark stood, resting hands on her hips. Despite the chill on his shoulders, his short hair felt thick with sweat. The scent of her skin filled the room like a vanilla candle. Every nerve tingled with anticipation.

Sliding palms up her curves until they ran flat over her stomach, he felt the convex belly button, continuing to the soft flesh of her breasts.

She folded her lower lip between teeth, eyes closed, rocking her head back, exhaling a soft sigh. Flattening soles against the mattress, her back arched into a bridge and she elevated hips to meet his loins.

Their muscles tensed, skin grew tight. Mark and Alison slithered together and locked, both grunting primal sounds of release.

Blood coursed into his temples; sound waves crashed around him. He concentrated fully on the here and now. All of history funneled into this moment. Time held no bearing. Only touch mattered.

Moments after their climax, he collapsed onto the bed. Mark's phone rang. He leaned toward the nightstand and raised the receiver.

Without greeting, George Pope said, "We got a black pross in the interview room who's a real devil. Swings a skillet at her live-in, came at me and your brother with a knife and is a three-quarters of a whack job. It's taken an hour, but she's calming down now."

"Okay," Mark answered neutrally.

"You should've seen this little vamp. Took a chomp out of my ankle. Had to kick her in the teeth just to get her off me. I'm not feeling real good about that, but what are you going to do, am I right?"

Light from the living room traveled down the hallway, lending a dimness to the darkened bedroom. Alison shifted onto her side, brushed a wisp of hair off her eyebrows, and exhaled, laying a hand on his shoulder.

"Why are you telling me this, George?"

"Oh, right," Pope said, as if he had forgotten the purpose of his call. "She says she was beat up a few nights ago by some hillbilly. Guy told her he threw a nigger off the top of city hall that afternoon. That's the word he used, nigger, along with some other unkind racial shit. Normally I don't put much stock in crazy hookers, but I tend to believe this broad."

"I'll be right there," Bennett said.

"You want me to call Connell?" Pope asked.

"No," he said, looking at Alison. "Not even a little."

*   *   *

Fifteen minutes later he entered the neighboring precinct house, climbing stairs two at a time until he reached the third floor. Bobby stood in the tiled hallway, acknowledging his brother with raised eyebrows.

"Hell, Marky, you look like you fell off a hayride."

Mark ignored him. "Where's this witness?"

"Being interviewed. Pope is watching from the observation room," Bobby said, crooking a thumb at a door behind him. "Wants me to brief you before you head in."

His brother's uniform was disheveled. Wrinkles and a loose tuck of the shirt suggested he had logged a long, eventful shift. Bobby was jittery, moving his hands as he spoke.

"What do you have?" Mark asked.

Bobby's fingers absently drummed against his hip. "Get a call on a domestic when this crazy fucking pross comes at me and Pope with a carving knife. We just reacted. I'm a little jazzed now, but when it happened I didn't even have time to shit my pants. We disarm her, link her up, and next thing she's singing like a canary. Her story is some john attacked her the other night, beat the hell out of her and said he did another black dame at city hall that day. She's got some pretty deep bruises. Had the shit kicked out of her all right."

Bobby blinked to calm dilated pupils and contorted his mouth unnaturally, stretching his lips. A plum-colored scratch rose along his neck.

"Yeah, Pope told me most of that," Mark said. "Hey, you okay?"

"Yeah, it's the end of my shift. I'm just wired is all," Bobby ran a hand over his forehead. "I'm telling you Marky, that was some action. This pross was swinging at me with a knife and biting Pope's ankle at the same time. I tackled her and he used her head like a soccer ball before we got control."

"Who's she talking to?"

"Ashford. We let her chill out for a half hour. Figured either of us might not get complete cooperation after Pope knocked out her teeth."

"Sounds like it was knock-down drag-out," Mark said.

"The old adrenaline kicked in, no question," A grin curled the edges of Bobby's lips, and his wink hinted of conspiracy. "Lucky thing I got experience in street fights."

Mark wondered if this was an apology for the other night. It was more likely that smashing bodies invigorated his brother.

"Come on, let me get a look at her."

The Bennetts entered the cramped observation room, where Pope leaned against a wall with arms crossed and watched through the one-way mirror. He raised his chin at Mark, muttering, "You're not gonna believe this," then turned back to the interview beyond the glass.

"Miss Malone, these are very serious allegations you're making," said a lumpy middle-aged detective in a shirt and tie.

"Think I don't know that? I'm telling the truth."

"And what was the cop's name?"

"Don't know the cop's name. Lonzo said his code name was Angel. He came to the house yesterday and his nametag started with a B. Battlefield or something."

"And he and Alonzo had a business arrangement?"

"Lonzo gave him dope, and he used some and sold the rest. If the narcotics cops started getting too close to Lonzo, he was gonna get a heads up call, like a warning to dump his stash."

The detective loosened his tie and turned to the mirror. Although he could not see Pope or the Bennetts, he gazed at them as if he could, a subtle headshake suggesting disbelief and wonder.

"And you could identify this officer if you saw him?"

"Hell yeah. Called me a stupid bitch. He was ready to slap me, but Lonzo stepped between us. Cop was mean to the core, you could see it in his eyes. Told me that I shouldn't complain about getting the shit kicked out of me because that's what happens when a girl works the streets. Like I deserved it or something. Said he needed a boost cause he was working a long shift."

Mark leaned toward his brother, whispering, "She's talking about Battaglia. Bastard was so damn dumb he used *Angel* as a code name. You understand why I wanted you to stay away from that scumbag?"

Bobby's expression remained stoic. Mark wondered how much of this his brother had known. Bobby was headstrong and a pain in the ass, but he wouldn't knowingly consort with a crooked cop, would he?

"And this isn't you just making up a story to get back at an officer you don't like, is it?" Ashford asked.

"Hell no," Sincere said calmly. "This is the real deal. On my daughter's life, I swear."

"I guess I'm going to have to call internal affairs," Ashford sighed. His shoulders rounded with reluctance. "Let them sort it out."

"Call whoever you need to," Sincere said. "I'll make a statement. I'm telling you, officer, these past few days have been like a wake up alarm. I gotta make some serious life changes. My daughter lives with my moms, and I ain't hardly ever seeing her. That's gotta change. Gotta quit Alozno, quit the drugs. And I sure as hell gotta quit working the streets. Cold out when the sun goes down. Get a chill up my cooch. This getting beat up mighta been the best thing that happened to me. Time to reclaim my life."

"Glad to hear it," Ashford said without enthusiasm. As he stood, a double chin sagged with regret. "I have to say, Miss Malone, I don't like busting other cops. Gives me a headache right here at the base of my brain." He pointed to scruff on his neck. "Let me get IA in here."

As Ashford emerged from the interview room, Mark left his cramped quarters and stepped into the hallway. He thrust a hand forward and introduced himself. The older man's face flashed recognition at Bennett's name, then dipped back to downtrodden.

"Yeah, Bennett. I knew your dad. We miss him."

"Thanks, me too. Listen, I only saw the end of your interview, so I don't know how much of this you covered, but before you call internal affairs, can I get a few minutes with her? Need to talk about this john that beat her up the other night. I'm working that city hall flier case and this guy might be involved."

"Yeah, you're working with Connell. How about that broad landing on a flagpole? Million to one odds, right?"

"Million to one is probably generous."

"Right." Ashford nodded gratefully, anxious for any delay to speak with internal affairs. "Yeah, go on in and chat with her. Let me know when you're done and I'll make the call." He massaged his own neck and shoulders. "Hell. When someone in cuffs accuses a cop of breaking the law, I'm usually pretty leery, but this one feels like she's telling the truth. Somebody's career is about to swirl down the shitter."

Just a matter of time with Battaglia, Bennett thought.

Ashford shuffled away, and Bennett took a deep breath before opening the door and entering the tiled room. Sincere looked up without changing expression.

"That was fast. You musta been right outside."

"I was."

"What's your name?"

"Detective Bennett."

"So if I talk to you about a wrong cop, I got any guarantees he gets off the street? Don't need him to come looking for me."

Bennett pulled a chair from under the table and sat opposite the girl. Her doe eyes were swollen, rimmed with purple bruises. Her skin had a leathery scent to it, like it had been used often and re-stretched over tiny bones. When she spoke, a gap was evident in a row of teeth.

"Actually, I'm not from internal affairs. I'm working on a case where a black woman fell from the top of city hall on Monday. There's some question whether she jumped or it was foul play. I think you met a man who might be involved."

"Oh... you want me to tell you 'bout my customer. You putting two and two together, thinking ahead like Sherlock Holmes. Cause Lonzo and that other cop thought I was making shit up. Dumb asses figured I got beat up by a ghost."

Bennett waited with sympathy.

"I'm pretty valuable to this department," Sincere continued with a note of pride. "Got internal affairs wanting to talk wit me, got you wanting to talk wit me. I'm the information queen."

"You're sitting in the catbird seat."

"Sittin' where?"

Bennett waved a dismissive hand. "Never mind."

"Can tell you stuff, yes sir. Saw the dude again tonight."

Bennett's neck straightened. "What's that?"

"What?"

"You saw the guy tonight?"

"Hell yeah. That's what started my temper. He was sittin'
in a car, picking up another girl. I came at him wit my knife, but
he saw me then screeched the tires and peeled away. Damn
smart of him cause I was gonna cut that motherfucker good."

Flipping open a notebook, Bennett's excitement grew. He
wrote the hooker's name at the top, added the date, then glanced
at the wall clock to record the time. *Calm yourself*, he thought.
*You've had other witnesses who have seen the guy too. None of
them led to results.* Still, this one felt different. There was
promise in Sincere's knowledge.

The tiny girl ran a tongue over her missing teeth while he
wrote. "Bennett. That was the other cop's name, the young
muscle guy."

"He's my kid brother."

"I see. So this job like a family affair. But you don't look
like him. My question to you, big brother, is what is Sincere
getting outta this? Cause I don't need to do no jail time. You
got a little brother and you look after him, right?"

"I try."

"Well, I got me a baby girl who lives with my moms. She
needs some looking after. Can't do that from jail."

"Well, Sincere, you did attack two cops."

"I wigged out a little, I admit that. But I was fed up wit
Lonzo. That was anger at him. Once I realized everything that
was going on, I cooperated fully with them guys. You ask your
brother. Told them all 'bout Lonzo's stash and the bad cop.
Now I'm willin' to tell you 'bout this cracker what beat me up.
All valuable information."

"That's true. So far, you've been very helpful. Let's
continue on that track."

"Be happy to if we take the jail time off the table."

"That's a call for the district attorney, Sincere. All I can do is lobby on your behalf. See, if I vouch that you've been assisting in our investigations, that works to your favor. By helping me, you're helping yourself." Bennett paused, hoping she would agree with his logic. "So tell me about this john."

"First I need some guarantees," she insisted.

Bennett paused and met her gaze. "Guarantees are going to be tough. All I can do right now is promise I'll work with you and make sure you're comfortable. In fact, you want a coke?"

Sincere leaned back and studied him. She had not expected such an offer. She knew the way these cops worked. Just take, take, take. Exhaling, she said, "Yeah, soft drink would be nice. Cigarette too. Calm my nerves."

Bennett nodded then stood. "I'll be back with both of those in a few minutes."

As Bennett stepped into the hall, pulling the handle shut behind him, the door to the observation room opened.

Although Pope was calm as he watched through the one-way mirror, now he appeared shaken, a delayed reaction from the confrontation in Alonzo's apartment. His smaller eye squinted to a narrow slit. Nostrils flared and his cheeks blushed red with restraint. He aimed a finger at Bennett.

"She's gonna try to squeeze you, Marky."

Bennett recognized the situation. He was walking a tightrope here, because he needed information from the girl. Pope was more concerned with vengeance.

"Watch me blanket her with kindness," Bennett said softly. "I'm betting she doesn't know how to respond when a man is actually polite to her."

"Keep in mind this little whore was waving a knife at me and Bobby two hours ago. I'm not crazy about you giving her the presidential treatment in there."

"I know," he answered. "But you taught me this technique. Soften her up so she'll talk."

Pope scowled, bent his leg at the knee, and reached toward his sock. "Want me to show you her dental imprints in my ankle? I gotta ride over to Buffalo General now and get a tetanus shot."

The young detective hesitated. "You prefer I slide on leather gloves and beat the hell out of her? I'm not Ken Connell."

Pope said nothing.

"This is a good lead and I've got to follow it. There was another killing today. We've got to make sure there's not another. I know what she did to you is serious, but you need to trust me on this one. I'm not going to forget about you. Right now we've got five murder victims and at least one assault."

Pope hesitated, exhaling a burst of air. "You're getting played," he said, then shook his head and stormed away.

Bennett watched him go, and questioned whether he was doing the right thing. *Stay focused*, he told himself. *Believe in your approach*. He waited for a moment, tugging his coat sleeves, then found a nook of vending machines at the end of the hall. He fished into his pocket for change and fed quarters through the slots, pulling the handle for a pack of Malboros and, at the adjacent machine, a can of cola. Both tumbled to the bottom trays.

No DA was going to let her walk after she attacked two cops. Bennett preferred not to lie to her, but he would if it was the only way to secure her cooperation. Was this hooker smart enough to recognize the situation? He needed Sincere far more than she needed him.

When he returned to the interview room, he laid the cardboard box in front of her, and like a host, pulled the tab off the aluminum can, tossing its curl into the corner. He smiled, asked if there was anything else she wanted. She took a long swig of pop, then used a thumbnail to split open the pack of cigarettes. She tapped one out and deftly moved it between her lips. Bennett fished into his jacket pocket for a matchbook, sliding it across the table. As Sincere struck a flame, both hands of the wall clock stood straight up.

As Saturday night gave way to Sunday morning, Sincere Malone began to tell her story.

Chapter 25

"White guy, stringy brown hair covered by a baseball cap, dark eyes, a patchy beard," Mark Bennett explained. "Mid to late twenties. No height estimate, because she never saw him standing. He had wiry arms and stubby, powerful fingers. He also had revolting breath. Drove a tan sedan, but Sincere wasn't sure of the model."

"What was he wearing?" the chief asked.

"Jeans and a plaid shirt. She noticed him scouting her from his car. Parked across the street with binoculars trained on her before making contact. There was another hooker with her, a transvestite who goes by the name Annette. Annette approached the car first, but our guy asked for Sincere. That's one of the reasons she charged extra, because she knew he specifically wanted her."

"He ask for her by name?"

Bennett paused. "I'm not sure, but Sincere had never seen him before."

His interview with the girl had stretched deep into the night. Afterward, Mark had phoned the chief, waking him at three a.m. Even in the empty hours, the boss' tone remained gruff and no-nonsense. *Would this new information*, he asked, *help prevent tomorrow's murder?* The men agreed to meet first thing in the morning. Mark had driven home, mind racing from the interview. He eased silently into bed. Alison turned over, laying a palm against his shoulder, but did not wake. He was too invigorated to sleep. It was still dark when he rose to shower.

By seven-thirty, he was back on the job, sitting in the chair opposite the chief's desk.

"So this john talked about the city hall flier?" the chief wondered.

"Right. He raped Sincere, beat the shit out of her and held a knife to her throat. When she begged for her life, he backed down. She watched the struggle in his eyes, like he wanted to cut her but was having conscience pangs. He mentioned city hall, and said, *I already met my quota for dead niggers today.* Then he shoved her out of the car."

Footsteps sounded from down the hall. Early Sunday morning, the squad was empty except for Bennett and the chief. Connell entered holding two Styrofoam cups. He set them on Lenehan's vacant desk, removed his jacket and tossed it toward his own chair, then stacked the cups and entered the chief's office, laying one of the drinks on the chief's desk blotter.

"Thanks," the boss said absently, perforating the slatted top.

"So some hooker saw our guy last night, huh?" Connell asked.

If the chief noticed Connell's slight toward his fellow detective, he did not acknowledge it. His attention focused on the open file in front of him. Absently, he blew toward rising tufts of steam.

"Yeah. Pulled out a switchblade and charged his car. He drove away, and she was pretty upset. I'm guessing that's what triggered the fights. She got into it with her boyfriend then with my brother and his partner. At that point she was probably psychotic."

Connell stiffened at the mention of Mark's brother. *That two-timing fucker.* A new angle sprang into the veteran's head, and he swallowed to conceal anticipation. *Jesus, it's almost too perfect*, he thought. *Get me on a case with Bobby Bennett. Then I can really probe the little rat.* Was it possible? He knew from Vietnam that sometimes guys got caught in friendly crossfire.

"Try to locate the she-man, Annette," the chief ordered. "Get him in here for an interview."

"Yeah, about that," Bennett said. "Bobby and Pope just signed up an informant this week named Annette who's a cross-dresser. It's gotta be the same person, so they're going to pick her up."

"Good," the chief said. He leaned back and slurped the coffee. "Do you say her or him?"

"What?"

"The she-man. Which pronoun do you use?" The chief compressed his lips like he was trying to squeeze away discomfort.

Bennett shrugged. "Her, I guess."

"Connell?"

Connell's mind was churning. He wondered if he could kill a fellow cop and make it look like an accident. Did he possess capacity for deception at that level? Could he take another life over a personal dispute? His expression didn't change. "Fuck if I know."

"It's a crazy world, kids, when you don't know if you're dealing with a guy or a girl. What are the odds that Sincere's making this up?"

"I don't think she is," Bennett said, running a thumb along the edge of his nose. "I had her go over the story a few times, and the details didn't change. The guy matches the description other witnesses gave in the street stabbings."

"Okay. Let's talk about the river killing yesterday. Any leads?"

"No," Bennett admitted. "We canvassed for hours walking upriver. Nobody saw anything and there wasn't any sign of a struggle."

"No way to even tell where the body entered the water," Connell agreed. He sipped from his coffee and laid the cup on the chief's desk.

"This guy is just brazen. Kills in the middle of the day, and nobody sees him."

"Nobody saw him this time," Bennett said. "But really, he doesn't care if it's public or not. We've had witnesses, but they haven't led us any closer."

"This hooker coming forward is a break," the chief said. "Opens up a whole new avenue. Now we know he's banging prostitutes. Odds are this Sincere wasn't his first time. That means other girls may have seen him up close, even spoken with him."

"Let's get a sketch artist to the Holding Center this morning to meet with this angry little pross," Connell said. "Sooner the better."

"Right," the chief agreed. "Get those sketches, make copies, and coordinate with Sex Offense. Tonight we get out there, work the corners, find hookers who know this guy. Tomorrow we show it around city hall. Somebody's got to recognize this asshole. So far we've been getting little breadcrumbs. This could turn into a whole slice."

"While we do that, how about we stakeout Chippewa?" Bennett suggested. "If the dude didn't get a piece of ass last night, he might show up tonight figuring he's due."

"After sundown," the chief nodded. "We'll put a couple extra cars there and hope for the best."

"I can rattle some cages in the meantime," Connell said. "I know a few hookers I can reach out to."

I'll bet you do, Bennett thought.

"I give them a good description," Connell continued, "you never know."

"Not sure how far you'll get without the sketch," the chief said. "Right now that description is too vague. Three quarters of the johns that get busted are white guys wearing baseball caps. I'd wait until you have something to show these girls."

"Besides, good luck finding a hooker who's awake at this hour," Bennett said.

The chief closed the three-ring binder and passed it over the edge of his blotter, where it laid on the desk's edge between the two men.

"I'm tired of this case," he said. "Tired of the bodies piling up. I'll get a good night's sleep if we can stop him today. We're close."

"Yeah, today's the day," Bennett said, reaching for the file. The plastic binder was two inches thick, filled with a week's accumulation of reports and paperwork. While grabbing the folder, he nudged the coffee cup, where it teetered then tumbled into Connell's lap. The plastic top loosened from its snug.

Connell leaped, a brown stain splattering his lap and legs in an inkblot pattern.

"Son of a bitch," he cursed, shaking droplets from his pleats. "These were freshly laundered. What the fuck, Bennett?"

"Whoops," Bennett said, stretching his mouth into repentance. "Didn't mean to do that. Look at the good news: it didn't hit the chief's desk. File didn't get wet either. I'd offer you my coffee as a replacement, but you didn't bring me one."

*   *   *

Joe's calves felt like someone twisted a tourniquet around his thighs. The new tattoo, a fifth matching chef's hat, had scalded his skin, and now itched like invisible fire. His stomach was swollen, neck muscles tight. He wondered if he had contracted a sudden infection. Could that fat hippie have forgotten to sterilize the needles?

The crusade needed to continue, but he could not muster the energy to raise himself from the couch. So he lay in his underwear and t-shirt, slipping in and out of consciousness, mouth falling open as his head toppled to the side. Cushions were scratchy against his cheeks and arms. He imagined the smooth, cool feeling of a freshly laundered sheet unfurled beneath him. But the act of getting up, shuffling to the closet and back, tucking in the edges... it was all too daunting.

He wished he had a mother, or a wife who loved him. Either would be skilled in pampering, nurturing him through these black holes that slammed without warning. He yearned for a tender touch to soothe his aching muscles, the proper mix of gentleness and compassion.

This might have all turned out differently, he thought, *if a woman had cared for me.*

But that kind of thinking was weak, and he scolded himself. No point crying over things he never had. Those bozos on TV with their mansions and nice clothes, pretty women and new cars, oil fields and pastures and weekly drama. None of that was anything similar to the life he knew. Loneliness and poverty filled his days. Still, he was thankful for things that did come his way, like his father's love.

If his father was here, there would be a blanket draped over him, a thick calloused hand to smooth hair back from his forehead. If only he could smell that musky scent, hear the footfalls of work boots tromping across the living room floor.

"Dad?" he said out loud. "Dad?"

Sightlines spun away in a vortex; vision turned cloudy. Furniture and discarded food wrappers filled the floor, but they existed in a faraway dimension, concealed behind a growing opaque haze.

He wanted to do a killing today to keep the streak alive, but time was skipping like a rock over water. Hours passed in a heartbeat, and soon it would grow dark.

Later, he told himself. *I'll feel better later.*

*   *   *

287

Mark Bennett spent the morning calling volunteer artists. Three were used regularly by the department. The best one, according to some veteran cops, was a middle-age guy, calm and collected, who understood that an accurate sketch relied on making a connection with the witness, getting him or her to recall details which might otherwise escape everyday notice.

It was difficult to line up a volunteer on Sunday morning. None of them answered their phone, and Bennett imagined the three artists were at brunch or church. *Keep trying*, he thought. *We have to get as much as we can from Sincere.*

As the day inched toward noon, he called George Pope at home and offered to buy him lunch. The old man was brusque, but agreed to meet within the hour at The Thirsty Bison.

*   *   *

"You understand why I did that?" Mark Bennett asked. They were seated in a booth, icy space between them. "I'm running a high profile case on zero leads. This Sincere Malone, she's my best witness so far."

"Call me old school, Mark." George Pope glared at him, but the use of Bennett's first name lessened the severity. "I get testy when it feels like I'm being thrown under a bus. That little whore nearly killed me, and two hours later you're serving her pop like a waiter at the Park Lane."

"I wasn't trying to throw you under the bus. I wasn't trying to minimize the danger you and Bobby faced. If anything, you guys are the stars. You don't bring her in, I never get that interview and we're still running in place, which I've been doing since this started. Right now at least there's hope. We get a good sketch, put it out on the streets... This could be a springboard to breaking the case."

Pope grumbled and turned his attention to the table, where a waitress dropped a plate of steaming chicken wings before them.

Two wooden bowls were overturned on the wings, trapping in heat. Bennett lifted them and laid them to the side.

"Need anything else?" the waitress asked above the bar's noise.

"Another round for us both," Bennett said. When she left, he hesitated until Pope met his gaze. "I understand your point, but I don't want you to be mad at me."

The big man shook his head, poked at a celery stick, and uncapped a plastic cup of blue cheese dressing. He looked back at Mark, age lines on his face like cracked clay. "No hard feelings," he said reluctantly, then he scoffed. "The Bennett brothers. How is it that I can be furious with both of you yet still find forgiveness in my heart?"

The waitress returned with twin mugs of beer. Pope's hand encircled the clear glass. "I'm telling you, Marky, for a few seconds, I was so pissed at Bobby I thought I was going to pop a blood vessel. I tried to clock him in the jaw. Thank God I missed or we might both be dead. He saw the whole scene when I didn't. Pushed me out of the way, turned, leaped up and wrestled with this little whore, and then disarmed her by himself. I was pretty much window dressing."

Mark bit a chicken wing covered by scarlet sauce. On one hand, he swelled with pride at Bobby's quick decisions and selflessness. But how could he be gallant for a ten-minute block and so shortsighted the rest of the time? The problem had baffled Mark since childhood.

"I never saw her coming," Pope continued. "She could have shanked me in the back of the neck. I might be paralyzed right now, or even dead. I'm telling you, the kid's made his share of rookie mistakes and he's a pain in the ass, but for those thirty seconds, he was a superstar."

And this, in a sound bite, was the life of Bobby Bennett, Mark realized. When his brother was recognized for what he could be, the kid glowed like a constellation. But Bobby never saw that side of himself. When he looked in the mirror he saw all the things he wasn't. He didn't have their father's wisdom, nor did he possess Mark's intelligence. Bobby was slowed by the burden. With a family name and expectations to fulfill, it was easier to kick at walls and knock them down than construct his own.

"Before this I was thinking of going to the Loot to request another partner," Pope confessed. "As close as I was to your dad, I didn't want to be on the streets with Bobby because he wasn't learning the job. I worried he was too distracted by little shit and that could get me killed. But in that burst of action I saw one hell of a cop. I've seen some great ones, including your old man, but I don't know anybody else who could have reacted that fast."

Mark chewed a carrot slice and drew a napkin across his lips. Was his brother a great cop or simply experienced in the center of tumult?

"Then came the kicker," Pope continued. "Our shift ends, and Bobby pulls out this envelope with a photo of me holding him as a baby. I hadn't thought of it in twenty-some years, but I remember your old man taking the picture. Now Mark, you know I'm not emotional. I didn't cry when Mac died. Hell, I haven't cried in thirty years. But I'm not gonna lie, today was as close as I came."

Bennett thought for a moment, then nodded. "Minute to minute, you never know which Bobby you're gonna get. He's a chimera."

"A what?"

"A chimera."

Pope moved the chicken wing away from his lips. "What the hell is that?"

"It's a mythical creature. Lion's head, goat's body and serpent's tail."

"Where'd you hear about this?" Pope wondered.

"Chimeras? I've read about them. It's an analogy for an identity crisis."

"Put down the books. You read too much," Pope reflected. "Anyway, regarding your brother I got a bit of a conundrum."

"What's that?"

"A conundrum? It's when you're torn between two conflicting emotions." Mark smiled at Pope's sarcasm. "You know, for a smart guy, sometimes you aren't."

"This is becoming an Abbott and Costello routine. What's your conundrum?"

"I'm going soft. If I tell the kid thanks and turn sentimental, you saved my life and all that jazz, how do I keep whipping him into shape? Does that shatter my hard ass personality?"

Chapter 26

We don't appear any closer, but at least wheels are spinning, Mark Bennett thought as he sat behind his desk.

No murders had been reported throughout the day, although that didn't mean none had occurred. After meeting George Pope for lunch, Bennett finally made contact with a sketch artist. The man had spent two hours at the Holding Center interviewing Sincere, charcoal pencils transforming her words into a composite. Bennett studied the result throughout the afternoon. A round face with small eyes, thin lips and a baseball cap covering the forehead, stringy locks feathered out above the ears. The chin was rounded, eyebrows neutral. There was little unique or distinguishing about him.

Who are you? Bennett thought, staring into two-dimensional eyes. *How do we get you?*

Copies were made and distributed to each precinct. Patrolmen were briefed to keep an eye open for anyone resembling him, likely driving a tan two-door sedan. Members of the Sex Offense Squad planned to hike up and down the hookers' hotspots, handing out leaflets and questioning girls.

Their quarry was becoming boxed in, Bennett believed. *Just a matter of time.*

Connell stormed into the squad without slowing or looking at Bennett. He went to his desk, shook out of his trench coat, and sat, flipping through the file and pausing momentarily on the composite. Bennett noticed he had changed into black slacks.

"Where you been all afternoon?" Bennett wondered.

"Don't worry about it," he scowled.

"It took a couple hours to find an artist, but we got the sketch. I guess that Sincere lived up to her name. Little head case, but the guy said she was actually pretty helpful—"

Connell cut him off. "Save your breath, Bennett. I don't need a minute by minute update."

Bennett inhaled, counting silently to five. He was tired of Connell's antics. Just when Bennett immersed himself in the case, this moody bastard came along to puncture him back down to reality. Connell had been a ghost for the past several hours, spent yesterday nosing around about Bobby, and continued to abuse Alison even though they had separated. How much longer could Bennett last without confronting him?

"Something on your mind today, or what?" Bennett prodded.

The detective looked up with narrowed eyes. "You scalded my legs with coffee. I'm gonna have scabs because of you. I had to go home and change, so you're damn right there's something on my mind. Want to know what it is? You're an asshole."

"Are you ever pleasant? Just once I'd love to see you act pleasant. You got any other angles on this case we need to talk about or have you been jerking off all day?"

"Today's not a good day for me to be talking to you," he said, shaking his head and turning attention back toward his desktop.

Bennett studied him for several seconds. He chose words carefully. "What does that mean, it's not a good day to talk? It's not a good day for blacks to be dying either, but that's what's happening. I don't think we should play word games during these homicides. It's our job to stop them."

"I don't need you to explain the job to me."

"You don't want to talk?" Bennett repeated. "Get over yourself. We can't be partners if we don't talk."

Connell raised his head and glared. "Maybe that's our answer right there." He closed the file, picked it up, and grabbed his trench coat, sweeping out of the room.

*   *   *

Angelo Battaglia was startled awake by plates of pain stinging his cheeks. He tried to retreat, but lying face up on his mattress, there was nowhere to go. Eyes opened to a blur of palms.

He grabbed wildly, locking fingers around thin wrists. When he squeezed, a yelp followed. Lisa's big saggy breasts hung above him like yesterday's laundry, bouncing out of synch with her swinging arms. Her knees jabbed his hips, weight pressing into his abdomen.

"You fucking bastard!" she screamed. "Let me go!"

"The fuck?" he wondered. "Why you hitting me?"

She let loose with a primal wail, untamed hair swirling around an angry expression, then corkscrewed her knee into his stomach, leaned forward, and sunk teeth into his wrist. A vice locked his bones. He flung his arm back, reflexively aiming at her head. The punch dislodged her, knocking her off the bed with a thud.

She sprawled on the floor, wearing Disney-themed panties and nothing else. A black and white image of Mickey Mouse covered the triangle of pubic hair. The left leg was crooked, a doughy roll of fat along her belly.

"You're a fucking bastard and I hate you!" she sobbed.

"Holy shit," he muttered, breath coming in spurts. He turned on his side to watch her, then ran a hand across his burning cheeks, feeling an oily warmth. Battaglia checked his fingers. The crazy bitch had flecked away skin and left him bleeding.

"What's the matter with you?" he asked.

Her breath heaved and she used spread hands to conceal her face, tears leaking through knuckles.

"Seriously, why the fuck you hitting me? Goddamn it, I wake up to you beating the shit out of me, you better have a fucking reason."

"I got a reason," she whimpered. "Believe me, I got plenty of reasons. But you don't care."

"You gonna tell me?"

She floundered onto her knees and stood, shoulders slouched. Half hopping, she stumbled to the bathroom and slammed the door.

Once his pulse had evened, he got up, slid into briefs and crossed the hall, knocking with impatience. When there was no response, he pounded on the bathroom door.

"Get out," he shouted. "I need the crapper."

Her sobs inflated the closed room, leaning toward hysteria. He knew Lisa was nowhere near opening that door.

Without thought he stepped back and swung his leg up, kicking it in. Handle and switch plate ripped from their screws, dangling splinters along the trim. The ball of his foot stung from the contact, but he was mad enough that it didn't matter. Lisa sat on the closed toilet lid, slouching against the wall, sobbing. Battaglia reached under her arms, picked her up and shoved her roughly through the opening. She was so far gone that she didn't know she was being moved.

Closing the door but unable to latch it, he moved the razor atop the medicine cabinet, tucking it behind the mirror's ledge so it wasn't visible. He didn't want the bitch to rush back with any wild ideas. He dropped his briefs to the floor, relieved himself, then showered and returned to the bedroom to dress for work. She still lay in the hallway, dime-sized goose bumps rising on her naked back. He stepped over her and shook his head.

Battaglia didn't know it, but this was to be the easy part of his day.

Arriving at work, he was summoned to the sergeant's office and ordered to surrender his gun and shield. Internal Affairs was investigating him, he learned, and until results were known, Battaglia was under suspension.

He sat speechless while a crimson haze burned behind his eyes.

*   *   *

Battaglia was escorted from the precinct house. The IA cop, a big Hispanic gorilla with a black mustache, stood at the door with crossed arms watching him walk away. As he moved up the block toward his car, Battaglia turned and looked back, shooting a middle finger toward the son of a bitch. He wanted to scream and beat his chest and yell that these rats were motherfuckers trying to pin some bullshit charge on him.

Cocksuckers, he raged. *They got nothing! Can't have anything! I've been careful.*

Yet in spite of his anger, Battaglia knew the truth. It wouldn't require much digging to learn that he was dealing. If they hadn't already, they would discover Alonzo, and that bastard would sing like a springtime pigeon. Any investigator worth his pay could construct a solid case to box him in as a crooked cop.

His eyes stung with shame. There was no going back to the job. His career was over.

What the fuck was he going to do with the rest of his life? He had planned to retire after twenty, move to Florida and buy a houseboat, live in luxury. Goddamn it, he only had nine years in, and he hadn't squirreled away nearly enough cash yet.

What would he tell his family and friends?

Mark Bennett was behind this. He didn't know how, but Battaglia was certain that holy roller had been the catalyst.

Bobby would know.

There was a phone booth on the corner. He got out of his car, fished in his pocket for a dime, and dialed the precinct house that he had just left. After being transferred, Bobby Bennett answered on the second ring.

"Bobby, it's Angelo."

"Hey."

"Did you hear?"

"Hear what?"

"I been suspended." Angelo waited, but there was no reaction from Bobby. To fill the silence, Battaglia relayed events of the past half hour.

"Huh," Bennett mused with disinterest. "Sorry."

That's it? Battaglia thought. *Sorry? He's not going to rage and get fired up and claim that I'm being railroaded? We drank together, we laughed together, I tried to show this rookie the ropes, and he's not going to react to my mistreatment by this fucking administration?*

"Is your brother behind this?" Battaglia asked.

Bobby paused. "My brother is investigating homicides. How would he be behind this?"

"I dunno. But he don't like me."

"Lotsa people don't like you," Bobby said. "You got any connection with this city hall flier?"

That little whore Sincere, he thought. *She was making noise about this. If she had been brought into custody...*

"No," Battaglia lied.

"Then why would Marky have anything to do with your situation? I don't know how you got into hot water, and I'm sorry about it, but maybe you need to look in the mirror."

So now this Bennett was needling him too. "Fuck you, Bobby. I took you under my wing from the first day you came on the job. I thought you were my friend."

"And I thought you were mine. My brother can be a pain in the ass, but he's right more often than not. I've earned the right to criticize him. You haven't."

"You're a douchebag."

"Yeah, well, I got work to do, Angelo. Unlike you. Call me when you realize you're not always a victim."

A sudden click, and Battaglia cradled a dead receiver.

*   *   *

The phone book listed three columns under the surname Bennett, justified in tiny seven-point type. Connell practically needed glasses to read it. There were two named Robert, although neither of the addresses corresponded to the one he knew. That proved nothing. Maybe the little punk had bought the house since this edition was printed.

He could investigate further, call Bobby's precinct to confirm where he lived, but that Sarge had turned suspicious yesterday on the phone. Asking more questions would raise a red flag, and right now it was better to minimize the chances of Bobby learning he was in Connell's sights. When Connell confronted him, he wanted the element of surprise, like a guerilla attack.

So as afternoon gave way to darkness, he found himself on Bobby's street, parked again beneath the overhang of an oak tree. Since yesterday, he had experienced open-ended nausea, spinning in a vacuum, unsure where this would end. He did not know what he hoped to discover on this reconnaissance, but the important part of a stakeout was gathering information. There was no such thing as too much information.

The house was one-story, with a low roofline and elongated bricks the color of sandstone. There was a picture window with drawn curtains and a flowerbox spanning the frontage. The lawn was dotted with new seedlings, probably planted last spring, although a mature evergreen grew off-center, near the yard's far corner. It was a single-car garage, its door painted tan, with a concrete driveway. Matching the character of the neighborhood, the home was small, but well tended.

Connell couldn't see a mailbox in front. *Must be on the garage side*, he thought. *Nothing was delivered today, but Bobby had worked late last night. Maybe the little shit slept in and forgot to pick up Saturday's mail.*

A station wagon backed out of a driveway down the block. A delivery boy's paper box dotted the curb. Inside houses, lamps had already been snapped on. The only potential witness was a fat girl standing under a streetlight on the narrow rectangle of lawn between sidewalk and road. She wore headphones like earmuffs, cord snaking to a portable tape player in her hand. Oblivious to her surroundings, she clapped hands out of time, like a defective metronome. Eyes were closed as she swayed without rhythm. Flab bounced between her chest and stomach.

If he was going to do it, now was the time. Bobby was on shift and the surroundings were quiet.

Connell got out of his car and strode with purpose up Bobby's driveway. The lumpy kid was singing off key. On the next street over, a dog barked. Connell stayed calm as he rounded the corner. As he surmised, a narrow black mailbox with scrollwork was screwed to the house's side. Its hinge squeaked as it flipped open. Empty.

Connell used his palms to shield light as he leaned into the window on the garage door. The inside was dark, however, revealing nothing. He jiggled the handle and found it locked. He continued along the concrete walk toward the back of the house, but was met by a redwood gate, padlocked, fully six feet high.

Frustrated to have learned nothing, he turned back. At the foot of the driveway, the fat teenager had crossed the street and stood staring with accusation. The headphones had been lowered from her ears and now curled around her neck.

"Y-y-you looking for Officer Bennett?" she asked, a stammer in her voice.

Connell felt relief. The girl had just confirmed what he knew. "Is that who lives here?"

"Yeah, Officer Bennett. B-b-but I'm not supposed to call him that any more." Her face appeared doughy, lower lip drooping. Connell realized she was retarded.

"Why not?"

"B-b-because he got a new job. Promoted. He's a detective now, but that's too hard to say. D-d-doesn't sound right, Detective Bennett. I'm so used to calling him Officer Bennett."

Promoted? The little runt just joined the force. Was Bobby Bennett really so desperate to impress a retarded girl that he exaggerated his job title?

"He's snowing you, kid," Connell said, glancing up and down the street. "You ought to be calling him Little Bobby. He's Officer Bennett, no matter how important he makes himself out to be."

The fat girl stopped swaying, confusion clouding her face. She clicked absently at the buttons on her walkman. "N-n-no, not Bobby. That's not his name. There was a Bobby, though. He gave me candy one day. H-h-he doesn't have much hair."

Connell hesitated. What was this kid saying?

"Who lives in that house?" he asked.

"Officer Bennett. I-I-I just told you." She started at Connell like he was the one with a learning disability.

"But not Bobby," he said.

"No, n-n-not Bobby."

"Do you know Officer Bennett's first name?"

"Yeah," she nodded smugly. "But I've never called him by his first name. T-t-that would be disrespectful. My daddy calls him M-m-mark."

Connell froze, consciously clamping his jaw so he didn't gape openmouthed before this fat retarded girl. He felt like he had collided with a tractor-trailer. Mark Bennett lived here. His chest tightened with the realization.

Not Bobby Bennett. Mark Bennett.

Mark was sleeping with Alison.

He had no proof, not yet, but with a certainty like the earth's rotation, he knew. Alison would never fall for some rookie patrolman like Bobby Bennett. Mark was just the type of guy she would be drawn to. In fact, Mark Bennett was the man Alison had always pestered him to become.

He was quiet, shy, reclusive almost, mired in his own little world where he never strayed outside the lines. He was the kind of spineless amoeba who did just what he was told at work, and when the shift ended, limited himself to one woman. His head was always buried in some book. He was slow to act, studious, a real egg-head.

And he's been fucking my wife right beneath my nose.

Connell's mind fluttered at the audacity of it all. He couldn't stand here much longer, before the potential gaze of neighbors who might see his rage.

"Thanks," he told the dim-witted teenager. He strode with purpose back to his car. He felt like craters were cracking his skull.

Inside, his palms wrapped around the steering wheel, gripping its contour until bones in his fingers hurt. Sounds and colors mingled, a psychedelic wash swimming through his senses. The world collapsed around him, focus narrowing to his blackened brain.

He had been made a fool.

He was the idiot husband, the cuckold.

That fucking whore.

That little punk bastard.

"Oh my God," he said. "Oh my God."

For the first time in years, his eyes grew puffy. Pride retained the tears. His throat scratched dry as he blinked them away.

Now what? he thought.

Chapter 27

"Ooh, this is gonna be fun," Annette said, her head and shoulders filling space between bucket seats. The smooth face split with a wide smile, a palm flattened on the back of each headrest.

George Pope was behind the wheel; Bobby Bennett sat on the passenger's side. Parallel parked along Pearl Street near its intersection with Chippewa, the engine was off, although Pope turned it on every ten minutes so the heater blasted warmth. The last wisps of light were fading from the day.

Despite scouring sex offense files and patrolling the streets, no one had been able to locate Jazz, the pregnant hooker who had seen the suspect up close. Recognizing that Sincere idled in the county lockup for assaulting two officers, the assistant district attorney was not willing to relinquish her into the custody of cops to participate in a stakeout. That could prove disastrous, both for police or the girl. So Annette was the only available streetwalker who might identify the wanted man. She agreed to post a lookout on a single condition: the cop who accompanied her needed to be Bobby Bennett.

"Bobby, let me ask you something," Annette cooed. "Can I reach up there and rub your head? I like a man in a brush cut."

Bennett turned and leaned forward. He spoke sternly.

"Annette, you are not allowed to touch me. Under no circumstances will you ever be given permission to lay those hairy-knuckled man-hands on me, so forget about it. Are we clear?"

The big prostitute wiggled her chin, tongue clucking. She remained upbeat, but it was clear she hadn't expected the harshness in his tone. Pope had always spoken to her with amusement. Why couldn't Bobby be more like that? Tonight anger boiled just below his surface.

"Wish you'd quit fixating on me being a man," Annette's falsetto voice remained feminine. "Just wanted to rub your head."

"Stop thinking like that, Annette," Pope ordered.

Annette turned reflective. "Well, you boys have been so nice to me already, buying me that slice with pepperoni, that I thought maybe we were all a little closer now. You know I like my pepperoni, don't you, Bobby?"

"I'm not going to last all night with this," Bobby scowled. "I don't want to be part of some drag queen routine." He stared longingly at ribbons of city sidewalks, overcome with a strange isolation, confined to this cramped space with an ancient partner who had cradled him as a newborn and a cross-dressing hooker who talked too much. Accepting this assignment was almost too much to bear.

"Now my Bobby made a rhyme," Annette chirped.

"All right, that's enough," Pope said. He pivoted in his seat and met her eyes. "You're done with the sexual innuendo, Annette. Bobby's not interested in you, and neither am I. Quit this little power play flirting game. We need you to point out a killer, so we're all stuck here. But if you don't clean up your mouth we're gonna tape it shut. You can't be nice, then you're not gonna speak. You can just clap your hands and point to our guy."

She blew out a breath and pushed herself away, leaning against the back seat.

"All right, all right," she lamented. "I was just kidding around. Officers of the law are too sensitive. Just thrilled to be here with you, doing my civic duty."

304

"I'm serious, Annette," Pope cautioned.

"I get it," she said, then made an exaggerated zipping motion across her lips and tossed away an invisible key.

Lord in heaven, Pope thought. *If catching this serial killer hinges on the good will of a tranny prostitute, the murders might go on forever.*

*   *   *

Valerie was perched on a barstool at a corner dive called Wreckers, exactly where Connell knew she would be. She surfaced here on weekends, like every dumb whore who followed a routine. A skinny Italian with grease in his hair tended bar on Sundays. He had done time for boosting cars, and the little weasel had an eye for Valerie. She probably would never sleep with him, but was able to tease enough to score free drinks whenever he was pouring.

Connell felt the collective clench of a half-dozen social outcasts as he entered the room. The cream-colored walls felt cold and impersonal. Even the greaseball seemed to deflate.

"Hi detective," he said, nose twitching.

"Hey," he nodded absently, then sat on the stood next to Valerie. "How you doing, babe?"

"Better now that you're here, Ken," she deadpanned, staring down at her drink.

"Let's cut the small talk," he said. "How do you feel about getting out of here?"

"Not so good." Her face twisted into a knot. "It's my period."

"Bullshit. It was your period two weeks ago."

Valerie bit a lip and swished blonde hair off her shoulders. "Well, okay. But I don't know about tonight. I think I'd rather just stay here."

He grabbed her arm roughly. "I don't give a shit what you'd rather do. I'd rather you weren't a whore, but there you are. I'd rather people didn't lie all the time. I'd rather not be a laughingstock, but—"

Connell cut himself off when he realized conversation had stopped and people were staring. Hot coals smoldered in his stomach. He had saved this girl's tight little ass more than he cared to remember. Now it was payback. If he could release this pent up rage and pound someone, maybe his mind would relax and he could figure out how to deal with Alison and Mark Bennett.

He let go of her arm, but leaned close and lowered his voice. The aroma of cheap perfume bit his nostrils.

"You're gonna fuck me like you mean it, then we're gonna walk up and down Chippewea and show a picture to all your stupid little whore friends. So what you'd rather do isn't really an option here, okay sweetie? We got a killer out there spreading terror and I've got a lot of shit I'm trying to wrap my head around. This, right now, is bigger than what you want."

Valerie recognized the intensity in Ken's eyes. Flesh had hardened and his muscles tensed. She had seen this look from men before, and knew that pushing back was useless. Best to submit and deal with the fallout later.

"Okay," she said softly.

From the far end of the bar, the Italian could not hear them, but was uncomfortable watching their body language. True, he had a sweet spot for the girl, but that detective boiled with a demon inside. Something bad was about to come down, he was sure of it. Yet he kept his mouth shut as Valerie glanced over her shoulder and raised a farewell hand while being hustled out the door.

*   *   *

As time stretched, they had seen businessmen, drunks, teenagers, hookers, a priest, and a hippie gliding by on roller skates. Trolling the streets had been blacks, whites and Hispanics of all shapes and sizes. Annette scrutinized everyone who passed by, saints and sinners alike.

There was no sign of the killer.

Bobby felt like he was sitting before a furnace vent. Pope would start the engine, blast the heat for a time, then turn it off. Three minutes later he grumbled about the chilly night air, and repeated the process.

Time to pack it in and move to Florida, Bobby wanted to say. *They've got perma-heat down there for all you old fogies.*

The trio had been crowded into the car for nearly two and a half hours. Annette had quieted after Pope's scolding, but gradually the injured feelings wore off. What began as a few innocent observations had morphed into full-blown chatter. Annette verbalized everything. When a thought popped into her head, she regarded it as a unique gift to bestow upon the world.

"I got this new lotion I've been using on my skin," she explained with enthusiasm. "Like a fine rich African butter. Kind of eggshell color when you squeeze it from the bottle. Put a little dollop in my palms, rub it all up and down my arms and legs. Goes on clear. You can't even see it, but my skin looks richer, you know? Smells like Hawaii. Coconuts, mangos, real tropical. Course, I've never been to Hawaii, but I imagine this is what Hawaii smells like." She pushed up a sleeve and extended her arm into the front seat. "You want to sniff?"

"No," Pope's answer was monotone. His head did not move as he continued to stare through the windshield. "Are you watching out there, Annette?"

"Of course I'm watching. That's why we're all here, isn't it? Think I don't know enough to do my job? I was just realizing that these fabric seats smell lousy, like grubby people have been lounging on them, which I guess they have. Criminals don't always smell good, do they? But my skin does. Don't you worry about me doing my job. You can count on me to wait here all night if we need to. And if we don't locate this creep tonight, I'm happy to come back tomorrow and the next night and on and on until we get this predator off the streets. It's a social duty."

How much longer can this last? Bobby lamented.

"Of course, I'm not making any money sitting here," she continued. "I mean, I know I'm being compensated by your fine organization, but let's be honest, it isn't much compared to the amount of green I can pull in when I'm actually working. There's a lot of guys out there who like a big woman and aren't ashamed to pony up their dough so they can get a piece of this.

"Now that guy right there," she pointed to a short, chubby man, awkward and nervous as he waddled tentatively up the block, "he's not our guy, but he's looking for a slice of love. He's an occasional client."

"Client?" Bobby echoed. "What are you, his accountant?"

"Don't like to say *customer*. Cheapens my profession."

"Oh my," Pope muttered.

"Name is Sam. Drives a Toyota Corolla, this guy. License number TX4 3K6. Says he's from Amherst."

"You know a lot about this guy."

"I talk with my clients. Make them feel comfortable."

There was a pause. "How do you know his license number?"

Annette shrugged. "I got a memory for stuff like that."

Pope turned in his seat to look at her. "Are you jerking our chains?"

"Naw, really. I was always good in school when teachers showed me flash cards. I've got this weird brain thing where if I see something once, I can remember it real good. Lots of people wanted me to go to college, but that path didn't fit my lifestyle.

Don't know many mathematicians who can get away dressing up like a girl."

"Huh," Pope mused, returning his gaze through the windshield. "Annette, you're full of surprises. Hey, look at this."

Ken Connell rounded the corner with long, purposeful strides. His dark trench coat was unfastened, belt ends flapping like twin pendulums. Behind him, a skinny teenager with bleached blonde hair tottered on heels, nearly jogging to maintain his pace.

"The hell is he doing here?" Bobby wondered.

They paused before a chubby Hispanic wearing a miniskirt and fake leopard stole. Reaching a hand into his coat pocket, Connell unfolded a paper and thrust it before the hooker. Her glance lasted five seconds before she shook her head.

"Working the strip," Bobby said.

"Asshole," Pope muttered.

"My brother says he's a son of a bitch, but one hell of a cop."

"He's a gutter dweller," Pope said. "Burns my ass when a cop steals a bust. Being a detective is political and you're judged on your numbers, but it's still a shitty thing to do." Pope hesitated. A day earlier, he would not have spoken his next words. "You ever make detective, kid, don't let me catch you doing that."

Bobby watched as Connell and the young girl continued up the sidewalk. Detective? Hell, his head was spinning as a rookie patrolman. Was that a promotion he would ever see? After a few moments to imagine it, he pivoted in his seat and addressed Annette.

"So you got this great memory," he said. "Let's use it. Impress us with recollections about our killer."

"I already told you all that." She waved a hand in exasperation. "Plaid shirt, short stubby fingers, baseball cap pulled low. Tan two-door car." Her tone became bitter, like a woman scorned. "Didn't say much to me besides *the other one, the other one*. He wanted Sincere. Still don't know why he'd prefer that little remnant when he could have all this woman."

Go figure, Bobby thought. *You're built like a tight end. He was probably afraid you'd kick his ass.*

Annette paused before her face leaped with an epiphany.

"Say, Bobby, would it help find this guy if I told you his license number? Cause I remember that one too."

Pope and Bennett looked at her and then each other.

Chapter 28

George Pope stared for five long seconds.

"If you're messing with us, Annette, so help me…"

"I'm not, I'm not," she insisted. "I'm pretty sure I remember that number."

"Pretty sure? Not one hundred percent?"

"Since that big dude scrambled my brains, I'm not one hundred percent about anything," she said. "Been wandering around in a fog, you know? Everything is cloudy, just outside my reach. If it wasn't for Bobby saving my life, who knows where I'd be right now? Could be laid out on a hospital gurney, or even in a morgue."

Pope exhaled, then scowled at Annette. "Why did we sit here for three hours before you shared this with us?"

She shrugged, licking her lips. "Wasn't thinking clearly."

"You were sure thinking clearly about your African butter lotion. I heard ten solid minutes on that."

"Is it even worth trying to track down?" Bennett wondered skeptically.

"It's as good as anything we've had so far," Pope said. With an expression like he was suffering stomach cramps, he nodded toward the radio. "Call dispatch and run a plate check. It's probably nothing, but what the hell."

*   *   *

Mark Bennett loitered in the squad room long after dinner, confident that his phone would ring with good news from the uniforms on patrol. In a perfect world, the killer would be caught soliciting, but that was too much to ask for. Certainly one of the hookers would recognize the sketch, providing the lead to bring this drama to its culmination.

Minutes clicked to hours, and frustration grew. By 9 p.m., halls remained quiet and hope evaporated. He slid on his coat, left the squad room and trekked downstairs, climbing into the car. Bennett exhaled, laying his forehead against the steering wheel, a sense of emptiness rumbling his stomach. It took several seconds before he composed himself enough to turn the key and nose the sedan away from the curb.

He drove into the night for several blocks and then raised the mic to his lips. "I feel it, Mac," he spoke with defiance. "We are so close to breaking this thing and it's just not happening."

The reply was delayed, distant. "Stay with it."

"I was sure tonight would be the night. Like you know it in your bones. I mean, I'm a new detective, so I've got no right to claim any instinct or sixth sense. But I really believe the end game is within reach. We just need the one little break."

"Don't hang your head, Marky. Some cases close easy, and some close hard. But you keep working until it closes. I know you've been going all the time, but that's all you can do." The voice grew stronger. "What about that other thing?"

"What other thing?" Mark wondered.

"That thing we don't talk about. Your girl."

Mark frowned. "What about it?"

"You need to deal with that too. Every day we don't talk about it makes it harder for you to come to terms."

"I'm not ready to talk about it."

"I know. If I can see that's a problem, how come you can't?"

Mark lowered the mic and held it near his chest, watching buildings he passed. He made a clicking sound with his tongue.

"You still there?" Mac wondered.

"Yeah. Listen, it's complicated."

"So simplify it."

"If I do that, then…"

"Yeah?"

"The only way to simplify this is to end it with her."

The pause stretched until a red light snapped green.

"I'm sorry," Mac offered.

"I'm not ready to break up. I love her."

"You love her right now," Mac reminded him. "That's what you told me last time. You love her now, but no promises."

"That's right. So what?"

"Hell of a way to live, Marky."

Alison's face assembled itself in his memory, dark hair knotted into a ponytail. He felt the pull of an empty evening, disappointment that the killer lurked just beyond their reach. Comfort came when he imagined Alison, her warm body contoured beside his.

"Maybe it's time to make some long-term choices," Mac advised.

These are issues to avoid, Mark thought. *How can my love for Alison be resolved when Connell and I work together? Neither of us wants to. When we solve this case, we can put some distance there. Maybe that's why I want this to close so badly, because only then—*

Crackling words through the radio brought him back to reality. Mac and thoughts of Alison scurried down a sinkhole. He depressed the mic's button and replied to the call.

Bobby's voice was patched through the speaker. Amid the static, his timbre was reminiscent of their father, leaving Mark uneasy. Bobby told of Annette and her remembered license number. Skepticism clung to his story.

"You thinking she's full of shit?" Mark asked.

"At this point, I don't know what to think," Bobby replied. "We're dealing with a dude who wants to be a woman, claims

313

she's got a perfect memory and could have gone to college, but makes a living giving hummers to poor saps who can't tell she's got a Johnson. And I was one of those guys who couldn't tell, by the way, so I'm guessing most of her customers don't know either. She flirts with me non-stop."

"So she's making up this license number to impress you?"

"Beats the piss out of me, Marky. I ain't so sure I want to get inside the head of a tranny hooker. But I just talked to dispatch. The plate matches a tan sedan. I'll give you the name and address and how you pursue it is up to you."

Mark hesitated. "Yeah, okay."

"Got a pen?"

He had that in his jacket pocket, but no paper, so he reached across the center console to the rind of an envelope buried under files on the passenger's seat. He turned it over and smoothed its wrinkles. "Go."

Bobby read off an east side address, and Mark scribbled it, immediately recalling the neighborhood, familiar from his days on patrol. Narrow old clapboard houses, lower middle class, clustered on a residential street between Walden and Genesee.

"Guy's name is Joseph Allen. He's twenty-five, got no priors. Did a stint in the army but was discharged on a medical."

Mark paused, jolted by a memory. "What's the name? Allen?"

"Yeah, Joseph Allen."

"Spell it."

"J-O-S—"

"No, the last name, jackass."

"Hey, back off. I'm giving you this tip. It's A-L-L-E-N. Why? You know the dude?"

I'll be damned, Mark thought. "Some psychic lady told the chief that our killer's name was Allen. But I was thinking first name, not last."

"Hmm..." Bobby said. "Maybe the dame knows something."

"Nah, it's probably nothing. I'm gonna head over there now and check it out."

"Yeah, good. Let me know, okay?"

Mark returned the mic to its cradle. He was overtired and his mind whirled. Had he just spoken with his father or his brother? And what about this withered old hippie who tipped them off to the name? Didn't she see some other vision too? A zoo with penguins or something...

"Coincidence, right?" he muttered. "Gotta be."

*   *   *

The day had been washed in a blur. He didn't recall getting out of bed that morning, but it must have happened, because now, after dark, he sprawled on the couch. He ate a fast food burger at some point too. Its stale taste clung to his teeth and a wax-papered wrapper lay crumbled on the floor. During afternoon hours, he remembered vague stirrings of clattering tools and the landlady clomping around the yard, mowing the lawn for what must be the final time before winter.

Now, as his mind focused, disappointment rose into reality. He had plunged into one of those pits that go deep enough to last all day. He had failed again.

Dad, he thought, *I've let you down. No killing today. Don't know why these black holes suck at my heels. Damned if I know how to stop them.*

Skin on his face felt like caked plaster. He swung his legs off the couch and stood tentatively. The back remained tender, tendons in his ankles strung tight. With his most recent tattoo, the arm ached as well. Moppy hair brushed his eyebrows. Shuffling to the bathroom, he sat on the toilet and listened to sounds his body made.

Through the open door he could see the kitchen's wall clock. Nine thirty-seven. Still more than two hours left today, so it was possible, although by the time he got himself together, it would be pushing things. He hesitated, then concluded that if he sat here and did nothing, the cycle of failure would stretch longer.

Tap water smelled of sulfur. He used a flatted palm to dampen and brush back his hair. When he looked into the mirror, he was startled by his appearance. His countenance had changed in the past week. Eyes had retreated deep into his skull; cheeks converged toward a center point near his teeth. Hard angles etched his nose.

Haggard, he thought. *I look fucking haggard.*

Just a little fight left in me. This can't last much longer.

He slid into a t-shirt and jeans then pulled a sweatshirt overhead. In the kitchen, he spread peanut butter over a slice of Wonder bread and ate greedily. Nine-fifty-five now. Could he get in a killing before midnight? Clock was ticking. Where the hell would he find a victim at this hour?

That dark bar on Ferry Street, he remembered, and the plan took shape. *Wait in the shadows for a drunken monkey to stumble out.*

Visualizing the scenario in his head, he leaned against the countertop, staring down at the front yard. Beyond the glass, cold evening air. Headlights crept slowly up the street, reflecting off fenders of curbside cars. Joe watched absently as a black sedan braked in front of his driveway. It paused for thirty seconds, then the engine stopped. Joe grew curious, forgetting his crusade, focusing on the now. The driver's door opened, and a tall thin guy stood. From the far side of the car, he gazed at the house.

Cop!

Joe's heart lurched.

Shit! Shit! Oh shit, they've found me!

He had planned to stay, to sacrifice himself as a martyr, but those were just adolescent fantasies. He scrambled to the door, slid into a pair of work boots and left laces dangling. Ignoring the pain in his legs, he clutched the railing like a drowning man and descended stairs two at a time. *Try to be quiet*, he thought, or that fucking landlady will hear me, but speed was more important than silence. His heels pounded. He couldn't exit the side door, because he would bump smack into the cop.

The basement. Calm, stay calm!

At the landing, he pivoted and continued down the next flight. Reaching the concrete floor, he felt like he was trying to outrun an explosion.

Quiet! Don't even breathe!

Joe shook out his arms and legs and tried to steady his breath. He would let the cop enter the back breezeway, then listen while he trudged upstairs. At that point, he could unfold the basement doors and escape. Was that hinge still squeaky? He planned to slip over the fence and be two blocks away before the pig even realized he had been there.

*   *   *

Mark Bennett turned onto Doat Street, passing a cloistered brick convent. Its nuns remained behind those walls for life, bracketed off from the world. The idea that a modern woman could maintain such a commitment to God, submerging herself into a tradition that harked back to the middle ages, was fascinating.

Then it struck him. The psychic had made reference to penguins. Nuns' habits, black and white, concealing everything except the face between eyebrows and chin. Could it be?

The tan car was parked along the residential street. He double-checked the plate against digits he had written. Then he eased his foot off the brake and crept ahead, searching for house numbers screwed to the corner brick. This was the address, all right, a typical old Buffalo home. An awning covered the narrow front span, driveway on the right leading to a backyard garage. Behind drawn shades, the first floor and second floors were lit. Above that, near the gable's peak, was a darkened third floor, probably an attic.

There was no movement, either here or anywhere in the neighborhood. He picked up the mic and pressed the button, providing his location and informing dispatch that he was checking on a suspect.

Bennett pulled to the curb, turned off the ignition and got out, walking up the driveway. He studied the house and its exit points. There were two side entrances along the blacktop. Closest to the street was an elaborate wooden door, the formal entryway. Bennett had been in homes like this before, and knew that behind it, three steps led up the living room. The second entrance was thirty feet back, with a cheap aluminum storm door that opened into a closet sized mudroom and stairs leading to the kitchen.

Glass block windows from the basement were at pavement level. Two mailboxes stacked atop one another, suggesting an upstairs apartment. Bennett leaned close. Dim illumination from the streetlights thirty yards away showed neither flap lettered with names.

He continued past the second door, to a backyard lit by a halogen lamp screwed to the garage's side. Nearby grew a massive oak tree, its textured bark and spreading limbs forming a canopy over the backyard. The base of a ceramic birdfeeder stabbed upward, its cracked bowl lying on the lawn with neglect. An add-on porch jutted from the lower floor. In the L made by conjoined walls, metal doors crooked at a thirty-degree angle covered the basement, handles polished smooth although rivets were flecked with rust.

He stepped closer, leaving a buffer between himself and the flattened steel. A noise, like bending wood. Was there movement below? A dim glow peeked between the door's seam. There had been no light through the basement windows when he walked up the driveway moments ago. Did someone lurk there now, or was the sound just a cat scratching its litter box?

Bennett felt a twang of concern. *Should probably have some backup on this,* he thought. But they had chased so many dead-end leads on this case. Odds were this was just the latest, that the tranny hooker had gotten her facts mangled and Joseph Allen was some nobody who had nothing to do with any murders. Bennett tried to reassure himself. He had followed protocol, informing the squad of his location. Still, it would help to have another set of eyes watching the house so no one ducked out.

A snow shovel was propped against the brick, early for the coming season. Bennett picked it up, felt the heft, and quietly slid its shaft through the basement door handles. If there was somebody inside, he was not going to leave through this route.

*   *   *

Joe clicked on the nightlight at the foot of the stairs. Four watts provided enough illumination that he could weave through the collection of stored shit without tripping. The cellar looked like a hurricane blew through, low-ceilinged, littered with boxes, wood scraps, even plastic branches from a disassembled Christmas tree. Its musty smell reminded him of soggy noodles. The concrete floor was gravelly, chipped from age. In the far corner, near the sump pump, rickety metal shelves tilted with instability. Glass panes leaned against them, draped with a plastic tarp. His shotgun was hidden on the second shelf. It would help to secure the gun, both for protection and because he didn't want them to find it, but fuck that, it had to be left behind.

He wasn't going to race through the neighborhood carrying an unconcealed weapon.

Joe slinked toward the escape doors and laid a boot on the first wooden step when he sensed a presence on the other side of the metal. He froze. Sure enough, through the narrow seam, a figure loomed above, quiet as death.

Slowly, to dampen any sound, he lifted his tread from the step and retreated into shadow, backing into a nook. His heartbeat, he believed, pounded louder than a jackhammer.

If the cop threw open that door, Joe would be caught, powerless to save himself.

*   *   *

Creaking below had stopped. Bennett cocked his head to listen, then looked up toward the windows and glanced at houses on either side. No movement, no change, no one staring down at him. Eyes glued to the basement hatch, he backed toward the second entrance, opened the aluminum frame and rapped lightly on the door.

A trudging sound within, then footfalls descending three steps. An interior hall light snapped on. Bennett stepped to the side, hand tucked into his coat, palm flattened on his gun.

The lady who swung open the door was in her sixties, with beady pupils and hair dyed California blonde. A flannel bathrobe covered stooped shoulders. Her hands were empty.

"Yeah?"

"I'm Detective Bennett with the Buffalo Police," he said. "I'm looking for Joseph Allen."

"Joey, huh? I was looking for him today myself. Hoping he'd help with the yard work." Her voice was harsh, masculine. "Didn't think he was home, but I just heard him tear into the basement like a devil fleeing heaven. Thought it was gonna knock the china outta my cabinet. He done something wrong?"

Joe remained paralyzed by the knock above, heard Mrs.
Boyd clattering through her kitchen and down the steps into the
back hall. Soles of her slippers squeaked against the linoleum.
Her brash words rang, as if she shouted through a megaphone.
He couldn't hear what the cop said.

Skin tingled like ants crawling over him. No good bursting
out the escape hatch until the cop entered the hallway, or the pig
bastard would see everything and he'd have a bullet lodged in
his spine.

A second pair of footsteps, quieter than the old lady's,
tapped the floor above.

That's my cue. Fuck this place.

Joe bounded ahead, too wired to be worried about echoes
now. He leaped onto the lower steps, ignoring the fire that
seared his calves, and threw his shoulder against metal, anxious
to breathe the chilled October air.

The whine of hinges was cut off. Instead of flaying open,
doors moved an inch then stopped.

Joe summoned a blast of adrenaline and hurled himself
again. It gave no further. Through the slit he saw a wooden pole
barring his exit.

*   *   *

"You'll have to head down there yourself," Mrs. Boyd said.
"Got the gout in my knee and I'm having trouble doing stairs."

Bennett started to say "Okay," but was interrupted by two
loud thuds and a groan. Senses, already on high alert, sprang
sharper. Gun drawn, he rushed into a dark abyss, leaping stairs
two at a time. Reaching the bottom, he lunged past the drywall
to the far side of the room.

Motion in the dim, a clattering movement from left to right. Instinct now. No time to think.

"Freeze!" Bennett yelled, tracking the blur with his gun. "Hands up!"

Bennett was grateful that his eyes were accustomed to darkness. A nightlight glowed near the foot of the stairs, but the room's far edge fell into shadows. Low joists forced Bennett into a crouch. The basement was a minefield of boxes and accumulated junk. He positioned himself behind stacked crates.

A skinny guy with stringy brown hair had stopped, concealed by a pile of cardboard boxes, open hands raised to shoulder height. His expression was that of a snared animal.

"You Joseph Allen?" Bennett asked.

"Yep."

"Don't move, Joe."

Difficult to tell his expression in the dim, but Bennett sensed malevolence filling the corners. "Don't worry."

"Where you going, Joe?"

"Ain't going anywhere."

"But you were trying to leave. Heard you rattle that door."

Joe's waist and legs were hidden from view, but hands stayed up with surrender.

"Okay, Kojak, what's next?"

The voice rang smooth, like oil flowing over water-rounded shale. Bennett wondered if he had ever worked as a disc jockey.

"Stay still. Are you the guy we're after?" Bennett asked.

"Depends," came the smug reply. "Who you after, man?"

"I'm after a guy who's killed five black people and beat the hell out of a hooker. I think that's you," Bennett said, pressure building in his eardrums.

The chuckle was guttural, touched with an air of pride. "Hell yeah, it's me. Five in the past six days. I missed Friday. Missed today too, but the day's not over."

So there it was, Bennett thought. *I've got the bastard.*
Damned if the withered old psychic hadn't been onto something.

"Yeah it is. Your day is over."

"I got even with those niggers," Joe continued, passion riding his voice. "Those fucking monkeys ain't gonna forget me soon, that's for sure."

"Got even with them? For what?"

"Where do I start? They killed my daddy, they beat me up, they leech all our fucking money from welfare." His voice took on a singsong quality, as if he had rehearsed the words before. "They suck from the milk of society. They smell like old shoes. Once slavery ended we should have packed them up and sent them back to Africa where they belong. Fucking Kunta Kinte. Killing them was something I had to do."

Shadows in the musty basement assumed a charcoal hue. Pine planks leaned against cardboard boxes that had been stacked into uneven blocks. Perspiration beaded along Joe's neck. Bennett smelled his stale odor, the pheromones of a trapped man.

"You need to come out. Keep those hands up."

"I'll keep my hands where you can see them, but I need a minute here. I'm not ready to come out."

"Why not?"

Because there's a shotgun two feet away from my knees, you stupid fucking pig.

"I wanna talk a little more," he said. "You're going to lock me up and I'll be put away, maybe even executed. This is my last gasp of freedom. Give me a minute, huh?"

I've got the situation under control, Bennett thought. *His hands are up. If he moves, I shoot. Dumb bastard is smart enough to recognize that. Let him gab. He might even reveal some information that I can use later.*

"Thirty seconds," Bennett said. "Savor this. Then we're walking out." He inhaled and blew out a calming breath. "Tell me about Rosa Greene."

"Who?"

"The woman who fell from city hall."

Joe squeaked with glee. "The pear-shaped ape that got skewered like a kabob. That's when I became the chef. If you'd let me roll up my sleeve, I'll show you my tattoos."

"Move and I shoot," Bennett advised.

Joe's grin was weary, insincere. "Fair enough. I'd like to say that monkey hitting the flagpole was planned, but it wasn't. Coincidence. That's when I knew this was part of a higher calling, because no one could have predicted that. A work of art, really. The others weren't that glamorous. Only bad part was I never got to look at her face when she died."

"Did you do that with the others?"

"Hell yeah. That was the best thing, just watching their expressions when they realized what was happening. I always meant to say, *this is for my dad*, but I got so caught up in the moment that I didn't remember until later."

"So your dad was murdered by a black man?"

Joe's nostrils flared. "Yeah, and you fucking cops never caught the son of a bitch."

"How long ago?"

"May 8, 1960. I was just a kid."

Standing in the shadows, he looked weak and harmless. But when his temper flashed, Bennett could see this skinny little runt channeling his anger into the arc of a swinging knife. Rawness brewed beneath the surface.

The two men squared off in silence, cop and killer, each contemplating the next move. Joe's chin and nose twitched the way a cat's do before it pounces.

"Okay, come on out," Bennett said.

"Not yet."

"Joe, I have to tell you, you're in a bad position here," Bennett cautioned. "I've got you cornered and in my sights. I don't want to shoot you, but I will if I need to. Any little bit of shit from you, and it's lights out. Probably I'd get a medal from the mayor for doing it."

Go ahead and shoot me, he thought. *We all know how this is going to end.* He tried to hide it, but fear compressed his heart. He didn't want to die here, in a dingy basement. He wanted his death to be epic, on a grand stage. *I need a distraction. Just look away for a second so I can grip that stock.* He adjusted his stance, shuffling his foot an inch closer to the shotgun.

If he wanted to be shot, he would have moved by now, Bennett thought. *For all his tough talk, like most cowards, this one planned to live.*

"Right now you've got two things going," Bennett soothed him. "You've been getting a lot of attention from the newspapers and TV. If you let me bring you in peacefully, they'll want your version of events. You can tell the world your story. You can tell them all about your dad, give him the legacy he deserves."

"What do you know about losing a dad?" Joe spat. "You know how hard it is to grow up without anybody loving you? You know what it feels like when the guy who gave you everything just vanishes?"

The pause was unexpected. Bennett swallowed. "Yeah, actually, I do."

This halted the rant.

"What do you mean?"

"My old man died last spring."

"He a cop too?" Joe spat.

"Yeah."

"Yeah, most cops have kids that turn into cops," Joe sneered. "It's like they breed them or something. I'll bet you and your old man would get together for coffee during the day on the taxpayers' dime, then have family dinners together every weekend, am I right?"

Mark thought fleetingly of days when he worked patrol and would meet his dad for lunch at The Thirsty Bison. The muted laughter, the subtle jokes, behavior restrained because both were dressed in uniforms and on the clock. But there was always pride in his father's carriage, knowing that his son followed his career path.

"Losing your dad hurts. Believe me, I know."

Joe's eyes narrowed, and for a moment his defenses waned. Maybe this cop struggled with the same demons he did. Maybe behind those droopy eyes he wasn't only a policeman following institution's orders. Perhaps he was a man suffering the same perils that Joe had.

"Okay, what's the second thing I got going?"

"You told me your dad was murdered on May 8, 1960 and it was never solved. You come with me peacefully, we get down to the station then we can talk more about it. You provide a location and your pop's name, and I promise I'll dig it out and read through the file on your dad's murder."

"So what? You read through the file? It was twenty years ago."

"I don't care when it was. Maybe the guy who did it is still out there and the thing could be closed."

"Don't bet on it," Joe said with disdain.

"Anyone else offered to look at it lately? I know one thing: if I don't pull it, that case is going to sit there and gather more dust. It will stay unsolved. You got one chance now Joe, and that's me. But everything depends on what you do in the next few seconds."

A knock and steps in the back hall above. Bennett heard the landlady's coarse voice, then a door thudded and footfalls clomped at the stairwell's top. Bennett's mind surged. How could he keep the killer boxed in if someone else rushed into the basement?

"Bennett, you down there?"

He recognized Connell, anxious and out of breath. Bennett exhaled with relief, eyes flicking away for a moment. Joe slivered closer to the shotgun.

"Yeah, but stay up there." He didn't want Connell entering the cramped quarters. He was making progress with the killer, negotiating in his own quiet way. He sensed Joe felt a connection. Losing a father had bound them together. If Connell entered, the dynamic would change, and they would return to square one.

"I've got him, Ken," Bennett announced. To soothe Joe as much as himself, he added, "We're going to walk out of here together."

He heard Connell advise the landlady to go to a neighbor's house and wait there. Shadows shifted to his left. The clump of boots descended the stairs. He wouldn't look that way, couldn't take his aim off the murderer, but he wondered why Connell hadn't listened to him.

"Did you hear me?" Bennett yelled. "Stay up there."

There was no response. Bennett focused attention onto Joe's chest. *Don't get distracted*, he thought. He sensed Connell in the room; from the edges of his vision he saw the detective's figure peering around the corner like a dragon's neck, assessing the situation. As Bennett watched, Joe's eyes dilated with disbelief. With the barrel unmoving, Bennett flicked his sight to the stairs again.

Connell's raised gun was pointed not at the bad guy, but at Bennett's head.

"You're sleeping with my wife, you son of a bitch," Connell snarled. "I thought it was your little brother, but it's not. It's you."

Bennett's heart expanded. Its thumping sound filled the tiny basement. How had he found out? Once glance at Connell's face embodied the accumulated hatred of the world. Quickly Bennett turned back to the suspect.

The endgame has arrived. Focus, he thought. *I don't want this conversation, not now, not ever. Certainly not here. But it's too late. Always knew the moment would come.*

"Put your fucking pistol down, Ken," he ordered.

"Fuck you, you little fuck." Connell's voice quivered with betrayal. "I don't take orders from you."

Connell teetered along the fulcrum of rage and duty. Bennett knew sudden movement would prove fatal. So they stood in silence for ten long seconds, three men, two guns pointing in different directions, fear, anger and mistrust filling the room like a meteor shower.

Joe watched the drama unfold. *Bring it,* he thought. *Caught between two bitter cops. Let these dickweeds duke it out over some piece of snatch.* The instant the young one twitched his gun, he would lunge. The shotgun was just outside his reach. Fingers tingled, nerves alert with anticipation. Wait until emotions peaked, then grab, pivot and shoot one of these pigs before he even saw the blast. Ignore his throbbing legs.

"I was actually starting to like you," Connell spat through gritted teeth. "But my instinct was right. I didn't want to trust you. You got promoted because you're Mac's boy. You're like a fucking Kennedy. All glam and no substance. Preppy little two-timing asshole."

"We've got the killer," Bennett said coolly, keeping his gaze on the suspect. "He's right here, he's admitted to it, and I'm trying to talk him out safely. Get that fucking gun off me. Don't blow this arrest."

"Fuck him. I'll put a bullet in him, blow your fucking head off and pin it on this runt. Saw it done in Vietnam."

"Don't be stupid," Bennett warned.

"Don't be stupid? Do you hear yourself? How long did you think you could fuck my wife before I found out?"

Joe's mind turned somersaults. The new cop was angry. He wouldn't allow Joe to keep stalling. This was a man of motion, somebody who couldn't be manipulated. *Act fast!* It wasn't a great plan, but it was the best he could devise, better than standing still. With his lower half concealed by cardboard boxes, he stretched his left leg, pain arcing into his spine, nudging warped planks with his toe. They clattered to the concrete floor, sound amplified by small space. He ducked low and lunged right, pawing for the shotgun as he rolled. His legs felt gooey, like warm candle wax.

Noise and sudden movement confused the cops. Bennett clenched, crouched, and leapt back three feet to avoid Connell's aim.

Connell swung his gun to the spot where the killer had stood. The space was empty, the floor's view obstructed by junk.

Little fucker couldn't have gotten far, he started to think, when he saw the twin barrels of a shotgun. The explosion of orange light was deafening. Searing pain shot through Connell's neck and shoulder. He dropped to the ground, lights spiraling before the room switched to black.

"Ken!" Bennett yelled. He couldn't hear his own words, but saw the shotgun swinging toward him.

"No," he screamed, then squeezed his trigger as the heat from a blast passed his cheek. Snapshots of movement were illuminated under the strobe of gunfire. Wood fragments and cardboard chunks leaped like popcorn in the half-light. Senses jumbled; he heard nothing but a tinny echo. The bitter smell of singed hair filled the room. Smoke streams rose like dry ice. He had fired three shots.

His breathing heavy, cheeks flushed, Bennett kept the pistol extended and swept the room, inching forward. Time froze as he crossed the concrete floor and peered over the boxes where Joe Allen had been standing. The killer was no longer there.

He was five feet away, sprawled on his back, the sawed-off shotgun angled below his upturned boots. Clothes were tattered like he had endured the apocalypse. His breath wheezed.

Bennett kept his gun trained there, then kicked away boxes so more light filtered through. Strings of Joe's arm and side had been shot away. He did not move.

"You'll look into that?" Joe rasped through hardened lips. "My dad's murder?"

Bennett studied the sallow face. Its complexion was flecked with stubble, nose sharp and unnatural.

"Yeah, Joe. You just shot my partner, so I'll get right on it."

"I killed a lot of fucking niggers, but I saved your life," he whispered. "That cop was angry enough to ace you." Joe's expression morphed like a drain plug had been pulled. Cheeks melted and flesh collapsed onto bone. Pupils washed blank and screwed upward into his skull. Shallow heaves in his chest went flat.

"Goddamn it," Bennett exhaled. In the quiet of the basement, he stabbed Joe's leg with the point of his shoe and drew no reaction. He picked up the shotgun and moved to the far side of the room, resting it on the concrete floor several yards away. Then he turned to Connell.

His face was static, eyes shut, and a golf ball-sized chunk was missing from the side of his neck. A yawning mouth of blood revealed murky veins and tendons. Bennett curled his lips and looked away. He inhaled, cordite settling into his lungs. He swallowed back the urge to vomit.

Bennett removed his jacket and ripped a sleeve from the shoulder. He wadded it and thrust the fabric into the empty gape, wondering if Connell could be saved.

The image flashed like a slide show: how much simpler would Alison's life be if this man didn't survive? His death would eliminate so many of their problems. She could live without fear or harassment. She would find financial security from his pension. Mark and Alison could pursue their love without any hurdles.

Connell's biggest obstacle now was time. He needed someone who knew first aid and lifesaving techniques. Bennett thought for a moment about dragging heels, finding a reason to delay.

But he couldn't carry that weight on his conscience. Connell might die, yet Bennett would do everything he could to save him. Otherwise he would be nothing but a common thug.

Pressure points. He pushed the rest of his jacket against the neck. A weak pulse beat there.

Bennett turned to be sure Joe's body hadn't moved. It was a corpse now, no longer human. The toes of one foot pointed upward, while the other lay perpendicular, collapsed on its side.

"You're both sons of bitches," he said.

Trying to stop the ringing in his brain, he clamped fingers into Connell's shoulder, shook his head and yelled, "Help! Help!"

Chapter 29

Hours stretched into decades as cops funneled to and from the scene, securing the area, processing evidence and trudging down narrow stairs to gape at the dingy basement where a serial killer had met his end. Mark Bennett was taken into the chief's car, returned to the squad, and grilled by his bosses about the shootings. Time lost meaning as he recounted details again and again. He was fed coffee and a cinnamon roll. Sometime overnight, as exhaustion swirled around him, he learned that Ken Connell had been transported to the Erie County Medical Center.

It was daybreak before Bennett arrived home. He phoned his mother and Bobby and George Pope, warning them that they might see his name in the papers or on TV in connection with the shooting, but that the case had closed and he was all right. Alison, however, was nowhere to be found. She was not at Bennett's house, nor did she answer her apartment phone at that early hour.

After a hot shower, Bennett lay in bed, body primed from caffeine and sweets and trauma, replaying events from the past twelve hours. The basement scene haunted him. He saw the skinny, scared kid with empty hands standing behind a pile of boxes, shadows darkening his sunken eyes as the head pivoted in dim light. Bennett heard that smooth voice, the muted rage as he recounted his father's unsolved murder.

I was going to cuff that kid and bring him out. No violence needed. Until the asshole showed up.

Self-righteousness inflated his chest, and Bennett slid into a brick of sleep, spanning fifteen minutes, then snapped awake.

He had not anticipated the shotgun. A new thought entered his head, and it was frustrating: Connell's appearance had been his fortune. When the bastard came barging down the stairs, Joe faced two targets instead of only one. Bennett had saved Connell's life after the shooting, but had Connell's presence in that basement saved his life?

If so, that made Ken Connell a hero.

Bennett swallowed and rolled onto his side. His bedroom felt constricting, air humid with confusion. *How in hell do I make sense of this?*

With morning light revealed through the curtains, Bennett rubbed his face and sat up. If only there was another way. But there wasn't. He needed to face Connell.

The guy was hooked up to machines, the chief had said, and would probably remain unconscious for a while. Critical condition, jaw wired shut, so there was no way they could continue their argument even on the off-chance he was awake. But looking down at Connell in a hospital bed would be uncomfortable and unsettling. The man knew about him and Alison now. That secret was out. Bennett wasn't sure how Connell could live with that.

*   *   *

Four dozen reporters arrayed themselves throughout the crowded room. Microphones clustered on the table, like metal tulips sprung from cords, propped at steep angles. TV personalities dressed in suits and ties hoarded seats up front, while print journalists and radio men peppered the remaining space. The two daily newspapers were rivals, but the timing of this story gave *The Buffalo Evening News* an edge, because they went to press before lunchtime. *The Courier Express*, a morning paper, had already printed its edition for the day, so would have to wait until Tuesday for the story's run. The *News* guy planned to duck out and phone in his report as soon as he landed a good quote. With deadline looming, he leaned against the back wall adjacent to the door, trying to restrain a flutter of nervous energy.

At 9:34, the Police Commissioner entered the room, surveyed the gathering, and stepped toward the table. With graying hair and a crinkled nose, he was a thick man. The buttons on his uniform strained to contain his rounded belly. As he sat, a reporter from the front row duck-walked forward to adjust his microphone's aim.

"Good morning, gentlemen," the commissioner began with a commanding voice. He enjoyed having the attention of everyone in the room, and paused to savor this moment. He knew that poised pens would scribble most of the words he said. Film would capture his stoic demeanor. His insights would appear in all the various accounts of the crime. Because of that, he had prepared notes, highlighting key phrases he planned to utter.

"I'm pleased to announce that the murderer who has been terrorizing black men in this city has been brought to justice. The killings that began last Monday from the top of city hall ended, paradoxically, in the damp basement of an east side Buffalo home late last night."

The commissioner thought the word "*paradoxically*" made him sound enlightened. *These are the sort of quotes that find a home in Time magazine*, he thought.

"The murderer was shot down in a gunfight with two detectives, one of whom was critically injured. I want to pause for a moment to think about Detective Ken Connell, currently in intensive care. Detective Connell is a decorated member of the homicide squad, a thirteen-year veteran who served two tours in Vietnam."

Ink continued to flow across pads while the commissioner stopped speaking for five seconds.

"The killer was a reprehensible twenty-six year-old white supremist named Joseph Allen," he continued, again pleased by his use of *reprehensible*. "He was employed at a factory but had recently stopped coming to work and therefore lost his job. All indications are that he was a loner and a racist. Right now there is no evidence that he acted in concert with anyone else.

"Another of our detectives, Mark Bennett, engaged in gunfight after this killer opened fire on Detective Connell. Bennett was shaken, but emerged uninjured. He behaved heroically by standing up to confront the face of evil."

The commissioner looked at the assembled media. The phrase *"confront the face of evil"* did not sound as impressive as he had expected when he wrote the notes. He continued, undaunted.

"While we mourn the loss of five Negroes and the serious injury to one of our officers, we are proud to say that the streets of Buffalo are now safe again for people of all races and colors." Another pause. "At this point, gentlemen, I'll take questions."

A din filled the room when everyone shouted at once.

*   *   *

"I have to see him," Mark explained to Mac on the ride over. "With all due respect to his parents, he's both a bastard and a son of a bitch. He was about to bleed out and I saved him, but he may have saved my life just by showing up on the scene."

"Why the hostility?" Mac wondered. "I know you butted heads when he was your partner, but he's a fellow copper."

Mark sighed and raised the mic toward his teeth. "Here it is," he said. "That thing we don't talk about. Ken Connell was married to Alison Keane, the girl I've been seeing."

The pause lasted as long as it takes to fill a balloon. "That explains the tension."

"Yeah, well, Connell didn't find out until yesterday. She and I have been flying beneath the radar."

"Huh," Mac mused. "Answers a lot of questions, kid. Now I get why you didn't want to talk about it. What are you going to say to him?"

What, indeed? Mark wondered. Bennett could visualize him propped in a hospital bed, white sleeveless gown exposing ridged muscles in his arms. Cords and IVs spiraled around him, drips vanishing into veins, jaw immobile. Face bandaged, burst blood vessels gave him the countenance of a wounded coyote, yet anger had evaporated from his eyes. He remained awake and alert, positioning himself straighter when Bennett entered the room.

First off, he would say, *thanks for being there and absorbing the buckshot that would have been marked for me. Thanks too for showing me the ins and outs of the homicide squad in the past few days. That stuff about investigating cases backwards and forwards, about not cutting corners, making sure you've got the right guy before you make an arrest. No one ever taught me that stuff. So I'm grateful.*

But this thing with Alison. How do we reach an understanding? I'm not sorry for dating her. Not one bit. She's precious, a shining light who loved you, and for whatever reasons, you let those feelings wither. You didn't treat her the way a loving husband should. You lied and manipulated her, fooled around while trying to control her life.

His car exited the expressway and he stopped for a red light at the top of the ramp. He had replaced the mic in its cradle, the dialogue with Mac morphing to a monologue which he directed at Connell. Up the block, a parking lot stretched the property's length. He pulled to an empty space in the third row.

I'm sure you have a different take, but I know her story. And having worked with you, seeing your behavior and mood swings, I believe her. Now when I asked her out I didn't even know she had been married. So I was shocked to learn she had shared a life with you. What are the odds that a girl I met in the library was married to the superstar who sits two desks away in my new job?

You two had split before we met. She left because of you. I understand your anger, but it's too convenient to put it on me. Don't go blaming me for your failures.

I could have walked away when I found out that she was your ex. There were times in the past week when I thought that I probably should have. It would have made life easier for her and for me. I would have dealt with you much better, instead of always clenching when you came around.

Bennett had not seen the inside of a hospital since his father's passing. Although Mac had died at Buffalo General, nevertheless he felt an aversion to the Erie County Medical Center, a behemoth building rising out of a low-income east side neighborhood. When sliding doors swished open, his lip curled at the anesthetic odor clinging to the walls and floors. Nerves fluttered as he approached the elevator.

But here's the thing. Here's why I'm talking to you now, Connell. I love her. I haven't told her that, because I'm scared, but in a short time she's become vital. When we're together I feel like I'm always the person I could be on my best day. Did you ever feel that way with her? She'll turn suddenly, and a lock of hair will fall across her right eye, and she'll brush it back and I just melt. Anyway, being with Alison is more important than keeping peace with you. I don't want to transfer out of the detective bureau, but if I have to find a new job, I will. That's how much I care about her.

Mark passed a young nurse wearing soft-soled orthopedic shoes and white scrubs, stethoscope draped around her neck like a boa. He gave her a room number and she pointed down a hallway to the left.

The reality is we owe one another our lives. I don't know if we'll ever be friends, but you should know that I respect you as a detective. Maybe someday, when you get out of here and get back on the job, we can work together out in the open, without having to hide things from each other. You said it yourself. We're more alike than different.

His heart pounded as he counted ascending room numbers. He stood before the closed door, inhaled, then knocked lightly. Bennett turned the handle and took three curious steps inside, peering tentatively around the corner.

It became clear why Alison hadn't answered her phone. She sat in a straight-backed chair beside Connell's bed.

"Oh," she mumbled, confusion rising on her face. "Hey."

*   *   *

Hours later, back home, Bennett's muscles were pulled taut, like tightened guitar strings. Exhaustion wracked his body. Collapsing in bed was a relief, a sense of finality to the watershed week. He knew that tonight he would not worry about the next murder.

Lying on his back, he unbuckled his belt and wriggled out of the pants. He sat up briefly, but was too tired to unfasten the shirt's row of buttons. He loosened the top one and stretched it over his shoulders, letting the oxford drop to the floor. Kicking off socks, he wore only boxers. The house was chilly, but for the moment, he felt too weary to slide under the blankets.

Unlike his body, however, his mind raced. Sleep would be sublime, but now there were other worries.

Alison was in the bathroom. Her explanation had made sense. The department's files still listed her as Connell's wife, his first contact in case of emergency. When the call came, it was a no-brainer. Of course she would go to the hospital.

Still, Bennett found it unnerving. Mark hadn't expected to see her there. In fact, Alison's presence next to Connell's bed was startling, like an apparition or a ghost. She proclaimed Ken to be controlling and manipulative, someone she had once loved but now wanted to keep far away. Yet there she was, watching with concern, hypnotized by the rhythmic blip of machines, the slow downward drip of an IV. Why? Did actions belie her words?

Bennett had been too flustered to say the things he wanted Connell to hear. Connell remained unconscious anyway, so words would not have taken hold. Alison seemed plagued by Mark's exhaustion. Connell had stabilized; doctors said he would sleep until the next afternoon. Alison suggested they return to Mark's house for the night.

Now, over the sound of running water, he thought he heard sniffling tears behind the closed bathroom door. A mixture of compassion and frustration welled inside him. Dammit, what was he supposed to do?

He released a sigh, rolled to the bed's edge and folded back the blanket before shifting underneath. The top sheet felt cool, and his body shivered. Despite the attraction, Alison had lived an entire life that would forever be foreign to him. He would never know or understand all of her, no matter how much he pondered. How could she have loved that selfish, arrogant man?

Maybe part of her always would. Regardless of her feelings, the connection would remain.

Can I accept that? Mark wondered. *Are Alison and I able to build a future together, or will Ken Connell forever wedge between us?*

Water stopped flowing in the bathroom, and shortly the door opened across the hall. A beam angled into the bedroom until Alison switched the light off. Her footfalls padded against the carpet, invisible in the darkness.

He sensed her groping the mattress' corner, then cold air tickled his skin as she lifted the blankets. Her chilled body contoured to his. It took a few seconds to realize she was naked. Despite exhaustion, desire sprang from his stomach. Mark brushed hair off the back of her neck and nuzzled her there, lips against her vanilla scent.

She let out a soft moan and arched her back, pushing into his loins. Mark tumbled toward paradise. Sore muscles were forgotten, sleepiness evaporated off the sheets, and he wrapped his arms around her stomach, squeezing her. She turned to face him, then pressed his shoulders back, slid off his boxers, and mounted him.

Holding her waist and hips, their lovemaking was fast, desperate, two lost souls searching for salvation. She came quickly, shuddering with a rush of relief. He felt himself rise toward the edge, but at the end of each approach, the final thrust retreated. After several minutes, she wiped sweat from his forehead and crawled off him with muted frustration.

"Why won't you come?"

"It's not that I won't," he answered. "I just can't right now. Too tired, I guess."

The yawn emanated from deep within. His mind was putty, stretching, turning foggy. Regret smudged his brain. He thought Alison muttered "I love you," but that may have been a dream.

Acknowledgements

There are many people to thank...

In addition to being a stellar detective and solid writer herself, Lissa Redmond gave me the idea for a story about a white serial killer during a conversation at Dog Ears Bookstore. She then arranged for me to read through police files of the .22-Caliber Killer case from the early 1980s, which provided background for this novel. She insists I refer to her as my muse.

My good friend and co-author Dennis Delano (a retired detective and current judge) let me see into the world of police work, providing clarification and details. Likewise, his brother Paul Delano, also a retired detective, was a gold mine of stories and anecdotes. Much of Paul's wisdom formed the basis for the character George Pope, sometimes verbatim. Tim Whitcomb, who has since become Cattaraugus County Sheriff, shared stories, one of which found its way into this fiction.

Britin Haller helped with hard edits in chapter one. I called her "the Butcher," but she was right more often than not.

Readers of early drafts include my dad and Kelly, Donna Laudico, Matt Chandler, Patty O'Shei and John and Karen Schleifer. Their comments and feedback helped.

Don Jackson is an amazing artist, as evident by his cover design and illustration. I am humbled that he agreed to share his talents for this book. Mark Pogodzinski, founder of No Frills Buffalo and a fellow writer and teacher, ushered the book through publication.

Friends, colleagues and students continue to lend support. Thanks to everyone who read *Undercurrent* and *Bike Path Rapist*. If you haven't yet, what are you waiting for?

About the Author

Jeff Schober has a journalism degree from Bowling Green State University and a master's degree in humanities from the University at Buffalo. A former journalist, he has written for several Western New York publications. He taught American history and Shakespeare in an alternative education high school for several years before becoming an English teacher at Frontier High School. In 1998, he was part of the National Endowment for the Humanities summer program, Teaching Shakespeare, in Washington DC. He has also acted in plays around Buffalo and in St. Catharines, Ontario. In addition to writing, he is an avid reader and hockey player.